MATTERS OF CHANCE

ALSO BY JEANNETTE HAIEN

The All of It

MATTERS OF CHANCE

A NOVEL

Jeannette Haien

▄ HarperCollins*Publishers*

HarperCollins books may be purchased for educational, business, or sales promotional use. For information please write: Special Markets Department, HarperCollins Publishers, Inc., 10 East 53rd Street, New York, NY 10022.

FIRST EDITION

Designed by Elina D. Nudelman

Library of Congress Cataloging-in-Publication Data

Haien, Jeannette.
    Matters of chance : a novel / Jeannette Haien. — 1st ed.
       p.   cm.
    ISBN 0-06-017003-4
    I. Title.
PS3558.A3255M37   1997
813'.54—dc21   97-15073

97 98 99 00 01 ❖/RRD 10 9 8 7 6 5 4 3 2 1

For Ernest Ballard

Author's Note

I want to name the four inspiriters who stood by me during the long time it took to write this book. They are Ernest Ballard and Mark Strand and Robert S. Jones and Peter Matson.

⋙

Matters of Chance is a work of fiction. All the characters who appear on the book's pages are imagined.

Insofar as the lives of the imagined people were profoundly influenced by the events of World War II, History looms large in the narrative, and speaks for itself.

As for that part of the book's action relating to the Liberty ship SS *John T. Stubbins*—to her missioned wartime voyage from Tacoma, Washington, to Port Said—I gratefully acknowledge the counselings given me by Captain Rōnān Maurice Henderson.

Afterwards

When the Present has latched its postern behind my tremulous stay,
And the May month flaps its glad green leaves like wings,
Delicate-filmed as new-spun silk, will the neighbours say,
'He was a man who used to notice such things'?

If it be in the dusk when, like an eyelid's soundless blink,
The dewfall-hawk comes crossing the shades to alight
Upon the wind-warped upland thorn, a gazer may think,
'To him this must have been a familiar sight.'

If I pass during some nocturnal blackness, mothy and warm,
When the hedgehog travels furtively over the lawn,
One may say, 'He strove that such innocent creatures should come to no
*   harm,*
But he could do little for them; and now he is gone.'

If, when hearing that I have been stilled at last, they stand at the door,
Watching the full-starred heavens that winter sees,
Will this thought rise on those who will meet my face no more,
'He was one who had an eye for such mysteries'?

And will any say when my bell of quittance is heard in the gloom,
And a crossing breeze cuts a pause in its outrollings,
Till they swell again, as they were a new bell's boom,
'He hears it not now, but used to notice such things'?

—THOMAS HARDY

Part One

1 ∾ The Beginning

November: 1925

Away from home for the first time at a boarding school he did not (then) much like, Morgan Shurtliff was a shy, lonely, fourteen-year-old dreamer, a bright though erratic student, a passionate reader.

"Shurtliff!"

He was seated in the back row of the classroom, his Latin book open on his desk but his eyes cast down, lower, into the region of his lap, where another book resided. "Sir?" he answered, looking up, forward, toward the lectern where Mr. Scudder, the Latin master, was standing.

"Are you with us, Shurtliff?"

"Yes, sir, I am."

"And just where do you think we are?"

"On page sixty-six, sir."

Mr. Scudder cleared his throat, then: "That was some time ago, Shurtliff. Since then, we, with Caesar and his legions, have trudged on. We are now encamped on page sixty-eight."

"Yes, sir."

"Tell me the name of the book on your lap."

"*The Arrow of Gold,* by Joseph Conrad, sir."

"Come forward, please, Shurtliff. Bring Mr. Conrad's book with you."

The silence in the room as he walked toward Mr. Scudder was of the weighted kind which precedes great moments.

He put the book in Mr. Scudder's outstretched hand.

"This page, Shurtliff—this one that's been dog-eared: look at it, please."

He did.

"Is it the page you were reading when I intruded upon your covert pleasure?"

"Yes, sir."

"And now, Shurtliff, as there are but a few minutes left in our class hour, and as we, even as you, enjoy a work of fiction, might you be so kind as to read aloud to us a paragraph or two of Mr. Conrad's prose?—starting, please, at the precise place you left off when I recalled you to the real world?"

"Yes, sir." He took *The Arrow of Gold* from Mr. Scudder.

"The *precise* place, Shurtliff—"

"Yes, sir."

"Oh . . . I almost forgot . . . When the bell rings, you won't mind staying on for a chat with me, will you?"

"Yes, sir. I mean, no, sir, of course I will."

"Good." Mr. Scudder folded his body into reclining position against his lectern. "Proceed, Shurtliff."

And so he began:

> "The upward cast in the eyes of Mills who was facing the staircase made us both, Blunt and I, turn around. The woman of whom I had heard so much, in a sort of way in which I had never heard a woman spoken of before, was coming down the stairs, and my first sensation was that of profound astonishment at this evidence that she really did exist. And even then the visual impression was more of color in a picture than of the forms of actual life. She was wearing a wrapper, a sort of

dressing-gown of pale blue silk embroidered with black and gold designs round the neck and down the front, lapped round her and held together by a broad belt of the same material. Her slippers were of the same color, with black bows at the instep. The white stairs, the deep crimson of the carpet, and the light blue of the dress made an effective combination of color to set off the delicate carnation of that face, which, after the first glance given to the whole person, drew irresistibly your gaze to itself by an indefinable quality of charm beyond all analysis and made you think of remote races, of strange generations, of the faces of women sculptured on immemorial monuments and of those lying unsung in their tombs. While she moved downward from step to step with slightly lowered eyes there flashed upon me suddenly the recollection of words heard at night, of Allegre's words about her, of there being in her 'something of the women of all time.'"

His throat being dry, Morgan paused to swallow.

All eyes shifted from him to Mr. Scudder, who, amazingly, was seen to be smiling. Furthermore, zephyr-like, there came forth from between his lips a low, drawn-out "Ahh—" which, as the exhaled breath of it ran out, was followed by the astonishing words: "Helen of Troy . . . Cleopatra . . . Petrarch's Laura . . . fair Beatrix . . . the eternal girl next door . . ." uttered slowly, in a milking, ruminative way. Then, still looking off, out the window, Mr. Scudder lapsed into silence.

The room, along with its transfixed occupants, waited.

The bell rang: a shattering trill.

At the sound, instantly, Mr. Scudder reacted with his usual master-to-dog look in the door's direction and the curt, unleashing words: "Class dismissed."

There ensued the noise and movement of departure.

Only Morgan remained in place. He stood, still as a statue, *The Arrow of Gold* clasped to his chest, the awful moment of censure upon him.

"Well, Shurtliff," Mr. Scudder began, "here we are, the two of us, left with Allegre's words echoing in our ears."

Morgan managed a weak: "Yes, sir."

"Relax," Mr. Scudder said.

In the circumstance, Morgan, though, could not.

"Let us agree, Shurtliff," Mr. Scudder recommenced, "that in future you will bring only your Latin book to this class."

Morgan nodded. "Yes, sir."

"I have your word on it?"

"Yes, sir."

"That's all then. You may go."

He could go! Had been told that he might. Yet he remained.

"What's your problem, Shurtliff?"

"I don't understand, sir."

"What, that I've let you off the hook?"

"Yes."

"Ah," Mr. Scudder murmured, "I see." Then, with an abstract smile: "Someday you'll understand, Shurtliff. Meanwhile, chalk it up to luck."

"If you say so, sir . . . Thank you."

"My pleasure."

In that seemingly unreal way, for the time being, the episode, as a portent, rested.

_✍

1937

He met her in early January at a noontime ice-skating party given by Lucy Blackett. Her name, Lucy told him, was Maud Leigh.

When he first saw her, she was skating alone, fast and rapt and hatless, straight down the middle of the long, narrow pond. Abetted by a strong following wind, she was all but flying, or so she appeared to be, and as she neared the pond's far end he began to fear for her—that she would not be able to stop herself—that she would slam headlong into the spearing branches of a low-lying clump of ice-bound alders. But just short of the hazard, as he held his breath, she dug the tip of her left skate blade hard into the ice and performed—angel of excitement—a most beautiful about-face jump, after which, without so much as a glance around, she shot off again, back, over the pond's gleaming reach, headed, as if he had called to her, straight toward him. She wore a coat of royal blue; her scarf and gloves were scarlet; the sun made a blaze of her fair hair. With an amazed heart he watched her, and—without knowing that her eyes were brown, flecked with motes of gold, and that her voice was low and alluring and as pliant as a divining Gypsy's—all in a moment, immemorially rejoicing, he became a man in love.

The most miraculous aspect of that fateful moment was that after the fact of it, Maud Leigh let him court her: first with small sprays of flowers; next, with a volume of Shakespeare's sonnets on whose fly-leaf, with a trembling pen, he wrote: "For Maud—Valentine's Day 1937"; then, in early March, with a first burning touch to her hand, followed quickly by the beginning kiss of a million lingering others whose glories left him awed and pale and Maud his own to marry in June.

During that six-month courtship, he existed on a plane at a height untouched before by the foot of any man and breathed of an air unknown but to gods. Life *was* Maud, lived in the changing weather of her eyes, in the tropical warmth of her holding arms, in her hair, freed of a hat, cascading over his hands like lit water, in the murred sounds she made of happiness, in the final, intent way she walked at his side as she led him through a gauze of rain across a field to a patch of blue and in it knelt to pick the first cold violets of spring, and handed to him one by one the fragile blooms and with each one, with a shyness so undone she dared not look at him, said, "I love you, I love you," bloom after bloom. Day and night, he drifted on a sea of desire deeper and vaster than his reason could chart or his soul comprehend. . . .

Where, in the realm of the actual, did these makings of memories take place?

—In Hatherton, Ohio, a flourishing, affluent county-seat community about thirty-five miles southwest of Cleveland.

And where, during the courtship, was Maud's beauty and witchery domiciled?

—In her father's house, large and solid and elaborately Victorian—it—the place where Doctor Leigh, sitting as straight and keen-eyed as a perched hawk, watched Morgan's pursuit of his adored only child, noting Morgan's suitable neckties, his habit of punctuality, his agreeable smile, his tact as regards to Mrs. Leigh's hypochondria (cause of her nervosity), his ease with a teacup, his young virility, the decent hour of his departure after evenings spent in Maud's company; and—on the afternoon Morgan came to seek his permission to marry Maud—he took in, with a physician's calibrate gaze, the death-like pallor of Morgan's face as, standing in the center of the rust-and-blue medallion of the Oriental rug that covered the floor of the front parlor, Morgan formally declared: "I love your daughter, Doctor Leigh; I wish to marry her"—the words charged with determination, barring of refusal. "I love her—" repeated deeply, hands calm, but eyes desperate.

Over his cruelly starched collar, Doctor Leigh listened and nodded his encouragement as Morgan continued his appeal. He was already satisfied of Morgan's qualifications as a husband to Maud: he knew all about Morgan's rising reputation as a lawyer, and his well-established family— that the Shurtliff name was held in high social and business esteem in Cincinnati and Cleveland; that Morgan's maternal grandfather had served for two terms as United States senator from Ohio and at the time of his death was a federal judge; that Morgan's father was the majority stockholder and president of the family's lucrative salt refinery and that he was, too, an orchardist (his apple plantation was famous), which fact verified the Shurtliff temperament as being a pastoral one—a trait Doctor Leigh valued as an indicator of a man's long-range resolve and durability. And so, at the end of Morgan's appeal for Maud's hand in marriage, Doctor Leigh told him: "You have my entire consent and warmest blessings," then held out his hand to be shaken and watched the speed with which the color of life flooded back into Morgan's cheeks.

The June wedding was in the Leighs' garden on a day graced by sunlight and birdsong. Beneath an ivy-covered trellis, Morgan, barely breathing, waited with his best man and the minister. On Doctor Leigh's arm, over a carpet of new-mown grass, Maud advanced toward him. A light breeze that smelled of apple blossoms stirred the long, filmy skirt of her white dress. Her face was golden.

Oh God!—Morgan thought as if outside himself—make me worthy.

2 ∽ The Handspike

1938

Somewhere, there is an old photograph on the back of which is written in Maud's handwriting, "The Stanton's party—June 9, 1938"—a date just three days shy of her and Morgan's first wedding anniversary. In the photo's background there are a few shadowy figures who have taken on the gray coloration of a garden wall. In the immediate foreground, Maud stands, gazing, in an assured, serene, almost confiding way, straight at the camera. She is compellingly beautiful. . . . It seems reasonable to suppose that whoever took the picture really meant it to be just of her, yet, there, haunting the picture's extreme right edge, barely in the frame of it, Morgan can be seen, standing very erect and absolutely oblivious to everything and everyone but Maud, on whose person his eyes are concentrated, sharp and intending and positively glittering with lust. When Maud, laughing, showed the photograph to him, Morgan stared at it with disbelief, then gleefully gave it the out-loud title: "Venus Being Ogled by a Sexually Insane Man."

In the most blatant way, the photograph tells the story of the first year of their marriage, a period marked, as Morgan came to remember it, by a kind of blind indifference toward and about everything but the pursuit of their own physical pleasures—entwinements of prolonged carnality performed thriftlessly on a sovereign amatory bed in a fragrant, still room so removed from the heat and stress of the outside world as to cause them to feel forever exempted from its touch. . . . (Once, very late, on a black, wind-driven winter night, they heard the whetting bark of a dog on the track of prey and Maud, in a whisper, asked: "Will it find us?. . . " "No," he whispered back, holding her: "Never. We're beyond discovery.")

⌁

1939

In June, at the very beginning of the third year of their marriage, they were at breakfast on a Sunday morning, outdoors, still in their bathrobes and slippers, idling on the terrace that abutted Maud's cutting garden. The day's beauty claimed Morgan's attention. "We should take a picnic to the lake," he said.

To which Maud replied: "I want to have a baby."

He would always remember how his lack of surprise, surprised him. It occurred to him to wonder if, perhaps, his lack thereof had to do with the very day itself, long risen in its beauty, advancing now with a steady increase of perfection toward noon. Against the sun's march, he half closed his eyes. "How long," he asked, as much to the iridescent air as to Maud, "have you known you want to have a—" he stumbled for some strange reason on the word "baby," and used instead—"child?"

"Long enough to be certain," she replied. Then: "What about you? Has the idea crossed your mind?"

He told the truth: "Yes and no," he said. "No, because not in so complete a way as it obviously has yours; but—yes. Yes. As a *feeling*. Especially lately." As a feeling (he qualified to himself) which had something to do with Time as currency—gold in his pockets, so to speak—but spendable only in an other, larger world than the one he had lived in with such unabated happiness for the past twenty-four months, and which, now, (this extraordinary moment made it so) seemed already legendary.

"So?" Maud asked.

Over the rim of his coffee cup, he met her eyes. "Yes," he said. "Let's do it. Let's have a child."

"A beautiful baby," Maud elaborated.

"Yes."

"You look so pale."

"Do I?" He laughed, and stood up and kissed her. "I'm terribly thrilled," he said. Then: "Shall we take a picnic to the lake?"

"Yes."

He went into the house to shave and dress. As he buttoned his shirt, two lines of a poem of de Vigny's, memorized as a school-boy, came suddenly to mind:

> I love the sound of the horn, at night, deep in the woods.
> God! how sad is the sound of the horn deep in the woods.

The mirror into which he looked to check his appearance showed back to him his tears.

ఆ

"We will have a child."

Those words, so easily and confidently spoken, lowered a curtain on the experiencing of sensual pleasure for its own sake. Eagerly, they put themselves at the service of the profounder difference, uniquely their own for its ardor of desired consequence as much as, for its rapturous void, the other had been uniquely theirs.

ఆ

(On Sunday, September 3, 1939, England and France went to war against Germany.

Morgan's father was visiting him and Maud that weekend.

From that fateful hour two days before when Germany had invaded

Poland, the radio had dominated their lives. As they listened to the transmitted announcement of England's declaration of war, Morgan's father began to sob. In the peaceful room, the sound, startling in the extreme, came out in three choked inhalations of despair followed by the wrung words: "My dear children . . ."

Morgan, cut to the core, remembered another day. "My darling boy—" his father had said, and, weeping, holding Morgan to him so tightly that the links of his gold watch-chain cut into Morgan's cheeks: "Your mother is dead." That had been long ago, when Morgan was twelve: it was the one other time he had seen his father so undone.)

‹ᴈ

1940

In January, the "verdict," as Maud called it, was given by two specialists: they could have no children of their own.

At the hospital in Cleveland, at the conclusion of the final conference, the senior doctor of the team centered his attention on Maud: "Think about adopting a baby," he advised. "In my opinion, the best agency is Tilden-Herne. It's run by a remarkable woman. Tell her I sent you. . . ." He wrote her name on a piece of paper which he handed, or tried to, to Maud, but she shook her head and refused to take it.

Morgan reached for it and slipped it into the breast-pocket of his suit.

The doctor continued to look at Maud: "If you should feel the need of some psychological help, Mrs. Shurtliff, I can refer—"

Maud, drawing on her coat, cut him off with: "That won't be necessary." She stood up and crossed the room and waited with her back to the door while Morgan went through the decent rites of departure.

"Let me hear from you," were the doctor's last words.

On the drive back to Hatherton, Maud slumped into the far corner of the car's front seat, closed her eyes, and fell into a silence which Morgan, mired in the thick of his own thoughts, made no effort to break. But when they reached home, he told her: "You must come for a walk with me." It was an order, the first of a few he ever gave to her.

She complied with a graceless shrug and fell into step at his side. In the field behind their house, in the chill of the sunless January afternoon, by the bend of the winter-running creek, she turned to him and wept in his arms: "My damn, deceiving body," she cried.

"Don't," he told her deeply. "Don't. It doesn't matter."

"But it does," she said with a violent quietness; then, in a warning voice: "You'll see. It will make a difference."

"Tell me what we're talking about," he urged.

"My body," she answered: "That it can't do what it should."

"*Should?* By whose decree? Surely not mine."

She stiffened: "I'm sterile," she said. "That's really what's on both of our minds, isn't it?"

He put her from him: "Not on mine," he answered, "and I resent the charge."

"Don't be lawyerly with me," she threatened, "and don't pretend on my account."

"Pretend *what?*"

"That my being sterile doesn't matter."

"I'm not pretending anything," he said, becoming angry. "As a matter of fact, I'm so far from pretending that I don't mind telling you I think you're behaving like a selfish fool." He saw the stung look on her face: he had never come close to speaking to her like that; never imagined that he would. Sorrowing, he felt the lash swing back on himself. He watched for a moment the creek's water, black and glistening, fringed, at its rapid middle flow, by a thin edging of ice. He turned back to Maud: "Please—" he said in an anguished voice, "we're in this together."

She met his gaze and under the sway of its appeal said: "Let me have a few minutes alone." And, because he stayed: "I'm sorry, Morgan. More than anything I wanted to have your child."

"As I wanted yours," he answered, barely able to. "But we can't, so let's accept that we can't and go on." He remembered then—even smiled— and with his right hand delved through the stuff of his muffler and over-coat and drew out from his suit pocket, the piece of paper. "Voila!" he said, waving it in the air, the very ass of an amateur magician: "'The Tilden-Herne Adoption Agency, Miss Zenobia Sly.'"

"*What?*" Maud asked with the first rise of a spontaneous laugh he'd heard from her in days: "What was that name?"

"Sly," he replied, and spelled it out: "S-L-Y. Miss *Zenobia* Sly."

"Imagine going through life with a name like that."

Her laughter encouraged him: "Wouldn't it be a good idea to give the lady a call?"

She sobered instantly: "Would an adopted child please you as much as our own?"

"Is the moon made of green cheese?" he shot back at her. "Oh, Maud, for God's sake—*try*."

"Give me a few days," she said.

But he knew it was his chance, so pled his case: "You've put the question to me, so you must hear my answer, and it's 'yes.' *Yes,* I can imagine being pleased by and loving an adopted child as much as I would our own. Maybe even more."

She visibly brightened. "At least," she said, "we can choose its gender." Then: "A boy," she thought aloud: "I'd like a boy." And then, with a gesture that undid him, she took off her gloves and put her naked hands in his. "Thank you, Morgan," she said.

≈

Starting in February, separately and together, week in and week out, they were scrutinized and exhaustively interviewed and their home minutely inspected by staff-members of the Tilden-Herne Adoption Agency.

"What's left for them to consider?" Maud asked of Morgan at the end of yet another wearying meeting.

"My tonsils," Morgan answered with a wry smile. "They haven't checked yet to see if I've had them out."

"Oh, Morgan—" she lowered her head. "What if we fail at this?"

All in a few weeks' time, she had lost the confidence that had so distinguished her. "We won't fail," he told her.

"What makes you so sure?"

"It's gone too far."

"What's gone too far?"

"Their interest in us," he answered.

"But how much longer do you think it will be before they tell us something definite?"

"I don't know, Maud. I don't know how they think or how they work."

He considered for a moment, then: "Meanwhile, we shouldn't talk about it so much, don't you agree?"

She nodded. "Yes . . . I'll try harder not to."

"I said *we*," he corrected.

"I heard you."

"Maud."

Thenceforth they practiced that brand of patience which shows in the faces of people who wait hourly in the thirst of drought for the coming of rain.

With Lucy Blackett as her teacher, Maud took up needlepoint. The close work sent her to the oculist for her first pair of glasses. In them, she looked older, more serious, more determinedly independent. "The new me," she knowingly said of herself the first time she wore them in Morgan's presence. . . . For himself, he went back to reading: during the prolonged, absorbed season of his bridegroomship, he had fallen away from the habit and came back to it now with a sense of thanksgiving. To read of the lot and destinies of others and of the tests they were put to and triumphed over or failed at, made him feel about his own life less amazed, less anxious, less—(he shied from the word for its hint of betrayal to Maud, but it persisted in his thoughts)—hermetic.

⁕

At last, in mid-May (they all but trembled as they read it), a letter came summoning them to appear the following Wednesday before the still unmet, by now fabled Miss Zenobia Sly.

("Miss Sly makes the final decision," one of the staff had told them. Another had warned: "Everything depends on Miss Sly.")

"Come in," Miss Sly greeted them, holding open her office door: "Do please sit down."

She was of average height, in her fifties, large-boned, stamina-stout, oddly graceful in her movements and, Morgan judged by one look into her clear blue eyes, extremely shrewd. The top of her head was crowned by a horse's-tail length of coarse brown hair wound into an immense, slip-shod bun through the center of which were speared, geisha-like, the sharpened lengths of two red-lacquered Tilden-Herne pencils.

Morgan found her fascinating.

She took her place at her desk, where, from a mercilessly straight, wooden-backed, uncushioned chair, she wordlessly stared first at him, then at Maud, before declaring: "My staff and I have met several times over your case. . . . We are all very impressed by your qualifications as adoptive parents." (In response to Maud's smile, Morgan thought he detected a slight easing of her mouth's firm set.) "You've specified your wish for a male infant," she went on, and, at their nods: "There's a long waiting list for male infants. A *very* long list. It will take time."

"How long do you think?" Morgan ventured to ask.

"At least a year, Mr. Shurtliff."

"Damn," Maud let slip.

Miss Sly took up her pen. "Take heart," she said. "As of this moment, your name has been added to the list. That's already a great advance."

"A year is such a long time," Maud said.

"Not when you're my age," Miss Sly tartly rebutted. "And remember, I said at *least* a year. It could be longer, but I'm sure no more than sixteen months at the outside."

Morgan said: "It's a comfort to know we're on the list. We're grateful for that, Miss Sly."

"Indeed you *are* on the list, and I promise you that in time you will have your boy."

But Maud, terrier-like, persisted: "Is there a chance—a *chance* that it might be sooner?"

Miss Sly appeared to soften: "I do wish I could tell you otherwise, but I don't see how it could be possible, given the length of the list. I'm truly sorry, Mrs. Shurtliff." Having dealt the blow, she did then what Morgan thought was very strange: she got up from her desk and with a kind of mighty languor wandered over to the window and looked out and up, into the branches of a maple tree whose furled, rust-colored leaf-buds were just beginning to open against the May sky. "It's lovely to see Nature come alive again after such a long winter as we've had," she mused as idly as a guest at a tea party: "I do so enjoy the spring, don't you?"

Morgan smiled and said a prompt "Yes"; Maud but nodded.

"My house is on a pond," she went on in a vague, contemplative way, "a *small* pond, but large enough to accommodate a pair of geese that come back every year to nest and rear their young. They afford me no end of pleasure."

"My father," said Morgan, "always speaks of wild geese as being the whales of the sky."

"What a very intriguing image!" Miss Sly smiled over it. She hesitated, then: "An idea's just struck flint in my brain—"

Morgan laughed: "That's a wonderful phrase—"

"It's one *my* father was given to using," Miss Sly responded.

"And the idea, Miss Sly?"

"Ah, well—" Again she hesitated, but now she narrowed her eyes.

"What?" Morgan urged.

She prolonged the silence—allowed it to positively settle in—nearly, Morgan felt, as if she needed to, or more, as if whatever she was considering depended on its certain drama. Then with a light, melancholy laugh, she broke it: "No . . . I see now the folly of the idea." And briskly, dismissingly: "It wouldn't do. . . . I can't, as I think on it, really suppose you'd be in the least bit interested."

"In—*what?*" Morgan earnestly insisted.

"In . . . twins, Mr. Shurtliff."

"Twins?" He gasped.

"Twins," Maud breathed, sitting straighter.

"Immediately available." Miss Sly's voice was made of silk.

"Twins," Maud said again.

"Twin . . . girls," Miss Sly amended.

"Twin *girls*," Maud echoed.

Morgan heard in her voice the note of wonder, of tremendous attraction, and turned to her, expecting to meet her eyes, but she was staring off, sitting absolutely still, her face suffused by a calm cast of womanliness heretofore unknown to him, the very strangeness of which immeasurably moved him and equally anguished him, as, almost at once it came clear to him that for her, just then, he did not exist. What saved him—saved, that is, his own dignity in his own eyes at that critical moment, was a certain obstacle in his character to self-pity; that, and, at the same time, the suddenly seen, suddenly experienced sense of himself as being, in the truest, garnering sense of the word, a husband. And so, at once, he determined to take from himself the dare of his calling, and, with his eyes in Miss Sly's waiting ones, he said: "My wife must of course speak for herself"—peripherally, he saw Maud, in the quickest way, turn in her chair and face him—"but as far as I'm concerned, I find the idea of twin daughters very appealing."

Instantly, the orderly room suffered the commotion of Miss Sly's upflung arms and incantatory cry of, "*Splendid!* Splendid!"—at the same time Maud exclaimed, "Morgan, so do I!" and delivered upon him an embrace so flung in its gladness that his chair teetered and threatened a backward fall, a disaster he averted by a jogo-like forward thrust of his body, which agile deed obliged the chair, somewhat against its will, to finally right itself.

"My soul, Mr. Shurtliff!" Zenobia Sly declared. "Are you all right?"

"I think so." Morgan laughed. "I think so."

"Isn't it astonishing the way things work out?" Miss Sly exclaimed.

"Astonishing," Maud trilled.

Like a proud ship under full sail, Miss Sly moved back to her desk: "You'll want to see the twins as soon as possible." She consulted her date-book: "What about the day after tomorrow? That's Friday. At ten. Is that convenient for both of you? . . . Good. Come here to my office: I'll go up to the nursery with you."

Maud's excitement was palpable: "How old are they?" she asked.

"Three weeks next Saturday," Miss Sly replied, "and they are beautiful. . . . But you'll see for yourselves." Then, her mood shifted and, in the shift, her eyes took on a darker cast: "I'm sure my staff has apprised you of the policy of confidentiality we practice here at Tilden-Herne as regards the biological mothers of the children we put up for adoption. It's a policy we believe to be psychologically sound and humanly decent—so, normally, I never speak to prospective adopting parents about the biological mother, but in this case—" she hesitated, reflected, made her decision, and went on: "in this case, I feel *inspired*"—Morgan loved the antique, lit way she stressed the word—"to share with you my knowledge of her character as being, in every sense, fine. *Exceptionally* fine," she concluded with a keen ardor.

Morgan, moved by the force of her sincerity, said: "It's very good of you to tell us this. It's a valuable thing to know."

But Maud brought her hands tightly together and held them so, defiantly: "I have absolutely no interest in the twins' biological mother," she said. "None at all." Her voice was petulant, tainted, Morgan thought, by jealousy.

He lowered his head, and from that posture of near dismay, heard Miss Sly's unruffled reply: "Yours is a quite usual and thoroughly healthy attitude, Mrs. Shurtliff. . . . We will speak no further of the matter." She adjusted the cuff of her blouse. Then: "It's understood of course that until you've *seen* the twins and had time to talk fully between yourselves about the undertaking of parenting them, I won't consider you to be in the least bit committed. You might, I mean, as you come to review all the ramifications, go back to your initial desire for an infant boy."

"No!" Maud broke in: "That's not possible now."

"My dear, long experience has taught me that nothing is impossible," Miss Sly countered.

But Maud, intent, disallowed the remark: "Please," she began: "I'm dying to know how soon—*when*—might we have the twins?"

"Well, Mrs. Shurtliff, let me think a moment. . . . You'll see them day after tomorrow. Then, over the next week or so, you must think in depth and search your hearts in order that you be *sure* you want these infants. When and if you *are* sure, you must call me and come again to see me. Then, providing the three of us are in complete accord, the legal process can be set into motion. Our Mr. Jackson is in charge of that. He will draw up and submit the necessary documents to the court. The court will receive those documents and, in due course, a hearing will be scheduled at which you will both appear in company with myself and Mr. Jackson and one of our staff members. That will be Miss Avery, in all likelihood. The court rarely denies a petition of adoption brought before it by an authorized agency of good repute. In my tenure as head of Tilden-Herne, an instance of refusal has never occurred." (She said the last words with a show of pride.) "And that's it! The adopting parents leave the court with the papers of adoption in hand, which papers free them to claim and take home the child—in this case, the children—as their own, for life."

"How long might all that take?" Maud asked.

"Oh, a month at the most," Miss Sly answered; then qualified: "A month at the most *after* I am convinced that *you* are *sure*."

"It's what I've prayed for," Maud said. Tears stood in her eyes. "I'm no good with words, Miss Sly, but Morgan is. Please speak for me, Morgan," she appealed.

But he could not, either for himself or for her—the condition of his thoughts being too deep, his world so suddenly altered, his view of it so brand new. All he said was: "We'll be here Friday at ten." He stood up, went around Miss Sly's desk, took her extended hand and, then, because and just as, for *her* reasons, she had earlier felt inspired to do the extraordinary thing, so, now, he was inspired for *his* reasons to incline his head, downward, and to kiss her cheek. To this action, her response—in that she evidenced no sign of surprise and remained silent—was nothing short of queenly.

⚭

It was late afternoon when they left Miss Sly and started on the trip back to Hatherton. Traffic was heavy. In the main, the drivers of the cars were men, husbands and fathers (Morgan reasonably assumed) returning to their homes at this tail-end hour of the workday. The expression on most of their faces was a classless one of release heightened by anticipation: soon, for each, an arrival marked by the humbling, age-old renewals of spousal greetings and children's kisses. . . . Such was the imagined ending he gave to their journeys, and in such way read in their faces his own future: saw himself as a soldier flanked by soldiers must see himself—as one of many, even as he feels in his breast the fervid beat of his own individual heart. . . . Ah, the astonishments of this day! . . . As he drove, he toiled with the issue of how and where to begin to approach what seemed to him to be a predestined reality into whose darkness of consequence, like a trusting blind man, he was allowing himself (and Maud) to be led. . . . And then he had a sudden image of himself as a thirteen-year-old reading *Moby Dick* for the first time. A picture. It was in February; he was house-bound with strep throat; outdoors, it was snowing. On a couch in his father's library, covered by an eiderdown quilt, he lay supine, devouring the book, enraptured, innocent: innocent above all. . . . *By heaven, man, we are turned round and round in this world, like yonder windlass, and Fate is the handspike.* . . . He read the sentence; read it again; then again. The words thrilled him, and under their influence he closed his eyes and conjured distant scenes of his life to come—scenes charged with extraordinary possibilities and great deeds—all already chosen by Fate for him and all just waiting for him in the run of his life to catch up to, and, as and when he did, in Fate's name, as Fate's servant, to faithfully fulfill.

. . . And now? Now he despaired at his lack of a determining faith by which he might account for all that had so suddenly, so incalculably befallen him. Infant twin girls! Had he been born twenty-nine years ago for them? Or had they been born three weeks ago for him? Like a deranged sailor who finds himself tied in the rope of his own knottings, he labored to free himself of the hold these questions had on him: worked his way in stages from the fastenings of perplexity to the sapphire lunacies of an extrinsic calm and from that calm to a kind of blasphemous merriment whose instantly recalled embodiment caused him to erupt into laughter. He caught his breath and in a voice that crackled with mirth, he said: "She's incredible."

Maud turned to him a charmed face and instantly affirmed: "Miss Sly."

"The one and only," he gleefully answered. "We've been had, my darling."

"Royally," she purred.

"And we're done for. Absolutely done for."

"Absolutely," Maud agreed. Whereupon, she reached out and took his right hand from off the steering-wheel and carried it with a slow solemnity to her lips: "I'm so terribly happy, Morgan," she said.

With something like a rush of pride, he assumed responsibility for her lack of need to call into question his own happiness. He only truthfully said: "So am I."

Her linking smile was entire. As its witnessing partner, he fleetingly allowed himself the pleasure of glorying in it.

❦

He dreaded going to bed that night. He was physically alert but emotionally exhausted. He anticipated hours of wakefulness and an early rising in a spent state to a day crammed with work assigned to him earlier
in the week by Judge Malcolm, not a page of which he had as yet put
thought or pen to. Imprisoned in the dark, he lay in the bed beside
Maud's dreaming body and waited, martyr-like, for the night's tortur-
ings to begin. Yet he slept like a rock.

It was Maud's touch on his arm that woke him. She was lying on her
side, looking at him: "Hello—" she said quietly.

"Hello yourself. . . . What time is it?"

"Early. Sixish." She pulled the blanket up over his shoulders. "I've
been thinking."

"Oh?"

"Shouldn't we name one of them Caroline, in honor of your mother?"

Spoken in the dawn light, her words—how could he possibly have
anticipated them?—struck him as fabulous. If at that moment a racing
herd of wild horses, white and perfectly muscled and in their transient
swiftness making of the air a whistle, were to be seen crossing the open
spaces of his windowed view, he would not have been more overwhelmed: all his boyhood memories of his dead, greatly loved mother,
he had shared with Maud: only with Maud. . . . In a voice thick with
emotion, he said: "What a beautiful idea."

"So—" Maud mused on: "Caroline for one. And the other?"

"Julia," he instantly answered, not entirely out of the blue: it was a
name he had always immensely liked.

Maud gave voice to the pairing: "Caroline and Julia." Then, in reverse:
"Julia and Caroline. . . . Perfection."

He got out of bed. "I'll be back," he said.

It was the last time in their marriage that they made love with all the
old, isolated, intact, clockless passion of their earliest encounters. When,
on succeeding dawns, they would turn sexually to one another, it would
not be as bold, confident invaders of a distant Eden, but as bound, abiding guardians of their imperfectly understood, imperfectly known
earthly lives.

The world, Morgan came to understand, had found them out at last.

On Friday, as planned, they saw the twins.

In the Tilden-Herne nursery, in a double-crib, the sleeping infants lay side by side on their backs.

They bent over them and gazed at them and in hushed, festive voices, spoke of them. The one on the left they named Caroline; the one on the right, Julia. Caroline had a tiny, brown, raised freckle at the base of her left earlobe, without which distinguishing mark it would have been impossible to tell her from Julia. When the twins woke, one of the nurses said that now they could be picked up and fed. With a tender ease, Maud lifted Caroline from the crib.

"Mr. Shurtliff?"

It was the first time in his life an infant was held out to him with the certain understanding that he was to receive it and house it in his arms. Or, rather, *arm*—his left one—as Maud was seen doing, with the globe of the baby's head nestled in the crook of her elbow, the diapered rump fitted into the shallow of her palm, the span of the fragile body connecting these two anatomical extremes accommodated—Lord!—*somehow*. . . . All as he was expected to do; all as he desired to do; all as—gracelessly, with a perilous pleasure—he somehow did. *(Bless thee, Bottom! Bless thee! Thou art translated. . . .)* In his right hand he took the offered bottle and shyly touched its nipple to Julia's mouth, then instantly laughed: he had seen puppies clamp like that with their jaws onto the teats of Dora, his father's old coon-hound. . . . He stared into Julia's face, impressed by her greed, enchanted by her pinkness, by the throb of a tendril-vein on her forehead, by her clear eyes, by the dwelling way she frowned at him. He had an urge to try out his voice on her, but the presence of three nurses and Miss Sly, who was standing off against the wall, viewing the proceedings with the calm, lit gaze of a lioness, acted upon his tongue as would a bit in the mouth of a horse. Not Maud, though, with her face bent down to Caroline's, whispering a series of half-sung, half-spoken fooleries that drew from the baby a chain of smiles drowned in spittle.

 . . . Long, long ago, the outcome had been fixed. Was deeply, deeply known. . . .

Still: he sought Maud's certain attention and said to her the given, single, ending word: "Yes."

"Yes," she whispered back to him; and again, with a celebrating passion: "Yes."

He turned to Miss Sly as to a witness. She nodded without expression, then startled with: "The condition still pertains: You must take at least a week to be absolutely *sure*," said with resolve, after which she smiled and glanced at her watch: "I must get back to my office. . . . But you stay as long as you like."

"May I come with you for a moment?" Morgan asked.

"Indeed," Miss Sly replied.

He told Maud he wouldn't be long; he allowed her to believe his purpose in going with Miss Sly was the missioned one implicit in her eyes' appeal: *vow to her our decision.*

As before, he sat opposite Miss Sly, who, as before, positioned herself behind her desk, from which place she looked at him with the full recognizing gaze of a practiced prelate. He all but expected her to say, "You have a confession to make. . . ." And, in a sense, she did: "You've something of a personal nature on your mind," she stated. And to his silent nod: "Am I correct in supposing it's one you feel you can't share with Mrs. Shurtliff?"

Neither her astuteness or frankness surprised him. "Yes," he immediately replied: "It's a concern I can't seem to rid myself of." He faltered: "I don't know quite how to put it."

"Don't try to be eloquent," she encouraged.

"Well," he began: "it's about the twins' mother—that she must be dying of sorrow."

Miss Sly sat straighter. A wary response, Morgan felt: protective: the equivalent of clutching tighter something concealed in the hand. Instantly he said: "I don't want to talk about *her*. Truly. All I would like—and I appreciate that it might be difficult to do—is that *somehow* she be given to understand she is"—he hesitated, trying to find just the right word, then, somewhat sure, concluded—"acknowledged."

Miss Sly sat, an immense presence, silent, for a frozen moment, then came to life and slowly put to him: "By *whom* acknowledged, Mr. Shurtliff?—" the words were posited not as a question but as a statement, gently, with genius: by saying his name, she spared him (he real-ized it at once) the blush of having to answer "Why, by *me*, of course."

He lowered his head. He had not thought it through, had not seen that to have the twins' biological mother "acknowledged" by him as their true progenitrix was to tacitly dispute the existence and workings of her own consciousness: that to add the surrogate conceits of his own mere sadness to the already scored sorrows of her intelligence, would be to apply salt to the rawness of an open wound. When finally he raised his head, his eyes engaged Miss Sly's waiting gaze. "I understand the nature of my error," he said simply. "Thank you for setting me straight."

She was prompt in her response: "You owe me no thanks. You cor-rected yourself."

He would remember afterwards the bond of her smile and how the wall clock ticking off the passing seconds did not act upon them as a prod, but as a complement to their established peace, "I mustn't keep you any longer. . . . We'll call you in a week's time."

She nodded. "Good-bye, Mr. Shurtliff."

"Good-bye, Miss Sly."

❧

Wednesday, June 12, 1940, was their third wedding anniversary. By the odd workings of chance, it was also the scheduled day for the adoption hearing before Judge Morton Thayer. . . . They woke early, turned to each other with a companionate restraint, got out of bed and dressed, all very quickly, as if there were someone still asleep in the house whom they wished not to disturb. He saw how Maud's hands shook when she poured their coffee. "We'll win the day," he told her. She disarmed him with a soft cry: "Oh, Morgan—" He held her and repeated: "We'll win the day." On the drive into Cleveland, they barely spoke.

Miss Sly was standing in the sunshine on the courthouse steps. They greeted her, then Morgan told her: "Today is our third wedding anniver-sary."

She smiled. "So it's a double red-letter day. What a nice coincidence."

Mr. Jackson and Miss Avery joined them. Miss Sly took command: "Let's go in," she said with a touch to the armor of her starched blouse.

The hearing was formal and splendidly contained—an example,

Morgan thought, of the law functioning at its cleanest, clearest best. Within half-an-hour all was over, the papers of consent in his briefcase—the proceedings capped by Judge Thayer's barked "Congratulations," tendered with a handshake first to Maud, then to himself. Maud wept. For the second time, Morgan kissed Miss Sly—and wondered: did tears always stand in her eyes on such similar occasions as had taken place under her aegis in these chambers? And again the notion seized him that she had some deep, ulterior, solemn interest in the matter of the twins' fate—that, in truth, she had gambled all the cards in her hand on the successful outcome of this final play. . . . They urged her to have lunch with them, but she had a Tilden-Herne board meeting, she explained, so must, with regret, decline: "But I'll see you when you come for the twins day after tomorrow. It's at ten you're coming, isn't it?" She cocked her head to one side: "I'll think of you tonight when I have my evening drink. Mine will be my usual dash of bourbon. I expect yours will be champagne. Oh—I mustn't forget to tell you: my geese have four goslings. I've counted them through my field-glasses. You know the way they gawk their heads up out of the nest, looking about. Spying on *me*, I expect. Well—good-bye until day after tomorrow."

🖜

(Emotionally, two days later, on Friday, June 14, for the first of countless times to come, they carried the twins over the threshold of their home. On that day too, half a world away, Hitler's army entered Paris. Morgan heard the news of this event as, with a tyro's awkwardness, he fitted a diaper around Caroline's tiny, hipless body. The sorrowing authority of Ed Murrow's voice reporting over the radio—a voice by now so familiar—brought a blur of tears to his eyes. By June 22—the day France accepted Germany's terms of surrender—he had become an expert at the task of diapering.)

🖜

On Sunday afternoon, June 23, in the First Presbyterian Church of Hatherton, the twins were christened by the Reverend Mr. William M. Halliday. Family and friends stood shoulder to shoulder around the flower-bedecked baptismal font. Maud held Julia; Morgan, Caroline. Large-eyed and red-faced with excitement, the children of the Sunday School choir, under Miss Sara Moore's direction, began the ceremony by singing "Oh, Happy Day," followed by all the verses (memorized) of "Fairest Lord Jesus."

Lucy Blackett was named godmother to both infants.

Geoffrey Barrows, Morgan's friend from his Harvard law-school days, was named as Caroline's godfather, and Peter Leigh, Maud's cousin, as Julia's.

Caroline Cunningham Shurtliff.

Julia Leigh Shurtliff.

Afterwards, at the christening party, Geoffrey charged Morgan with: "You used to be an Episcopalian."

Morgan smiled: "*Officially*, I still am. But not here in Hatherton. For starters," he went on, "there *is* no Episcopal church. It's a given in these parts that if you're gentry and a church-goer, it's as a Presbyterian you worship."

"So when in Rome—" Geoffrey interposed.

"Exactly." They were alone for a few minutes in Morgan's study.

"Does it ever come up as an adversative question? The Episcopal church versus the Presbyterian church?" Geoffrey asked.

"For me, personally, you mean? No. And it's never remotely come up as an issue between Maud and me. She goes to church with a fair degree of regularity, and as often as not I go with her. The Reverend Mr. Halliday's never sought to convert me and I'm always made to feel welcome at the services by him and the congregation. I suppose it's possible they're all just tolerating me pending the day I see the Light on their terms." Morgan paused, then laughed: "I did have one agonizing moment with Doctor Leigh when I was courting Maud—"

"I like him. He's entertaining."

"He is. He's a damn good doctor, too. But it sure the hell wasn't easy getting past him as a suitor to Maud."

Geoffrey asked: "What was the agonizing moment?"

Again, Morgan laughed: "You have to bear in mind that it happened early on after I met Maud—the third or fourth time I called on her—I don't remember which for sure. Doctor Leigh—not Maud—answered the doorbell. He took my coat and told me Maud would be down in a minute and meanwhile, if I'd come with him into the library, he'd show me a book I might find interesting. It was a cold winter night and there was a fire blazing in the hearth—all very cozy. Incidentally, the library in the Leighs' house is an interesting room, paneled in oak, with a fine, elaborately carved mantel of flowers and vines and birds. If we have time tomorrow before you leave, I'll take you to see it. . . . The book Doctor Leigh showed me turned out to be a history of Hatherton written by his father for the Pioneer Society. He told me I was welcome to borrow it and I thanked him, and then—I couldn't help feeling he'd *planned* to do it—he began to reminisce about what he called his 'growing-up years.' I figured right off that it was his way of letting me know the rules he'd been taught to play by and, by imitation, they'd be the ones I'd be judged by as a suitor to Maud. . . . He began by telling me he'd been raised in a strict Presbyterian tradition—that on Sundays as a boy he'd only been allowed to read Fox's *Book of Martyrs* and Gorman's *Bible Stories* and that the only recreation permitted him was the putting together of jigsaw puzzles depicting such edifying scenes as the Taj Mahal, the British Houses of Parliament, the Eiffel Tower, and the Great Wall of China. Those were the only ones he mentioned that I remember. . . . Then he went on to say that it had been implanted in him to believe that, quote, all Democrats were unrespectable, all Methodists uneducated, all Catholics slaves to the pope, and as for the Episcopalians, the only thing its founders had succeeded in doing was to construct the largest needle with the largest eye through which the most camels could most comfortably pass. Unquote. All of which views," Morgan continued on over Geoffrey's guffaw, "he said he took for granted in precisely the same way he took for granted the cake of Babbit's soap on the washstand in his room and the bottle of castor oil in the family medicine cabinet. . . . By the time he finished, my balls had withered to the size of sunflower seeds. . . . But I figured what the hell—I'd better bite the bullet and tell him then and there that I'd been reared as an Episcopalian, and do you know what he said? He said he should have guessed it from the fact that I wore shirts with unstarched collars."

Geoffrey howled. "*Then* what?"

"Well, nothing really," Morgan answered. "He offered me a cigar—a very good one, I might add—and just as we were lighting up, Maud came in. The three of us talked together for a few minutes—I have absolutely no memory about *what*—and then Doctor Leigh said he had to catch up on his reading of a current crop of medical journals, so he'd repair to his study and leave us to entertain ourselves. . . . End of story."

Geoffrey's long mouth sustained its smile. "It's a—"

—but whatever he was about to say was never concluded: Morgan's father, clad in cutaway and striped trousers, appeared in the doorway, "*Pa,*" Morgan greeted him; "Come in."

"Sorry to interrupt, but Maud's wielding her camera. She wants you both in the garden."

"Ah, the camera," Morgan said: "Posterity's revenge." He made a head-to-toe, prizing sweep of his father's figure. "You do look splendid, Pa."

"I'm glad you think so," Ansel Shurtliff laughed. "I felt the occasion warranted resurrecting the rig from the cedar closet. The last time I wore it was two years ago when old Senator Cleary's granddaughter was married. The bride's father assigned me the task of keeping the senator sober."

"And did you succeed?" Morgan asked.

"We mutually suffered," his father replied. He turned to Geoffrey: "It's very touching to us, your coming the distance from Philadelphia for today's doings."

"I wouldn't have missed it for the world," Geoffrey answered.

"We'd better go," Morgan urged, "or Maud'll have our hides," on which note, with a hand-touch to the knot of his tie, he led his father and Geoffrey from the room.

෧

That night, after dinner, after Ansel Shurtliff had departed, after the twins were asleep and Maud had gone to bed, Morgan and Geoffrey talked late. Over brandy, they sat in the lamplight, the thick pungencies of clipped boxwood-bushes drifting in through the open window, and from the yonder meadow the calling of a whippoorwill, lonelier in sound than an owl's bark. Relaxed, sure of one another, they spoke of the past and present, the exchanges intimate, made with a renewal of the old sequestered languor that had so characterized the long confabulations they had used to have in the large, book-lined, randomly furnished room shared throughout their law-school years.

. . . In their senior year, Geoffrey had resisted Morgan's decision to begin his legal career in Hatherton. "With *your* marks, law review and all, and your connections, you're a shoe-in with the best Cleveland firms. For God's sake, why *Hatherton*?" Because (Morgan had defended) over the next ten years Cleveland would grow *out* to Hatherton, and he wanted to be in on the ground-floor makings of zoning-restrictions and the like: wanted to use the law as an overseeing instrument of control so that there would be a reason and *plan* to the expansion—not just an expedient, free-and-hard-dealing suburban and industrial raping of the rural lands he loved. *Plus*—he'd pressed on—the man in Hatherton with whom he'd be practicing was Judge Eustace Malcolm—a powerful figure in Ohio legal circles—retired as a federal district judge, but still active in the gold-plated Kissel, Chandler firm in Cleveland, of which he was a founding partner and in which he still retained a majestic "Of Counsel" relationship. "Professionally, I'll have the best of both worlds, urban *and* rural," had been Morgan's closing argument. But the issue had remained an internecine one between them: For weeks they had chewed it over, Geoffrey aggressively; Morgan with a stubborn sureness.

. . . And here they were, these few, fleeted years later, just as they had positioned themselves into being: Morgan, in Hatherton, a partner in Judge Malcolm's bristling, gaining firm; Geoffrey in his father's *echt*, long-established, staid Philadelphia firm. . . . Geoffrey had reported in considerable detail about what he was up to legally these days, and then it had been Morgan's turn, after which Geoffrey had conceded: "You sure have a greater variety of cases than comes across my desk and about a hundred times the responsibility. . . . I never thought I'd be saying this," he went on, stroking his cheek, his voice confiding, "but it was a wrong move, my going into Dad's firm. He wanted me to and I wanted to please him, but being the son of a senior partner in a shop rife with legal talent—all hard-breathing contenders for the big prizes—is a stickier proposition than I ever imagined it would be. . . . Dad bends over backwards not to show paternal favoritism, but he keeps tabs on the work I do for the other partners and he does it in a way that really burns me; you know—that convivial, intramural, inter alia approach: 'How's the boy doing? How's he proving out?'" Geoffrey's mouth twisted into a wintry smile: "Maybe I do him an injustice. Maybe the problem's all in my head. . . . *However*,"— Geoffrey drew out the word—"*as* a problem, it's about to go away. I've been waiting to tell you: I've decided to join the Air Force."

"Geoff!"

"Look: it's only a matter of time before we get in the war. Do you want to bet it'll be within a year?"

"No," Morgan said, "because I think so, too. . . . The Air Force . . . as a pilot?"

"If I qualify. I've been led to believe there's no reason why I won't."

"Sometime soon I'm going to have to decide what I'm going to do about the war. I've been thinking a lot about it."

"It's an easy call for me, Morgan. It's different for you, especially now with Caroline and Julia. You've powerful ties. . . . Speaking of which"— he brightened—"I had a positive twinge of envy this afternoon seeing you standing with Maud at the baptismal basin in all the accrued glory of your marital bliss. For a minute"—his smile was open now—"I almost regretted that I'm still single."

"No permanent attachment in sight?"

"None. Lots of activity, but nothing deathlessly significant. It's probably just as well, considering."

"Don't say anything to Maud yet about the Air Force, will you, Geoff? Any talk of war upsets her. I can't get near the subject with her."

"Right."

They sat in silence for a moment, then, acknowledging the lateness of the hour, agreed that they ought to turn in. The whippoorwill was still calling, its plaint coming now from the woodland west of the meadow. Even after Morgan closed the window they could still hear it. Geoffrey said: "It's a haunting sound."

"I hope it won't keep you awake."

"Not a chance."

Upstairs, at the door of the guest room, Morgan whispered a last question: "When do you expect to know about the Air Force?"

"Soon. I'm scheduled for a physical on Thursday. I'll keep you posted."

ᥕᴓ

(A letter came from Geoffrey about two weeks later: "I've just learned I've been accepted as a 'fly-fly' candidate. The examining medics were impressed by my good eyes, my sound heart and the health of my entrails. Their findings and those of a psychiatrist who certified me sane, did the trick. I'm to report in three weeks' time for training at Pensacola, Florida, particulars of address etc. to follow. I'll telephone soon. Pick your moment to tell Maud. Meanwhile, love to her, to *my* Caroline, to Julia. As ever, Geoff.")

ᥕᴓ

Over the course of the following weeks, Morgan came to marvel at Maud's stamina and equanimity. Hercules's labors in the Augean stable (he often thought) must have been an easier task than was hers as an attender to the twins' myriad, often fracturing needs. Each dawn, at their wakened cries of hunger, she would be out of bed like a shot, eager to see them and to serve them, and in that spirit went on through the arc of the day. Evening after evening, he would return home from the office and find her in the twins' room, singing to them, bent over their crib, or, sometimes, holding both of them in her arms (how did she do it?), showing them something out the window—the sunset, or the silver of a rising new moon—telling them about it, laughing. Her hair would be loosened, her face flushed, her beauty wanton. All in a rush, in one breath, he would cross the room and kiss her, then each twin. . . . It became an evening ritual that deepened in a meaning like the plot of a great book. . . . He felt for her a tenderness that sometimes verged on fear. "You're tired," he would say, touching her brow with the cushion of his thumb. And she would yield: "Yes, I am." But the satisfied look she gave him was the vital one of a victor.

Of their old, larky evenings, no vestige remained. No more the nights theirs to do with exactly as they pleased—a dinner in or out; a new movie at what older Hathertonians still called the "Opera House"; a dance at the country club; a rapidly conceived and executed supper party; a drive into Cleveland for a symphony concert or a play or a black-tie "do" at the grand house of a relative or older, nabob family friend (oh, those lovely, late homecomings); and gone, too, the simple, spontaneous act of leaving the house on a whim—a stroll together in the meadow before bed, or a spin downtown to Milar's Drug and Fountain Emporium for a suddenly yearned-for hot fudge sundae.

Now, when they sallied forth into the world of an evening, it was by a carefully worked out Plan, with Caroline and Julia left in the care of a Hatherton Hospital nurse recommended by Doctor Leigh. (Maud would never have considered using one of the high-school baby-sitters whose services were so popular with her friends.) Now, evenings out were Events, charged with the excitement of rarity.

⊸§

He became what is called "a light sleeper."

As a boy, in the earliness of certain calm evenings, he had liked to take his canoe onto the large pond that lay past the south-ending tree line of his father's orchards. (This was the same deep, spring-fed pond which, in his grandfather's time, had provided the winter ice for the summer tea.) He would paddle out to the middle of the pond and as the canoe glided forward under the impetus of a final stroke, he would take a balancing hold of its sides and in one deft action, swing his body off the thwart onto the canoe's cedar floor-boards, from which place, with his legs stretched out full length and the back of his head pillowed in his hands, he would close his eyes and sightlessly drift: drift with the lambency and oblivion of a floating feather, letting whatever thought strayed into his mind wander free over the surface of his consciousness in the same unguided, will-o'-the-wisp way the gentle evening breeze ferried his canoe, wherever, over the pond's surface. . . . There would be sounds so familiar he almost didn't hear them: the taking, snap-jawed, last-of-the-day feast of a bass; the solemn wing-beats of a low-flying, homing heron; the flicked rise and plop of a playful perch; the tuning up, setting-sun thrums of bullfrogs. . . .

. . . Now, neither fully asleep nor fully awake, he would lie in the dark beside a soundly sleeping Maud, and, in feel, be again on the pond in his canoe at the hour of twilight, drifting. Once, in the dead of the night, he laughed silently (or did he imagine his laughter?) over the fact that at age twenty-nine he had become the ghost of himself as a twelve-year-old boy.

⁓ঔ

It was mid-October. He had been a father for four months.

"You've become ambitious," Judge Eustace Malcolm said to him one morning in the office. "It shows in your work."

"Mouths to feed," Morgan replied.

"That'll do it." Judge Malcolm laughed. "Mind if I sit down?"

"Please do, sir."

The judge's portly figure complemented his love of conversation. "Did you know I was in the great war, Morgan?" he began; and to Morgan's affirmative nod: "I was well above the upper draft age when we entered the fray in 1917—married seven years, father of three young children—obviously not a foot-loose lad. But I wanted to serve in some capacity, so applied for a place in the Judge Advocate General's Corps. I was sent to Washington for a training course that lasted about three months and after I received my commission, to my considerable surprise and great delight, I was assigned to General Cornell's staff in Paris. . . . General Robert John Cornell. . . . Does that name mean anything to you?"

"I'm afraid not."

"It crops up now and again in the odd history book. I'll tell you about him another time. . . . Anyhow"—the judge exhaled—"I was billeted with a family who lived outside Paris; a very Catholic, hard-working, bourgeois family. The rather elderly paterfamilias—Monsieur Machavoine—held to the views of his ancestors with the same zeal a wise dog holds on to a bone that's still got a bit of marrow in it. He was a strict man, but charming in his way. Very well-mannered. Morally four-square. He'd inherited his land—quite a considerable tract—from his father, who'd inherited it from his, et cetera, going back God knows how many generations. You get the picture. . . . My French was pretty good; it still is, as a matter of fact. To put it simply—I could understand Monsieur Machavoine, and he could understand me. He liked to talk history with me and to mull over his life, and one evening he told me that when he heard the cry of his first-born child—a *son,* he was quick to tell me—he left his wife's bedside and went out into the field behind his house, and for the first time in his life, gazed on the land with a *possessor's* eye. . . . You follow me, Morgan?"

"Yes."

"He then went on to tell me that the next morning, he committed the only cruel act of his life. He rose at sunrise, he said, to a fair day—the first fair day after a long stretch of rainy ones. The month was April, and he had some plowing to do, a *lot* of plowing, and he wanted to get it done as quickly as possible so that he could set in his crops. . . . So he did that old, savage thing—long outlawed, by the way—that was once the habit of impatient peasants: he attached, as a prod, a bit of barbed wire to the inside of his plow-horse's crupper. He wanted, you see, to make the horse move faster, and, of course, the poor beast *did,* what with the barb pricking its rump every time it lifted a hoof. But then, Monsieur Machavoine noticed the blood. . . . With tears in his eyes, he told me of the shame he felt for causing his horse to suffer. He took his sin to his priest and confessed it, citing to the priest his son's birth on the previous evening as his reason for committing the sin of cruelty, claiming that, just in a matter of hours, a desire to conquer the world—that was the phrase he used—had taken possession of him." Judge Malcolm paused; then: "I'll never forget how *perfectly* I understood what he meant."

A parable, Morgan thought. But he did not attempt a grand response. He only sat back deeper in his chair, and with a smile, said, "Well, sir, I can't say I've developed a desire to conquer the world, but I know for sure that before long I'm going to have to add a new wing to my house."

Judge Malcolm laughed: "That's a sufficient prod, Morgan." He stood up: "And how *are* Caroline and Julia?"

"Marvelous."

"And Maud?"

"She admitted to me yesterday that once in a while she feels like a one-armed paper-hanger. But other than that, she's fine, thank you. Wonderful in fact."

"Might you all be home next Sunday afternoon?"

"Yes."

"Clara and I might likely drop by for a visit."

"That would be lovely. Please do."

"We'll phone first to make sure you're not in the middle of a nursery crisis. Meanwhile, give Maud my love." He glanced at the papers on Morgan's desk: "Is that the Veblen matter you're working on? . . . Durance vile . . . Slog on, young man, slog on. . . ." In the doorway he turned and bowed: "I'm off to the county courthouse. Marston against Baines . . . God help me."

~§

At home one night (this happened in early November), he worked late in preparation of an impending hearing which involved a client's right-of-way over a large parcel of land recently purchased for an unprecedentedly high price by an overly ambitious, opportunistic Cleveland developer. He finished writing the brief around midnight and, on his tardy way to bed, crept into the twins' room, expecting to find them as usual—that is to say, lying apart, asleep in the large of their double-crib, their pink faces silhouetted against the white sheet, the action of their breathing a gulping one, like that of birdlings. This was the sight he anticipated as, by the muted glow from the hall light, he peered down into the crib's latticed depths. . . . But—no! On this night, as if each were a magnet to the other, they had come together and were clasped at the crib's center in so merged and involved a way that for a moment he could not make out which arms and legs were Julia's, and which Caroline's. . . . And then—the sight rocked him—he saw that the thumb in Caroline's mouth was Julia's, and that in Julia's mouth, Caroline's thumb was fastened and being dreamily sucked.

The thought rushed upon him: *they are each other*: and he stood amazed, and truly for the first time and, with a gasp, took in the confounding implication of twinness as being a riddle of divided wholeness. . . . Until this moment, he had been reasonably confident that with will and a bit of luck, he could fulfill the basic tenets of responsible paternity: as provider, as protector, as instructor and nurturer. Now, though, as he gazed at the infants in the enigma of their girdled unity, his confidence was flawed by the question of a first sorrow: was he capable of being the severer of such an innocent phenomenon of oneness?

Had Maud ever found them thus immingled?

He put the question to her first thing the next morning. No, she had never seen them like that. Perhaps the time had come, she suggested matter-of-factly, for each to have her own crib. "I'll call Doctor Franklin and find out what he thinks."

Her practical response did not ease his lingering mood of sorrow.

"You're brooding," she mildly accused.

"It was an extraordinary thing to see," he defended.

She frowned: "You sound as if you think it was—unnatural."

"I didn't mean to," he instantly rejoined.

"After all, they're still tiny, and they had all those close months in the womb—"

"Yes," he interrupted, "but still . . . there was something about them that went way beyond just *physical* closeness, something—"

Maud held up an arresting hand: *"Don't,"* she said; then quickly, urgently, "You'll do a great wrong if you turn what you saw into a big mystery."

He made a movement of surprise: "Go on," he said.

Her response came like lightning. "Each has her own *soul,*" she told him fiercely, "and each human soul is independent. If we don't believe that, we'll queer them for life." Before he could speak, she surprised him further with: "It's Scripture."

"Scripture?" asked not as a test.

Which she understood. Quietly, she answered: "Mr. Halliday told me so."

He smiled: "Bless the Reverend Mr. Halliday," he said genuinely.

She came back with: "He's not the total ass you think he is."

"Maud! When did I ever say he was a total ass?"

"Well—"

"It's only his eternal smile, his everlasting fair-weather optimism and perpetual good-will, his persistent willingness to spend half his life praying for my salvation, that puts me off—but that he's a total ass—why the thought's never crossed my mind."

Her laughter exploded like sudden sunlight. Then she sobered. "He's right, though, about each twin having her own soul."

"He is. And you are too, to know it." He met her eyes: "But what we need is another crib."

"I agree," she said. "I'll see to it this afternoon."

So ended that day's lesson.

Lillie Ruth Newhouse was the Leighs' cook.

She had "come" to the Leighs back in 1918, when Maud was four years old. In 1940, twenty-two years later, she was still reigning in the Leighs' kitchen, turning out the best biscuits under Heaven, the juiciest roast chickens, and for special occasions, an eight-inch-high angel-food cake without equal in the world. And still singing . . . When you entered the big, high-ceilinged front hall of the Leighs' house, you could hear her giving drawn-out, worshipful voice to the line of a spiritual as she did some quiet, ruminative task like putting together the stuffing for a bird, or peeling potatoes, shelling peas, cleaning greens and the like; but if she was involved in some livelier chore—whipping egg-whites, or turning the handle of the ice-cream machine—the bouncier beat and peppy tunes of "Camptown Races," "Patty-cake Joe," or "Oh, Susannah" would pour forth, rendered in a weird mix of tooth-whistle and song: the repertoire you heard was an indication of what you'd eat later on.

She was small in build, spry, and, to quote Mrs. Leigh, "darling in heart." She had a smooth-complexioned, light brown face, a wide, high brow, a fine mouth, and fine, heavily lashed eyes. In 1918 when Mrs. Leigh hired her, she laid claim to being "around forty years old"; perhaps she was a bit older, perhaps a bit younger. By 1940, her hair was rapidly graying, and she was given to dyeing it, but laughingly said she didn't know why she bothered: "The white comes in faster than I can black it out," she'd say, lowering her head for you to look at, whether to show the white part that was blacked out or the black part in white ascendancy, was never clear.

She spoke of the Leighs as "my people" and called Maud "Baby," or "Maudie," depending. To the Leighs, she was "family."

No one knew better than Doctor Leigh how much and how well Lillie Ruth understood the terrible reach of what she had once described to Morgan as "the dark place in Mrs. Leigh's mind," this being the cause of Mrs. Leigh's removing herself to her room from time to time and drawing down all the shades, and in a lost way, with clenched hands and closed eyes, weeping. . . . "She's had one of her bad times," Lillie Ruth would report to Doctor Leigh on a now-and-again evening, and Doctor Leigh would know that Lillie Ruth had spent hours sitting at Mrs. Leigh's side, rubbing her hands in an effort to unlock the fisted fingers, and talking to her in a soft, dove-like, repetitive, bridging tongue whose meanings he had never been able to fathom, or, for himself, on his wife's behalf, to master and put into practice.

These "spells," as Lillie Ruth called them, had begun in the late 1920s. Doctor Leigh had at first thought they were symptoms of early menopause, but that had been a wrong diagnosis: their source, as proved by time, was mental, not physical. ("A malaise of the spirit" was the phrase a colleague used.) Over the following years, the "spells" seemed to pattern themselves like cut-outs traced from a master design: they did not lengthen in duration or occur with greater frequency, nor did the mute sorrow or cosmic weariness or skewed vision of the world (whatever the nature of the problem), appear to intensify: they but came and went in the predictably uncertain way of weather. About them, Mrs. Leigh refused to speak. When Doctor Leigh would appeal to her to tell him why she wept, her body, along with her facial features, would freeze, and she would stare off, stiff and still as a joss, her thoughts her own, unreadable, Doctor Leigh felt, even to her own eyes. Once, only once, he confided to Morgan that his wife's tendency to gloom hung over his life "like the sword of Damocles."

When Morgan was courting Maud, she had told him her mother was "prone to moods." She had gone on: "Sometimes she gets very sad. Never for long though; Lillie Ruth knows how to bring her around." Then she had added: "Lillie Ruth's a saint." It was early in the spring. They were seated side by side on a bench in the Leighs' garden, their hands in their laps. The profound physical tension between them acted as shackle and gag: sustained conversation was impossible. When they did speak, it was in spurts—fragments of thoughts spoken in thin, fervent, almost furtive voices that would not carry beyond their hearing. The nearby incessant churr of an April cricket acted upon their nerves as would a last, testing tug on a rawhide binding already strained to the breaking point. Pale with desire, Morgan received Maud's confiding words about her mother as an intimate gift, intimately given: a bond between them. He wanted Maud to know he understood her dread of her mother's moods—the strangeness of them and how they set Mrs. Leigh apart from other people—but he did not (yet) feel free to particularize, so broadened the perspective: "Everyone feels sad from time to time," he said; and, after a moment: "You surely love Lillie Ruth, don't you?" Maud had nodded: "Almost as much as I love mother." . . . So of course, in the agony of his love for Maud, Morgan too loved Lillie Ruth: gave himself over, first, to the notion of loving her, and in time genuinely came to.

It was not surprising then, that in early November of 1940, he sought out Lillie Ruth and told her: "I need your help."

Lillie Ruth waved him to a chair drawn up at the kitchen-table. "Sit down and have a cookie. I'll make you a cup of tea."

"Maud will listen to you, Lillie Ruth."

"Not always, Morgan. What is it?"

"I can't get her to see she needs help with the twins."

"I told that to Doctor Leigh last week," Lillie Ruth hastened to say. "I told him there isn't anybody can keep on like she's going. She's thin, too."

"I know, but whenever I suggest we try to find someone to help out, she resists the idea. She says there's no one on earth she'd trust to look after them."

Lillie Ruth laughed, showing a tongue red as fireweed. "Maudie can be stubborn sometimes. She's got a jealous streak, too."

Morgan spoke to the charge of stubbornness, but he left the other alone. "Do you know of anyone who could help her, Lillie Ruth? Because if you do, and if she thought the idea came from you, I'm sure she'd take to it."

Lillie Ruth went through the lengthy process of pondering. "I'm familiar with plenty of girls looking for work, but they're all too young. Not *serious* enough. You have to be serious where babies are concerned, Morgan." (As if he didn't know.) Then Lillie Ruth said: "Lucinda's niece, maybe."

"Ah." Lucinda was Lillie Ruth's best friend—sharer of her days off, a member of the Blue Choir in Lillie Ruth's church, a wearer, like Lillie Ruth, of important hats on Sunday. "Lucinda's niece—" Morgan repeated.

"She's been with a family in Elyria, but they moved last month to Wisconsin. They all but promised her a place in Heaven if she'd go with them, but she didn't want to uproot herself and go off somewhere so far away." Lillie Ruth handed Morgan another cookie. "Lucinda brought her to church last Sunday."

"Oh? . . . So you've met her."

"I surely have."

"Is she married?"

"No, and not likely ever will be."

"Why's that?"

"She blotched."

"Blotched?"

Lillie Ruth nodded. "Uhm . . . has little white patches on her skin. Men don't take to that, leastways no men I've ever heard of." She laughed the issue away. "There's only a couple of blotches on her face— *little* ones—no bigger than snow-berries. The big ones Lucinda says are on her legs, but stockings cover those, and the ones on her arms, well, she wears long sleeves."

"How old is she?"

"Around thirty, I reckon. Old enough to be serious." Lillie Ruth looked straight into Morgan's eyes: "I'll talk to Lucinda tonight. Stop by tomorrow and I'll tell you what I've found out." She bagged cookies. "Take these with you. See Maudie gets one or two."

"I'll save at least three for her."

"She's too thin, like I said. . . . She *needs* help. *Steady,* serious help. Don't you worry, Morgan. Myself and Lucinda, we'll put our heads together. It'll work out."

"I feel better already."

Lillie Ruth walked him to the front door. "One thing's for *sure,* Morgan: Caroline and Julia are the prettiest babies I ever about saw *anywhere.* When they grow up, the boys'll come from all directions looking for a smile from them. We'll all have to stand around with flit-guns in our hands to spray them off like you would flies."

Morgan threw up his hands: "If we live that long, Lillie Ruth! At the rate things are going—"

"It'll work out, Morgan. You leave it to Lucinda and me."

That was how it came to pass that Lucinda's niece, Tessa Jackson, entered their lives.

᪣

The year was vanishing into memory.

At Christmas-time, Morgan sent a note and a picture of the twins to Miss Sly. One the back of the picture, he wrote: "Caroline and Julia Shurtliff—December 16, 1940." . . . Miss Sly responded with a conventional greeting-card of a seasonally decorated tree. Beneath the large sprawl of her signature were the underlined words *Thank you*. That was all.

In the late afternoon of December 31, it began to snow. Morgan put the tire-chains in the trunk of the car ("just in case") and through the white of the wind-driven storm, he and Maud drove into Cleveland to attend the annual New Year's Eve party given by his Aunt Letitia (his mother's sister) and her husband, Lewis Grant. On this night, the Grants' tall, pillared house, of the so-called Greek revival style, was ablaze with lights. Seen distantly, through the densely flying snow-flakes, it looked detached from the earth, as if afloat: "Like a child's dream of an ocean-liner," Maud said.

They were to spend the night, their first away from the twins. Tessa, by now well proven, had shooed them into the car with the words: "I know as well as both of you put together exactly what to do for Caroline and Julia. *Exactly*. So—*git*—!" said with a back-door, banishing wave of her hand.

As they drove off, Maud told him of the careful arrangements she'd made with her parents and Lillie Ruth and Lucy Blackett for any "back-up aid and comfort" Tessa might require. "They've all promised to look in on her," she concluded.

Morgan laughed: "I hope she survives all the attention."

In a near whisper, Maud said: "I feel like I'm running away with you. Eloping."

"It's been a long time since we larked off," he answered.

"I bought a new dress for tonight."

"Ah . . . I can't wait to see it. . . . It's starting to sleet. I may have to stop to clear the wind-shield wipers. . . . What color is it?"

"Deep red."

"My royal wife," he murmured. "You'll be the belle of the ball."

"Are you as happy as I am, Morgan?"

There was in her voice the charm of an appeal that went back to their first months together. Morgan heard it as being so: as a sudden revived interest in self and sexuality that of late had been eclipsed by maternity—reawakened now by the blustery night, by their closeness in the warm, enclosed car, by the fragrance of the scent she was wearing, by the fugitive stimulation of their isolated progress over the snow-strewn ribbon of road: by the fact of the dying year.

He said: "I love you more than I have ever loved you." Not in a suitor's voice, but in the viewing, consequential voice of a fulfilled man.

In the soft light from the dashboard, he saw the slow descent of a tear snail its way down her cheek. He touched her arm: "If you cry," he told her, "I will, too, and we'll end up in the ditch."

❧

At eleven o'clock, the Grants' sizable company sat down to a festive, formal feast that in duration linked the final hours of the Old Year to the first of the New. Morgan's father was present, seated at his sister-in-law's right. Opposite Morgan, Maud was placed. Across the wide span of the table's mahogany gleam, their eyes kept meeting, surprised each time by the force of a promise made for later keeping. Close on to midnight, by the fictions of candlelight, toasts were proposed. Morgan caught a fleeting look of alarm on his father's face: War, he thought: he's thinking about the approach of war.

On the clock's stroke of twelve, Lewis Grant rose to his feet and lifted his champagne glass and solemnly spoke the momentous words: "To the year nineteen hundred and forty-one."

3 ✑ Unto Nations Wide

Wars and alarums unto nations wide.

—EDMUND SPENSER, *THE FAERIE QUEEN*, 1590

1941

In April, Morgan and his father met for lunch. Morgan had requested the meeting; requested, too, that it not take place in Hatherton. "I have to be in Cleveland on Thursday," his father had responded: "Is that soon enough? . . . At my club, then, at twelve-thirty"—where, settled at a quiet table in the tall-windowed, portrait-hung dining room, Morgan asked: "Do you remember that time we had a problem with a snake, Pa?"

Ansel Shurtliff nodded: "I do indeed. Vividly."

. . . It had happened the year before Morgan's mother died, when he was eleven. . . . On a fine mid-May day, Morgan—intensely proud to be allowed to—had helped his father and Crosby with the spring-clearing of the rose garden. (Back then, Crosby had been his father's gardener.) In the large rectangular plot, the three of them had worked amiably together, pruning the bushes, feeding the roots with Crosby's special blend of fertilizers, then, with measured, smoothing strokes, raked the freshly turned, moist soil. When the task was completed, Morgan had stood, feeling manly, between his father and Crosby and listened as they voiced their satisfaction with what had been accomplished. "Order! Sublime order," his father had crowed. "You were a great help, son." Morgan said: "I liked doing it," to which his father looked directly into his eyes and told him: "I'm glad."

Crosby began to gather up the tools: a spade, a three-pronged weeder, pruning shears, the bamboo rakes. And then Morgan heard his father's surprised voice: "How did we miss *that?*" said with a gesture toward a long stick, blemish to the otherwise pristine scene, lying between two bushes at the far end of the rose-bed. Morgan felt a certain sink of spirit: the stick reposed in that part of the plot he had been assigned to rake. He said quickly: "I'll get it—" and hared away to pick it up. He got to within three or so yards of it when he slowed, then abruptly stopped: the stick was moving—curling back upon itself in a complexly deliberate way. "Pa—" he cried.

His father came running, Crosby too, and he heard with a thrill Crosby's ejected oath, "Jesus, it's a copperhead."

The length of the snake's body was now fully coiled upon the throne of its tail, the triangle of its head, raised.

Ansel Shurtliff seized Morgan's arm. "*Come—*" he commanded. Morgan could still remember the sensation of the lightness as his father sped him over the ground and how, at their heels, Crosby's weightier footfalls sounded like those of a pursuing bull. Near the house, in the haven of its high-roofed shadow, they drew up, panting. "Stay here, son," Ansel Shurtliff breathed. Then, to Crosby: "I'll get my gun."

A moment later, the two men went back across the lawn's broad reach to the place of the snake's lie. Morgan, trembling, covered his ears in expectation of the gun's report. But then, he saw his father's shoulders drop at the same time Crosby spat, and he knew the snake was gone. He watched patiently as they searched for it. Finally, though, they gave up. "May I come now?" Morgan shouted, and his father called back, "Yes, but be careful."

Crosby vouched they'd likely never see the snake again.

"So you don't think we should warn Mrs. Shurtliff and Maggie?" Ansel Shurtliff asked of Crosby. (Maggie was the cook.)

"I wouldn't," Crosby answered. "Especially Maggie. She's Bible-minded about snakes. Went into hysterics over that little garter one she saw in the kitchen-garden last summer."

"So we'll keep this between ourselves, right, Morgan?"

Morgan was engaged in reconnecting his drooped and wrinkled socks to the knee-band of his corduroy knickers. He said, "Yes, Pa," then, looking up, appealed: "Can I tell David Hicks? I'll swear him to secrecy."

"All right," his father consented. "You can tell David, but no one else."

Some two weeks later though, Crosby, in Morgan's presence, reported to his father that he'd just seen the snake again: "Sunning itself on top of the mulch pile, sir. I tried at it with my hoe, but it got away under the tool-shed."

"So we have to suppose it'll turn up again. I feel I must tell Mrs. Shurtliff and Maggie to watch where they step."

"I guess you should."

Morgan was told not to play near the tool-shed.

A few more days passed before, twice, in rapid succession, the snake showed itself, first, in the morning when it slithered away in front of Ansel Shurtliff as he was measuring off the wicket-points on the clipped grass of the old croquet court. (When Morgan was told of this sighting, he thought instantly of the old, large, elegantly framed photograph of his dead grandmother, clad in croquet-bloomers, mallet in hand, bending over a ball, gauging her shot). . . . On the afternoon of that same day, his mother saw the snake "coiled like a rope" she said, in the shallow water of the big, tri-pedestaled bird-bath. "A peril," his father said, disturbed to a palpable degree: "A peril."

But again, a few lulling days passed before it reappeared, this time virtually on their door-step. Morgan spotted it. . . . He had been excused from the luncheon table and had gone for no particular reason into his mother's small sitting room—an alcove off the front hall—not on his usual beat when he was at loose ends, trying to figure out how he would pass the rest of the day. . . . The wide French doors that led onto the terrace were closed against the outdoor heat (it was June by now), and he wandered over and looked out through them, thinking he might jog up a friend for some afternoon fishing on the pond. Would the perch bite

with the sun still so high? Wondering, he settled his eyes on the closer
scene—on the inviting look of the double-seater go-go swing: he might
take a new *National Geographic* magazine out to it and, for a while, look
at the pictures: just until the sun lowered itself a bit. . . . And then he
saw it, the dark, sluggish, mordantly patterned length of it stretched out
on the warmth of the terrace stones, its jeweled eyes agleam in its wide
head, the thin end of its tail, slack. . . . He moved back from the door
into the center of the room; then, still on tiptoe, with his heart atrip, he
crossed the hall and at the entrance to the dining room, in a dusky voice,
announced to his parents: "The snake's on the terrace."

His mother breathed the single word: *"Gracious"*; his father did not
waste an instant.

Morgan clung to his mother as, through the sitting room window,
they watched his father, shot-gun in hand, round the ell of the house
and, with steady, determined steps, move toward the snake. For the
longest-seeming time, it remained still, as if blind to his approach. But
then, quite suddenly, it livened: lifted its head in a wary, wicked way,
flicked its tongue, and, by now thoroughly informed, gathered its
strength and made to thrust itself forward. It had difficulty though,
gaining traction on the smooth terrace stones, yet by means of a series of
persistently performed sinuous twistings, it managed a sure, if slow,
advance in the direction of the terrace's boundering grass. Ansel
Shurtliff placed the butt of the gun to his shoulder and took a following
aim. In a hot whisper, Morgan asked his mother, "What's he waiting
for?" She tightened her hold on his arm. "He can't shoot against stone,"
she whispered back: "The shell pellets would ricochet." Her hushed
explanation ended just as the snake's head touched the grass, and with
that win of its element, summoned its power of speed. The instantaneous shot came like a world-ending crack of thunder. Vitally wounded,
the snake writhed. With the second shot, its flailing weakened. The
third settled it into death.

Awed, Morgan croaked: "He did it! Pa did it." But as seen through
the glass of the terrace door, there was no look of triumph on his father's
face: it was gray and fallen, and as Morgan understood years later,
creased by sorrow.

. . . Now, Ansel Shurtliff said to his son: "I'm very curious to know why you've brought up the episode of the snake."

"Because it applies to my current feeling about the war," Morgan answered.

"The continuing threat of it, you mean," his father interposed.

"Yes. That, and my need to decide what I'll do when and if we get into it."

His father frowned: "Not *if*, Morgan, only *when*. I have no idea what the deciding provocation will be, but whatever form it takes, I think it won't be long in coming." He sat straighter: "I can hardly bear the thought of your involvement." Then, in a stronger voice: "It's wise of you to be considering the role you'll play in it."

The waiter, plates in hand, was beside them. "The trout looks delicious, Frank. Thank you. How are you keeping these days?"

"All right, Mr. Shurtliff, thank you, sir."

"Your arthritis?"

"It's off and on," Frank replied.

"You're due to retire soon, aren't you?"

"The end of the year."

"The place won't be the same without you. How long have you been here?"

"Forty-four years next month." Then, with a grin: "Mr. Flagler—he's going to do a write-up about me in the club newsletter."

"I look forward to reading it. . . . Thank you very much, Frank."

Genuine interest and unfailing courtesy, Morgan thought as he listened to this exchange: his father's engaging way.

And, as they were alone again, Ansel Shurtliff picked up with: "I hope our trout's as good as it looks." Morgan had no chance to reply before: "In my judgment, you'd be better off to volunteer *before* the fact of our entry in the war than to wait and be drafted. That way, you can choose your service."

"Ah—" Morgan began: "You've stated my thoughts precisely." He put down his fork: "The problem is Maud," he went on: "She's appalled by the idea of my volunteering."

"She feels as I do," his father cut in with a helpless gesture: "Would that our feelings could alter the facts."

They ate in silence for a moment. His father again took the lead: "What branch of service are you considering?"

"The Navy."

"That would be my choice for you. Shipboard life is cleaner than foot-soldiering. I guess of all the services, the Air Force is the chanciest."

"Speaking of which, Geoff Barrows writes that he's being sent to England soon. He wangled it through some Royal Canadian Air Force channel. He's very pleased; very excited. Very sure of himself."

Ansel Shurtliff received Morgan's last words with an ironic, impatient look: "A bravura attitude," he said. "A cover-up of fear." He paused; then, after considering: "I take that back. In Geoffrey, such an attitude is more likely the muscle of courage. . . . I guess the time has come to add his name to the growing number on my prayer-wheel."

This final comment, spoken gently, with masculine grief, lay between them like a stone. Morgan, though, eager to continue the discourse of his own cause, thrust it aside with the abrupt question: "How can I convince Maud that the best thing I can do is to volunteer?"

"By not trying," his father instantly replied. "Credit her, Morgan. She's no fool. She knows there's no escape. It'll break her heart, but she'll yield soon enough."

"I've given myself until the middle of June."

"That's a reasonable dead-line." Then, in quite another tone: "I'd like to plan a visit to you and Maud sometime in May. . . . Maud and I can commiserate together." The remark held no conspiratorial hint, no intimation that he intended to posture himself as an exerting abettor to his son's plan: its only thrust was that of resignation. He touched his lips with his napkin, then squared his shoulders: "I recommend the brandied peaches for dessert."

They launched into a discussion of other matters, of books they were currently reading, of the twins' progress as walkers and of Maud's plans for their first birthday party, of how the spring weather thus far augered well for Ansel Shurtliff's orchards. But the conversation, for all its promise, struck Morgan as wistful: the kind of chat two people engage in as they take a last fond look of land from the deck of a departing ship.

A light rain was falling when they finished lunch. Beneath a raised umbrella, Morgan walked his father to his car. "Thank you, Pa. I'll be in touch about your visit in May."

Ansel Shurtliff nodded: "Love to Maud," he said. "Embraces for Caroline and Julia."

᪐

On Tuesday, May 27, President Roosevelt addressed the nation in what was called "a National Emergency Broadcast."

The event took place in the concluding hours of Ansel Shurtliff's four-day visit with Morgan and Maud. The three of them listened together to the broadcast, their eyes fixed on the radio as if it were a person: the king's messenger in the disguise of a box. The living room windows were open to a breeze that stirred the curtains and let in the pastoral scent of freshly mown grass. Tessa was upstairs with Caroline and Julia.

"The war," President Roosevelt was saying, "is approaching the brink of Western civilization itself. It is coming very close to home. The Battle of the Atlantic now extends from the icy waters of the North Pole to the frozen continent of the Antarctic." He went on, citing the number of merchant vessels already destroyed by Axis planes and submarines "within the waters of the Western Hemisphere." "We have," he said, "accordingly, extended our patrol in North and South Atlantic waters. We are steadily adding more and more ships and planes to that patrol." The president concluded the broadcast by declaring, as of the day, "an Unlimited National Emergency."

Morgan rose from his chair and switched off the radio. His father roused himself as from a dream and in a detached voice suggested that they might all have a drink—"a pony of brandy for each," was the way he put it. Morgan left the room to get a tray. . . . When he returned, his father was sitting as before, but Maud was at the window, gazing out, her head up, her back rigid. She looked as she had that long-ago evening when he paid his first formal call on her: slightly aloof, even a bit arrogant; intense, yet presciently vulnerable. In the prevailing silence, Morgan poured the brandy and carried a glass to her. He touched her arm. She looked at him briefly, her eyes immense; she took the glass from him, then turned away, and more to the walls of the room than to anyone in it, she said: "It's no use to hope anymore."

⊸§

On Friday, June 16, he signed up as a volunteer in the United States Naval Reserve.

The chief petty-officer on duty at the recruiting headquarters in Cleveland handed him a set of papers to fill out and pointed him toward a table at which two youths, writing implements in hand, were already seated. As he joined them, one raised a naked forearm and said a bored, "Hi—"; the other, also with rolled-up shirt-sleeves and markedly grubbier hands, set his eyes on Morgan in a curious and candid study of his combed hair, his shaved face, his necktie and vested suit, his age—(*that*, above all, Morgan felt), the hunch affirmed by the youth's following, deferential remark: "Nice day, sir."

Morgan nodded: "I guess it's one we'll always remember."

He settled himself then on the iron chair, uncapped his fountain pen, and with a clear brow began the tedious task of filling out the blank spaces on the pages redundantly referred to by the petty-officer as "the official government documents."

4 ✑ Giving Rise to . . .

Nor would we have all the stories of Atlas holding up the sky and Prometheus nailed down on the Caucasian range and Cepheus elevated among the stars in the company of his wife and daughter and her husband, if there had not been men who, in their mortal days, achieved some genuine, marvelous discoveries of supra-terrestrial truths, capable of giving rise to these fictitious fairy tales.

—CICERO, *DISCUSSIONS AT TUSCULUM*

She was a Liberty ship: the SS John T. Stubbins.

At Tacoma, Washington, on a windy, overcast day in early November of 1942, the lieutenant who would command her Navy gun crew when next she put to sea, boarded her, dockside, for the first time. A merchant seaman conducted him to the pilot-house: there, bent over a table in close scrutiny of a chart, was the *Stubbins's* master.

"Sir—" the lieutenant addressed the captain's posterior.

At once, though in a peculiarly mechanical way, the captain's spine began to straighten and the body slowly to turn around (the process reminiscent of a life-size Bavarian clock-figure regulated to show itself on the stroke of the hour) until, at full face, it solemnly stopped and, fixed so, met with its own eyes those of the waiting lieutenant's. After a seemingly faulty moment, the figure came further to life: lifted its right hand to its braided cap in acknowledgment of the lieutenant's held salute, and then, though still wordless, it made the gesture—suddenly fluid—of extending a hand to be shaken.

Visibly relieved, the lieutenant began anew: "Sir, I'm—"

"Morgan Shurtliff," the figure, now vocally human, cut in: "I have
your papers; I've been expecting you. . . . Names interest me. *Morgan.*"
As spoken this time by the captain, the two syllables sounded solid,
like dice thrown onto the baize of a gaming table. "It's not an everyday
handle. Almost as unlikely as my own: Rupert. Rupert Wilkins in
full." He pronounced his surname formally, precisely, as would
(Morgan thought) a good butler. In quality of sound, the captain's
voice was temperate—at odds with his physical appearance, which, in
bearing, suggested truculence—the body stocky—(not quite as tall as
Morgan felt he would have liked it to be); legs the slightly bowed ones
that men of the saddle and the sea seem often, strangely, to have in
common; grizzled, wiry hair; a wide intelligent brow over a rather
thin, acute face; very blue, alert, steady eyes: but the voice, for all its
agreeableness of timbre had a thrust to it that conveyed of authority.
"As I said, I have your papers," the captain now went on, still looking
at Morgan: "I don't mind telling you how glad I am you're not green at
your job."

Morgan considered, then said: "If by not being green at my job you
mean that I know all I should about a ship's weaponry, you're right. But
I've never seen action, so in that sense I'm as green as they come."

At this piece of information the captain gave a concurring smile. "As
to not seeing action," he said, "I can match you green for green. But
you're a full-grown man, not an inexperienced Navy princeling" (the last
two words said with an abrasive twist). "Given the run before us, it's that
I'm glad for. . . . You know, of course, where we're headed."

"Yes, sir, I do," Morgan answered. (All too well: when he'd received
his orders to report to the *Stubbins,* the officer at Naval Headquarters in
Tacoma had told him: "You'll be going to the Red Sea," then added:
"Good luck," in a tone of such grave sincerity as to cause Morgan's heart
to sink) . . . But what now was most racing through his mind was the
captain's phrase "Navy princeling," spoken as it had been in a way that
suggested the ugly possibility that Rupert Wilkins might be one of
those separate-minded merchant mariners who hold grudges against
Navy men (especially of junior rank and in the Naval Reserve)—which
possibility of attitude, if in fact it did exist on the captain's part—
Morgan was determined not to aggravate by word or deed—a determi-

nation put to immediate test by the captain's next question: "How do you view the assignment?"

Unsure of the question's exact meaning, Morgan asked: "In what sense, sir?"

"Your *feelings*, Shurtliff," the captain said a bit impatiently, with a look away: "How do you feel about it?"

The question seemed to Morgan both unprofessional and feckless: unprofessional because testingly intimate, and feckless for reasons so obvious as to merit little more than a hollow laugh. But he answered without hesitation, and with deep honesty: "I dread it," then forwarded with: "And you, sir? How do you feel about it?"

The captain's eyes tore back to him. "Turnabout is fair play," he said. Then: "I dread it too. I'd be a fool if I didn't. I expect to apply my skills and to pray a lot. In this case, dread's a spur to survival, wouldn't you say?"

Put that way, Morgan's affirmative reply came easily.

"What do you do in civilian life?" the captain next asked.

He's summing me, Morgan thought. "I'm a lawyer."

"A lawyer," the captain repeated, mulling; and: "That takes a lot of training. Where did you get yours?"

"I went to Harvard Law School."

"Harvard's an expensive place. . . . Did you work your way through? Support yourself?"

Morgan could not tell which the captain was: a petty niggler or just possessed of a goat's haphazard curiosity. "No," he answered.

"You don't look as if you would have had to. . . . Are you married?"

"Yes."

"Children?"

"Twin daughters."

"How old are they?"

"Two and a bit."

"When did you last see your family?"

"Eighteen months ago."

"That's a considerable time." The blue of the captain's eyes had a way of changing intensity, and over his last comment the irises darkened— into sympathy, Morgan thought at first—but the virility of the lingering gaze caused him to reconsider: a kind of wrath coupled with resolve was behind the brush-stroke of the deeper hue. *"War,"* the captain muttered. To the single word, spoken with vehemence, Morgan remained silent. The captain, though, kept considering it, astare—perhaps at the concreteness of his private view of it—until, rather wildly—he made a gesture, an agitated kind of ridding toss, as of an object thrown into a waste-basket, after which, in the most usual of voices, he said: "We'll be carrying lumber in the cargo holds and as many tanks as can be fitted on the deck. The loading starts this afternoon."

"How long might the loading take?" Morgan asked.

"Five, maybe six days, by my calculation."

"Good," Morgan said, adding by way of explanation: "My crew will all be new men to me. I have a hunch I'll need every minute with them before we leave."

"It's your command, Shurtliff. You see to the guns, and I'll see to the ship." The captain looked at his wrist-watch. "I'll show you to your quarters—" and, as they moved off together: "I know from your papers you've not served on a Liberty ship before."

"That's right, sir."

"Are you aware that Liberty ships are regularly named after American patriots?"

"I am now."

"This one's named after a colonel who fought against Burgoyne at Saratoga in 1777. . . . *John T. Stubbins* . . . It's a very sturdy sounding name, don't you think?"

"Very."

Now that his attention was directed on matters pertaining to his ship, the captain seemed more relaxed, more willing (Morgan felt) to expose himself to be liked. He slowed his steps and said: "I haven't been able to find out what the 'T' stands for . . . Thomas, maybe."

"That would fit," Morgan replied.

"Thomas was my father's Christian name," the captain jogged on. "He died two weeks after I was born. Struck down by lightning while he was raking leaves in the backyard. My mother saw it happen from the kitchen window. If he'd lived, he'd be seventy-six today."

Arrested, Morgan asked: "Today, sir?" then turned the question into a statement: "Today's his birthday, you mean."

The captain nodded: "I guess that's why the name 'Thomas' is particularly on my mind."

"I understand. . . . If I had the proper stuff in hand, I'd offer a toast to his memory."

A first full smile lit the captain's face: "That's good of you to say, Shurtliff. . . . Here we are." They stood in a narrow passageway before the open door of a stateroom. "It's small, but it's all yours."

Morgan glanced inside. "It looks fine."

Then the captain said the revealing thing: "I like to know about people, especially ones I'm going on a long voyage with. When I was asking you about yourself, I didn't mean to give the impression I was just idly prying." He gave Morgan no chance to reply. "Settle yourself in, then have a look around the ship. I'll see you at lunch." He turned, and with his rolling walk, swung off.

≈§

Since that seemingly ancient day back in July of 1941 when Morgan had been sworn into the Naval Reserve, he had served on three other ships: the first, a training vessel, the USS *Argosy*—an old, sturdy, broad-beamed tub of a boat on which, as an able-bodied seaman, he'd spent a month "cruising" from New York down to Cuba and back; the second (after he'd been commissioned as ensign), the light cruiser USS *Minneapolis,* on which he'd remained from early October through Christmas week of 1941, patrolling the waters between Maine and Florida. On December 7, 1941—the day Japan attacked Pearl Harbor—the *Minneapolis* was off the Virginia coast. As the captain announced the news of the attack to the assembled crew, Morgan thought of his father: that the "deciding provocation" (Ansel Shurtliff's phrase spoken the previous April) had come at last: that, now, the battle would be joined in earnest.

His third ship had been the SS *Myddleton,* a fine heavy-duty freighter built in the mid-1930s. He took up duty on her as gunnery officer (second in command) on Tuesday, April 7, 1942, five days after he'd completed a three-month training course at the gunnery school in San Diego, California. The *Myddleton* first made a fast run from San Francisco to the Hawaiian Islands and back, which voyage, undertaken in the relatively new circumstance of war, comprised his initiation into the unearthly disquietudes of fear. . . . Next, the *Myddleton*, carrying a tightly packed cargo of army vehicles (jeeps, ambulances, trucks) set off, solo, on the long Pacific voyage to Brisbane, Australia, and from Brisbane, via Melbourne, to Wellington, New Zealand; from Wellington back to San Francisco Bay, in which safe waters, she dropped anchor on Saturday, October 24, 1942. When, then, he put foot ashore, he learned he had been made a lieutenant (j.g.). "Mirabile dictu!"— he wrote his father of this promotion.

&

Among the books he brought aboard the *Stubbins* was a small but excellent atlas. Spanning pages three and four, under the heading "Elliptical Equal-Area Projection," the world was shown. With his thumbnail, he traced the voyage ahead: (from Puget Sound, south to Panama; from Panama further south, down the length of South America, around Cape Horn, then east across the South Atlantic to Cape Town, South Africa; from Cape Town further east, into the Indian Ocean, then north, to the crown colony of Aden; from Aden, through the Red Sea and the Suez Canal to, *finally*, Port Said).

He chose a quiet moment to put to the captain his question: "Might I ask, sir, how long you think it will take?"

The one-sentence answer came without hesitation: "Three to three and a half months, depending on how much zig-zagging we're forced to do."

. . . Even before they embarked from Puget Sound, it had been his conviction that the crew knew where they were headed. All it would have taken to inform them was a piecing together of certain gleanings picked up and shared by a couple of savvy, old-hand merchant seamen: a slipped remark, overheard, made between dock workers, the remark added to the fact of the *Stubbins*'s cargo (tanks and lumber), *that* fact linked to the latest rumor about the geographical location of the war's

most current hot-spot (the African campaign against the Germans)—
and scuttlebutt would have done the rest. . . . He never had any solid
proof that the crew knew: his certainty was based solely on the feeling
he had when he engaged their eyes, that the strain of his own knowledge
was fully met.

☙

On Friday morning, November 13, 1942, the *Stubbins* sailed from Puget
Sound. The day was sunless and blustery and cuttingly cold.

"Dearest," (he wrote to Maud that night): "We made our departure
early this morning. You will note the date. After being in port for a
while it seems strange to feel the roll of the sea again. As I write, I imagine you and Caroline and Julia and Tessa several hours closer to dawn
than I am, but all still asleep in our quiet house. I wonder what your
night is like, if it is clear, if there are stars, if there is a frost. I remember
how lovely it is this time of year when the cold begins to set in in earnest
and you bring out the winter blankets from summer storage, and how
the wool smells of lemon verbena. I am the very soul of a home-sick,
longing husband. As I always do when we are under way, I'll add a line
or two to this letter each day."

He capped his pen, stood up, stretched, then took to his berth, where,
prone, he saw himself as might an imaginative stranger: as looking like
an effigy of a knight-crusader sculpted to fit in the niche of a remote
European church: hands crossed over his chest, feet upright on their
heels, eyes closed, lips compressed in a line of death-like resignation.

. . . *Loneliness:* about which, before the war, he thought he had some
knowledge, learned initially at the time of his mother's death and
enlarged upon two years later by the thorny period of his first bleak,
miserable days of "adjustment" at boarding-school when he had wondered if by jumping out the window of his second-floor room above the
house-master's quarters, he would be killed in the fall or merely injured,
just enough to require being sent home, there to be warmly, lengthily
nursed to full recovery; and farther on in time, to his seventeenth year,
after he had sweated through the heat of a first passion with one
Margaret (called "Mudge"), a sloe-eyed, slightly older, russet-haired,

sexually vivacious chameleon who, after several summer weeks of steamy encouragement, had finally "squared" with him—she didn't, after all, care for him—leaving him denied and trembling at the end of a stone-strewn path that dropped abruptly down into the murky shallows of a stale pond; and still farther on in time to his university and law-school years—to all the confident conceits of young manhood honed to a fine edge among a secure group of friends whose deathless energy in com-bine with a Gargantuan appetite for free-wheeling parlance, inspired an alpine consciousness of Self, which consciousness, in rare moments of solitude, he had construed as being that brand of Ultimate Interior Isolation which is the authentic, verifying mark of Maturity. . . . In a word, bunk. . . . Now, simply and terribly, he knew loneliness as a starv-ing man knows hunger.

Behind closed eyes, he considered a further strew of feelings and adjustments having to do with life as he had known it over the previous months: the men he had worked with: the admirable ones who would be recalled as having performed their diverse, difficult jobs with dignity (a few, even with style and wit); and the opposite, the onerous ones, impos-sible to deal with: the belchers and bullies and foul-mouthed brag-garts—to name but a few traits whose ways tried one's tolerance. It always struck him as miraculous that in the crowded, confined circum-stance of shipboard life, day after day could go by without murder being committed by one man (upon another) who had been rubbed by one of his fellows just once too often, the wrong way. . . . In all truth, it could be said that among the rag, tag, and bob-tail of an all-male crew cast together by chance on a wartime ark, there were but two, in common, abiding concerns: Fear—about which no word was ever exchanged—and Boredom, the cud of which was chewed around the clock, though for all the mock and blasphemy heaped upon it, secretly valued: to be bored was to be safe.

. . . And yet, and yet—what of that singular happening aboard the *Myddleton* which, by its radiant properties, had united the crew in so complete a way as to cause all to forget their individual enmities and, for a moment, to behave as one—. . . . The drama, for such of a sort it had been, had taken place on the long-awaited day when, after weeks at sea, the *Myddleton* was due to make her port of destination: Brisbane, Australia. . . . For the two previous days and nights, a teeming rain had fallen, pounding down with the sound of castanets onto the *Myddleton's* decks, lashing the faces of the men at their stations, blinding the lookouts, sharpening tempers to a knife's edge. At the third dawn, though, the downpour abated, but the sky remained black and the sea continued to run in long, sullen, sickening swells. . . . The noon meal had few takers. . . . Still, as scuttlebutt would have it, they *were* nearing their destination, and among the ship's company, a tension of anticipation set in, and with it the animations of pride: by luck and sweat, the *Myddleton's* cargo was virtually delivered. By mid-afternoon, every man whose duties permitted was topside, standing or sitting on whatever free deck space was available. Surely, *soon,* there would be some evidence of imminent landfall: beneath the dark clouds, a shorebird would show itself in flight, or a tree branch with its green leaves still on it would drift into view. . . . *Wait,* as Noah had waited; so too, Job. . . .

And then, as happens in that part of the world—with a terrific, flushing suddenness—the sun came out, and tandem with its exploded brilliance, a blast of yeasty wind blew in from the *Myddleton's* port side and sang its elate way through her rigging—all, as at the same unbelievable instant, land was sighted, forward, afar, rising fabulously, leviathan-like out of the sea; and, briefly, as one, the crew went crazy. A great cheer went up. Hats were sent aloft, forever away. There was a collective spasm of in-place, March-hare jumping; ear-splitting whistles; the lurid howl of Tarzan's jungle yodel, in response to which the galley utility man became a lewd Jane—sprang onto the hood of a lashed-down ambulance, and from that stage, with his red hair ablaze in the sun, performed a rapturously obscene belly-dance. . . . Yet even in the midst of that galvanizing dance, it was the risen land that dominated consciousness, and as the reel of exuberance wound down, all eyes turned toward it with moist celebration. . . . For himself, Morgan, agog, had been filled with the insane sense that it was being momently created: that he was witnessing the borning of Eden. . . . Even now, these months later, he could not think of the episode without a feeling of spiritual elation; and what he could never understand was the *why* of the memory's soothing effects: that its balm could still relieve the tortures of loneliness and fear, yet at the time of the memory's making, all had been bedlam and din.

. . . To recall that experience was to think, too, of Zenobia Sly: it had been in a letter to her that he had given a full account of it. . . . Over the last eighteen months, he had written six letters to her. From her, he had received five—the last three sent to the Armed Forces Headquarters, Treasure Island, San Francisco Bay, California—the envelopes addressed in her distinctly large, looped handwriting, the enclosed pages conversational in tone and reflective of his last communication to her. . . . He knew she wrote to him against all the scruples of her professional ethics; that, at some large, searching moment, she had made her decision to waive her rule about remaining in personal touch with a Tilden-Herne adoptive parent: what had decided her, of course, was the greater reality of the war. He knew too that once the war was over, given survival and his return home, what was now active between them would quickly cease, and with tacit understanding, they would again distance themselves and become but silent rememberers of this time when they had been close. This shared knowledge of a curtailed future lent to the present-tense of their relationship a peculiar vitality. . . . "Dear Mr. Shurtliff" (she used his rank only on envelopes); "Dear Miss Sly . . ." She was a kind of human safe in whose locked interior were already housed so many confessions and left-over artifacts of dislodged and dislocated lives that he felt free to add to the accumulation the baggage of his own thoughts and feelings, no matter how flawed or of what order of strangeness, which now, almost hourly, his wartime existence gave rise to. . . . And there was something more; something *other:* in a removed, credulous region of his mind, and for the quirkiest of unexamined reasons, she was enthroned as the earthly, overseeing goddess of his luck.

Her most recent letter was a typical ramble and typically surprising:

> *You write of your difficulty in getting to sleep. It is a misery I understand, having inherited the tendency from my father who was a great insomniac. I offer you the following mental twister which is more entertaining than counting sheep. My father taught it to me a very long time ago. To my regret, I did not think to ask him during*

his lifetime how, when, or where he came by it. He was a witty, imaginative man, so I suppose he might have made it up. Out of sentiment and anxiety that overuse might dilute its power, I have been chary about sharing it. It pleasures me to pass it on to you now. You must first memorize it, then, as you lie in bed, say it over and over to yourself, and the next thing you know, it will be time to get up! Or so it works for me. I do so hope it will prove as effective for you. Here it is:

One good hen
Two ducks
Three cackling geese
Four plump partridges
Five Limerick oysters
Six pairs of Don Alphonso tweezers
Seven hundred Macedonian horseman dressed in full battle array
Eight sympathetic, apathetic, diabetic old men on crutches
Nine brass monkeys from the Sacred Sepulchres of Ancient Egypt
Ten lyrical, spherical heliotropes from the Iliad Missionary Institute

He had duly memorized the incantation, his mind, as he did so, filled with endearingly witchy images of Miss Sly. . . . In the safety of Tacoma's harbor, it had worked to perfection: the dust and noise and grandeur of the seven hundred Macedonian horsemen had so addled his senses he had closed his eyes on the scene and fallen instantly to sleep.

⋘

The passage down to Panama went smoothly. They drew a certain dim comfort from an occasional friendly plane that flew over, and had the further solace of sighting on the horizon, at widely spaced intervals, three ships of their own kind. At the oil-depot in Panama there was a back-up of vessels waiting to be refueled. The *Stubbins* took her place in line: her turn came some twenty-three hours later; to those hours was added the seven required to fill her tanks. The crew passed the time in its various ridding ways: on-going games of poker were played with a greater vehemence; books changed hands; some beards that had been grown were shaved off; one man set himself the homely task of mending his clothes—a button here, a seam there—then volunteered his skill with the needle for the benefit of a few chosen mates. Two gunners, Climson and Vodapec, teamed up on the guitar and accordion, and for a while "Don't Sit Under the Apple Tree with Anybody Else but Me," "Kiss Me Once, and Kiss Me Twice, and Kiss Me Once Again," "I've Got a Gal in Kalamazoo," "Run, Rabbit, Run," and songs of other such familiar ilk, echoed throughout the ship. . . . The purser gave out word that letters would be collected for mailing; in addition to his daily extended one to Maud, Morgan handed in two to his father, one to Geoffrey Barrows and one to Miss Sly in which he first thanked her for sharing with him the palliative power of her father's Morphean incantation and secondly, described to her the performance of a school of whales that had sported one morning in close formation alongside the ship. To her, he called them "finned pachyderms." One of them had come very close to the *Stubbins,* and, blowing, had thrown itself out of the green surf in a vaulted arc, ousting a geyser of white, creamy froth, a cool spoonful of which had fallen on his cheek. For a moment, he had seen the black gleam of its whole body. Then, nose-aimed and powered for China, it dove, immensely down, and was seen no more. . . .

☙

At ten knots, the *Stubbins* inched her way down the length of South America. There were daily "Abandon-Ship" drills. Awake or asleep, life jackets were worn. The faces of the three radio officers, in feature so unalike, began to bear a resemblance each to the other, the gaining resemblance composed of that kind of crazed, haunted, listening look associated with madness or martyrdom.

Off the coast of Chile, far out at sea, they were hit by a savage storm that slowed them to a near standstill: against the terrific seas, the *Stubbins's* engine was cut to minimum revolutions. With his gut in his mouth, from behind a bridge window, Morgan watched an endless train of immense waves ("rollers," the captain called them) advance upon the *Stubbins,* and heard with an awed, admiring ear the captain's cajoling orders given calmly to the wheelman:

"Ease her down."

"Ease her bow around a little to one side so she doesn't nose directly into them—"

"Watch her revolutions and compass to see she's still steering—"

All the while the *Stubbins* bucked like a horse.

. . . On another day (he had by now given up a regular tracking of Time), under clear skies, in moderate seas, they rounded Cape Horn. . . . Recalling the pages of Melville's *White Jacket*, he thought of the hazards of sail in older days and marveled at how the alarms and frights of life had kept pace with the change from canvas to steam. . . . He was on the *Stubbins*'s flying-bridge, port side (the captain having said he'd be welcome), straining his eyes for a glimpse of the Cape's famous nub. "It's out of range, Shurtliff," the captain said: "We're too far south of it. You'll have to imagine it." Which is what he did, sufficiently well to cause in his mind a flicker of amazement that he, Morgan Shurtliff, was in such proximity to it as to have become, for a few hours, a part of its continuing, legendary past.

. . . The liquid wilderness between Cape Horn and the Cape of Good Hope (lengthened further by an increased amount of zig-zagging done to thwart the hunt of enemy submarines) began to seem as eerily infinite as the very universe. . . . The twenty-fifth of December came and went, a barely observed Christmas spent in the limbo of a time-zone that queered any bridging thoughts of celebrations at home. Ditto the thirty-first, as, at midnight, it was quietly noted by the men on watch that a year had passed: that it was now 1943.

&

He wrote letters (whose fate as to if, when, and where they might be mailed, he had no idea), the several packets of which, held together by the elastic embraces of rubber bands, he kept on the top shelf of his locker. Mostly, they were short communications telling of some diversion supplied by nature that caused in his mind a vivid recall of a contrasted or analogous memory:

> . . . *We see a lot of flying fish. They rise up out of the water, shoals*
> *of them sometimes, and glide along just over the water's surface.*
> *Their "wings" are two elongated side fins, attached to their bodies*
> *behind the gills. They make me think of the big flocks of grackles that*

fly up in a body from a harvest field and skim over the stubble of
corn stalks.

. . . It rained all day. I thought of that flowery umbrella you like
so much, and of how it becomes a big, gay bouquet when you open it.

Et cetera, et cetera.

In such lingerings, there was clearly nothing for a pale, glassy-eyed
censor to get excited about.

ᵈ§

He would oversee his gun crew at their diurnal tasks of oiling and polishing and checking the lethal workings of the *Stubbins*'s weaponry, and
wonder if *his* face, like theirs, bore the look of a dog owner who loves his
animal overmuch, and in a continuum of infatuated concern obsessively
grooms and otherwise cares for it: the men bent so over the guns, frowning, palming and stroking the gleaming steel, almost, it seemed, in a petting way. . . . Once, as he observed a couple of gunners so engaged, he
fantasized the weapons as kinds of dogs: the twenty-millimeter Oerlikon
anti-aircraft guns as sleek, intelligent greyhounds; the three-inch, fifty-
caliber cannon as blood-thirsty, feral mongrels; the lighter machine guns
as feisty terriers.

. . . There was one gunner, Malkerson, who was called "Owl" by the
rest of the gun crew, and referred to at large as "the Owl." He was a West
Virginian, a hill man: a near-illiterate, sublimely unworldly, free-spirited,
immensely likable youth who told Morgan early on that he "fancied"
night-duty, it being his claim that he could only sleep in the daytime.

"Why is that, Malkerson?"

The boy had a beaming smile. "I'm used to taking to the woods at
night," he drawled. "To hunt, sir."

"Ah—"

"Let the sun go down and I'm off with my dog for the night," he went
on. "It's my gift to see in the dark. My daddy passed it on to me."

"Do you have brothers and sisters?"

Malkerson's grin broadened. "Ain't one girl, sir. Only eight boys. My
ma says the Lord ordained it so."

"What do you hunt?"

"Anything you can eat. Possum, pig, deer, squirrel. Any kind of pot bird. My daddy, he can sniff out game a mile away and name you what it'll be. He's a wonder," said with an active pride. "You ever eat possum, sir?"

"No. Maybe I will someday."

"You *should*. It's best stewed, with turnips and carrots and taters and strong onions throwed in." Malkerson's smile suddenly disappeared. "It makes me sorry just to think of it."

For Owl the Devil was real; he told of a man he knew who had the print of the Devil's hoof "set" on his right arm. "He kilt a man in rage," was his explanation of this avowed phenomenon. "My daddy has a nose for the Devil, too. He says the Devil smells like squirrel-moss, real damp and spoiled, like a haunt."

"I've never heard of squirrel-moss. What does it look like?"

"Kind of an ailed brown, sir. You can't never dry it out. There'll be a long spell of dry weather, leaves all crisped out in the woods so's you have to step whole-footed not to scare game, and there'll be a plot of squirrel-moss wet as *that*"—pointing off to the surround of sea—"drops of water on it big as hawberries."

"How did you ever end up in the Navy? Did you volunteer?"

The Owl flashed a confiding smile: "Hell, no." He turned red: "Sorry for the oath, sir. . . . The sheriff sniffed me out. Came to our place one day with a paper in his hand and told me my time'd come. I didn't hardly know about a war's being on. Next thing I knew, they put me in it." He ran his hands shoulder to hip over his Navy blues: "My ma'd laugh at me, dressed up like this."

Owl had two songs he sang softly on the night watches; one, secular: "Take Me Back and Try Me One More Time"; the other, a gospel hymn: "In the Sweet By and By"—crooned low, in a believer's voice. The crew treated him with a gentleness devoid of the least condescension: in the truest of protecting ways, they had made him their mascot. One gunner in particular—Sutter, by name—a tough, city-bred, casual cynic, was, ironically, the greatest appreciator of the Owl's touchingly foreign immaculateness: it was Sutter's often-made assertion that the *Stubbins* was kept afloat by what he referred to as "the Owl's faith."

. . . Sarkis was the first mate. He was a middle-aged, tight-mouthed, relentlessly conscientious man with fast, noticing eyes. The captain's working relationship with Sarkis fascinated Morgan for the reason that, as with two ascetics bound together in the service of the same deity (in this case, the sea), communication between them was conducted in the main by means of a kind of doppelgängerish intuition: a nuanced glance, an eyebrow raised just so, or a shaded gesture whose subtlety of import was instantly understood and, accordingly, acted on.

. . . With Crawford, the chief engineer, the captain's relationship was more complex, the *Stubbins* being their in-common body: the captain, her brain; Crawford, her pulse—the measure of her well-being dependent, therefore, in equal part on each. In the hierarchy of command, Crawford of course was the deferrer, yet from his person, like the lingering smell of grease and oil that marked his presence, there exuded a whiff of personal autonomy which occasionally irked the captain (or so Morgan thought). There was no doubting, though, the magnitude of respect they bore for one another. It was the sense each had of his absolute importance that made them, to the degree they perceived themselves to be, *rivals* of the *Stubbins's* destiny.

. . . The captain continually showed wisdom in the way he discharged what by law was an absolute, god-like authority over the lives of the *Stubbins's* men, the rendered manner of which won him an across-the-board respect and loyalty (and, incidentally, scattered to the winds Morgan's first apprehensions about him). His faults, if such they might be called—occasional displays of impatience, a steamy intolerance for sloppy work, that maddening curiosity about the personal lives of those around him—proved to be minor faults in an otherwise estimable character whose greatest virtue was that of a sentient decency.

(Of all the men under whose jurisdiction of command chance might have thrown him, Morgan was by now convinced of his good fortune in having Rupert Wilkins as his captain.)

❧

Even in Eternity, time passes.

❧

In mid-January of 1943, they put in to Cape Town, South Africa. . . .

As the *Stubbins* was being refueled, the captain and Sarkis went ashore to be briefed about how best to proceed on the next lap of the voyage. Scuttlebutt had it that in the waters between Cape Town and Aden, enemy subs thrived like cockroaches. . . . The question arose: would they depart Cape Town and, from the tip of Cape Agulhas, head a bit east, then north, through the Mozambique Channel, up the African coast to the Gulf of Aden? Or, from Cape Agulhas, would they hold to a longer-lasting course, leaving the island of Madagascar to port, seeking by this farther means the greater obscurity, perhaps safer reaches of the Indian Ocean before turning north? . . . On the captain's and Sarkis's return to the ship, Morgan was summoned to the bridge. He arrived at the same time Crawford made his appearance. The captain greeted them; Sarkis settled for a nod to each. "We've been warned against the Channel," the captain began: "I'm just as glad. I don't like the tight passages. . . . We'll take the longer course. . . . Either way, though, I have to tell you there's no lack of submarines around. There've been eight sinkings between here and Aden in the last three days. We'll go steady, at the best speed you can give me—" This last remark was aimed at Crawford, who stood, grave-faced, with the bulk of his weight resting on his right leg.

Crawford's response was quick in coming, and firm: "I'll see you get it, sir."

"Shurtliff—"

Morgan met the captain's eyes: "I get the message, sir."

"Good . . . We'll leave tomorrow morning." The captain made one of his movements of dismissal: of having said all he had to say, except that, from the way he looked at Sarkis, Sarkis knew to remain.

❧

And so again, nakedly, the *Stubbins* put to sea.

Everyone knew this lap of the voyage posed the greatest threat, and the ship's company rose to the challenge by exercising its individual fears in the best though not always the most usual of ways: by an increase in civility, simple in kind, but the properties of its gentling influence benefited morale. Morgan credited the captain for setting the style of conduct.

(One good hen, two ducks, three cackling geese . . . There were nights composed of such intense anxiety that he knew Miss Sly's incantation could not possibly induce sleep: at such times he did not attempt to invoke it, feeling that to put it to such an unreasonable test would be to play false with what he deemed to be the affectionate, original facets of its usually undoubtable, albeit obscure, power.)

By luck, or God's will—whatever—they made it through to Aden. . . . There, where in ancient times the then-world met in exotic commerce, word was given out—qualified by some pithy remarks about venereal disease—that the crew would have a twenty-four-hour general liberty. In the way crazed lemmings are said to quit the land and rush headlong into the sea, the released men, in a reversal of the lemmings' scurry, rushed ashore to Aden's famous red-light district. Morgan watched them go. The Owl went with Sutter, who told Morgan: "We'll have a walk around, then I'll bring him back, *whole*."

That night, the captain stopped by Morgan's stateroom. He was carrying a pint bottle of bourbon and two glasses. "Do I disturb you, Shurtliff?"

"Not at all, sir. I've just finished a letter to my wife. . . . Sit here. The bunk will do for me."

"I feel we owe ourselves a drink."

"It sounds a grand idea."

The captain's face was jubilant. "We've all but got it made. The Red Sea's safe; and the Suez. From now on, it's only a matter of time."

Morgan took the offered drink and raised his glass: "So here's to Port Said, and to you for getting us there."

"It's good of you to put it that way, Shurtliff. I appreciate it. . . . When we get there, I'm going to take a couple of days off and go into Cairo. After the cargo's unloaded, of course. You'll have time off too. Would you care to join me?"

The attraction of the unexpected invitation took Morgan by such surprise that he lingered over it, which lingering brought from the captain: "You may have other plans for yourself," said blandly, as an avenue for a negative reply.

"I'd like very much to join you."

"Good. We might take a ride out from Cairo to see the pyramids."

"Ah . . . the tombs of the pharaohs!" Morgan said. "Imagine our doing that! . . . I can't tell you the number of times in the last weeks when I've wondered if I'd ever set foot on land again."

The captain kept his gaze on Morgan's face. "You sound a bit low. . . . It's the let-down of being safe. That, and—well, the fact that Port Said's only the half-way point; that we'll have to turn around and do it all over again. *But,*" he leaned a little forward, "when we get back to the States, you'll have a long leave. A real stretch of time with your wife and daughters."

This man, Morgan thought, knows all about me. . . . Then, though, it struck him afresh that in personal degree, he knew little about the captain. *Nothing* really, beyond the fact that he was not now, nor ever had been, married (which bit of information Sarkis had once let slip). Still, Morgan supposed, he *must* cherish someone and in turn be cherished. Yet he had never intimated of any such attachment and in temperament seemed ungiven to any such bond as would form the basis for sustained and ardent reveries. There was no question, though, that he understood in others the call and case of love—which understanding his last perceptive words had demonstrated. . . . A direct inquiry would be imprudent. Morgan took the indirect approach: "And you, sir: I can't think of anyone more deserving of a long leave than yourself." The remark, as Morgan heard it back, took on the suspense of a put question.

The captain fairly rushed to say: "I don't do well on land, Shurtliff. I'll have a week or so with my mother and that'll do for me. . . . She's on my mind. It's going on two years now since I've seen her."

"Where does she live?"

The answer was given in a dry voice: "You won't ever have heard of it. Suffern, New York. In the house I was born in. The same house with the backyard my father died in. . . . I told you about that. . . . 'Struck by lightning while he was raking leaves': I was brought up on those words. If I had a dollar for every time I've heard them I'd be a rich man." The captain refreshed their glasses.

"Does your mother live alone?"

"She does. But she has a cousin who lives next door, so she's got close company. The cousin's married to one of those men who never stops complaining about his health, but he'll bury us all. You know the type. You name it and he's got it: everything from chronic dyspepsia to a permanent migraine. He wears out chairs, sitting and whining."

"Has the town changed much over the years?"

"I wouldn't say so. Oh—it's more sprawled out than it was when I was growing up, but it still has the same feel to it. Small. *Limited*. . . . I never liked it; couldn't wait to get out of it"—said with a verbal thrust that invited elaboration.

Morgan was quick. "How so?" he asked.

The captain smiled: "It's a long story."

"If you don't mind telling it, I'd like to hear it."

"Stop me if you get bored."

"Don't worry."

"To say I didn't like it and couldn't wait to get out of it is a half-truth. . . . I won't say anything negative about my early childhood. I owe too much to my mother. Can you feature what it must have been like for her, widowed at twenty-three, left with a two-week-old boy to rear on her own? . . . If she ever felt sorry for herself, she never showed it, at least not to me. . . . It wasn't until I got to be twelve or so that I began to get restless. It was my grand-father—my father's father—who drove me up the wall. He owned a store in town: Wilkins Feed, Grain and Hardware, it was called. My father'd worked in it. . . . When my father died, my grand-father shouldered the care of my mother and me. God knows he didn't lack for sorrow in his own life: he'd lost his wife at a fairly early age—I never knew her—then his son, so my mother and I were all he had left. . . . He was a well-meaning man, but cautious and careful beyond all reason. Timid. Fussy to a point that drove me crazy. You could walk twice around the block in less time than it would take him to itemize and add up a bill of sale. To begin with, he'd check his arithmetic three times, then go about dotting every *i* and crossing every *t* of every item purchased. It used to embarrass me to watch customers waiting around while he did his paperwork." The captain raised an agitated hand: "You know me, Shurtliff. I'm a stickler for details. You can't captain a ship and not be. What I'm talking about is the *spirit* behind a task, the *attitude*. Energy. You know what I mean. It'll do to tell you my grand-father sighed a lot. . . . It sounds like I'm talking against him. I don't mean to. He was a well-meaning man at heart. It was the *rote* of his life I couldn't stand. The way he tethered himself to habit. . . . The hell for me was that starting when I was twelve, I had to work for him every Saturday at the store. I say I had to: I mean I was expected to by him *and* by my mother. They used to tell me the store would be mine someday and wasn't I lucky to have my future cut out for me like that. . . . The summers were the worst because with school out, I was required to be at the store every day. But the summer I turned fourteen everything changed for me, and believe it or not, by my grand-father's doing. . . . Are you hearing more than you bargained for?"

"On the contrary."

"Here: let's have a splash more." Then: "How old are you, Shurtliff?"

"Thirty-two."

"A babe. I'm fifty-three. You don't have to be a genius to figure out when I was born. 1890. Add fourteen years to that and you'll get the year 1904, which is when, as I said, my life changed. . . . I don't know what got into my grand-father to do it, but that summer he took it into his head that he and my mother and I should go on what he called 'a week-end junket' to the New Jersey shore. . . . It was the most daring thing I'd ever known him to consider doing. It meant his breaking routine and stirring himself to buy the railroad tickets and arranging somewhere for us to stay overnight. When he sprang the idea of the trip on my mother and me, I didn't know how to feel about it. The farthest away I'd ever been from home was ten miles or so outside of town, and that on my bicycle or by horse and buggy. . . . The tracks of the Erie Railroad ran right through Suffern, but I'd never ridden on a train and I really wanted to. But my grand-father's everlasting tendency to fuss and worry cast a long shadow over the plan, as far as I was concerned. I knew in advance what it'd be like: how he'd sweat over every possibility of what could go wrong, that his wallet might get swiped, or the store catch on fire in our absence, and harping on me every second to sit up straight and look smart, and asking my mother every third minute if she was comfortable and if she was, fretting that in five minutes time she might not be. . . . Just to think of how it would be made me squirm." The captain paused, then, with vigor: "God, Shurtliff, I must be drunk, going on like this."

Morgan laughed: "I'd be willing to sign an affidavit that you're not."

"Thanks for the reassurance. . . . I'll get to the point of that week-end. . . . The trip went off better than I'd supposed it would. My mother and grand-father sat together on the train, and I sat by myself behind them. When we got to where we were going—a little resort town called Bellstone—we were picked up at the railroad station by the husband of the woman who ran the boarding-house we were booked into for the night. That we'd been met in a horse-drawn, closed buggy threw my grand-father into one of his worry fits: how much was the ride going to cost? Or was it included in the price of the rooms? He whispered the issue to death with my mother. . . . Anyhow—we made it to the boarding-house. Mrs. Gamp—I'll never forget that name—showed us to our rooms, then told us that the beach was a ten-minute walk away, to just go out the front door and continue straight down the lane. . . . We set off, and sure enough, ten minutes or so later, we crossed up over a set of sand dunes and there it was. The sea!" The captain's eyes widened, and he said again in a voice that weighed of passion: "The *sea* . . . I couldn't believe my eyes. . . . The *extent* of it and the way the waves folded over on them-selves, one after another. I just stood, goggle-eyed. . . . And you know those lulls between the time one wave crashes on the shore and the next one breaks? I started in timing my breathing by the intervals, they seemed that *natural* to me. The *smell* stirred me too. . . . I didn't know a flying thing about the workings of the sea—about currents and the like—but I formed the idea straight off that in the water before me was a bit of every named ocean in my geography book and that if I held a few drops of it in my hand, I'd have a grip on the world. It was the most exciting idea I'd ever had. . . . What happened next was my grand-father's putting to me the question: 'Well, what do you think of the ocean? and do you like it?' I was in such a trance that the sound of his voice made me jump. I knew if I tried to tell him how much I liked it—what I thought of it—I'd start to bawl. Why? Because the next day I'd have to leave it. . . . In my mind, you see, just in those first few minutes in its company, it was already established for me that I *belonged* to it." As if he was embarrassed by the expressed fervency of the remark, he bent his face down toward his lap. "It's what I meant earlier when I said the week-end changed my life."

Morgan, deeply immersed in the captain's narrative, avowed: "That's what it is to fall in love."

The captain raised his head. For a moment, his face bore a look of predicament, as if he were uncertain how to respond to a comment made with such emotion and which, Morgan supposed, ran counter to his own prescriptions of masculine reserve. At last he said: "I'd not have put it that way. I lack your ease. But I won't argue the point."

Morgan bridged a brief silence with: "On the terms you wanted, it must have taken a lot of doing for you to get out of Suffern."

To that observation, the captain laughed: "We'd be here this time next week if I ragged on about all I went through. . . . But I will tell you this much: the next summer I went back to Bellstone and got a job as a hand on a boat—a thirty-foot sloop called *Elaine*—owned by a grand old man named Adams. He'd had a heart-attack and didn't trust himself to sail alone anymore. He was a fine yachtsman. . . . After a month with him aboard the *Elaine,* I was solidly hooked on the sea. I was fortunate. I mean—I don't know many men who've had the luck of finding out at such a young age what they were born to do with their lives." He smiled: "I've chewed your ears off."

"It's the best time I've had in weeks."

"At least it's been peaceful." The captain stood up. "It's time we turned in. . . . Thanks, Shurtliff."

"Many thanks to you, sir."

≈§

Spent and reeking from its Babylonian excesses, the crew struggled back to the ship the next day.

Sutter, never given to subtleties, let Morgan know he'd been true to his word: that he'd returned the Owl "whole." "We walked around and had a good meal, then took in a Gary Cooper movie. Owl liked it."

"So you were back early last night," Morgan commented.

"Yes and no, sir," Sutter answered, and, as Morgan did not rise to the ambiguity, Sutter, being Sutter, smiled his worldly smile and explained: "After I returned the Owl, I went back ashore—"

—on which note, by turning from it, Morgan retired the subject.

≈§

They departed Aden and passed through Bab el Mandeb ("The Gates of Hell") into the Red Sea.

Sarkis had "done" the Red Sea as second mate on a vessel of American registry back in 1936, and described the region's summer temperatures as being "hot beyond belief." Each day, he said, the sun had burned "at a flaming pitch"; that the humidity had been "thick as mold"; the nights of the passage "gummy sweats." He shrugged and ended with: "It's a bit cooler this time of the year, so we'll have it easier."

≈§

It took the best part of a day to go through the Suez Canal. . . . For this penultimate fraction of the voyage they anchored twice, the first time at Suez to have the cargo inspected and to take on a pilot; the second time at about mid-point of the canal's length, in the lay-by of Great Bitter Lake (named after the taste of its water), so that three ships proceeding from the opposite direction, could pass. At Al Qantarah, near the site of the old landmark railroad bridge, the captain announced in a winner's voice: "*Now!* Now, by God, we're within spitting reach of Port Said."

The date was February 25, 1943.

The voyage had taken one hundred and four days.

≈§

They anchored in the roads of Port Said and for three days lay waiting for a berth. Phelps, the second mate, set up a dart-board and dragooned the crew into a ship's competition—a diversion that but feebly relieved the ugly agitations of boredom and the lingering, dispiriting effects of the cruel fact that no mail awaited them in Port Said. In the purser's sorry, abstract words, none had "slipped through."

≈§

In all, the time spent ashore in the captain's company was an oddly benign interval. He and the captain sought no diversions of an altering sort, so had none: in the main, their mood stayed pensive, almost to the point of melancholy—absurdly so, given that the interlude was meant to be (in the captain's wry words) their "great moment."

In the end, they were ashore only for a day. . . . Sarkis had gone to Cairo the previous week and suggested to them what they should do, starting with a drink at the legendary Shepheards Hotel, followed by lunch at a restaurant called Lulu's (owned by a friend of his, Des Milburn, who had been chief cook on a ship they'd served on together before the war); then a walk through a bazaar, after which, if they wanted to, they could go see some pyramids. . . . Sarkis had also "set them up" with a driver who'd agreed to be at their service from the time in the morning when they left the *Stubbins* until they returned that night—which driver, Magdi Mohammed, awaited them, as arranged, outside the dock gates. Magdi was a ghoul-eyed, slavishly deferential, congenital grinner. His car was a dusty, ancient Mercedes, which bore a sign attached to one of its doors: TAXI TRANSPORT BY EXCEL-LENCE. Morgan thought it marvelous and with a laugh said so.

Under way, the captain said: "Well, Shurtliff, this is it—the start of our great moment."

"The way Magdi drives it may be our last. . . . Do you agree that our 'transport by excellence' could use a new set of shock-absorbers?"

"You've read my mind." The captain took off his cap and hung it over the knob of his knee. "But the shock-absorbers aside, I can't get over what a motherly sort Sarkis is."

. . . Cairo's traffic moved at a snail's pace; the blaring horns deafened. Beggars—tragic grotesques of all ages and degrees of pathos—pounded their hands on the car's closed windows. To Morgan's murmured "Christ—", the captain said in a hollow voice, "Too many people." And after a moment: "Would you mind, Shurtliff, if we forgo that drink at Shepheards Hotel and go straight to Lulu's? I'm starved."

Morgan's consent was made with a vigorous nod.

The entry into Lulu's was through a closed, latticed iron gate guarded from the inside by a tall, barrel-chested man of indeterminate racial origin dressed in what seemed to Morgan's amused eyes to be the dimly romantic, yesteryear regalia of a Foreign Legionnaire. The man appraised Morgan and the captain, head to toe, and then, as if they had passed some occult test, he unlatched the gate and admitted them with a wordless bow. Immediately audible were the sounds of a popular eatery in full noon-time swing. They crossed a well-planted courtyard and passed through a narrow hallway into the region of the dining room—a spacious, coffer-ceilinged chamber whose natural coolness was abetted by the slow-moving propellers of numerous overhead fans. Memories formed of Somerset Maugham's descriptions of similar colonial haunts in Singapore, Kuala Lumpur, Bangkok, Rangoon: places now all fallen to the Japanese. There were even potted palms, rooted in immense urns painted over with vivid flowers and resting dragons. But what aston-ished—what caused the captain to draw in his breath and to mutter "Good God—" was that the room was thick with officers from most every branch of the Allied military services, some of positively celestial rank. The active feel these noisy eminences gave off was of spiff and prance: of that thoroughbred air captured for the eye in gravure pho-tographs of the winner's circle at celebrated racetracks. The high-stakes impression drew a smile from Morgan.

They were led to a table by a turbaned headwaiter whose demeanor was a cross between a Levantine Jeeves and a bodyguard to Al Capone. His manner changed though, instantly, when the captain told him: "We'd like Mr. Milburn to know that two friends of Mr. Sarkis are here."

"Indeed. I'll tell Mr. Milburn straight-away."

"Hold on. . . . We're in need of a drink. What'll you have, Shurtliff?"

Morgan's reply was cut off by a voice that came from the table most adjacent to their own: "Welcome to Cairo, gentlemen." They turned in their chairs and faced a British lieutenant-general (in company with a Free French colonel) who raised a large hand and in resonant tones said: "These days, the only drink available in this part of the world is gin and orange."

Morgan watched the captain handle the general with a thin smile and the simple comment: "Thanks for the tip—" and, to the lingering waiter: "Two gins, please; no orange."

The waiter moved off.

From surrounding tables, authoritative intonements on the progress of the war in Africa drifted their way: "—the remains of Rommel's forces on their last legs—"; "—knew the tide had turned in our favor when the Martuba airfields were captured—"; "—Leclerc's victory at Kasr Rhilane—"

"They're a confident bunch," the captain remarked. Then, with yield: "I guess they've earned the right to be."

The waiter returned quickly, bearing on a tray two soup cups and two glasses filled with what Morgan assumed was gin. He placed himself between Morgan and the captain, lowered his torso and with a mighty discretion told them: "It's water in the glasses. The stuff in the soup cups is Scotch whiskey, compliments of Mr. Milburn." He stood straight again: "I'll get menus for you now."

The captain said, "Thank Mr. Milburn for us—" and to Morgan: "Always trust Sarkis."

The food was excellent. They took their time over it, glad for the change of dining on land and in a stead so opposite from the *Stubbins*'s officers' mess. That the view let on to the courtyard, and that the berry-laden espaliered trees which flanked its walls attracted a species of small, sparrow-like birds, contributed, for Morgan, the more touching part of the difference. The captain, though, kept returning his gaze to the worldlier scene: "It's an interesting crowd," he said. "I never thought I'd be lifting a fork in the company of a Royal Navy rear-admiral. . . . No . . . Over there, with the two commodores."

Morgan followed the direction of his gaze. "Dazzlers all," was his only comment.

The captain touched the knot of his neck-tie: "I feel like I'm at a costume party."

Morgan guffawed: "Would that we were!"

At some point well along in the meal, the captain confided: "I've been putting off telling you. . . . We'll be leaving next Friday. I got my orders day before yesterday."

"Going back the same way we came?"

"The very same."

They retreated for a bit into their own thoughts.

"We're a scintillating pair," Morgan finally offered.

"Aren't we just . . . It's a bazaar we're up for next, right?"

Whether or not Magdi's choice of bazaar was of the best, they would never know. . . . He put them out of the car into the seethe of an immense plaza carpeted with sheep and camel dung and furnished with stalls presided over by bearded, gesticulating native merchants hawking wares that ran the gamut from the gaudiest of seraglio scarves to "guaranteed" Roman vases. As in all such crowded, venal places, there was an air of menace, heightened at every turn by a human tide of beggars, fakirs, and whores—the last in startling abundance. Toward them all, Morgan felt only sorrow. He turned to the captain: "You don't seem to be enjoying this any more than I am. What about the pyramids? Shall we ride out and see them?"

"The sooner the better. This is a zoo. . . . I've never liked zoos."

Rated against the perspective of expectation, the set of pyramids Magdi drove them to impressed Morgan as being small. He found this sense of lesserness oddly disconcerting, for of course and in fact, they were immense. In the end, he decided it was the more silent, more solemn, more amazing experience of the circumjacent desert that scaled them down and created for him the greater, conjurable sense that, finally, they were no more or less than gestures at immortality made by mortally affrighted kings.

He had come to them replete with interest and an open curiosity, only to find that what existed and happened around them—all, it seemed to him, of a dark aspect—put his enthusiasm at hazard: above the tombs, against the sky's unbroken blue, a congregation of buzzards wheeled in huge, ritualistic circles, round and round, round and round; cutting the horizon, far, far off, the silhouette of a caravan moved in slow degrees toward a goal he felt was beyond his capacity to imagine; a bit away from where he stood, a group of cowled native women sat without speaking in attitudes of such unaliveness and indifference as to suggest their silence was more fated than chosen; and nearer, again and again, he met the gaze of tenebrously gowned men as they walked toward him, but their eyes held nothing for him, no greeting, no surprise, no wonder, no passion either of exclusion or inclusion—only a sepulchral remoteness— itself, he concluded, a form of concurrence that he was, as they were, but another timeless soul timelessly met in the shadow of death.

"Shurtliff."

He welcomed the call. He looked at his watch: nearly six in the evening.

He squared his shoulders, reset his cap on his head, and with long, determined steps—as if on the challenge of an uphill path—he strode forward over the sand to where the captain was waiting by Magdi's car.

❧

Friday night, March 19, 1943

A star-filled sky, but no moon; a calm sea.

They were a week out from Port Said, in the Indian Ocean just south of the Mozambique Channel, bound at full speed for Lourenco Marques.[1]

On this night, as on all others, the *Stubbins* showed no glimmer of light. By order, life-jackets were worn by all. In every quarter of the ship, tasks were performed as quietly as possible. When words were exchanged, voices were kept low. Morgan, making his nightly check of the armament, was greeted in such a way by the Owl, who, with Sutter, was stationed forward at the dual-purpose gun. In a near whisper, Owl remarked on the fair night, the brightness of the stars; the peace. "I've almost come to like the sea, sir," he added with a soft laugh. Sutter told him he was out of his skull, but to keep talking anyhow: gab broke the boredom. . . . Midship, at one of the anti-aircraft guns, Vodapec too commented on the night, calling it "nice," and the sea "smooth as silk."

"Shurtliff."

He was on his way to the ship's stern: the hushed imperative came from behind. He turned around: "Sir—"

In the diffused starlight, even standing close as they immediately were, the captain's face under its darkened cap was barely visible. His voice, though, for all its quiet, was distinct, and the message conveyed, clear as glass: "We've received word of submarine activity in the area. . . . I've decided not to alert the crew. If nothing happens, it would only strain

---

[1]Now called Maputo.

them unnecessarily, and if the worst happens—" The captain wavered, then finished with: "I can't see that foreknowledge would arm anyone to advantage. Sarkis agrees with me. . . . Anyhow, there it is, Shurtliff."

"We've been lucky so far, sir. Chances are we'll stay so."

"Right," the captain replied. Then, simply, "I'll get back to the bridge."

Morgan went to his cabin. There, from its keeping place, he removed a small kit, prepared long ago: contents: an initialed, brandy-filled silver flask (a present from another era, from Maud); a Bible, bound in soft leather (given him by his father when he first went off to boarding school); and a tin of sulfa powder—the lot wrapped in oilskin and tied with linen twine, an end length of which he used now for securing the kit to his belt.

He took his time, surprised by his calm. He consulted his watch: 9:01. He drank a glass of water. A mistake. With the last tepid, tank-tasting swallow, by an imperial trick of mind, he was in the meadow behind his house, kneeling beside the creek on a mound of willow-shaded grass, filling his cupped hands with the stream's clear water, putting his lips to the pleasing chill, his eyes, the while, following the swim of a charming newt . . . *Christ* . . . The past that had risen before him clashed with the present and he stood, frozen by the sudden animal lucidities of fear. The pity of it all! . . . He suffered through a moment of resentment that took the form of a soundless weeping. And then his anger shifted to himself, and to himself he posed the issue of his manhood's strength, and thereby, albeit slowly, worked his way back to the south side of a stoic courage. Finally, and for the numbing fact of its being the only next thing he could do, he returned to his duties on deck.

An hour passed, and nearly half of another.

. . . The first torpedo struck the *Stubbins* on her port bow. At the rending blow she trembled mightily and, veering, began almost at once to lose way. As much for her as for themselves, her men cried out—a wild plaint of shock and disbelief that came from every quarter and continued at full pitch until, whether by force of will, habit of duty, or the savage compulsions of terror, they recovered their senses and, acting on the "Abandon-Ship" order that came almost at once from the bridge, set about to save themselves. The conduct of most was near automatic: a result of the disciplines practiced and perfected by the relentless drills the captain had insisted on, himself observing each exercise, and timing it, seeing it done, each time, instanter. The blackness of the night, though, confused: and the unrehearsed contingencies of the injured: and the impediments of strong metal and loosened rigging and broken glass and the hindrance of huger objects that shifted in a greased way over the deck as the sea began to pour in through the cavity of the *Stubbins*'s open wound, flooding her, and causing her to tilt slowly onto her nose. Yet, somehow, and with amazing speed, the four life-boats were released from their chocks and, with each one manned by an inboard officer and two seamen, lowered to the sea's surface where, launched and holding at a safe distance from the foundering ship, they stood by as the men came down the ropes. For that act, some helped others: Sutter, for one. Holding the wounded Owl, he inched him down the hemp ladder, down the entire cliff of the *Stubbins*'s side, encouraging him all the way by the charging offense of his language, that he *could* the fuck make it if he'd *try:* "Come on, Owl. I won't drop you. Come on, you lovely shit . . ." And Kenner helped Williams (whose right arm was a mangled mess) bringing him down, seated, on his shoulders—the success of the carnival stunt made possible by the agile way Williams put his left hand to use during the descent, shifting it swiftly from one hemp vertical to the next, by which action he both lessened his weight on Kenner's shoulders and kept himself from falling over backwards. Morgan took charge of Anderson, the chief petty-officer (whose left leg was brutally injured) by positioning himself below Anderson on the ladder and guiding Anderson's good right leg downward, rung by rung. Just before they dropped, Morgan told him: "Take a deep breath . . ." In a sea thick with the spillage of fuel oil, he retrieved Anderson, and with Anderson gripping his belt, he began to swim. They were fantastically lucky: Garvin—in command of one of the lifeboats—saw the closely paired bob on the water of their life jacket lights, and with Rhode and Tamworth working the oars, instantly came to their rescue.

Incredibly, most of the men were in the water now. . . . Morgan hauled Hughes into the boat, then with Hughes's turnabout help, the near-lifeless Owl, and after him the exhausted, still cursing Sutter. They picked up others: Vodapec and Climson and Browne.

The captain, too and last, left the *Stubbins*, abandoning her after sending the others before him. Three-quarters of the way down the ladder he stopped and turned his body full around and, faced so, away from his stricken ship, he let go his hold on the ropes and jumped, feet first, into the sea.

No more than fifteen minutes elapsed between the strike of the first torpedo and the hit of the second—just time enough for the bastard sub to swing around and take a murderer's aim and discharge its next blow—delivered to the *Stubbins*'s starboard side, midship, with a killing accuracy that ruptured the rest of her bunker tanks and set off the deck ammunition. There were, then, explosions of blinding light and scythed concussions of sound, like machine-gun fire, and the greater deafening blasts of the larger shells and a downpour from the sky of debris, and on the sea, spreading rapidly, greater spills of oil. As seen now in the flashes of exploding light, the *Stubbins* looked as if she were in the grip of some extreme, empowered underwater hand that was pulling her firmly down and under. . . . There was a chaos of unpatterned waves, two of which came together and formed a single, imposing, crested undulation that poured itself broadside into the captain's boat (the only one with a motor), casting its occupants back into the sea and—direly—swamped the craft. By the illuminating bursts from the still-exploding ammunition, Morgan and the others in Garvin's boat saw it happen. Garvin barked out the order to row: "*Row. Row!*" in the direction of the catastrophe. Rhode and Tamworth strained at the oars, but because of the need to maneuver against the hazard to themselves from another such making wave, their approach was indirect and painfully prolonged. By the time they reached a position relative to the swamped boat, its outcast members, seven in all, including the captain, were widely scattered—calling out—all of them choking from the oil and slippery as eels when it came to handing them into the boat.

At some point during the rescue operation—certainly long before it was completed—the *Stubbins*'s stern heaved up and out of the sea. She was seen pitched on her nose: doomed. For an eerily long moment she remained so, as if staying herself by her own will: as if she were deter-mined—even odd and tragic as she looked now, with her propeller exposed and her fine, orderly, substantial beauty all undone—to be remembered as resisting her death to the very end.

Those who could kept their eyes on her, watching as all mourners do, with a terrible attention and an opposing prayer that the inevitable come not and that it come fast.

She lurched again, this time with an incalculably immense, dispelling sigh. There was an ear-splitting crash as her masts fell and a storm of ruin racketed down her decks. Some of her men wailed out—"She's going!"—and even as they gasped, she plunged, and with an unimagin-able speed, vanished from their sight, taking with her the strange poetry of their instantly remembered lives aboard her and leaving them in the night's darkness on a sea thick with oil and the floating wreckage of their lost world.

◆

. . . In time, the sea regained its calm.

In the lifeboat, Anderson lay under a thwart. Now and again he would moan and Morgan would reach down and touch his hand. Across from him, Sutter held the Owl, now mercifully unconscious. Five men were sprawled on the bottom of the boat. The others simply sat, mutely erect, or slumped forward, holding their heads in their hands, some leaning against one another, clumped so for support. There was a perva-sive stink of vomit and oil. In the stern, alone, the captain's crouched fig-ure had the rigid, hulked, dark look of a chained dog.

For a while this was the way they remained, resting, under the stars.

(. . . In law school, the course in criminal law had been taught by a much admired legal scholar named John Caddell. Mr. Caddell had a swift mind and he looked like a gambler on a Mississippi steamboat, which is why generations of law students referred to him as "Blackjack Caddell." He was a broadly read man and he would often open a class-lecture by quoting from this or that book written by an author or "thinker" deemed worthy of his respect [the leaps in kind could be prodigious, ranging over centuries]. And so one day he had entered the lecture room and, after giving out his usual languid "Good morning to you all," had turned to the blackboard and written on it the single phrase "the fatal futility of Fact"—after which he had faced back to his audience and in his deep, leading voice said: "Those are Henry James's words. They appear in his novel *The Spoils of Poynton*. . . . Notice that the word *fact* is capitalized, not by me, by Mr. James. . . . For a moment, let us delete the word *fatal*, which leaves us with the pithier 'the futility of Fact.'" [A weighted pause.] "Now, let us reinsert Mr. James's qualifier—'fatal.'" . . . [Another pause.] Then, briskly: "And now, let us proceed to the case of today's discussion.")

It was as they rested that Morgan heard in his mind's ear Blackjack Caddell's voice saying again the words of James's sentence, and began, wearily but genuinely, to ponder which "Fact" of his present circumstance was the mattering one: that of the demising torpedoing of the *Stubbins*, or the more mysterious, unresolved one of his still being alive, and being so, as yet unwilling to consider a preference for one form of death over another. And it was then, out of a passionate, obedient love of life and loyalty to it, that he prayed to survive, vowing to himself that if he did, he would never make of his continuance an earthly boast.

&

By midnight, the three life-boats had come together, the raw comfort of the joining made possible by the glow from the stars and the sea's prevailing calm.

A head-count was taken:

—Eighteen in the boat Morgan was in (commanded now by the captain), (two—the Owl and Anderson, seriously wounded);

—Eighteen in the boat Sarkis had the charge of (one—Williams—injured);

—Sixteen in Pfeiffer's boat (no physical injuries, but Staines and Norreys in shock).

In each boat, most were suffering from the effects of having swallowed salt water and oil.

Of the vanquished *Stubbins*'s total complement of fifty-seven men, fifty-two were accounted for; five were dead or missing.

The boats rocked in close proximity and the captain spoke quietly through the dark to his men. He made a kind of sermon out of what he called "our decent chance of making it through." He gave two reasons for his optimism, the first one being that before the "Abandon-Ship" order was given, Jacks, the radio officer on duty, acting on orders, had transmitted an SOS, giving the *Stubbins's* position and the time of the initial torpedoing, so it was logical to assume that friendly ships would conduct a search for survivors; and the second reason—the luck of the weather: the light, steady breeze and the easy seas.

He told what he thought was the best thing to do: that the two boats under the command of Sarkis and Pfeiffer should take immediate advantage of the favoring weather and set sail together for the coast of South Africa (which he calculated to be some ninety miles away); that he and the men in his boat should stand by in the area for the rest of the night on the chance of picking up at dawn any or all of the five missing men, and that then they too would sail for the coast.

He was masterful: he gave shape to hope.

⋅§

Saturday, March 20, 1943

At around two A.M., the two boats set off. The captain stood up for their departure: "Good luck," he said into the darkness. From the departing men, good-byes were murmured. As the white sails disappeared into the night, Morgan heard Vodapec's whispered words to Tamworth: "Now we're for sure on our own."

Dawn came slowly. By its first gray light, they looked about with horror at the floating mass of debris and vast extent of the oil slick and—wordlessly—at each other: at their filthy bodies, their weary, fear-ridden faces, at Anderson's mangled leg and the Owl's slight breathing. . . . Rhode was the one who snapped them out of their silence. He had been staring off with a dazed, reclusive look on his face (Morgan thought him in shock) when, without the least change of facial expression, he said: "I think I see a raft."

The captain was quick: "*Where*, Rhode?"

Rhode pointed: "Focus on that third streak of oil, sir . . . the widest one, way beyond the end of it . . . that black form, sir."

Against the rising sun, the captain hooded his eyes with his hands. "I don't see it, Rhode."

But Browne did. "*Something's* there. It's riding low, sir. It *could* be a raft with a drogue put out to steady it."

Most were involved now, straining to see.

The captain sounded desperate: "I can't pick it up. . . . You're *sure,* Browne? Do you still see it, Rhode?"

"Yes, sir."

"Yes, sir."

The captain sat down. "We'll row toward it. Guide us, Browne; Rhode."

Hughes and Magrath manned the oars. The captain told them: "Set a pace and don't exert beyond it. It won't do to use up your strength hurrying."

Certainty set in soon enough: just as Rhode and Browne had said, there was something ahead—a goodly sized object darker by a bit than the sea, riding low and fairly steady on the water. "Keep on as you're going," the captain said. And when they'd progressed about half-way to it, he cupped his hands to his lips: "Hello," he shouted: *"Hello!"* . . . There was no answer. To Hughes and Magrath he said: "Say when you want to be relieved. Vodapec and Tamworth can take over."

Hughes said: "No need yet, sir."

They went on for a spell in a silence broken only by the rhythmic sloshings of the worked oars. Then the captain tried again: "Hello . . . Hello."

In the raft, a figure raised itself. Against the sky, its upright substance looked like a huge bird perched on a floating log, and it stayed so, still, for a long minute. And then, from its sides, not wings, but arms were lifted to shoulder height and extended outward full stretch and commenced moving, up and down, up and down. Like an animated crucifix, Morgan thought. Three other figures lifted themselves to view. Then a shrill sound rent the air—a piercing glissando—and Climson whipped to his feet: *"Bowen.* That's Bowen's girl-whistle . . . Hey, *Bowen!"*

"Sit down, Climson," the captain commanded, not sternly, not—obviously—to squelch Climson's joy, but for the serious sake of the task at hand. In the strengthening light, Morgan could see his eyes: that they were intensely blue and in concentration hard as steel. . . . "Hughes, Magrath, go on a bit more, and when I say to, bring the raft's midship part to windward. We'll let it drift down on us. Rhode, you get ready to throw a line to it when it's close enough." He was in complete control of a conspicuous excitement. "Sutter. . . . *Sutter—*"

"Sir?" Sutter's voice was barely audible.

"We're going to have to shift you and Malkerson to the other side. . . . *Sutter?*"

"I hear you."

"Browne will hold Malkerson's feet in place and Shurtliff'll help you ease him across. I'll tell you when." And then, with a direct look at Morgan, the captain made a sign: *Easy,* it said: *Sutter's on the edge.*

Myers.

Fuller.

Bowen.

Underwood.

By turn, each was transferred from the raft to the boat. From the way they let themselves be helped, Morgan got a sense of how spent they were: even Bowen, whose whistle had been so spirited. Fuller was barely recognizable: his blond hair was black with oil, his face and mouth bloody, lips grotesquely swollen, his front teeth gone. When Underwood was handed aboard, he looked into the faces of his mates and at the captain. He said, "Thank you." Then he began to weep.

Myers told the captain: "We lost Davis, sir."

❧

In the small boat, crowded together, there were now twenty-two men. They set about to tidy up the boat: cleaned up the vomit; bailed out the water; coiled the lines. . . . The captain and Morgan went to work on Anderson's leg: on the worst of the open wounds, they sprinkled the sulfa powder from Morgan's kit and applied a loose wrapping of bandages supplied by the boat's first-aid kit. About the Owl's condition, all was mystery: he had no visible injuries, but his pallor was deathly and he breathed with obvious difficulty. Once in a while his eyelids would flutter: when that happened Sutter would speak to him, trying to rouse him, but the Owl did not respond.

. . . "Breakfast," (the captain's wry word), was a leathery concentrate of nourishment described on each packet as "Emergency Issue." The intake of fluid was a two-ounce-per-man mix of water and orange juice. The captain put Morgan in charge of meting out these rations which would, he said, be dispensed, on his orders, three times to each man, each day.

Then: *then* they stepped the mast and rigged shrouds and a forestay. The captain reseated them for a better ballast. (Sutter would not be separated from the Owl, and the captain did not force the issue.) Garvin took the tiller. The captain raised his arm and with an arrowed gesture said: "*That* way." Vodapec and Hughes hoisted the sail. The breeze took it and winged it out and as the boat spurted forward, Climson began to sing the child's song:

> *Old MacDonald had a farm,*
> *Ee–i, ee–i, oh.*
> *And on the farm he had a cow,*
> *Ee–i, ee–i, oh.*

His voice was joined: "With a moo-moo here, and a moo-moo there—"

No barnyard creature lacked honoring.

Thus they departed the site of the *Stubbins*'s grave.

It stayed breezy all day. The sun was warm, but not tropical, so they did not suffer from it. The terribly cramped conditions made for stiff bodies and limbs and induced that kind of large-eyed, resigned lethargy a tethered animal displays. Generally, though, morale was good. There were even intervals that were vaguely lively, vaguely funny, as when a long litany of knock-knock jokes were exchanged, and after that, riddles, and a few dumb stories, all clean enough to tell to your sister. It was as if a kind of shyness had seized them: as if each wanted to be seen in an innocent light. Such constraint applied too in the matter of urination and defecation: in an attempt to bestow privacy, heads were turned away: the attempt mattered more than the fact that no privacy of the least sort was attainable—except of course as one sought and found it in his own thoughts, by which means, for suspended lengths of time, each became his own hermit. Closed eyes and a sealed-off look were the clues to these individual absences.

... Maud, dearest ... Without pen or paper I write to you from nowhere. ... What do lovers live by? Everything that has no limits: Eternity; memory; regret.

And so the first day passed.

When night came, they took their bearings from the stars.

Throughout all the previous hours, Anderson had borne his pain with a heroic bravery. Somewhere around eleven, though, he went a bit berserk, shouting out in the darkness that he could bear it no more. That was when the captain gave Morgan permission to give him most of the brandy from Maud's flask.

Sunday, March 21

Dawn broke fair. The sun came up strong, blazoning the sea with a golden light.

Mid-morning, the Owl died. It was a vanishing of a kind sudden and soundless, made known by a trickle of blood that came out of the right corner of his mouth and dripped down onto Sutter's hand. Sutter's tears were the streaming agent: "He's stopped breathing."

Corcoran was sitting next to Sutter. By a gesture, the captain indicated to Corcoran that he was to change places with himself. At Sutter's side he confirmed the Owl's death. He spoke directly to Sutter: "I'm very sorry, Sutter. . . . You must let him go." His tone was as gentle as a woman's would have been. He began to ease the Owl's body out of Sutter's hold. Morgan, watching, considered one of a string of Latin phrases drilled into him at school: *Basis virtutum constantia:*[2] an epitaph for the broken Sutter.

Without looking up from the task of undoing the Owl's life-jacket, the captain told Brey to keep his eyes on the sail, and to Sanderson, now at the tiller, to head the boat closer into the wind. "We'll say the Lord's

---

[2]Constancy is the basis of the virtues.

Prayer, then we'll slip him over the side." He turned back to Sutter: "Shaw will help me do that if you'd rather not, Sutter."

"I'll do it," Sutter answered.

They followed the captain's lead: "Our father, who art in heaven, hallowed be thy name. Thy kingdom come. Thy will be done"—their heads bowed and their voices, in the great containments of sky and sea, near lost:—"but deliver us from evil, for thine is the kingdom, the power, and the glory, for ever and ever." At the "Amen," as they raised their eyes, the captain was seen to brush the Owl's hair back from his forehead, exposing to sight the completeness of his vividly young face on which he gazed for a singular moment. When he next spoke, it was in a carrying voice that shook with feeling: "The Breastplate of Righteousness, the Shield of Faith, the Helmet of Salvation, the Sword of Spirit." Then: "*Now,* Sutter."

The boat heeled sharply as they put the Owl over.

With the act done, the captain resumed his place in the stern.

"Trim the sail," he ordered, "and resume course."

⌇

There is a pull of water which runs off the east coast of Africa called the Agulhas Current, and they faced the danger of getting caught in it and of being carried by it down around the Cape and out into the South Atlantic: into oblivion. Sutter made the mistake of mumbling aloud, somewhat wildly, what he was thinking: that the Owl's death was an omen of their collective doom. The captain's response came with the force of a whip: "Hear me, Sutter. I'll not stand for that kind of talk. Understand?" Sutter straightened his back: "Sir," he said. The captain insisted: "Say '*Yes,* sir,' Sutter"—which, immediately, Sutter did.

⌇

Around noon-time, the seas began to make. By midafternoon, the swells were heavy and very turbulent.

At dusk, the captain took the tiller. The waves by then were immense: deep and steep and topped by white, wind-driven spray that blew upon them with the fierceness of a teeming rain. They took shifts bailing the boat. The captain steered with a god-like skill, not as one in contest with the sea, but as if he were a willing accomplice to its savagery. He would crab the boat, quartering it through the canyon of a trough, then straighten the tiller just in time to meet the loom of the next coming-on swell. He did that for almost seven hours: all through the deepest part of the night: *how*, Morgan would never know. Perhaps, he thought, by some uncanny gift of strength endowed by a high and subtle kinship to the sea itself: by that "belonging" to it he'd discovered in himself that sharp day he'd first encountered it as a land-born boy from Suffern, New York.

. . . Sometime around three A.M., the tempest began to moderate. With the coming of dawn (on Monday, March 22) as the waves leveled off, they all kept their gaze forward to where, by the calculations they'd been proceeding under, land ought to be. They'd been going, after all, since Saturday morning—two full days—and ninety miles, as Climson dared to say, wasn't all that far. . . . To Morgan's surprise, the captain expanded on Climson's remark, calling it reasonable, and stating his own disappointment at a lack of evidence of their being on the right course: at the absence, for instance, of any bird life in the sky. . . . But they'd made it through the storm, he said, and by God, they'd make it all the way. . . . He looked a bit mad, with his oil-smeared face and torn clothes and gesturing hands that were raw from his hours at the tiller and with, inside the blood-shot whites of his eyes, the blue pupils sharp as razors, taking in the perdition of his men—five of whom (Morgan among them) had broken out head to toe in a fiery rash from the oil; Myers's skin an oozing mess of salt-water boils; Fuller's swollen, disfigured face; Anderson's leg, rotting; and the sufferings of all from exhaustion and thirst. . . . He looked mad. . . . And then, as if he knew it and was ashamed, he lowered his head toward his lap and for about an hour, slumped so, he appeared to sleep.

Garvin had the tiller. No one talked. In a silence that grew heavier by the minute, they but sat, absorbed in their thoughts and unspoken fears that they were caught in the current and were being taken from land.

❧

Early in the afternoon a plane flew over.

They heard first the faint, steady throb of its engines, which alien resonance caused them, with a hushed gravity of focused attention, to scan the heavens in the direction of the gaining sound. . . . Then they saw it:

saw it for what they supposed it to be: as their avenging angel of deliverance. . . . It was flying at a high altitude on a straight course, emerging swiftly toward them through the open sky. In an urgent, wild scurry of movement, they began to wave their arms and to vent their praise of it by yells and shouts of excitement and celebration. With their eyes and arms and voices raised to it, there was a moment of inattention to the boat, fatal in kind: with a sudden sheering velocity, the main boom jibed, snapping the mast in two—*that* as—without the merest dip in altitude or a wagging of its wings in the known signification that the pilot had spotted them—the plane passed overhead and sped away.

By the two calamities—loss of sail, and the plane's annihilating snub —the last of their rational hope was taken from them.

From the stricken look on the captain's face, as Morgan vividly beheld it, it was obvious that he blamed himself for the loss of sail. Out of a combination of conviction and respect and a kind of despairing affection, Morgan addressed him over Browne's and Tamworth's bent figures: "It's not your fault, sir," he said.

The reply was a low denial that carried: "But it is."

Anderson—until then mute in his suffering—cleared his throat and rasped out: "Mister Shurtliff's right, sir. It's not your fault. It's the fault of the whole circumstance." Then, in a tone of appeal: "I'd have some brandy if there's any left."

Morgan shook the flask: "I'd say there's a swallow." He unscrewed the cap and put the flask in Anderson's hand.

"At home," Anderson croaked on to no one in particular, "my wife heads our local chapter of the WCTU. . . . It would distress her to see me take liquor. I'm going to, though. And tonight, after it's dark, I'm going to put myself over the side."

The captain said: "It's a while till nightfall, Anderson. We'll talk about it then. . . . Would you like us to shift you a bit?"

"No. I'll stay as I am for the time being."

❧

Over the next two hours, the breeze weakened and the sea turned slack. Cramped, numb, thirsty, itching, sickened by their individual filth and the reek of Anderson's festering wounds, they drifted aimlessly under the clear of the unchanging sky, detached in bodily attitude from one another; in spirit, joined entirely in a silent despair.

ᴇᶴ

Midafternoon, from his place in the stern, the captain roused them with a single word: *"There."* He was pointing into the distance. And, as they peered: "I'm sure it's a boat."

A dot on the horizon.

A dot that was moving.

Moving, in a willed way, toward them.

Toward them, though not directly: in slow, measured, criss-crossing laps insinuative of a vessel on the hunt.

As the minutes ticked by, and as it attained in size, their hopes began palpably to rise.

The captain by now was on his feet, standing just *so*, rigid and wordless. He looked cast in iron.

He allowed a longer interval of time to pass.

When he broke his stance, it was by way of one of his old, abruptly made gestures, this one triumphant: "I make it out a British Corvette," he said deeply. And then, in a voice of sudden thunder: *"WAVE:* Wave your arms off. Yell! *Louder. WAVE."*

They were seen.

They knew it from the way the ship veered from her angled course and turned toward them in a manner presenting. Faced so, head-on, even from so far away, there was something of pomp about her—an impression that strengthened as she increased her speed and began, steadily and surely, to advance upon them. The distance to be covered was not inconsiderable. Progressing, with the sun agleam on her upswept prow, she looked winged. But she could not be fast enough for them—they, with their reaching eyes on her, waiting, the ultimate minutes of her coming the longest of their lives. . . . Yet when she was all but arrived, that is to say, when she was quite near and for obvious reasons had to slow her pace, the accumulated minutes took a backwards, disappearing leap, so that—*now*—as she made a sweeping circle of approach and at last hove alongside and was manifestly there, the length of time her coming had taken seemed, in immediate review, strangely swift.

Forever after, Morgan would wonder at their behavior in those first psalm-like moments of knowing they were saved: that no one went to pieces: that they held to a self-control achieved at such a cost that it turned them "cool" (the word, used so, learned years later from another generation and applied in retrospect): the precarious pose maintained throughout and as, in strict accordance with wartime rules, they were boarded and inspected. During this formality, the Corvette, sleek and bristling, held to her removed position. On her decks, her crew remained a silent, stony-faced, on-guard assembly of watchers.

The petty-officer in charge of the inspection was middle-aged, deeply tanned, meticulously groomed, sharp-minded in his interrogation of the captain, and toward them all supremely respectful. With the inspection completed, he raised his hand and made a releasing signal to the Corvette's crew, who bellowed out at once a loud cheer, backed up by jolly and cordial displays of friendliness. Then, with an efficiency and considerateness that verged at moments on tenderness, they went to work to remove the rescued from the life-boat to their ship: Anderson first, after bedding him on a stretcher; Fuller next, the awful grotesqueries of his mutilated face shined by sudden tears. Then Myers, with his erupted boils, babbling his gratitude through lips that trembled like a fledgling's wings. Rhode. Underwood. Browne. Magrath. Sutter. Tamworth. Vodapec. Bowen. Climson . . . One by one. Garvin. Brey. Corcoran. Sanderson . . . Each after the other. Hughes. Larivey. Dunne. Shaw. . . . It took a long time. . . . When his turn came, Morgan, until then sealed in that aforementioned control, broke: he opened his mouth to thank the bosun who stretched out a hand to him, but the intended word never came. Instead, the choke of a feral sob. He could no more have suppressed it than he could have held up the world in his two hands.

A seaman took charge of him. It took three washings down with heavy soap to get the oil off him before he was salved over with a first remedy for his rash.

He never saw his uniform again.

❧

They were taken to Durban, South Africa.

There, they formally delivered themselves over to the British.

A staff of military bureaucrats briefly detained them: "Just long enough to sort you out for the records," one of them explained.

Clothed in the humble extremes of a too-large pair of pants (clean, though) and a too-small short-sleeved shirt (also clean), naked-footed but for a pair of white gym socks (his shoes, like his uniform, had been cast away), dispossessed of everything that was his own (his confiscated flask and Bible were later returned to him), Morgan, as in a dream choreographed by Kafka, answered as sensibly as he could a series of questions put to him by a balding sergeant who seemed more interested in proving (on paper) that he, Morgan Shurtliff, was not dead, than in acknowledging his flesh-and-blood presence as evidence that he was alive.

Eventually, he was taken to an infirmary. There, in a quiet ward, he slept for hours. The captain visited him on the second day. He pulled a chair close to Morgan's bed and peered at him: "They seem to have your rash under control. You're a bit fragrant though."

"It's the ointment," Morgan said. "The ward orderly calls it 'Essence of Rhinoceros Piss.'" Then: "And how are you, sir?"

"All right, I think. . . . I had a bad time yesterday morning, but it only lasted about ten minutes. Some sort of delayed reaction, I guess."

"What happened?"

"I was shaving and all of a sudden my hands began to shake. I couldn't get them under control. . . . Fortunately, no one was around." He held out his hands: "They're steady enough now," he said of their stillness. Then: "I once heard one drunk say of another, 'For the shape he's in, he's in pretty good shape.' That about describes me. . . . But I've a lot to tell you—" (said with a sudden livening, eyes charged by an intense blue); and, at once: "Sarkis's and Pfeiffer's boats made it through. They stayed together—were about thirty miles off the coast when a British patrol boat spotted them and took them on. They're all in Cape Town, all of them fine—except for Williams, who's in the hospital, but—to quote my informant—the Brits by the way are very decent about sharing what they know—his arm is 'fixable,' which turns out to mean he'll have the full use of it when the medics finish with him." The captain's clean, brief narration, occluding of an imposed drama, revealed in unsaid full his depth of joy and humility that the story's end was of a marvelous best.

To it, emotionally, Morgan nodded.

"I've more to report," the captain picked up. "I've seen all our group. They're scattered about the place, but they're comfortably billeted and by and large they're in good shape." He paused, but only for an instant: "Anderson and Fuller were removed to Cape Town yesterday. . . . I'm told the hospital there is first-rate. Anderson's the one to be worried about."

"I've been afraid for him," Morgan said. "I expect to be let out of here tomorrow, the day after at the latest. I'll make the rounds of my crew then." He spoke next of what he'd come to believe: that he owed his life to the captain: "For the way you brought us through the storm, sir. Your skill with the tiller."

"Oh, I don't know, Shurtliff," the captain replied. "I've been thinking about that. About—everything. . . . In the end, I'm inclined to the feeling that what brought us through is beyond my understanding." He leaned forward in his chair: "Just between us, I keep being surprised that I'm alive. If I sound a bit 'dotty,' as my mother would say, it's because I haven't quite got used to the idea yet."

"That makes at least two of us."

A commotion at the door of the ward—two doctors followed by a nurse pushing a cart loaded with a supply of medicinal mysteries—broke their mood. Morgan said: "Tell me about your suit."

For the first time the captain smiled. "A blinder, isn't it?" said with a touch to the plaid lapels. "The padre who runs the local seaman's mission supplied me with it. It's not that I'm ungrateful, but I have to tell you I don't feel myself in it."

"It's not a bad fit though. God knows what I'll find to wear when I get out of here."

"If you think I'm eye-catching, you should see Sutter. He's cocked out in somebody's dead uncle's smoking-jacket. Velvet. With a crest embroidered on the handkerchief pocket. You know Sutter. Out to kill." Then, with a look down: "I'm sorry I said that. The truth is he's using the jacket to cover up his grief."

"Malkerson, you mean."

The captain nodded. And after a moment: "I'm told that as and when transport becomes available, we'll be shipped home. Not as a unit, of course. Individually. It'll take a while, so don't hold your breath." He stood up. "I'll see you later."

"Thanks for coming by, sir."

For a month he remained in Durban, billeted the while in one of a forest of tents set up on the old, very English, once thriving racetrack, now an R-and-R center—converted to that use sometime back in 1940 or '41. As seen against the vine-covered, architecturally resolved structures of the old colonial club-house and grandstand and near-by stables and grooms' quarters, the rows and rows of exactly spaced, precisely staked, dun-colored canvas shelters had the fixed, grandiose look of a Hollywood set: a military encampment à la Cecil B. DeMille.

In the beamed stables, in stalls still vaguely redolent of horse, battle-weary soldiers and tired airmen and ship-wrecked sailors could sit opposite a psychiatrist and confide their wartime nightmares. In the club-house, they could play billiards or cards or chess, or just sit around drinking and shooting the breeze. At night, in the arms of Red Cross girls and closely chaperoned, patriotic Durban damsels (even, by dint of discreet infiltration, a few "professional" ladies), they could dance to the music provided by a stack of records, the "smooth" ones vintage American, played by the Big Bands of Glenn Miller, Harry James, Tommy Dorsey, Artie Shaw, Benny Goodman. . . . There were plenty of jitterbug and bebop discs too, and hip morale rousers:

You've got to AC-cen-tuate the positive,
E-lim-inate the negative,
LATCH onto the affirmative . . . etc.

But the records whose waxed surfaces showed the most wear were the nostalgic, slow, romantic ones with lyrics and melodies that licensed you to hold the girl you were dancing with a bit closer: "Deep Purple," "Stars Fell on Alabama," "Let's Face the Music and Dance," "The Man I Love," "As Time Goes By," "Dancing in the Dark," "Stardust" . . .

Wafted on the late-night sea breeze, the wistful lubricities of such songs would reach Morgan's ears as he lay awake in the tent shared with a mix of

British officers. There were three men whose cots regularly remained empty until the bar closed, which was roughly about the time the dancing stopped. (Not infrequently, these three spent the night elsewhere.) The others, like himself, were mostly married men who tended to turn in early. One such—a tall, reticent infantry officer (decorated) in his early forties— was a fabulous snorer: you could wake at any hour of the night and he would be at it—a hundred-and-fifty-pound cicada thrumming away. The tent smelled of canvas and hemp and the roughly sawn wood plankings that formed its floor. If he balled up his pillow and turned his head just so, Morgan could see through the screen door, a few stars. He would set his eyes on the distant constellations and think of Maud, and with a wired, aching anxiousness, wonder about her. He knew well enough the changes the war had wrought in himself, but of the ways it might have changed her, he had no idea. He supposed it was possible that, bearing the responsibili- ties of parenting alone, she had settled into a maternal state of daily habits and patterns of mind that his presence, when he returned, would inevitably skew. She was a person of passionate dedication; of passionately held con- victions. How would he fit into them? How, and to what degree, might the realities of reunion betray their memories of one another? . . . Heretofore, he had dwelt only on their love—a love (for him) which time and distance had heightened and idealized to a point perhaps impossible of fulfillment. He must guard against that danger.

Difficult almost beyond bearing was the lengthy time ashore with its empty leisure and sexually torturing nearness of women. Yesterday, for instance, he had gone for a long walk on the strand at the head of Durban's harbor: he had seen a leggy, blond girl strolling with a soldier. Over a white blouse she wore a flowered scarf draped across narrow shoulders. When she passed him, her stride in step with the soldier's, he had looked for an instant directly into her eyes. Brown. The soldier had whispered something to her, his face hidden in her hair. Her throaty laugh had stirred him to the point of pain.

At the one "dance" he had briefly attended, an RAF pilot had identified to him a girl who was "available. Worth the price. Terrific." Why not, he asked himself as he walked on—why not seek her out? He recalled the flyer's cold-eyed, recommending words, the toughness of his voice authen- ticating the remote nature of such a purchased coupling; that one need not ever know her name; that it would be a fleeting, emotionless act of sexual solace. Nothing more. So why not? . . . Before him, at his approach, a flock of small, long-billed shore-birds rose up from the sand and flew off. . . . Walking once with his mother in his father's orchards (he must have been about six years old) on a gray, windy autumn day, they had similarly startled into flight a scavenging clutch of blackbirds. His hand was in his mother's. He could still remember the warmth and lightness of her touch. As the birds flew up into the sky, she had counted them:

One for sorrow
Two for joy
Three for a wedding
Four for a boy
Five for silver
Six for gold
Seven for the story never to be told.

The verse had captured his imagination (probably, as he thought of it now, for the hint of mystery implicit in its last line), and at his urging, then and there, she had taught it to him.

On the beach in Durban, he mulled over the verse's final line and reached the conclusion that there are two kinds of stories "never to be told": one, the secret that gives birth to a lie, and the second other, a suprapersonal experience whose bold and lingering effects on the soul forever mute the telling of it. On the aboutness of the second, his grasp was firm—a result of a recently realized intuition that, while a bare-boned factual account of the *Stubbins's* torpedoing would be easy to relate, the profounder elements of the experience—the Owl's death and the Hadesian trials in the lifeboat and the strange reality of his survival—comprised a story—*his*—never to be told: that, even were he to live to be Methuselah's age, he would never be able to reduce it to an impersonal measure sufficient to make it the listener's story as equally much as it was his own. . . . This knowledge brought to mind the vow he had made in the lifeboat: that if survival were granted him, he would never make of his continuance an earthly boast. . . .

So *no:* he would not seek out the airman's "terrific" assuageress.

⋖ঽ

On Wednesday of the second week, the captain left Durban (on an armed British trawler for Cape Town where he would next board an American freighter that would eventually land him in Buenos Aires, from whence he would be flown on a military plane to Miami, Florida). "That's the drill as I understand it," were the captain's summing words.

"I envy you being on your way," Morgan said.

They were having a last drink together on the eve of the captain's departure. "There's other news, Shurtliff. Not good." The captain's eyes raced away from Morgan's gaze, then back. "I heard yesterday that Anderson's leg had to be amputated."

"God . . . I wonder if he'd rather have died."

"That's what I keep asking myself. He's been a merchant mariner since he finished high school. It's the only life he knows and it's over for him."

Morgan said: "He spoke of his wife. Remember? So he does have *that* life, love and a home—" He was searching, trying to dredge up something remotely promising.

But the captain would not have it: "That can't fill his time," he cut in with a passion almost of outrage: "I mean, what the hell will he *do*, Shurtliff? Can you answer me that? What will he *do*?"

There was a silence. Then the captain, in that unexpected way he had of shifting moods, asked in his usual voice: "Do you believe in this war, Shurtliff?"

Morgan was fairly certain he understood what prompted the question, but it surprised him nevertheless. He was quick in his response: "Yes. Yes I do. I think that men with too much power—*evil* men like Hitler—must be stopped. *Have* to be: that not to stop them licenses them for greater evil. That was my reason for signing up. I still stand by it." He paused: "I don't mean to sound like a bloody Christer," and, as the captain remained silent, with his eyes still full on him: "All wars become more complex as they go on. God knows this one has. But at its core, I believe it's a right-minded one." Then, because he wanted to know for sure: "Why do you ask?"

The captain opened out his hands: "Because I need confirmation of my own feelings about it as against the cruelty of it." He looked suddenly frayed: "I'm tired, Shurtliff. I don't mind telling you that I am. I was awake all night trying to figure out what I can say to Anderson when I see him in Cape Town. . . . What *can* I say to him?" he appealed.

"I don't know, sir. . . . Anderson's a hero of sorts, but if I were Anderson, left without a leg, I don't know if the idea of a heroic sacrifice would be very comforting. I suppose it's possible that by the time you see him, he will have figured out a lot for himself and on his own terms." Then: "Will you remember me to him?"

"I will." The captain looked at his watch: "I'm due to report in in a few minutes. There is one other thing, though: if you'd like me to, I'll telephone your wife when I get to Miami."

Morgan's heart leapt: "*Would* you? That would be wonderful."

"I won't be able to tell her much, you understand. Nothing, really, except that you're all right and ought to be headed home fairly soon. Here—" he took a small notebook out of his suit-pocket. "Write down her telephone number."

"In case you can't reach her, I'll give you my father's number too. He'll pass on your message to her." Morgan handed the book back to the captain: "I can't tell you how much I appreciate your doing this."

The captain stood up, as, immediately, Morgan did. At that final moment and as they looked at one another, all the junctions of their relationship came together. For Morgan, there had been the long-ago partings from Maud and his father: this one, of a third kind, was no less wrenching.

Quietly, in a manner intimate, yet remarkably open, the captain said: "We have a lot between us worth remembering." He stood very straight; he held out his hand. "Let's try to stay in touch."

Morgan nodded. "Thank you for everything."

"Good-bye, Shurtliff."

"Good-bye, sir."

�

Time limped on.

Toward the end of the third week—result of findings ground out by the interlocking gears of the Allied military machine—he received his orders: on Thursday, April 22, he would depart Durban, berthed on a

Dutch freighter bound for Buenos Aires: thence, from Buenos Aires, on an American military plane to Miami, Florida. (It interested him that his passage would virtually be in the captain's wake.)

He was jubilant.

That night he got drunk. It hadn't been his intent, but, as was later pointed out to him, "It's what happens after you've had five hundred drinks." The next morning, a hangover: head of a size that eclipsed the risen sun. He never found out who it was that delivered him back to his tent and deposited him on his cot and loosened his tie and took off his shoes and left the scrawled, classic, three-word message tucked between his shirt-buttons: "Sweet dreams, darling."

⁓

On the deemed day of the next week, he boarded the Dutch ship.

As a guest-passenger (by alliance) on an armed foreign vessel urgently engaged in the business of war, he was that weirdest of all military anachronisms: a healthy, experienced officer on hold. Everything about him—his appearance (he was dressed in mufti, but always wore a tie); his idleness (empty of all responsibility, he strolled aimlessly on deck or sat on fair days in the sun in the fallow way of a park-bench habitué), and, devoid of a common language with any member of the ship's company—his gestures (disengaged and made often with a cigarette in hand)—all marked him as the odd man out.

On his own terms, he defined himself as a mute in limbo.

. . . The captain, Hendrik Tjeenk, had a heavy Teutonic brow, a stern mouth, and gray-blue eyes hard as flint. He was bulky in build and tall, and when he walked he bent his torso forward and kept his head down, as if facing into a perpetual gale. He had but one feature that relieved his general look of ferocity: his ears: huge ornaments the color of smoked salmon set close to his head, with richly fleshed pendulum lobes it was his habit to toy with: to pull on or to stroke, sensuously, up and down, or twist between his thumb and forefinger. At meals in the officer's mess he sat, bear-like, devoting his attention to the endless curries served up by the ship's Dutch-Indonesian cook. But he regularly prefaced each meal by a gesture of insistence that Morgan occupy the chair at his right, and, ritually, he offered the salt to him before reclaiming it and applying it liberally to his own food. Thus he played the host. . . . Beyond that he made little effort in Morgan's direction: early on in the voyage, the two of them had reached an agreement, arrived at by hand-signs signifying futility, that the language barrier was beyond their ability to surmount.

⁊

Sometime during the first week of the voyage to Miami, he wrote to the Owl's parents. . . . He had an image of them in his mind, formed by the Owl's own words spoken under calm conditions on the long watches—on nights when the sky had been open and filled with stars and the seas running quietly, the *Stubbins* slipping through them, and suddenly the Owl's soft voice telling something marvelously remote to the circumstance: "My ma's *tall*." And, another time: "My brother Winston" (such an elegant name, Morgan had thought) "—his aim's as good with a sling-shot as it is with a rifle"; and, another time: "My daddy helped a fawn get born once. He was walking in the woods and came on the doe. About stepped on her. She was down, near dead, the fawn not coming on like it ought and he did for her the same as you would a cow with a queered calf. Reached in up to his elbow and got a right hold on the fawn and brought it out for her. He stayed by her till she was on her feet. The fawn was fine. Did you ever hear tell of a wild thing letting a man do for her what she couldn't do for herself? But my daddy's a wonder in that way."

Such was what the Owl told of his people.

The fact of the Owl's remembered near illiteracy caused Morgan to suppose that the letter to his parents might need to be read aloud to them, perhaps by the mule-riding, Bible-carrying, sin-cleansing itinerant preacher the Owl had once spoken of; or ironically, perhaps, by the same sheriff who had "sniffed" him out and sent him thereby off to war.

Dear Mr. and Mrs. Malkerson,

Your son, Henry—(the need to write of the Owl as "Henry" provided for him just enough of a veiled remove to steady the pencil in his hand)—*served as a Naval gunner under my command on the SS* John T. Stubbins. (He deeply hoped the censor would let stand the reference to the *Stubbins*.) *The sorrow of Henry's death was shared by our crew who loved him for his goodness of heart and for his faith which sustained us all. He spoke often of both of you and of his brothers.*

(He faltered, then pushed on, writing, crossing out and starting again, wresting from his million thoughts a few; word by word) *. . . steadfast to his duties . . . ever thoughtful of his shipmates . . . might be of some small comfort to you to know he did not suffer . . . died peacefully, surrounded by friends. We said the Lord's Prayer . . . buried in the clean sea.*

With deepest sympathy,
Sincerely,

The short letter, eternally meant, eternally incomplete, took him hours to write.

He put it in the zippered side-pocket of his new waterproof duffel bag. In Miami, he would copy it out on decent paper (perhaps revise it), then hand it in for mailing via the proper military channels.

৵

As on the *Stubbins*, the specter of fear haunted the ship, and, as on the *Stubbins*, procedural similarities pertained against possible disaster: at night, navigation lights were blacked out and the ship's inside lights strictly obscured; lifeboats were permanently swung out ready for lowering; progress was a dog-legged one (never a straight course); life-jackets were always worn.

Often in the dead of night, he would go up on deck and listen to the foreign whisperings made by the officer of the watch to the man at the wheel, or to the closer exchanges of the hunkered-down gunners, and see the dark figures of the posted lookouts, gazing off, covering the horizon round. The pricks of diamonds on the sea were the reflections of stars. . . . *I am going home. Very, very slowly, I am going home.* . . . In his own language he would say the words to himself, believing them against all odds, taking his assurance from the irresistibly beautiful heavens. . . . *I am going home.* . . .

❧

Back in Durban, he had chanced on a bookstore owned by an antique Englishman who dealt mostly in obscure tomes from a remotely remembered, revered England of a past era. From the dusty, myopic old gentleman, he had purchased (at a steep price) the first two volumes—published in 1837—of what the dealer had called "a history of *lives*." (The third and fourth volumes of the set were "regrettably lost.")

The title page of the extant volumes read:

A Genealogical and Heraldic
HISTORY of THE LANDED GENTRY;

or

Commoners of Great Britain and Ireland, Enjoying
Territorial Possessions Or High Official Rank,
But Uninvested With Heritable Honors

———

BY JOHN BURKE, ESQ.
*Author of The "Dictionaries Of The Peerage and Baronetage,"
of the "Extinct and Dormant Peerage," Etc.*

———

IN FOUR VOLUMES

———

LONDON: HENRY COLBURN, PUBLISHER,
13, Great Marlborough Street.

———

MDCCCXXXVII

Combined, the number of pages of the two volumes totaled 1,388.

The print of the written text was blindingly small. Each day he read about twenty-five pages. His eyes could stand no more.

He was often awed by what rose at random from the page to confront his imagination.

> . . . John Arthur Moore "blown from a porthole of the *Ajax*, when that ship was destroyed by fire near the island of Tenedos, in the night of the 14th of February, 1807, but was saved by a boat belonging to the *Canopus*."

> . . . Robert Byng "smothered in the black hole of Calcutta, June, 1756."

> . . . Sir Robert Drury "killed by the falling of a stack of chimneys, in 1703."

> . . . Helen, daughter of Alexander, Lord Abernethy, of Salton, "who had twenty-five sons and eleven daughters, seven of the sons fell at Pinkie, in 1547."

> . . . Thomas Waite "killed as a boy in 1743 by a schoolfellow (William Chetwynd) at Clare's Academy, Soho-square."

Consider the broken hearts of Charles and Frances Robertson (County of Ross) by the deaths of their far-roved sons:

> Hugh, a planter in Jamaica, "died of the yellow fever";

> Archibald, a planter in Demerara, "died of the yellow fever";

> Robert, in the East India Company's medical service, "died of locked jaw, occasioned by the bite of a snake";

> Duncan, a merchant in New Orleans, "died of the yellow fever."

Think of the women who "died in childbed": Sarah, Genesia, Joanna-Law, Selina, Fright-Marie, Lilia, Emma-Admonition. . . .

Some named men "rose from a lowly birth to high and influential situation." Some, of mighty birth, "fell afoul in adulthood to the habits of gaming, the juice of the grape, and the charms of the fair." And some "died by the swords of conceit"—like William Gower—"unfairly killed in a duel at a tavern in Drury-Lane, February, 1725, by Major Oneby, who was tried at the Old Bailey, found guilty of murder, and ordered for execution, but during the night he cut his throat in prison."

Twins: Nicholas and Andrew Tremayne: "Yea! such a consideration of inbred power and sympathy was in their natures, that if Nicholas was sick and grieved, Andrew felt the like pain, though they were distant and remote from each other; this too without any intelligence given unto either party. . . . Yea! so they lived and so they died. In the year 1564 they both served in the wars at Havre de Grace. Being both to the last degree brave, they put themselves into posts of greatest hazard. At length one of the brothers was slain, and the other instantly stepped into his place, and there in the midst of danger, no persuasion being able to remove him, he was also slain."

THRWITT, Richard—(alive and flourishing at the time the volumes were printed in 1837) acquired his surname in A.D. 1109 from one Sir Hercules: "This Sir Hercules—severely wounded in defending a bridge, single handed, against numerous assailants, at the moment he succeeded in forcing them to retire, he fell exhausted amongst the flags and rushes of an adjoining swamp, while the attention of his party, who in the interim had rallied, was fortunately directed to the spot where he lay by a flock of lapwings (or as called in some counties *tyrwhits*) screaming and hovering above, as is customary with those birds when disturbed in the vicinity of their nest."

. . . In 1185 Philip, (nephew of Giraldus Cambrensis) "was the first man wounded in the conquest of Ireland, and was also the first who ever manned a hawk in the island."

Trestram and Hannah Bennerstom: husband and wife. Writ on Trestram's tombstone: "He Died of Contagion of the Moon's Lunacy." On Hannah's tombstone: "Devoured by Time at Age of 106 Years."

And of such droll names as Pexall Brocas, Grills-Vivyan Pendarvis, Gamaliel Milner, Slyde Peregrine Walmestit, Marmaduke Slingsby, Bulstrode Peachy (by linear entanglement a forebear of Jane Austen)—it pleasured him in his great idleness to conjure for each name, feature and mien: which one given to a Hell-all raffishness? which to a dour piety? which to ordinariness?

For a mute in limbo, the two volumes were perfect companions.

∾

Sarkis had once told him that as they approach their home waters, sailors often get "the Channels" (or "Channel Fever")—a malady, he explained, which manifests itself by an inability to sleep and a lack of interest in food. Sarkis said he had never suffered from the Channels himself, but that over the years he had seen many a strong man brought low by it or turned by it "to conduct of an awful queerness."

Was it then the Channels that Morgan fell victim to three or four days out from Buenos Aires? Buenos Aires being, in his mind, a kind of foot-in-the-door entrance to his home waters—still far away, but by airplane speedily reached. Quite suddenly, he ailed of an exhausting nervousness. Time—at sea always slow in passing—ceased to pass at all. . . . Through the last nights he thrashed in his berth and in the morning's mirror viewed himself swollen-eyed and blank-faced, the new day a shroud on his spirit. He could not read with concentration; could not track a single thought to its conclusion. His mind was a circus of conflicting tensions. The smell of food repelled him.

In short, all the symptoms—magnified and multiplied to maddening pitch—of Channel Fever as described by Sarkis.

∾

He was on deck, pacing back and forth with the crazed fatigue of a caged beast, when they let down the anchor in Buenos Aires. Before him the sprawled city: blurred sound of distant traffic, trails of smoke rising skyward, a Catholic dome, a Protestant steeple, the carrying barks of dogs. . . .

Captain Tjeenk appeared at his side. He pointed to a harbor launch coming toward the ship, then made a gesture that linked Morgan to the launch.

"Ah!" Morgan breathed.

He went to his stateroom and from his berth grabbed his packed duffel bag. He was back in no time, buttoning up his coat at the captain's side.

Incredibly, a mere twelve hours later, he boarded the plane for the flight to Miami, (the intervening hours another story for another time).

Unbelievable—the fact that he was strapping himself in: that, already, the plane's outside starboard propeller was turning over, its sound augmented in staged degrees as, in succession, the three other propellers whirled into action, the engines revved to a high, testing wail sustained at peak before being cut back, *diminuendo,* to a honed thrum. . . . A slow crawl forward to the run-way. A ninety-degree turn into the spectral wind. A pause, equivalent to the taking of a deep breath . . . *Go!* Over a ribbon of tarmac a charged, gradual gathering of terrific speed and then—oh God!—the Icarus ascent, up and up, higher and higher, closer and closer to the stars.

He felt a mystical elation that the flight was by night.

Aloft, lost in wonder, he fell asleep.

5 ⁓ The Dominions of Memory and Expectation

Toward the end of May, 1943

He would read one or two paragraphs, then look up from his book out the window of the speeding train to the surprise of a different scene: the crow-inhabited woodland of a moment ago replaced by a pasture with a stream running through it; the pasture replaced by a waterfall cascading down a wall of shale; next, a poor rural church in need of paint, but the burial plots in its adjacent cemetery well tended. To view the world thus, in occurrences of separate display, reminded him of rainy boyhood afternoons spent with his grandfather's old-fashioned stereoscope. From a set of leather-covered boxes he would draw out, one at a time, a tinted photograph, insert it into the holding-slots of the wooden-handled "viewer," then raise the viewer to his eyes and be amazed by the pulling depth of the three-dimensioned image that sprang before him ("As in real life"—to quote the fulfilled promise printed in tarnished silver paint on the shank of the viewer). Now, on a pond, a great blue heron arrested near a stand of reeds.

The train—a long one—rounded a curve. From his seat in its next-to-last car, he caught a fleeting glimpse of the engine before it disappeared behind an embankment, the signature of its on-going transit a trail of smoke visible over the rim of the verge.

He stole a glance at his watch: in an hour and twenty-eight minutes, the train was scheduled to arrive in Cleveland.

All in all, as regards this overland journey, he had been lucky: had had the break yesterday afternoon of obtaining a place on a Navy cargo-plane making a routine flight from Miami (via Washington, D.C.) to a military air base in New Jersey from whence, by hook and by crook, he had gotten himself into New York where, from Grand Central Station, at this day's dawn, he had caught this train—caught it with only a few seconds to spare—for he had taken time before boarding it to telephone Maud, waking her from sleep, his voice jubilant: "I'm in New York. If I hang up right now, I'll be able to make a train that'll put me in Union Terminal this afternoon."

Over her gasp, he stated the time of the train's scheduled arrival. "Don't drive into Cleveland alone, will you. . . . I'll get out to Hatherton somehow—bum a car from Aunt Letitia maybe. I'll call you when the train gets in. *Soon.* We'll be together soon. . . . I must go."

In the past he had traveled many times over this same stretch of track, homeward bound for vacations from his schools in the East. Those long-ago journeys had been overnight ones, immensely anticipated, made frequently enough for him to know and be known by a troop of genial, white-coated Pullman car porters ("Regulars," they called themselves) who remembered his name from trip to trip and greeted him by it as they waved him aboard and saw to him throughout the journey in a way that made him feel, in his gray-flanneled, tweed-jacketed youth, Important. Of those earlier journeys, his most affectionate recollection was of waking at dawn in a lower berth: of raising the window-shade and turning his head on the pillow and briefly scanning the fleeing terrain; *briefly,* for he would not be able to stay awake very long, what with that mesmerizing sound going on and on, so lulling: that rhythmic clickety-clack, clickety-clack made by the train's wheels as they passed over the evenly spaced rail-joinings (the sound harmonized once in a while by the romantic drear of its whistle, let at road crossings). The porter would wake him in plenty of time to wash and dress for breakfast, which marvelous meal was taken in a carpeted dining-car agleam in the morning light with mirrors and tinkling glasses and silver-plated knives and forks and spoons engraved with the letters NYC (the trinity of initials known in an almost folkloric way as standing for "New York Central"), and, at nearby tables, faces lit too in anticipation of the journey's end, always, for him, marked by his father's waiting presence and unrestrained embrace (modified, when he turned eighteen, to an intensely rendered handshake). Back then, the journey had always been perfectly predictable.

This one, to the nth degree, was different.

This was wartime travel. No luxury of Pullman and dining-cars: instead, coaches, all similar, with fixed, upright seats filled to capacity with servicemen (beside him, a Marine captain; in the two seats in front of him, a Navy CPO and a paratrooper; directly across the aisle, an Army lieutenant and a Medical Corps corporal); and against hunger, coffee and cellophane-wrapped sandwiches and cookies dispensed at canteens set up at the front of every third or fourth coach. There was a low babble of talk around him and, at the end of the car, a noisy crap-game in progress. Some men (like his seatmate) slept, their neckties loosened, chins inclined onto chests, or heads loped over onto a shoulder, legs akimbo. A few though, like himself, were sitting in an alert, private way that suggested interior anxiety. Toward these few he felt a kinship, it being his guess that they too were freshly on leave, with, after long absence, the terrors of reunion still before them.

Distinct from today's dawn telephone call to Maud was the first one he had made to her after his arrival in Miami: after he had been "cleared" (for reasons of security), and "checked out" by two doctors (one medical, the other, a psychiatrist), and after that, put through the tedium of filling out a myriad of forms, each a different kind of attestation of his bodily and martial resurrection, the entire process infinitely more intricate and prolonged than the vaguely similar, brief interrogation undergone at the hands of the British back in Durban. But eventually, an officer told him: "Go down the hall. Second room on your right. You can use the phone to make two calls."

He could almost smile, now, as he thought back on that first call. Then, though, it had been a desperate affair. The room was windowless and stale-smelling and very small, its only furnishings a desk and a collapsible iron chair and a large poster tacked on one wall: LOOSE LIPS SINK SHIPS. He had picked up the telephone and given to a male military operator the code-number assigned to him for the allowed two calls (the second would be to his father). At the sound of the first ring his heart had begun to swell inside his chest in a way never before experienced. After two rings, the sensation of ballooning increase caused him to fear it might burst; by the third ring he was fighting for breath. The fourth ring was interrupted mid-point of its trill by Maud's instantly recognized, unique "Hello?"—followed by the operator's voiced need to be sure that the number reached was the correct one, after which, satisfied that it was: "Go ahead, Lieutenant." But before he could—

"Morgan"—called out through space in the wild, convulsive way the mad shout at clouds; then repeated: "Morgan," low, this time, and directed, as if at an arm's length away, she suddenly saw him.

"Maud."

There are stories of amateur mountain climbers who unwittingly dislodge a pebble crucial to the mountain's stability, causing thereby an avalanche. Such was the effect of his saying her name; the words came so, then, between them, tumbling, one atop the other, each one a precious assurer that all which had pertained between them in the past, pertained still. It was from the memory of that call that now, in the great grip of expectation, he felt safe in his imaginings of their being together again: how it would be—be *like*—instead of the other way around, the other way around having been for so long an unpresumptive one.

In about twenty-five minutes . . .

He stood up. The action roused the Marine captain who drew his sprawled legs into line, looked at his watch, and said, "God, we're almost there!" "Almost," Morgan replied. He stepped over the captain's sizable feet and, swaying in accord with the train's movement, made his way down the aisle to the toilet at the end of the car, in which rank cubicle he did the best he could to make himself, in his mother's remembered word, "presentable": washed his face and hands, combed his hair, reknotted his tie, gazed in the cracked mirror at the shoulder-fit of his new uniform. ("What you do next is you go and get yourself totally reoutfitted," had been the loonily phrased order given him on his second morning in Miami, which order, duly acted on, resulted in the motley clothes he had obtained in Durban being relegated to a trash bin—except for the loose gray linen jacket he had regularly worn at meals in the officer's mess aboard the Dutch freighter, and which, for reasons he then did not try to understand, he chose to keep.)

⋖৯

With a shudder, the train came to a stop.

In a rush of movement they were all on their feet then, collecting and shouldering their gear, yawning with impatience, shuffling their way down the aisle and out the car's doors into the dank, murky, underground world of tracks and idle locomotives and ghostly, drifting steam and the choking, immingled smells of coal and hot pistons and oil. On a grime-encrusted platform he moved apace with the hurrying others, the march a lengthy one from the train's end forward, past all its now emptied-out cars, past, at last, its huge resting engine, on, up the rise of a ramp to a set of open iron gates beyond which lay the teeming immensity of the station's lobby.

If she were there, would he ever find her?

He had the advantage of being tall, but so, at that bewildering moment of entry into bedlam, everyone else seemed too to be. Deafened by the noise, stunned by the sheer number of people, he stood still, embarrassed almost, by his despair that she was nowhere visible. He forced himself to order his thoughts and recalled his words spoken to her in such haste that morning: that he would telephone her on arrival; that he had urged her not to drive to Cleveland alone; that there was perhaps the problem of gas-rationing; that, all things considered, and imagining as she might have the untidy chance of missing him in the station's throng, she had decided to remain in Hatherton; to await him there.

He must find a telephone.

The touch to his arm came from behind. He turned. Having herself found him, she stood, wordless, exploring his astounded face, her heart in her eyes. Afterwards, and for as long as he lived, he remained awed by the easy, tranquil way, then, they claimed each other, like two long-parted, never-doubting souls met in the allegories of a promised Beyond.

When they did speak, it was to say in *his* voice and with appeal: "I must sit down for a moment."

And so they did, on a newly-quit near-by bench. At the marvelous first sight of her, he had uncharacteristically kissed her with his cap on. He made the formal gesture now of removing it and of looking fully at her. And she at him. "Are you all right?" she asked, and before he could muster an answer: "You're very thin," her eyes cast over with tears, a hand laid to his cheek: "Very handsome, but very thin." Those were her first barely audible but lighting words.

"Very much in need of a shave," was the ridiculous response he made, thankful for being able to speak at all, the while gazing at her, seeing how her beauty had deepened: that it was now fully mature, *established*, like a fine sculptor's achievement.

"You *are* all right?" she asked again.

"Oh, yes," he answered at once. "Only overwhelmed."

His assurance, made so readily and positively, cleared her brow and she smiled with something like audacity, with that high look which in the past had always, always sexually stirred him, and which now, as he met it, caused him for a wild moment to read it as the harbinger of some plan she had made and arranged for and was about to verbally disclose: an intimate plot—the dreamt of, longed for very thing—whereby for a day or two they were to be alone somewhere where they weren't known, somewhere terribly *quiet,* or that desire, sated, would make so. But he was wrong: wrong, that is, to the degree that what he had taken from her smile was a wrong inference, though that she *did* have a plan, he had no doubt; no doubt, too (as was affirmed by the sudden rush of color to her cheeks) that her plan was far other in kind than the one he had fleetingly imagined, and further, that it was a plan already irreversibly in force, beyond her power to change, the happy outcome of which (his intuition instantly informed him) meant everything to her. The crisis of her blush quickly faded, and in its place her face took on the cloaked look of a high-stakes gambler who holds a set of cards filled with risk: "Dennis drove me in," she began mundanely, clearly with the greater thing to follow.

"Dennis," he murmured. . . . He had not thought of Dennis for a long time. Dennis: a mainstay in the Leigh household, proudly self-described as "Mrs. Leigh's driver"; responsible for taking her around and about Hatherton and, once in a while, into Cleveland for a day's shopping or an afternoon symphony concert at Severance Hall, the latter excursions undertaken when, by her own say-so, she "felt equal to the occasion."

"He's waiting for us outside," Maud drew him on. Then, in a rush, squared him with: "Caroline and Julia are waiting with him."

Ah! He saw it in a flash—*her* image of *him:* the one she had cleaved to throughout their near two years of separation: the *entirety* of it, the sum of whose parts (lover, husband, father) she had long since molded into a completeness of expectation which, now, entirely, she posited in his very lap.

He took it up: "Caroline and Julia . . ." seen last as infants; loved out of emotional habit and on glad principle, the love tender, soft, illusory: one that had often occupied his daytime thoughts at sea but had never materialized as an invader of his night-time dreams. "I can't imagine what they must be like," he said in slow reflection. "How they must look now."

She showed surprise: "But you have all the recent pictures of them," said with a hint of protest, "—all the ones I've sent so regularly."

He shook his head. Now was not the time or place. "I haven't received any mail for a long time," he said. "A lot's happened. I'll tell you about it later." He tried for a dismissing smile that failed to strengthen.

He might have gotten by if only she hadn't said: "We're together. That's all that matters."

She took his hand and, as his protector, held it: he had come so suddenly undone. She ignored his tears; went beyond them: "Last week," she began in a once-upon-a-time way, "I went to the lake and opened up the cabin. Got the remains of winter out of it. We'll go there tomorrow, just the two of us. You can tell me everything then. . . . I was going to surprise you . . . Morgan?"

"Glorious," he brought out. And, after a deep breath: "I swore to myself I wouldn't fall apart."

"Oh," she said, almost laughing, "when you called this morning, after you hung up, I cried and cried and cried. Sopped the pillow."

Her words fell on him like a mantle and for a moment more he sheltered under their cover. Then, insofar as he was outwardly restored, he picked up with: "I can't wait to see the children. You *are* marvelous."

"I knew you'd understand," she said, passing over his view of herself in the matter, keeping to the core of it, "understand, I mean, how important it is for *them*."

He thought it remarkable that the words they had thus far spoken, comprising as they did the unmasking text of their reunion, were being said so quietly in the hive of a railroad terminal with, all around them, the great industry of life going on, loud and churning and otherwise independently bent. He put on his cap and stood up: "Will I be able to tell them apart?"

"No," she smiled, "but don't worry. You'll figure out how to soon enough."

And, as they walked: "I hope they'll like me."

"Oh, but they *do*," she wonderfully replied. "They *do*. They know all about you. All they need is to see you in the flesh."

Outdoors, on the sidewalk, the crowd was thinner. He had the strong pleasure of seeing Maud's hair take fire in the sunlight. *"There,"* she said, pointing off to her left down a line of waiting cars drawn up beside the curb. *There* indeed: the Leigh's remembered "family car," a maroon-colored, seven-passenger Packard with whitewall tires, and standing next to its polished bulk, Dennis, holding the hands of two little girls. Maud hurried toward them. At her approaching call, the three of them turned and began to run toward her.

Toward him.

Of that moment, what stayed longest in his memory was the look on the children's faces of terrific curiosity.

Dennis was the first to speak: "Welcome home, Mr. Shurtliff. We're all mighty pleased to have you back."

He dropped his kit-bag and rung Dennis's hand, then took another hand, tiny, that was tugging at his sleeve, its owner a stranger of a child in a blue flower-sprigged dress who told him in a high, positive voice that pierced him through: "You're Morgan."

He knelt to her and looked into her eyes: "Yes," he affirmed, feeling from Mars: "I'm Morgan."

The other child, mirror-image of the first, but wearing a green dress, stepped up to him. "My name is Caroline," she said.

"Ah," he murmured. He looked from one child to the other and said back their names (their identities secured for them by their different dresses), and, in as serious a way as they were seriously regarding him, he said to them: "You were this big the last time I saw you," measuring off in the air a mite distance between his two hands. "You're very grown up now."

"We had a birthday party," Julia rushed to say. She made the important point of holding up three fingers.

"You're three years old," he acknowledged, touching first the stub of Julia's nose, then Caroline's. He stood up and whispered to Maud: "They're beautiful."

Her returned smile was radiant: "*Bright*, too," she whispered back. She looked at her watch and made a herding gesture: "Let's go."

In a degree of almost forgotten comfort he sat beside her on the car's back seat whose velour upholstery retained a whiff of the attar-of-rose perfume Mrs. Leigh regularly applied to her handkerchiefs and to a small swatch of gauze she tucked between her breasts (the gauze visible sometimes when she leaned forward). The twins sat on the swivel jump seats. Dennis, in Mrs. Leigh's remembered words, "manned the wheel."

Within minutes, certain of the children's character-traits were established for him: in equal measure they were immensely friendly, immensely trusting; laughter came easily to them; they were interested in the world and alert to its surprises. Caroline was an instantaneous reactor, a hasty, dispelling chatterer who thrived in the present tense and was competitive; Julia was quieter—a gazer and a listener who thought ahead: "When we get home," she told him, "you can play with Ralph."

"*Ralph*," he said, looking directly at her. "Tell me about Ralph."

Julia frowned: "Well," she slowly began, "he's yellow and he has big ears."

Maud, he saw, was going to let the mystery of Ralph unfold on Julia's terms. "How many legs does Ralph have?"

Caroline interjected: "He's got a long tail," dismissing the numerical question.

Julia, though, said: "Four."

He asked her: "Is Ralph a cat?" But her concentration had strayed: her eyes were on his and Maud's hands, on the clasp of their intertwined fingers, and he thought: she's wondering about *me*—the arrived myth—sitting before her with a hand joined to her mother's in a hold she perhaps senses as one that separates her from her mother in a way heretofore unknown, and he felt a kind of pity for her innocence and her plight of adjustment. He would have liked to be able to explain to her that he too was adjusting: that he was as new to the task as she was.

Caroline said, "He's *not* a cat. He's a dog," and, swinging her legs: "Pip gave him to us."

"Ah," he exclaimed. "So Ralph's a dog. And who's Pip?"

"Your father," Maud stated.

"Pa! 'Pip'?" he charged, as surprised as he was amused.

"He chose it." Maud smiled: "He said he couldn't bear the thought of being called 'Gramps' or what he described as 'some other age-inducing term of grandpaternal veneration.'"

He could absolutely hear his father saying that sentence. "When did Pip"—he *had* to try out his father's new name—"give Ralph to you?"

Julia looked to Maud for the answer; Caroline kept swinging her legs.

Maud put a stilling hand on Caroline's knees: "Gently, Callie." (It startled him: took him way back in time: "Callie" had been his father's sobriquet for his mother.) "About six months ago. Pip found him lying in a ditch by the side of the road. He's a young dog. Somebody just abandoned him, we guess. He was pretty far gone. Pip thinks he'd either been grazed by a car or mauled by a bigger dog. Maybe a fox." (From the intent way the twins were listening, he could tell that Ralph's story was a favorite with them.) "Anyhow, Pip picked him up and took him to the vet and the vet patched him up and gave him a rabies and distemper shot, and then Pip nursed him along for a couple of weeks and by the time he brought him to us, Ralph was thriving."

"Who named him?"

"Tessa. The first day we had him, she kept calling him Ralph—I don't know why—and it just stuck. It suits him."

"What breed is he?"

Dennis, until then silent, guffawed. "*Dog*, Mr. Shurtliff," said in the voice of a base-minded vaudevillian; "Complete *dog*."

He saluted Dennis's summation.

Maud though, elaborated: "We're *sure* collie. *That* mostly, with maybe a bit of beagle and cocker spaniel and golden retriever thrown in."

"Lord! Is he smart?"

Maud hedged: "He's—eager. *Very* eager."

The way she said it and the loaded look she gave him was terribly funny; sexual somehow. He exploded into laughter.

He was having a marvelous time.

৺

The twins had no dimples; their hair wasn't curly; their bodies were not cherubically chubby. Of cuteness, none, or of the darling that draws exclamations from sentimental strangers. Fair hair, thick and shiny, framed their oval faces. Their long eyes were heavily lashed, the irises a dark, deeply-welled blue. Noses are unpredictable, but for now, theirs were formed in a way that augured well for the future. Expressive mouths. Good hands, the thumbs articulate. Legs straight as masts. But what was rarest was the stamp of *laterness,* seen on their faces as they gazed out of the car windows or were otherwise quietly engrossed: their beauty would outlast childhood: it was of a kind to be taken seriously at all stages of life. . . . As he studied them he couldn't but think that their biological parents must have been a handsome pair, attractive to the world: attractive to each other in the costliest of ways. . . .

"We know some songs," Caroline said.

"Sing them for me."

Baa, baa, black sheep . . . Polly, put the kettle on . . . Three blind mice . . . Bobby Shaftoe's gone to sea / Silver buckles on his knee / He'll come back and marry me / Pretty Bobby Shaftoe.

Caroline, the leader, switched from song to verse, reciting: "Ride a cockhorse to Banbury Cross / To see a fine lady upon a white horse / Rings on her fingers and bells on her toes / She shall have music wherever she goes."

Julia took a deep breath: "Two blackbirds, sitting on a hill / One named Jack, one named Jill / Fly away, Jack, fly away, Jill / Come again, Jack, come again, Jill." Finished, she said, "Now *you*, Morgan."

Maud turned to him and said in a fast, whispered aside: "We'll settle about the first-name bit later."

(Hint of a cloud. *What*, he wondered, was there to "settle"?) He asked: "Do you know about the crookéd man?"—and to the children's negative nods—"who walked a crookéd mile, who found a crookéd penny against a crookéd stile and bought a crookéd cat which caught a crookéd mouse and they all lived together in a little crookéd house."

The children laughed. "Again . . . Say it again."

He did, pleased to be a hit.

ৡ

They were out of the city now, in deep country, fields and woods distributed all around them, greened in the thousand tones of spring. It was that fading hour of the afternoon when even on the stillest days the leaves of the sycamore trees shiver. In the merging harmony of the land's immense calm and the warm nearness of Maud's body and the children's prattlings and the smooth ride over the familiar road, the tensions of the day began to fall away. He felt them going, like burdens lifted off his shoulders.

ৡ

(Old Argus—Odysseus's beloved hound—who died of joy when his master at last returned . . .)

Toward the stopped car, Ralph came, robust and juvenile, streaking over the lawn, barking with excitement.

And from the steps of the front porch, Tessa hurried toward him with outstretched arms, her face with its little white-berry blotches remembered as vividly as the generous face of his house with its imperfect fenestration, seen behind her, through tears.

Stirred by a risen twilight breeze, the trees communed in whispers. A mocking-bird sang.

At last, at last, he was home.

⋙

Indoors, he went from room to room, certain that were he blindfolded he could easily have done so, yearning and absence had so memorized them for him, their spacial encompassments and the contexts of their individual atmospheres like stanzas of poetry learned by heart—seen in the mind's eye as on the page. And the stability of *things*, felt most in his study: on one of the wall-shelves, the novels collected and read in adolescence, their plots conveying of thrilling risk and a hero's incorruptibility; and on his desk, his grandfather's hour-glass, the float of its mercury placid in the clear cup of its bottom chamber; and over the desk, the Landseer water-color of sheep grazing on a hillside (a gift from his father on his twenty-first birthday). He picked up the amber globe of a paperweight, remembered as much for its beauty as for its fecklessness, tending as it did to roll off on its own, its stopping-point the brass lipping that bordered the desk's surface—

"I'm sorry about the spot on the rug," Maud startled from the doorway. "Ralph. Before he was fully house-trained. Tessa and I went at it with everything we could think of, but it *does* still show."

She came into the room's twilit luminance, entering its evocations.

From upstairs, Caroline and Julia were calling for her.

She didn't care, she said in a whisper.

He put down the paperweight, staying it against an ink-well.

They kissed with all the rapture of their first encounters—as when, in the Leigh library, they would steal their chance before Doctor Leigh's firm surgeon's tread would be heard approaching the threshold.

"Where *are* you?" The children's imperative question came now from down the hall.

As of yore—torture of Tantalus—they stepped apart.

⋙

In the pantry, he poured a drink of whiskey. A small window in the pantry door afforded a slotted glimpse into the dining room. Two places were laid on the table. Flowers. Candles to be lit. He turned around, his view now into the kitchen where Maud and Tessa were overseeing the twins at their supper, the scene a timelessly domestic one, a living model of a Dutch genre painting, even to the inclusion of the family pet: Ralph, over by the sink, was muzzle-deep in his own bowl of food.

Maud and Tessa cajoled: "No custard until you finish what's on your plate." "Use your spoon, Julia." "Careful, Callie. Try not to spill."

Julia acknowledged his presence in the doorway by raising a hand and fluttering it. He waved back. Caroline covered her face with her bib, then lowered the curtain: "Peekaboo." "Peekaboo yourself," he told her, ducking his head up and down, opening and shutting his eyes, making gargoyle faces. Giggles from Julia, now in the game. Caroline shrieked. Ralph barked.

Maud's and Tessa's glances informed him: he was gumming up the works. "I'm going to have a bath," he announced. "I won't be long."

"We get a story before bed," Julia said.

(Ah . . . sacred routine.)

Maud looked at him: "Take your time, darling. Have a nap if you want to." And, with a full smile: "You're *home*."

⋑

Their bedroom. Its fragrance. Its remembered spring shadings made by the day's last light coming through the windows emerald from the tree-tops.

The long mirror showed him in his uniform. In this room of all places, it bore no application, and he took it off with the haste of an actor shedding the costume of an uncongenial role. Then the droll moment when he opened his closet door and stood back, surprised to the point of silent laughter by the sartorial choices displayed within: jackets and pants and suits, all having to do with civilian life. From his kit-bag, he took out the wrinkled Durban jacket and hung it, honored, next to what had once been (might still be?) his favorite summer suit. But his uniform he hung apart.

In complete contrast to the accustomed military shower was the long bath taken in the commodious, old-fashioned lion-footed tub he'd stubbornly insisted on keeping when the bathroom was modernized. "In such a tub," he'd told the plumber, "one could be a hippo." The plumber—a bulbous-nosed, strong, noisy worker—had vowed he'd never wanted to be anything but the human being God had made him, but it was surely every man's right to be what he wanted to be, even if it was such a soulless thing as a beast.

Out of his bath, he toweled himself dry and finished off the last of his whiskey. "Have a nap if you want to," Maud had said. He did want to, terribly, after his soak, tired as he was from the long trip, and faced with the sight of the bed and its cool, turned down sheets. So he just would, he decided. Just would lie down for a few minutes and take a tight-eyed, short, restoring nap, one such as—as a fourteen-year-old Latin student with a sexually rhapsodic imagination—he had fancied a Roman centurion would have allowed himself at the end of a day's march, enabling him, afterwards, to display to a soft-skinned, moist camp-follower a pair of testicles hard as agates and a penis erected of iron.

A risible fabulation . . .

Simply put, it was a nap from which he never wakened. Never, that is, until the next morning when dislocating sounds unknown at sea roused him (a dog's bark, voices of children). He sat up, alert and knowing and appalled by what had happened: that he had spent the first night of his homecoming alone in his marriage bed. He put on a bathrobe and went down the hall and from the top of the stairs, wailed out her name: "Maud."

She came and stood smiling up at him from below.

"I can't believe what I've done."

She was all mildness. "What?"

"*What?*" He reaccused himself: "Slept through the night is what. Exiled you to the guest room. God, darling—"

She raised an absolving hand: "I knew when we arrived home you'd never make it through the evening. I told Tessa so straight-away. . . . I'm very glad you conked out." (At the end of a watch, Sutter would always put his lips on the gun and kiss it and tell it in his mock Edward G. Robinson gangster's voice, "It's my conk-out time, baby. But stick around; I'll be back." The act always drew a laugh from the Owl.) "Hello?" Maud said. "Breakfast is ready when you are."

He snapped to: "Give me fifteen minutes. I could eat a horse. After breakfast I'll call Pa. Then we go to the lake. Right?"

"Yes." Said with that high, heart-stopping look: Eve's very own.

❧

They drove out to the lake in the small, snazzy Chevy convertible he'd bought back in the summer of 1939 and promptly named "the Harold Teen," in honor of the adolescent boy in a then-popular, syndicated comic strip. Although the day was beautifully clear and sunny, they did not fold back the car's canvas top: what they were up to, even before the fact of its being indulged, wanted sequestering.

Some things, once learned, you can do for the rest of your life. Like driving a car. But if you haven't done it for a goodly while, when you are again in the driver's seat, you reexperience all the charms of first mastery: that *you* are in control; can negotiate curves with ease; brake to a smooth stop; turn on a dime; obtain a speed that outraces the wind, and glide—one hand on the steering wheel, the other on the knob of the stick-shift, ETC.

He had always liked driving, and never more than he liked doing it today.

Their departure had been delayed by Caroline's protesting tears that she and Julia were being left behind. "We'll be back this evening," Maud kept telling her, stroking her hair back from her eyes. Julia but watched. Tessa, though, handed the picnic hamper to Morgan with the words: "You should just *go*. Callie'll stop her bawling before you're out of the drive. She likes to put on a show." She told Maud the same thing: "You and Mr. Shurtliff should just go."

At last Maud conceded and at last disengaged herself from Caroline's clutch.

He bent to Julia: "I'll bring you and Caroline a bouquet of wildflowers. All right?" He kissed her.

Julia nodded, and in her sober, peculiarly adult way, said: "Good-bye, Morgan."

Which Maud heard and now, under way, alluded to: "She must have picked up calling you 'Morgan' from listening to Pip and me talk about you."

He needed to know more, so was cautious: "Caroline hasn't called me anything yet."

"I always speak of you as 'Daddy' when I talk with them about you. I think that's what they should call you. You *are* their father, after all."

He sensed to tread lightly: "It's possible they'll come to it in their own time and way."

But Maud continued to frown: "They don't call me 'Maud,' and it strikes me as wrong, Julia calling you 'Morgan.' You should discourage it."

"I'll do my best. But whatever they end up calling me, I want to feel they're comfortable doing it." Then he dared: "Perhaps with adopted children—"

He got no further. He had struck the old chord of discord between them. Maud all but flared: "They don't know yet that they're adopted and they don't have to know for a long time. It's up to us to establish for them who *we* are; that *we're* their parents."

The groundwork of her reasoning was sound, but he feared its dangers of future illusion. For now, though, the topic was one best not pursued: as long as the war was on, leaving Maud to cope with parenting alone, he must reconcile himself to having the lesser voice. So he addressed instead what he believed and what was in his heart to say. "They're marvelous children, darling, because you're a marvelous mother to them. I don't know how you've done it, all on your own. It can't have been easy."

Her eyes had a sudden, moment way of skimming over with tears, and now, in a low voice, with intimate force, she said: "Oh, Morgan, there've been times when I missed you so I thought I'd die."

He understood that she bespoke the two sides of the coin of longing: of a boldly-minted, fully aspected sexual visage on the obverse side, and on the reverse side, encircled by a wreath of modest leaves, an engraved head shown in profile, its chasteness a propounder of the plainer aspects of conjugal life.

There wasn't a car in sight. He stopped in the middle of the road. "I know," he whispered, kissing her. "God, how well I know."

And when they drove on: "Your captain telephoned Pip about five weeks ago," Maud said. "He told Pip he'd tried to reach me but hadn't gotten an answer. It made me cry that I'd missed his call."

Ah, he thought: the moment's come. "Rupert Wilkins. He promised me he'd call you or Pa."

"He told Pip he'd left you and the other members of your ship's crew somewhere in Africa—he didn't say where—and Pip got the impression he shouldn't press him. It seemed fantastic, your being in Africa. We'd had no mail from you for ages, so to hear that you were all right was wonderful." She turned on the seat and fully faced him: "He told Pip it'd been a pleasure for him to serve with you. He said you'd been a tower of strength to him."

He kept his eyes on the road.

"You seem very far away. What are you thinking about?" she asked.

> Still questioned me the story of my life
> From year to year, the battles, sieges, fortunes
> That I have passed. . . .

He had no idea how to proceed; how to bring together the rags and tatters of his scattered thoughts. It was futile, absurd to try, there being no logic to the experience, and its tragic shades too harsh to thrust in whole upon her. Not, anyhow, conveyable.

"Morgan?"

"I was going to tell you later, but it's just as well to tell you now." He stated the simple fact: "We were torpedoed in the Indian Ocean."

"Morgan! *When?*"

"March nineteenth." He wanted to get it over with quickly: "As torpedoings go, ours was a relatively lucky one. Our ship went down and I spent about three days I'd not like to repeat in a lifeboat before we were picked up. Beyond that, there's not much to tell." He looked for an instant directly at her.

Her eyes were wide with wonder and spectral fright: "You might have died," she whispered.

And because she touched his hand in a way that made confession possible: "I've spent a lot of time wondering that I didn't."

"How many did?"

"Two." He felt a sudden need to raise them from anonymity: "A merchant seaman named Davis, and one of my gun crew, a boy named Henry Malkerson."

"And wounded?"

"There were some."

She remained for a moment silent; then, with lowered eyes, quietly: "I don't know what to say." But she did; exactly: "I love you."

> My story being done
> She gave me for my pains a world of sighs:
> . . . She loved me for the dangers I had passed
> And I loved her that she did pity them.

His tears almost blinded him. He slowed the car. They were at that point in the trip where the road dipped down into a wooded valley, down to the turn-off lane that led to the inland lake. She touched his arm again: "We're almost there," then drew from the pocket of her skirt the key to the gate and displayed it, solid and gleaming in the sunlight. "I love you," she told him again.

❧

Maud's grandfather had bought the hundred-odd acres of land back in 1889. In 1891, the so-called "cabin" was built—a deceptively simple name for the commodious, two-storied, hand-beamed, Adirondack-style dwelling set on a hill above the large lake. Doctor Leigh was fond of the place (he referred to it as his "retreat"), but, ironically, Mrs. Leigh found it too remote, too lonely for her liking. In recent years, Doctor Leigh used it almost secretly, slipping away from his medical duties, coming out to the property on the odd afternoon for a couple of hours of solitary fishing or a hike in the woods. He kept the cabin in immaculate repair and had the land regularly patrolled by an old loner who lived in a small, narrow-windowed house down the road from its gates: Fred Canoose—said to be a full-blooded Indian, remnant of the region's Iroquois tribe: an untalkative man with dark, undomesticated eyes set in a lean face, a man seldom seen, but given to leaving "things" on the cabin porch as evidence he was minding his duties as care-taker—a collection of pheasant or raptor feathers; a pyramid of dried alder branches for starting a fire, the boughs cut by a beaver's teeth; bunches of wild herbs tied with a hide-string; a rabbit's scut. Those kinds of lonely things. Now, propped up against the front door, an old, found, two-pronged deer antler. Maud picked it up: "It wasn't here last week," she said. "I'll put it on the mantel."

⋙

In one's entire life, there are but two or three days when only the lyrical happens.

The cabin smelled of ancient wood-smoke and pine boughs and the dried brown tufts of bulrushes. In an upstairs chamber windowed on the sunlit lake, they made love the first time with a hard, emphatically self-ish passion; afterwards, with an encyclopedic range of sexual indul-gences, languorously.

In the early afternoon they ate their picnic lunch and between them, drank a bottle of wine. They were a bit heady afterwards and sleepy, and napped under a light blanket in each other's arms. When they woke, he took her rowing on the lake. Red-winged blackbirds whistled. Jesus-spiders walked on the water. A flock of ducks came, circling, quacking, splashing down. There were yellow irises blooming in the shore-line shallows, and with the knife Doctor Leigh kept clamped to the under-side of the boat's middle thwart, he cut a bunch for Julia and Caroline. The sun was three-quarters down. In a voice already cast in reminis-cence, Maud said: "We have to think about getting back."

He rowed toward the pier and let her off. "I'll be along in a moment," he told her.

He secured the boat and stored the oars in a near-by shack. A loon appeared and swam near but dived out of sight when he lit a cigarette. It came up farther away, eyed him, and let out the shiver of its call. He stood watching it, pleased by its presence, thinking it had probably been hatched on the lake and recently returned to it to seek a mate and bring into being another clutch of its kind. And then he had a sudden image of himself as being someday an old man. A premonition that really, someday, he *would* be: that it was his fate to outlast the war, outlast his youth and the flood and ebb of middle years, and live to an age when he would walk with a cane. He had never imagined himself so, and that he did so now, sated as he was in body, and stupendously happy, struck him as a strange, evincing curiosity.

He stubbed out the last of his cigarette and picked up the bunch of water-irises lying at his feet.

Tonight, for the first time, he would read a bed-time story to Julia and Caroline.

᪐

The next day, in the morning, he went to see Lillie Ruth and Mrs. Leigh. (He had telephoned in advance. "Come at ten," Lillie Ruth told him.) At the front door of the Leighs' house, she hugged him and praised sweet Jesus he was home. "Safe with us," she said.

"I'm so very, very glad to see you, Lillie Ruth."

The lines on her forehead had deepened and she had allowed her hair to go completely white, but her smile was as rich as ever. "You're thin, Morgan. We'll fatten you up. . . . They've had you roaming the world." (It sounded biblical, the way she said it.) "I thought you'd be in your uniform." She ducked her head down and wiped her eyes with her apron. "I've never seen Maudie like she was when Dennis took her into Cleveland to meet you. Crazy with excitement, so happy . . . You must have crowed when you saw the twins. . . . Doctor Leigh's gone to the hospital, same as usual. Mrs. Leigh's in the library. She's different, Morgan. I won't be long bringing you some refreshment."

Mrs. Leigh rose from her chair to greet him. She looked in perfect health, her figure as ample as ever, the color in her cheeks and lips her own, her abundant hair glossy, wound up on her head in a neat French twist. "Morgan, my dear." The alto of her voice (inherited by Maud) had lost its beguiling deepness; was thin and airy and wanting in draw.

He moved a chair close to hers and sat down. "You've been gone such a long time, Morgan."

To this conventional opening, he made the conventional reply that yes, it *had* been a long time, but here he was, back, and as she could surely imagine, thrilled to be. She nodded, though without animation. He spoke of Maud and the twins, and she seemed to be listening, but her eyes never fully met his own, and the way she sat, so still, and in such a majesty of self-absorbed calm, left him with a sense of disengagement. (Maud, too, had warned him.) He would have been at home with her nervousness that in the past had used to send her hands rummaging through the air or fluttering up to her throat—gestures of her affrightments—for, as quirky reminders of his own devils, they had peripherally involved and included him. But now, her unfathomable tranquillity distanced her from him to what he felt was an unbridgeable degree.

In a footling way, he rambled on, talking of the lovely morning and the cloudy beauty of the white field-daisies flowering everywhere over the landscape, even, with the hope of eliciting a smile, of Ralph. "Our dog," he said, to remind her. Her face was blank: the dark side of the moon; and he gave up and fell silent.

He loved the room, the solemn oak paneling, the visual affronting spontaneity of the mantel's carvings, the book-lined floor-to-ceiling shelves, the old brocade pillows strewn on the couch, the tall windows—

"When you were away, Morgan, did you see death?"

It was as if a rock had gained a voice. The sound, and the dark question, stunned him. Yet having posed it, she did not wait for his answer, but went on in her paper-thin, commandingly tranquil voice, now a confider's one: "I used to see Death often, but not so much anymore, and when I do, I'm not a bit afraid of him. Not in the least."

Him, Morgan noted. Death (if that was what she was really talking about), to her, in gender male.

"I envy you your lack of fear."

"You must learn to *accept,* Morgan dear."

He would never forget the teaching tone of the admonition, never, in the future when he thought of her, be able to set aside the collected power of her composure, separate and arcane, a temple without exit in which she resided alone in the exampled logic of her advanced madness.

He thought again of Maud's warning made to him at breakfast. . . . Of course, Lillie Ruth, knowing, came in then bearing a tray set with cups and saucers and a china pot filled with freshly made coffee. "And cookies, Morgan," she said over a glance shot at him at how he was holding up.

"Sit with us, Lillie Ruth," Mrs. Leigh said with a first smile.

Conversation was easier with Lillie Ruth present, but he was spent, and stayed only a few minutes more, and when he left the house, he closed the front door carefully, noiselessly behind him.

↝

Sheriff Gary Mills was conducting traffic at the juncture of Main and Barnes streets. "God, if it's not Mr. Shurtliff!" he said through the rolled-down car window.

"How are you, Gary? And Mrs. Mills?"

"Good, thanks, both of us."

"And young Gary?"

"Joined the Marines last year. On the day he turned eighteen. Couldn't wait to sign up. He's off somewhere in the Pacific now. There's three cars behind you, Mr. Shurtliff—"

In front of the courthouse, he spotted Bob Dulrich (chief clerk of the court) talking with Byard Williams (the court stenographer). He steered the car curbside. "Gentlemen—" he called out.

"Morgan Shurtliff!"

"None other."

"Judge Malcolm said you were due back," Bob Dulrich said. "You're a welcome sight."

Byard Williams—a great questioner and a great talker—had a waxy voice and the fluke deformity of a hare-lip, the line of the vertical fissure extending from his left nostril down to his mouth, giving that portion of his face a tucked, perpetually tortured look. "How long you home for?"

"Nearly a month. This is my first drive around town."

"Have you seen our new industrial complex?"

"No. Where is it?"

"On Geddes Street, about a half mile down from Seton's Hardware. It was built so fast we hardly knew it was happening. It's big. You'll see. 'Dawson's Manufacturing,' it's called."

"What do they turn out?" Morgan asked.

"Trigger parts for machine guns, government contracts, of course. They work three shifts a day, seven days a week. A lot of women. You've heard the song, 'Rosie the Riveter'? We've got plenty of Rosies around these days."

Bob Dulrich put in his oar: "The plant's brought in a whole new breed of folks to town, Mr. Shurtliff. Men past draft age and their families, moved out from Cleveland. The high school's overcrowded"—Bob's wife was the tenth-grade math teacher—"and like Byard said, a lot of single women in overalls working eight-hour shifts, earning more than my wife does at her teaching. . . . As you see it, how's the war going?"

It was a question that would dog him for the whole of his leave. "I don't know anything you don't know."

Bob Dulrich's lip twitched: "It's sure taking longer than any of us ever thought it would. Everybody's showing the strain."

Morgan nodded. "Are things frisky at the courthouse?"

"Never busier. Judge Malcolm'll tell you."

Morgan started the car's engine: "I think I'll go take a look at the new plant. Let's the three of us get together soon. Give me a few days."

On the railroad side of town the large, hastily built, utile structure of Dawson Manufacturing, Inc., scarred the landscape. Compared to the solid, brick Victorian facades of Seton's Hardware and Tyler's Agricultural Outlet and Garrison's Lumber and the picturesque New York Central Branch station with its oval stained-glass windows, and the well-laid-out abutting strengths of its loading platforms and grain silos and holding sheds for cattle, Dawson Manufacturing, Inc., was an affront to the eye. Morgan viewed it with the sadness of disgust; saw it as a forerunner of more such abominations to come, the legal endorsement of its ugliness a precedent difficult, if not impossible, to undo.

He re-crossed the railroad tracks, following a route that skirted the edges of plowed fields, and so returned to the heart of Hatherton, to its Green—a proud, elm-shaded, carefully tended square with a fine, conciliatory Civil War statue (rendered by McMorrison) of a Union officer supporting in his arms a Confederate soldier; and, the Pioneers Museum, the Atheneum Academy, the Shaker Club, the bank (People's Trust and Loan), the county courthouse, and the pillared, steepled Presbyterian church (dominant on the Green's south side), and on its north side, the Van Sinderin Building (designed by Joseph Stoddard at the behest of Clarence Van Sinderin, who caused it to be erected in 1895 after he'd made his first killing in iron-ore). Among other enterprises of the so-called "professional" order, the Van Sinderin Building—as shown by a large, signifying brass plaque given into its granite exterior—housed the offices of:

MALCOLM AND SHURTLIFF
Attorneys-at-Law

He entered the building and crossed its lobby, climbed (two steps at a time) the reach of its exuberantly curved, iron-railed, marble staircase, turned left at the top and strode down the corridor to a massive pair of closed teak-wood doors, opened one, and—like a returned fox at the mouth of its lair—paused, and took a verifying breath: *ah:* exactly as he remembered: the accordant smells of law books and leather chairs and Judge Malcolm's Cuban cigars, and floating out into the hallway from the offices of the Misses Dorothy and Ellen Hart (sister secretaries), the workday odors of newly sharpened pencils and rubber erasers and the inks of typewriter ribbons and carbon paper, and now, in the immediate vicinity, face-to, the opposing scent worn by Mrs. Forshay (receptionist) (Yardley's Lavender).

"Glory be! Mister Shurtliff!"

"Mrs. Forshay." He was ridiculously pleased to see her.

"Ellen; Dorothy," she sang out, "look who's here! . . . I must tell Judge Malcolm."

—already in sight, coming down the hall from his office, his advancing steps impressive for their lack of hurry.

Mrs. Forshay drew herself up like a sentry: "It's Mr. Shurtliff, Judge Malcolm."

"So I surmised. *Morgan.*"

"Sir."

A privy stranger, watching and listening and knowing nothing about the two men (the one venerable and rotund and measured of movement, the other relatively young, intense, tall, lean) might have been stirred to wonder at the seeming lack of connection between the bluntness of their spoken greetings and the ardent, felicitous look of established relationship that passed between them.

Mrs. Forshay and the Misses Hart stood silently by, a *tableau vivant* trio depicting Interest, or, like the imagined stranger, Wonder; or of their individual sentiments, Sweetness.

He spent a fast hour with Judge Malcolm, the first of several during his leave. At the judge's urging, he supplied details of his two years away, filling in gaps of information left out in letters written under the constraints of censorship, and ending with a bare-bones account of the torpedoing.

"Such an experience!" Judge Malcolm murmured. "I expect it'll take you a while to parse out its effects on you. There's an old proverb—maybe you've heard it, I think it's Russian—'If you look back at all, you'll lose the sight of one eye, but if you don't look back at all, you'll go blind.' In my war, nothing happened to me of so scoring a nature; I was never in any personal danger. But the fact is, from whatever perspective it's viewed, war inevitably alters the viewer. It doesn't matter a scintilla who you are or what your rank or calling. I see evidence of that truth every day, all around me, written on the faces of all of us *here*—'left behind,' as the saying goes, 'keeping the home fires burning.' You know the song: 'Though your hearts are yearning.'" (He sang the words.) "I fritter away a lot of hours wondering what we'll all be like when the conflict ends. How we'll settle down as individuals and as a nation. How the *world* will settle itself." Somewhere along the track of this running discourse, he had reached for a cigar and after puncturing its lip-end with a small gold spike attached to his watch-chain, he lit it. "Back in the sixteen hundreds, they jailed John Bunyan for preaching in the fields," he mused on through a cloud of exhaled smoke: "You'll plead leniency for me, won't you, when they take me away for committing the crime of airing in public my overly morbid dreads of things still to come." And then he laughed: "Clara told me the other day she'd stop dining out with me if I don't get what she called my 'jeremiad tongue' under control."

Morgan smiled. Coming from so formidable a source as the conjured Mrs. Malcolm, the threat warranted consideration, and he was about to say as much, but lost his chance to a well-remembered diversion: a Vesuvian fall of cigar ash onto the desk, and the judge's head bent at once over the spillage, blowing at the ashes, scattering them over a residing mass of legal papers referred to now with a broad gesture as "A minefield of impending matters." And then: "But *here!* These are for you." He picked up a batch of bulging file folders: "An accounting of the cases we've handled during your absence. Also an accounting of your take in the firm's profits."

Morgan received the hefty bundle and rested it on his knees. "God,"

he said, "it terrifies me to think of the time I've lost, and more to come."
A cry of resentment. He turned back the flap of the top file and looked
at the first page: "The Murray case," he murmured. It was the last case
he had worked on before he went away.

"I followed your advice and took it to trial," the judge said. "The verdict came down in our favor. You might want to see the transcript of the
proceedings. There were a couple of amusing moments." Then, shrewdly:
"I'm only going to say this to you once, Morgan. Don't brood about your
professional life—about the time lost, as you put it. The law's in your
blood. You'll come back to it better equipped than ever to serve it." He
pointed to the files: "Read them. I want your thoughts about the spill-
over effects some of the cases might have on our future practice. You'll see
what I mean as you read along. . . . Now tell me, what does the Navy have
in store for you next?"

"Miami," Morgan answered: "SCTC. Submarine Chaser Training
Course. I think it's about a four-month course. Maybe a bit more. I'm
not sure. After that, I haven't the vaguest idea. . . . When I received my
orders, the guy who gave them to me said I'd lucked out—that Miami in
the summertime is the Eden of Hell." He shrugged: "At least I'll be able
to telephone Maud once in a while."

"Speaking of Maud, she's put you down for dinner with us next
Wednesday evening. Roger Chandler and his wife will be there too."
(Roger Chandler was the head of the stellar Cleveland law firm of
Kissel, Chandler, in which Judge Malcolm still retained an "Of Counsel"
position). "Roger's been talking to me about establishing closer ties
between our practice and theirs. When the war's over, of course. He's got
his eye on you, Morgan."

Morgan said: "Thanks to you, Judge. I'm flattered—"

"No. Not thanks to me. Thanks to your legal merit. Your name keeps
cropping up in Cleveland legal circles."

Morgan's smile was a dim one: "That's nice to hear, but it all seems a
bit remote to me now. I don't seem able to think with much clarity
beyond just making it through the rest of the war." It seemed necessary
to expand the remark: "What I mean is that for now I have to settle with
life on a day-to-day basis. It's my way of staying sane." He thought he'd

said too much, and in the despised voice of a complainer. He sat straighter: "At the moment, I'm just so damn glad to be home. So glad. I still don't quite believe that I am." He didn't trust himself to say more.

The judge said: "I understand." His eyes were glistening. "One would have to be a fool not to understand." This time, carefully, he guided his hand to an ashtray and stamped out his cigar. Then, looking up, he changed gear: "Am I correct in remembering that Maud told Clara, who told me, that your father's arriving this afternoon?" And to Morgan's nod: "News does travel." He smiled. "Your homecoming's the talk of the town. There are a lot of people outside your family who want to see you." Then he laughed: "Popularity is a mixed blessing. By the time your leave is up, I expect you'll feel you've been feted to death. If I were you, I'd take a look at Maud's date-book."

Morgan laughed too. "That sounds like good advice."

"Forewarned; forearmed." The judge stood up. "I'd like to walk you to your car. . . . It will improve my image to be seen with you."

◆§

Lunch on the terrace. His first meal as paterfamilias: Maud opposite him; Caroline in a high-chair on his left, Julia in a high-chair on his right; Ralph stretched out at his feet.

Unbelievably beautiful, the tall sun-shielding elm tree. He kept looking at it, up, into it, into the jade of its leaves; into its age. At sea there had been only the sky.

◆§

After lunch he read to the twins for the second time. *Uncle Wiggily Goes Swimming* was their choice (the book a frayed one from Maud's childhood). On the first page was a large, giggle-inducing picture of Uncle Wiggily in top hat, blue vest, and red trousers, standing by a pond, contemplating a swim; and eight ("Count them") bandy-legged, pop-eyed, big-mouthed frogs in crazy bathing suits—three of them lazing on the pond's bank, three others already in the water, two poised on a log, about to dive in; and, on the edge of the action, in a torn shirt and disreputable, patched pants, the lurking, wily Fox; and worse, meaner and hungrier-looking, the Wolf ("Really *bad*," Julia said). The scatter-brained narrative was rapturously funny and threaded with pendent halts: "You may read on only IF: if the spoon holder doesn't go down cellar and take the coal shovel away from the gas stove." And two pages further: "You may read on only IF: if the rice pudding doesn't put on roller skates to ride down the hill with the chocolate cake" (wild laughter from the twins). Then a big, new picture: Uncle Wiggily, out of his snazzy clothes, stripped down to his yellow underwear, wavering at the water's edge, no longer sure that he *wants* to go swimming, and oh!—the Wolf, grinning his terrible saw-toothed grin, bellying his way out of the bushes, sneaking up on Uncle Wiggily from behind.

Suspense! "You may read on only IF: if the egg beater doesn't try to catch the automobile and bite it full of holes so that it looks like a lace curtain."

Maud came into the room. "Nap time," she said.

"No! No!"

"Yes, yes. Daddy'll read the rest to you later. . . . Pip's coming, remember? You don't want to be tired for Pip, do you? . . . Tessa's waiting for you upstairs. Run along."

Embraces, as of a great parting.

They had not been alone since early morning. On the couch, he held her in his arms, her head against his chest, his lips on her forehead.

"Tell me about your visit with Mother," Maud said. "Were you appalled?"

"No. No."

"Were you able to get her attention?"

"At moments, yes."

"Was she rational?"

"In her way."

"Sometimes when I go to see her she hardly seems to know me."

"Oh, I'm sure she always knows you, darling. She certainly never lost track this morning of who I was. I think it's more a matter of how she perceives us—as liking life for reasons that don't interest her anymore."

"It terrifies me. You won't ever let me get like that, will you, Morgan? *Promise*. Kiss me."

It was like being asleep, holding her so, unaroused, a quiet hand on her breast, as if they were dreaming together an ordinary dream about an ordinary sorrow, their solacing kiss a faith of waking from it. And then, low, still under the mood's influence, Maud said: "There's a letter you must read." She shifted her body, and from the pocket of her shirt removed an envelope addressed to herself. "It came about a month ago. It's from Geoff's father."

It was a handwritten letter of an easily legible period penmanship, a senior lawyer's brief summary of a large event, elaboration left to the reader: "We want you and Morgan to know that Geoffrey is a prisoner-of-war being held somewhere in Germany. As of this date, April 26th, his prisoner-of-war status has been officially confirmed. In addition to the official verification, we have received a letter from his Squadron Commander giving a few allowable details to the effect that on return-ing to base in England, but while still over enemy territory, Geoffrey's plane took a fatal hit, but that prior to parachuting out, Geoffrey radioed that he was not injured, which latter information will hearten you and Morgan as it heartens me and Geoffrey's mother. You will please forward this news to Morgan." There was a bit more: closing lines of affection, of ... "our continuing prayers for Morgan's safety. Sincerely—"

"*Christ.*"

Maud was quick: "I called the Barrows the day I got the letter and spoke to Mr. Barrows. He promised to let us know as soon as he knows how we can write to Geoff. I probably should have showed you the letter yesterday, but—" She let her defense go. Then: "Morgan?"

She had that way of saying his name, of calling him back.

He looked down, onto her face, into her eyes: "Oh, not yesterday," he said with great feeling. "I wouldn't have wanted to know yesterday. . . . I think I'll take a walk."

"Would you like me to go with you?"

"No, darling. I'll work it through faster if I'm alone."

He headed across the lawn toward the open meadow. At the line where the mowed grass ended and the scrub meadowgreen began, he turned and looked back toward the house and saw Maud standing at a window. She raised a hand and set it on the window's broad glass whose transparency provided the boon sight of her, and he waved to her, then turned and walked on.

For himself, after the torpedoing, there had been the leap away from the stricken *Stubbins* into the sea, and almost at once, by compatriot hands, the miracle of deliverance into the lifeboat. For Geoff, a leap out into infinite space from his crippled plane: a wingless free-fall drop, a hand-tug intelligenced by reflex to his parachute's rip-cord, the 'chute unfolding—billowing out to the sudden instant of its fully ballooned "take," then the immensely occurring groundward waft lower and lower on wind routes that made of the 'chute a gliding raptor, and earth when attained and touched—the enemy upon him.

In his mind's eye, he saw it happen.

The meadow creek was running fast and he stayed on the path beside it, walking slowly against its flow. At the bend in its course where it briefly widened and formed a pool, he sat down on the bank, close enough to the water to touch it. Before the torpedoing, when he'd gone to his stateroom to get his emergency kit-bag, this was the place whither, by a trick of mind, he had been transported. The center of the pool was deep; he could not see its bottom. . . . The fancy seized him that on the pool's mud floor, invisible to him, there might be the motto remains of a toy boat, treasured yestertime property of a now grown-up man, and that around the jollity of the plaything's hull, minnows and crayfish and salamanders were celebrating their lives. The notion magnified itself and became the *Stubbins*, lying distantly on the ocean's floor, its crew's quarters now the abode of deep-sea creatures, and in his own stateroom an octopus perhaps, one of its tentacles suctioned onto a page of his drowned atlas. "Morgan." It was a part of the fantasy, his thinking that he'd heard his name called. . . . "Mor-gan!" This time the call was not to be doubted as real. He scrambled up the creek-bank and, over the extent of the open view, he saw a man standing on the far edge of the meadow and he began to run toward the man as too the man hastened toward him. They met with a flung clasp, the man breathing hard, uttering through sobs the long message: "I know I'm early, but I couldn't wait any longer."

"Pa," Morgan said, *"Pa."*

Two men in a meadow weeping together out of gratitude and awe and innocency at the way fate works.

Their recovery, when it came, was entire, and they set off on a long walk that followed the creek's course, turning with it at a meander that faced them into the westering sun, going on, farther afield. Straight off, Ansel Shurtliff asked Morgan if his ship had been torpedoed, and at Morgan's affirmative reply, he said that the captain's phone-call to him had "sponsored a suspicion of such a disaster" (which suspicion, he hastened to add, he had kept to himself). "If it won't distress you too much to talk about it, I'd like to hear about it."

It was the one time in his life that he ever approached a telling of the experience inclusive of its harshest, most painful particulars. What abetted his emotional control, even during the accounting of the Owl's death, was the upholding, absolutely silent, mandarin-like way his father listened.

When he finished, Ansel Shurtliff, dry-eyed, told him: "Life's a web woven of improbabilities. Whenever I feel overwhelmed by events, I visit your mother's grave. In time, you'll find a resting place for your sorrows, one you can go to in thought if not in body, and come away from strengthened." Then, virtually at once: "Where was it in Africa you said the British took you?" His abrupt change of topic bespoke a mutually tacit need.

"Durban," Morgan replied.

"Tell me about Durban."

He was surprised at how much he enjoyed picturing for his father the former racetrack and the rows of Army tents, the old grandstand, the clubhouse and the adjacent horsey building—("The stable-block still fully intact?" Ansel Shurtliff queried; and with a laugh: "Don't ever tell your Aunt Letitia. She'll want to buy it.")—and the outlying harbor and sweeping beach and shoreline and the town-city of Durban itself, and about the myopic antiquarian book-dealer from whom he had purchased the two volumes of Burke's *Landed Gentry* ("My kind of reading matter," Ansel Shurtliff said).

They had long since turned their steps in a homeward direction. Now, nearing the end of their walk, Morgan asked: "Were the twins still napping when you arrived?"

"Yes. They're fascinating, aren't they."

"Beyond words." Morgan smiled: "Maud tells me they call you 'Pip.'"

"At my request. . . . Soon after they began to talk, I ran into Warren Bassett one evening at the Hunt Club, and he chewed my ears off talking about his grand-children. He's got three of them, two boys presented to him by his daughter, Louise—do you remember her from your cotillion days?" (Morgan had a flashed image of Louise Bassett with whom he'd once warmly necked in the front seat of her father's racy white Cord.) "She married into the Cincinnati branch of the Walsingham clan. Warren junior sired a grand-daughter. So there you have the three grand-children of Warren senior. . . . At the time I saw Warren at the Hunt Club—that would be about two years ago—all his grand-kids were under age four, but he touted their intelligence in a way that led me to suppose they were prodigies fluent in Greek, masters of Euclidean geometry, tying their own trout flies. No limit to the Bassett brains," Ansel Shurtliff flared on. "But when Warren told me, proud as a peacock, that his grand-kids call him—brace yourself—'Chief-daddy,' the whole construct of his grandpaternal glory tumbled in my eyes. . . . That's when I decided to be Pip to Caroline and Julia. *Pip.* It's spirited and easy to say and I very much doubt my borrowing of his hero's name has set Dickens spinning in his grave. Honestly, *really,* don't you think my being Pip is an innocent egotistical aberrance next to Warren Bassett's enthronement of himself as Chief-daddy? . . . May I take your laughter as a display of agreement?"

They had stepped from the meadow onto the lawn. Before them, a view of the house and terrace that showed Maud and the twins sitting together on a bench, their heads bent toward their laps, absorbed in something, the dressing of a doll perhaps. Morgan whistled. Ralph, as yet unseen, answered with a bark. Maud raised her head. "Hello," she called. And then, in a tumble, at their best speeds, they came: Ralph first, Caroline next, Julia after, and, goddess-herder of them all: Maud.

Morgan, standing in place, arms opened out to catch, thought: *This. This* is happiness.

Doctor Leigh came by before dinner. "Hello, hello. A drop-in," he told Morgan, "to welcome you home."

He looked exactly as he had the first time Morgan ever saw him: righteous, terribly clear eyes, a jaw firm in its set, complexion burnished of health and sensible living, brindle hair parted as by a bread-knife, chest-span imposing.

He refused the offer of a drink, even of a chair, stressing that he couldn't, mustn't linger, citing "duty": "Evening bed-rounds at the hospital." Thus, like a sudden valley wind, he blew into the family circle, dispelling its prior ease and intimacy and, by his continued vigorous insistence that he not allow himself the luxury of sitting down, causing, too, Maud and Ansel Shurtliff and Morgan to remain on their feet and Julia and Caroline to wilt and linger in large-eyed silence as he railed on about the wartime paucity of doctors and nurses at the Hatherton Hospital (of which he was the head), and at the clinic in Cleveland (on whose surgical staff he served). Aside from his admirable, high-ethic dedication, Morgan had never been able to figure out what Doctor Leigh was all about. What fueled his heart and mind . . . Maud spoke often of his religious faith. Maybe that was his motor.

He stayed not a second longer than his self-allotted respite from duty permitted. "Good-bye, good-bye"—quitting their company, backing carefully, as if he were a large car, out of the room.

In the hall, momently alone with Morgan, he made a glancing reference to Morgan's morning call on Mrs. Leigh: to "her increase of psychological dislocation." That was his phrase, chilling to Morgan's ears. And, half-way out the front door: "I'll make time next week for a longer visit with you. Grand to have you home." And, in his hurry, as he walked down the porch steps: "I never doubted you'd return just as you have, sound as a dollar." On which last remark, flung over his shoulder, he completely departed.

A picture surfaced in Morgan's mind. Of Sutter. Sutter in Durban, describing with his twisted smile a decorated British infantry officer whose path his own had briefly, haplessly crossed: *"Him,"* Sutter had said, "with his swagger-stick and boots polished to a shine a blind man could see his face in. From the time they're hatched right up to the day they get their heads axed off, turkeys have his kind of confidence."

⋥

After the twins were bedded down for the night, dinner: a wonderful affair that provided him his first glimpse of the friendship which had developed in his absence between Maud and his father, its fastness independent of their in-law relationship and, as fascinatingly exists in most opposite-gender friendships, its latent spice of sexual attraction.

⋥

It was nearing midnight. The house was cloaked in silence.

In their bedroom he stood with Maud by an open window, admiring the lit globe of a mounted moon. Then a slow, kissing progress toward the bed, the end of the second day of his leave, determined.

⋥

. . . Reunions with kin—cognate, agnate, and affinal (in legal parlance). Reunions with friends; with acquaintances.

. . . Celebrations: of his thirty-third birthday on June 1, and on June 4, of his and Maud's sixth wedding anniversary.

. . . Church on Sundays: prayers of Peace; for the safety of those serving in the armed forces; for Mercy to the enemy.

. . . The daily routine of reading in the *Cleveland Plain Dealer* about the progress of the war, and of hearing about it each evening on the radio. At sea, for weeks on end, absent of any news, they had floated in ignorance of the war's history as it was being made. Now, an assailing currentness: reports of land, naval, and air battles being fought in Europe, in Asia, the regions referred to as "theaters." Defeats, gains, setbacks, fresh attacks, surrenders. Estimates of losses: men, ships, aircraft, tanks. Accounts of bombing raids, pigsties and cathedrals alike destroyed. The jungles of never-heard-of Pacific islands blasted skyward by shells sent from the weaponry of off-shore flotillas and by explosives let from the bellies of skimming planes. Ended lives mentioned in numbers and with a candor that awed and which in his mind he saw as individual faces with surprised eyes like the Owl's . . . No let-up, everyone said. No escape.

. . . The eerie arrival in one afternoon's mail of a letter from himself to Maud. "February 25, 1943. Darling," it began. Exclaiming on the date, Maud asked: "Where were you when you wrote it?" "Port Said," he answered: "February twenty-fifth was the day we arrived there"—marveling as much at the fact of the letter's existence as that it had been composed in a place so fantastically far away and at a time previous to the altering experience of the torpedoing, therefore (almost) as if written by a stranger. And equally weird: being in the room with Maud as she read it: a certain confusion: himself a postscript to the letter? or the letter a postscript to his presence?

. . . And on another day, a letter from Lucy Blackett, serving now with the Red Cross in England. Lucy: quiet, conscientious, unpresumptuous, well-born, *shy* Lucy. Unsung until now. In her small, tidy handwriting, the one-paragraph text of her letter covered only one page: "I'm writing this, dearest Maud, in an underground shelter while an air-raid is going on. Such a lot of noise! Imagine me in such a situation! I'm scared to death, but so is everyone I'm with, so it's a shared fear and cozy in its way. I've been reassigned here (London) to work at the American Red Cross Club for Women. The club is on Charles Street, just off the famous-of-song Berkeley Square. ('Nightingales sang in,' etc.). The club's a haven for American nurses, WACs, WAFs, etc. I've been so surprised by the number of women pilots there are who ferry cargo planes from the United States here to England! 'My goodness' (as my Mother would say) 'what ladies *do* these days!' The noise is really loud now and getting louder. I'd best bring this to a close. Hug C. and J. for me. Stay cheerful and please keep writing as regularly as you do. I count on your letters. Love ever, Lucy." Maud read the letter aloud to him. . . . Lucy's odyssey, he thought. Brava, Lucy.

. . . Games: played with Caroline and Julia and Maud and Tessa and anyone else who might be around. Tag. Follow the Leader. Blindman's Bluff. Rover, Rover, Try to Come Over. Hide and Seek, liked best at dusk for the shiver of hiding in a place more secret for being sunless, and for the darker sound of the called-out "dare": "Come out, come out, or you'll be *it.*" Caroline always called him "Daddy." Sometimes Julia did too, but in the heat of the game she would forget. "*Run, Morgan!*" she would yell as he was sprinting toward the "home" tree, Maud hot on his heels: "Run *faster,* Morgan—" windmilling her arms, thrilled through, loving the moment, absolutely loving the moment when he would reach the tree—touch it, and crow: "Ollie ollie oxum, Freedom!"

. . . The Captain and Sarkis and Sutter and Anderson and the others of the crew. At the oddest times one of them would enter his mind and take possession of it. Sometimes they would *all* appear before him and he would see their faces clearly, as in a group photograph; and that was very strange for the reason that *his* face was in the picture, *there* in their sovereign midst. This image was the one that most filled him with a sense of loss, their unity being now all scattered. It felt wrong that he had no current knowledge of them: wrong, not to know where they were and how they were faring. . . . As often as he thought of them, he thought of Geoff.

. . . In the woods, on a bed of moss. On the way home from a late-night party in Cleveland, unable to wait, in the car, parked in the obscurity of a conspiring off-the-road lane. At the lake one night, after a swim, naked, in the aerie of Maud's childhood treehouse. Over and over in the constancy of their own room, again and again at that remotest, blackest, stillest hour of night, owl-to-lark; and fabulously during rainstorms. It was as if Time had cast them back to the first sexually obsessed days of their marriage.

❧

On the thirteenth day of his leave, they quarreled.

The twins had just been put down for their nap. Maud asked him: "What would you think of some tennis and a swim at the club?"

"A good idea, especially the swim. I'll be a cripple on the court," he laughed.

Maud laughed too: "So will I. It'll be the first time I've played since last September."

She was a very good tennis player. . . . Before the war, on such summer weekend afternoons as they had chosen to spend at the club, he had always preferred to watch her play than to play with her, he enjoyed so much observing her on the court in contest with a first-rate opponent, she was physically so well suited to the game's demands: long legs, free stretch of arms, the limbs attached to her body's slender frame in a strung, ready way. She played with concentration and a peculiar kind of glowing esprit that men found stimulating, and responded to by sending her hard, fast shots that were flatteringly difficult to return and when the set was finished, by flirting with her off the court.

"Can I have a few minutes before we go?" he asked her. "There are a couple of things I want to do."

"Anything I can help with?"

"No, love. It's telephone stuff. I told George Colgate I'd call him today, and I'd like to try to reach Miss Sly."

"Miss *Sly?*" Maud froze in place. "Did you say Miss Sly?" She did not wait for an answer. *"Why?"* She was furious. "Why in the world do you want to call *her?*"

He searched her face, her eyes, and saw she had made of him an enemy.

"Why?" she demanded again.

"For reasons of friendship," he said gently.

"Friendship?" she jabbed: "On what basis do you claim friendship with her?"

"Through an exchange of letters," he said. "I wrote to her after I enlisted and she very kindly replied, and we've written back and forth since then. Her letters helped me." He was prepared to go on, to tell her about the diverting nature of their correspondence, but she cut him off.

"You mean you've kept up with her! Behind my back!"

"Oh Maud, for God's sake, calm down. . . . You asked me why I want to call her and I've told you. Now you tell me why you're so angry."

"Because she's Tilden-Herne is why, and I put Tilden-Herne behind me three years ago. I thought you had too. You've misled me," she accused.

"Maud—"

But she would not be stopped: "Your staying in touch with her," she began, not looking at him—addressing the wall—"it keeps her in *my* life *and* in Caroline and Julia's. It's mean of you. *Awful.*"

He strove to stay calm: "You're way off base," he said quietly. "Let's talk about it later."

Perhaps it was his restraint that pushed her on: "*My* feelings don't matter to you."

"You know better than that."

Now she looked right at him: "But you're going to go ahead and call her anyhow, aren't you?"

What he couldn't stand was her affronting tone and manner. "Yes," he said, and walked out of the room.

＊

Until the quarrel, he had languished in a marital Garden of Eden, gamboling and feasting and drinking and making love, all as if his occurring brilliant sojourn in the Garden might, as an opportunity, never come his way again. For all its perturbation, the quarrel, for *him,* had one good side effect: it kicked him up from off his sybaritic ass and sent him forthwith to his desk, where, with the door of his study firmly closed, he got out the files Judge Malcolm had given him nearly two weeks ago. Faced with the task of reading them he sighed and gazed at them, piled neatly as they were now in front of him, representing to him a kind of *instrument*—the equivalent of a violin to a violinist, or a piano to a pianist—and he thought of that famous broad-browed legal scholar, Joseph Story, who, in 1829, on the occasion of his inaugural address as Dane Professor of Law at Harvard, had said the words known since by every lawyer worth his salt: "The Law is a jealous mistress, and requires a long and constant courtship." Considering those words, he suffered fear that through long disuse, the gallantries and tendencies and exuberances and processes of legal *thought* which in the past had been so fluently his, might now be rusted beyond application. . . . To his everlasting surprise he was wrong. Which isn't to say that all came immediately easy (as in the instant of driving his car) but that, a few pages into his reading of the first file, his juridical faculties began to limber up, and by the end of an hour, were flexed enough to make him feel he could competently appraise the files' contents. In all, the exercise took over three hours—a defining time as it turned out, for it focused his critical attention on his professional life to date and set him musing on the ways he would alter its course when the war was over.

He came out from his study in time to hear the six-o'clock news. Maud was already seated in front of the radio. "Would you like a drink? Your usual?" he asked her. She was cold as ice, but worse: monumentally polite. "Yes," she said, "as you're getting one for yourself; yes, thank you." He had a partial recall of a tune and its lyrics: "It's June in January." La *laaa*, la *la*lalala. The tune didn't work, though, if the words were reversed: "It's January in June," which unsingable reversal aptly described her unseasonable marital chill.

From out of the brown radio, a Voice was theorizing about the ongoing great build-up of Allied forces in the Mediterranean region. "There is speculation," the Voice was saying, "that Sicily will be the likely first target of an Allied campaign designed to bring Italy to heel. General Eisenhower and General Sir Harold Alexander Cunningham will—"

He went to the pantry. In the kitchen, Tessa was giving the twins their supper. In their world, all was as usual. He chatted with Tessa for a moment, then told the twins that when they were finished eating he would take them for a quiet, evening walk.

"Ralph too," Caroline said.

Julia said: "And then a story."

&

Maud turned from him that night in bed, as if his touch, made peaceably to her hand, was a scalding one. She fell asleep at once. Beside her, awake, he pondered deeply on their quarrel, on what—as he saw it—lay behind it: namely, that any brush of reference relating to the matter of the twins' adoption triggered in her an armed reaction reminiscent of the bitter, self-abusive anger she had heaped upon herself at the time the doctors had told her she could have no children of her own. Intuition forged the link. Sense affirmed his conviction that during this brief interval of his leave, it would do no good to force the issue into the open, particularly if his hunch was correct as to the psychological make-up of the problem. When the war is over, he thought: when I'm home to stay and when we have Time on our side, we'll face it together and set it right. . . . It began to seem as if everything that mattered depended on the war coming to an end. . . .

❧

He telephoned Miss Sly the next morning.

She said at once how "relieved" she'd been to receive a recent letter from him, mailed from Miami. (He had written it his last day aboard the Dutch freighter.)

"I'd like so much to see you," he told her, stating it that way, as a kind of wish for her to fulfill or not.

"And I you, Mr. Shurtliff."

From her absence of a following qualifying remark, he risked the single word: "When?"

"As it happens, I've a fairly easy schedule this week. Tomorrow would be fine. *Or* Friday. Would a time on either of those days suit you?"

"Tomorrow," he said. "May I take you to lunch?"

"How very nice. . . . There's quite a good restaurant not far from my office. It's a quiet place." She gave him the name and address. "Could we meet there at twelve-thirty?"

"Perfect," he said. *"Perfect."*

❧

He waited for her outside the restaurant, under the awning that announced its ordinary name: THE CARRIAGE STOP. He had already spoken to the elderly headwaiter and secured a table in a windowed alcove that overlooked a small garden.

He saw her coming down the street, walking at an easy pace that suggested a pleasure of exercise taken at noon under a fair sky. She wore a summer dress of a soft, flowered fabric that floated around her large-boned body, the drapery of its ample skirt trailing her forward steps, and he had again the impression of a deeply feminine woman, who, for this occasion, had dressed for *him;* as he had dressed for *her:* he was in uniform. He went to meet her. "Miss Sly."

"Mr. Shurtliff."

They sounded each other's names in unison, and laughed, and stood on the sidewalk for a moment, face-to-face, in a first near look, holding to the clasp of their handshake. She was remarkably solid, like a mature tree or a hill: a fact of Nature that doesn't change except so slowly as to be almost unnoticeable. She had that effect on him, of completeness and continuance.

They were seated. Their food was ordered. Having agreed that their meeting warranted celebration, the waiter promptly brought their chosen drinks: a glass of very dry sherry for her, bourbon on the rocks for him. She raised her glass and, her head cocked a bit to the side, looking him through, she smiled and said: "Now we can talk." She meant of course not ponderously, not in a solving way *about* huge subjects, and not for vain ends, but *of* things, in the spirit of their letters, this and that, as spring kindredly to mind. A multitude of leaping topics:

—People. (Of how, in her words, "difficult times sort out individual human virtues and vices and become a proving-ground of character.")

—The world's varied and vast geography, and its antiquities: for him, the solemn pyramids, which (he told her) haunted and impressed him in memory more than they had when he'd stood in their stony presence; and, for her, the Rosetta Stone, seen in London some six years ago, its effect on her a remaining one of "pure awe."

—The chance medley (which he briefly touched on) of the torpedoing, and her comprising nod and one sentence story-response about her father's Army surgeon brother killed in 1917 by a sniper's bullet as he walked with an orderly down the main street of a small French village "secured" the previous day by the AEF troops: how, in different guises, Chance changes our lives.

—Ralph: the comic canine of his homecoming, and her following inspired account of Passepartout, the "dizzy, one-eared dachshund" of her childhood, her laughter as she described the dog so vigorous that one of the tortoise-shell pins that held the flummoxy knot of her hair slid loose and dangled over her fillet of sole, and he leaned across the table and fully abstracted it and held it for a second before handing it to her, and was touched by her charming blush and expressed disparagement of what she called "my unruly mane."

—President Roosevelt's health: "He looks so *frail* in the newspaper pictures, so *weary*," she said. "Do you think so too, Mr. Shurtliff? That he's physically exhausted? It does make one wonder if he ought to seek election again next year, though changing leaders midstream of the war"—the hazards of the thought left unexplored. "In the 1940 election," she went on, "I voted for Wendell Wilkie. I liked so much his ideas about the world combining itself in purpose for its collective good."

—(How? from speculations about political figures, did they get onto the subject of movies?) "I do *adore* Chaplin," she said, "but I'm not a committed movie-goer. The last movie I went to I walked out on at the point where Freddie Bartholomew turned into Tyrone Power."

—Bill Maudlin's wartime cartoons; and, laughing, about Kilroy: *Kilroy was here*, "here" being Everywhere; Kilroy, Everyone.

—A moment, over dessert, devoted to telling her of Julia's and Caroline's beauty and brightness and of his and Maud's parental happiness: only a moment, but during it his awareness of her fierce attention to every word and the tremble of her lips, but her strict silence that precluded elaboration.

—Books.

The speed of their communication reminded him of being a boy on a snowy winter day hurling downhill on his Flexible Flyer—so much so that when she glanced at her watch and exclaimed, "My soul, it's after three! I'm long overdue at my office," it was like the sorry end of the sled's sped course—*though*—"Tell me quickly," she said: "I *must* know what you'll be doing when your leave is up"—and he quickly told her as much as he knew. "I'll write," he said.

"And I'll write to you," she said, rising from her chair but still looking at him: "because I *want* to." She refused his offer to accompany her back to her office. "You understand," she said. "I know you understand."

And so, outside the restaurant, they embraced, and parting, said their usual words: "Thank you, Miss Sly."

"Thank *you*, Mr. Shurtliff. Until we meet again." Then, in her summer dress, she walked away.

He had long since given up trying to define exactly what she represented to him, or what, together, they represented to each other. All that

he knew for sure, and did not question, was his absolute sense of connection with her: that she was a *meant* figure in his life. It was in that
way, mystically thinking, and with emotion, that he watched her go.

❧

He called Maud. He said "Darling—" when she answered the telephone. She immediately asked if he would be home in time for dinner.
He took a light approach: "Your wish is my command. I'll be there if you
want me to be."

"It hadn't occurred to me you'd think otherwise," she answered in a
voice more present than at any time since their quarrel.

(She would have made a good litigator, he thought.) "I'm seeing
George Colgate at the Union Club at four. If I'm home by seven?"

"Fine," she said. "Give George my best."

Ah . . . the January thaw, and the melting despite the fact that she
must have suspected he'd seen Miss Sly. Or hadn't she? "Maud—"

"There's news about Geoff, Morgan—a letter from Mr. Barrows
telling how we can write to him." He heard the background squeal of a
child. "I *have* to hang up, Morgan. We're about to give Ralph a bath. He
rolled in something. He *smells* awful." She was almost laughing.

"*Wonderful* about Geoff," he roared. "Sorry about Ralph. *Seven*, at the
latest."

"Don't drive too fast."

Then the click of disconnection.

Love, he mused, standing in the phone booth. *Love:* plaything of the
gods. How can anyone rationally think that the deities of myth aren't
still at work in our lives, spending the energy of their whims upon us,
conspiring, casting us alternately into Darkness, into Light? Ah, their
mischief . . . Miss Sly. Maud. Geoff. (Don't forget the dog.)

❧

His leave was in its final days.

As often as he could he went to see Mrs. Leigh. He never stayed long.
He would sit beside her and try to amuse her; try to raise her out of her
silence. But you can't fly a kite on a still day.

Spurred by Judge Malcolm, he composed a "memorandum of projection" about the future of their law firm's practice.

He wrote letters: to Geoff, sent through the Red Cross to a numbered STALAG; to Lucy in London; to two of his cousins serving in the military, one at Camp Lee, in Virginia, the other in the Pacific (APO San Francisco); to Rupert Wilkins, hazarding the long letter to the address he'd been given back in Durban.

He spent one afternoon in Cleveland with Frederick Selby, lawyer to the Shurtliff clan and trustee of its residual wealth (gained from iron-ore and salt mines and railroads), the fortune amassed in the previous century by his paternal great-grandfather. Mr. Selby had bidden Morgan to the conference. The reason for the conference? A "layered" trust, established years ago by that canny, enterprising ancestor, "the principal of which," Mr. Selby told Morgan, "is due to kick in for distribution at the end of this year." The gold-rimmed, round lenses of Mr. Selby's glasses somewhat enlarged his eyes. "You and your paternal cousins are the beneficiaries, and as there are ten of you, you'll receive a tenth of the principal."

Morgan, listening, thought of his cousins. The ones who were domiciled in Ohio (four in Cleveland, two in Cincinnati) were the ones he knew best. (Three, in the Ohio set, he regarded as close friends.) The two who lived in Pittsburgh, and the one who lived in New York, he knew with that kind of interested but distant affection which pertains between admired blood relatives of the "visitor, or to-be-visited, status." (That was his father's phrase.) All the cousins were male; all, in age, within a twelve-year range of one another; all, save one, married. Two were intellectuals (a classicist professor at Columbia University) (an Episcopal prelate); two, like himself, were lawyers, and, like himself, now away at war; one was a stockbroker; another, (the oldest) a banker, brother to the next oldest who was a would-be senator; another (referred to in the family as "our confirmed bachelor"), was an architect. In the lot, there was one disgrace, a perpetually bad-news rotter (bane to his wife, a casual philanderer, an untidy liar, always in debt). Such was the way the cousinly clan was distributed.

Morgan of course had always known of the trust's existence, known that one day he would be one of its inheritors, but his orchardist father had always played down the Shurtliff money. ("You'll come into it in due course, Morgan, but by the time you do, you'll be mature enough to know it's by an accident of birth. Meanwhile, boy, your primary obligation is to prove yourself *to* yourself in ways as admirable as possible.") That was the creed Ansel Shurtliff had reared Morgan on.

"It's a very substantial sum," Mr. Selby said. "You'll be a well-to-do man." (He named a figure, impressive by any standard.) "Between now and the end of the year, you must make a new will. Start thinking about it." Mr. Selby smiled his thin smile. "Your father was in last week. He brought me up to date on your doings. I understand you've got a while ashore."

"At least four months, maybe more," Morgan affirmed. "I've got to digest all this." Then he gave voice to the old cliché: "'A lawyer who represents himself has a fool for a client.'. . . I'd like you to go on representing my interests."

"It will please me to," Mr. Selby said. "Let me know your thoughts about your will, and I'll hammer them into a first draft for your perusal. Do it as soon as you can. Feel free to call me here at the office or at home, evenings *or* weekends. Anytime at all that suits you."

They shook hands and Morgan departed.

The afternoon had been a dazzler.

❧

They were to spend the last week-end of his leave at his father's home.

On Friday afternoon, he packed the Chevy's trunk with what he thought was an insane amount of gear, and they set off, Maud beside him in front, Tessa and the twins and Ralph on the back seat. At a fast clip, the trip could be made in a couple of hours; with this cargo, though, he was more concerned with safety than with speed.

Maud conducted a lesson from Hardy's *Alphabet Book:* "A for Apple" (the twins repeated after her), "B for Broom, C for Cat," through to "Z for Zebra." They sang songs. Stopped at a railroad crossing by a clanging bell and a criss-crossed set of blinking red lights, they counted the slow-passing freight cars. "C for Caboose," Morgan said as he restarted the Chevy's engine. He read aloud a first sign nailed on a fence post: "The Queen of Hearts," (and a bit farther on, the second sign), "Now loves the Knave," (the third sign in sight) "Because the King," (the fourth and final sign) "Ran out of Burma Shave." They passed through the dusky hollow of a long covered bridge. Maud remarked that Ralph was behaving awfully well. Tessa said, "I told you he would." The country-side was lovely. The twins fell asleep.

All in all, a sweet, uneventful journey.

❧

The visit was crowned by the presence of his aunt and uncle, Letitia and Lewis Grant. ("A family house-party," Ansel Shurtliff said: "Like old times.")

He did with the twins many of the things his father must have done with him when he was their age: canoed on the pond; lifted them up onto a strong low branch into the leafy realm of one of Ansel Shurtliff's oldest apple trees, then perched himself on an adjacent branch and heard Julia say, "We're birds"; rocked them in his old swing; played with them *at* croquet (their grasp of the game meager, but the time spent at it lively, especially when Ralph joined in, mouthing a ball and rollicking off with it).

With Maud, on Saturday afternoon, he walked down to the pond. They sat at the water's edge, holding hands, not talking, thinking the same thing: that in two days' time they must say good-bye. . . . Right before their eyes, then, exquisitely compelling, they saw a nuptial pair of dragonflies. By a series of minute maneuverings, the male adjusted himself over the female's body and embraced her. She shivered, and they commenced their great exertions. The reed bent beneath them and moved with them. Believers say that God is conscious of each mating as it occurs, whether between humans or creatures. . . . *This* frail one took an oddly long while to complete, and the end was unceremonious, marked by the male's departure and immediate disappearance into a near-by forest of bulrushes, the female left behind on the reed, her diaphanous wings opened out at her sides, motionless, like a pair of forsaken arms. "Oh, Morgan," Maud cried.

❧

"Drinking time," on Saturday evening—the twins in their nightgowns, but allowed to spend a few more minutes with the grown-ups, Letitia taking off her jewelry, slipping the strand of her pearls around Julia's neck, pinning a sparkling brooch on Caroline's nightgown. "Now rings," she was saying: "Hold up your hands." Bedecked, the little girls walked with a somber importance around the large room.

"Music," Ansel Shurtliff said. "We must have some music." From the record cabinet he removed an old album and, laughing, struck a pose beside the Victrola.

"You look satanic, Ansel," Letitia told him.

"Prepare yourselves" was his response.

He put three records on the Victrola's "holding arm." Then, wickedly, he flicked the switch that set the turntable spinning, and they waited. Waited, as the first record made its slow descent onto the turntable and the bamboo needle its ponderous approach of audible connection. Then, at peak decibel: "AH! SWEET MYSTERY OF LIFE AT LAST I'VE FOUND YOU." Nelson Eddy and Jeanette MacDonald: *his* rancid baritone, *her* piercing, life-threatening soprano—"AH! AT LAST I KNOW THE MEANING OF IT ALL—"

"Morgan!" Letitia keened: "Call the police! Your father needs restraining."

But Morgan, howling, had already seized Maud and was dancing with her, or *trying* to, stopping, freezing in place whenever the singers settled on a high note and milked it to breath's end.

The twins' eyes were enormous.

"Blue Moon" fell next onto the turntable—during whose peroxide sentiments, there was a stampede to the liquor tray. . . . To "Rose Marie," Morgan took Caroline and Julia in his arms and dandied them around the room, gliding and turning, their knees knobbed into his ribs, their arms in a stranglehold around his neck, his ears ringing with their ecstatic squeals and with the applause and cheers from the onlookers. . . . Maybe he was a bit drunk. Maybe not. Maybe it was the shining beauty of Maud's face, watching, as he danced with their children, that made him feel, in reflection of it, golden.

ঌ

On Sunday morning he went with Maud and his father and Letitia and
Lewis to the eleven o'clock service at St. James Episcopal Church. Here he
had been baptized and later confirmed. Here, as a choir-boy, he had sung
many times the hymn the congregation was singing now. Here too, in a
guise of spotlessness, he had sat in the choir-loft trembling in fear of eternal damnation as a visiting prelate preached on the Seven Deadly Sins:
only the day before he had perpetrated his first and final theft: a Mars Bar
lifted from the candy counter of the local drugstore. And here had taken
place his mother's funeral; (she was buried in the nigh cemetery). Sit, for
the Lesson. Stand, for the second hymn. Sit, for the sermon. "Let us pray."
Kneel. Stand, for the third hymn: "Eternal Father, strong to save." Sit, as
the collection was taken. Stand, for the reading of the 126th Psalm:

> When the LORD restored the fortunes of Zion,
>> then were we like those who dream.
>
> Then was our mouth filled with laughter,
>> and our tongue with shouts of joy.
>
> Then they said among the nations,
>> "The LORD has done great things for them."
>
> The Lord has done great things for us,
>> and we are glad indeed.
>
> Restore our fortunes, O LORD,
>> like the watercourses of the Negev.
>
> Those who sowed with tears,
>> will reap with songs of joy.
>
> Those who go out weeping, carrying the seed,
>> will come again with joy, shouldering their sheaves.

Remain standing, head bent floorward, for the benediction. Amen.

The service over, they made their way down the aisle, out of the church, into the fresh air. In his uniform (worn at his father's request) he felt conspicuous amidst the conventionally suited men and hatted women who were standing about in comfortable clusters, familiar to each other, talking, exchanging Sabbath pleasantries. Most were strangers; some though were his father's friends, and with them he fell into easy conversation.

A group walked toward him—two middle-aged couples, a young woman, and a white-haired man with a tired face. They took up a position near him, and when he finished chatting with the Dillards, one of their number (clearly their elected spokesman) stepped forward. "My name's Bill Ritter," he said, "and this is my wife, Emily." He was a short, plump man with willing, slightly popped Pekingese eyes. Morgan shook their extended hands. "We have two sons in the Army," Mr. Ritter said. The husband of the second couple said: "Our boy's in the Navy too—a machinist-mate on a PT boat." Then the young woman: "My husband's a bomber navigator." They shuffled their positions, making more space for the white-haired man: "My grandson," he began, then lowered his head and fell mute. Morgan took in the black mourning band sewn on the left sleeve of his light summer suit. "Your grandson, sir?" he asked. The man looked up: "My *only* grandson," he corrected: "He was a captain in the Marines." "I'm truly sorry," Morgan said. They all stood a moment, searching. Then, from the willing Mr. Ritter: "We just wanted to say hello to you." Morgan looked from one face to the other: "Thank you," he said: "I'll always remember that you did." The white-haired man was the first to turn away. After a gentle saying of good-byes, the others followed in his wake.

❧

Caroline Cunningham Shurtliff
Born—28 March 1887
Died Age 36—3 April 1923
Beloved wife of Ansel Osborne Shurtliff
Mother of Morgan Cunningham Shurtliff

The text was inscribed on a bronze tablet embedded in a flower-carved slab of white marble. Near-by, there was a spring-fed pool, lily pads afloat on the water's surface, and at the pool's southerly rim, a pussy-willow bush.

They stood in a half-circle facing the tombstone, Maud next to Lewis Grant, Letitia with her hand through the bend of his father's elbow, himself at his father's right side, completing the arc. . . . The April day his mother was buried had been bright but chilly, and he remembered that the pussy-willow bush (today in June leaf) had been then in silver bloom and that all the time the coffin was being lowered into the earth he had kept his eyes on the bush, on its thousands of silky catkins shimmering in the cold sunlight and that he was up to a rapid count of over three hundred when he heard the first spill of spaded soil hit the sealed lid of the coffin, at which instant he had burrowed his face in the folds of his father's dark overcoat and given way to all the perplexities and sufferings of his young grief. . . . "Do you tend to that pussy-willow bush, Pa?" he now asked.

"Only a bit," his father answered. "I take out the winter-kill and cull the sterile new growth, but that's about all. I like it to look wild, not kept."

"It's lovely," Morgan said.

"Determined," Ansel Shurtliff mused. "It keeps going on, year in and year out. That's what I like best about it." He consulted his pocket watch. "We ought to be on our way or we'll be late for dinner. We're having roast beef," he boasted, "and as I used up most of this month's meat-ration stamps to obtain it, I don't want Mrs. Cromey laying the blame on *us* if it's overcooked."

But Letitia—never one to be hurried—kept staring at her sister's tombstone, squinting at it.

"What are you thinking?" Ansel Shurtliff asked her.

Slowly, with a developing, deepening smile, she turned full face to her brother-in-law: "That she did have *the* most divine figure of any woman I've ever known."

Morgan glanced at his father: to instantly catch his reaction to the remark; to the extraordinary remark.

His father's richly intemperate, unsacred laughter shattered the cemetery's quiet: "Didn't she just!" he trumpeted: "Divine's the only word!"

(Later, when they were alone, Maud asked him: "That exchange
between Letitia and Pip—about your mother's figure—did it surprise
you as much as it did me?"

Morgan threw up his hands: "It absolutely bowled me over.")

అఈ

In Ansel Shurtliff's house, Sunday-noon dinner was still treated as a ceremonial Occasion. A kingly banquet given by the king in his castle. To
Morgan, the dining room seemed filled with the radiance of other such
feasts, hugely, hugely enjoyed—savored in a bygone time of peace that
predicted an aftermath of nothing more or less than an afternoon nap or
a long read in a soft, big chair. But today, in the melancholy stimulation
of his imminent departure, the protracted meal was an agony. If he could
have been the designer of a best farewell, he would have risen from the
table and, after a fast embrace of its beloved occupants, fled the scene.

When, *finally,* the break came between the main course and dessert,
he asked his father's permission to be excused, apologizing to him and
the others, touting his supreme sacrifice of passing up dessert. "But
if I don't," he explained, "we'll be awfully late getting back to
Hatherton." And then, to Maud: "Don't hurry, darling. I'll round up
Tessa and the twins and get them going at collecting all their
stuff. . . . *None* of you should hurry: it'll take me forever to get them
organized."

The king, reminded, was truer: "The time's almost come," he said.
"Almost."

అఈ

Maud and Tessa and the twins were in the car; beside it, Letitia and
Lewis, maintaining to the end an appearance of cheer, chatting, petting
Ralph's head, stuck out through one rolled-down window, and shaking
his repeatedly lifted paw. A bit away, in a sought privacy, Morgan and
his father. "Open it when you get home," Ansel Shurtliff was saying of a
package he had just given Morgan. "It's a companion book to those you

bought in Durban. I found it on a dusty shelf in the back room of Tim Buchanen's establishment. God knows how it found its way there." He looked distraught. "I'm gabbling," he said. "Holding you back." His offered hand trembled.

Morgan couldn't but wonder how he must look, standing there beside a young holly tree, taller than the tree, but in his distress slack and lanky in comparison to it.

He fumbles up into a loose adieu. . . . That was Troilus's quirky line. "Good-bye, Pa."

"Good-bye, Morgan. Good-bye, my boy."

❧

Dawn of Tuesday, June 21, 1943

The sky was just beginning to brighten, just tingeing up into silver. It had been a cool night and over the lawn and meadow there was a lingerence of ground mist.

For his train's seven A.M. departure from Union Terminal, Dennis was to drive him into Cleveland—breakfast to be eaten somewhere along the way. The evening before, Morgan had parked the Chevy on the street, away from the house. Now, by first light, he looked out their bedroom and saw Dennis leaning against the car. "He's here."

They had planned it so, this their farewell, that it be swift and quiet, made while Tessa and the twins were still asleep.

"Don't come downstairs," he pleaded. Then he bent and picked up his kit-bag. "I hope Ralph won't bark."

"He won't," Maud sobbed.

Down the length of the silent upstairs hall; down the stairs, taking from the banister its oaken strength; stealthily, across the dim interior of the downstairs hall; past his study, out the front door, into the impersonal day.

He never looked back. "Hello," he said to Dennis. "Thank you for being on time."

Ralph had not barked.

❧

THE

YEAR BOOK

OF

DAILY RECREATION
AND INFORMATION,

CONCERNING

REMARKABLE MEN AND MANNERS,
TIMES AND SEASONS,
SOLEMNITIES AND MERRY MAKINGS,
ANTIQUITIES AND NOVELTIES

ON THE PLAN OF THE

EVERYDAY BOOK AND TABLE BOOK

or

EVERLASTING CALENDAR OF POPULAR AMUSEMENTS, SPORTS, PASTIMES,
CEREMONIES, CUSTOMS, AND EVENTS, INCIDENT TO EACH OF THE THREE
HUNDRED AND SIXTY-FIVE DAYS IN PAST AND PRESENT TIMES:

FORMING A

COMPLETE HISTORY OF THE YEAR

AND A

PERPETUAL KEY TO THE ALMANAC.

———

BY WILLIAM HONE.

———

Old Customs! Oh I love the sound,
    However simple they may be:
What e're with the tune hath sanction found,
    is welcome, and is dear to me.
Pride glows above simplicity,
    And spurs them from her haughty mind,
And soon the poet's song will be
    the only refuge they can find.

Clare

———

WITH ONE HUDRED AND FOURTEEN ENGRAVINGS.

———

LONDON:

PRINTED FOR THOMAS TEGG, 73, CHEAPSIDE;
R. GRIFFIN AND C9., GLASGOW; ALSO J. CUMMING, DUBLIN.
1832

This is a copy of the title page of the book his father had given him—a volume of 1,643 pages, the text printed in letters small as gnats.

The train was gaining speed.

He opened the book to June 21 (1832). Page 731.

Below the given date there was first a five-stanza poem titled "The Season," described for the reader's edification as "a Norman song of summer, written in the 14th or 15th century, taken from the 'Lays of the Minnesingers.'" It was a fragile lyric of love and nightingales and weather "Mild as the tender lamb / And as the red rose bright."

—Sun rises—3:43 A.M.

—Sun sets—8:17 P.M.

—Foxglove begins to flower under hedges: in gardens there is a white variety.

—Spanish love-in-a-mist blooms.

—Chili strawberry begins to fruit.

—Scarlet strawberries now abound.

—Madock cherries begin to ripen.

—Charlock and Kidlock, terrible weeds to the farmer, cover the fields with their pale yellow.

—Readers of the Everyday Book may remember, in an account of "Cannonbury Tower," incidental mention of the beautiful marble bust of Mrs. Thomas Gent by Betnes. That lady, distinguished by scientific knowledge and literary ability, is since dead. She was born on this day.

. . . So much for June 21, 1832.

In Miami the next day, Morgan looked with astonishment at the headlines in the morning paper: of what had happened on June 21, 1943.

RACE RIOTS, (he read). In Detroit. 34 killed. Estimates of injured above 700. In New York's Harlem, 6 killed.

"My God," he gasped.

A Navy captain, sitting with him over lunch, said: "It's unbelievable, isn't it, a thing like that happening in America? It's sure as hell's pushed the war off the front page." The captain qualified: "Not for long, I guess."

6 ✑ Over and Out

Miami. 1943.

In the off-the-street entry that fronted the SCTB (Submarine Chaser Training Building), marooned behind large panes of protective glass, was a lifeboat. Around it, the SCTC captain gathered the new men. "Look at this boat," he told them. "Look hard at it. Look at those dark stains on the thwarts and interior sides of the hull and on the floor- boards. Those stains, gentlemen, aren't the work of a surrealist painter. Those stains are dried blood. The men who briefly occupied this boat were survivors of a daytime torpedoing. Their ship—one of a large convoy on its way to England—developed engine trouble and lost her position in the convoy while repairs were being made. As a conse- quence, she was trailing behind the convoy. A perfect target. Shortly after the torpedoing, and by 'shortly after,' I mean within an hour, one of our escort ships searching for survivors, found this boat. All its occupants were dead. They had been machine-gunned. *Murdered*." The captain paused; then: "This lifeboat is here to remind us that toward an enemy who would do such a thing, no mercy can be shown."

వ

"We're a mixed lot," Morgan wrote his father:

> *For purposes of quick communication I'll divide our mix into three groups, though of course, no such distinctions officially pertain. The group I fall most naturally into is comprised of older men who have been in the service a goodly while and spent considerable time at sea. The second group is made up of newly commissioned graduates of Navy sponsored V–12 college programs, all of them very "gung ho" about the war. They seem awfully young to me, being mostly in their early twenties. Lastly, there are some Russians whose presence here devolves on the turning over by our navy to their navy (delivery in process) of a fleet of sub-chaser boats (plus new weapons).*
>
> *We are all comfortably housed in a former sun-worshiper's hostelry called the Columbus Hotel. By what I can only guess is a fluke of good luck, I've been allotted a room to myself. You will appreciate how much the privacy means to me. The Russians live as a unit on the hotel's top floor. They are a friendly bunch given to inviting the rest of us up to their lodgings for what their commander, in his patois English, calls "the enjoy taking of some vodka." Their quarters include the hotel's old ballroom, an eye-shattering, gold-painted arena with huge chandeliers appropriate to my imaginings of how an Italian bordello is likely lit. It's in this weird salon—perfect setting for an under-budgeted movie about the Tzarist times—that we drink the Russians' vodka, of which they have a seemingly endless supply, pouring it out as if it were as easily come by as tap water.*
>
> *If the gods favor me, they will arrange my future so that I'll never have to return to Miami once I leave it. The summer climate is hot and humid, perfect conditions for mosquitoes and seedy real-estate developers. There are huge tracts of outlying land covered with door-to-door cheaply constructed houses, the odd palm tree supplying*

*scraggly shade against a blistering daytime sun. The native populace
transacts its business with a tropical lethargy. Their speech,
especially the women's, is an out-of-tune drawl, twangy as a
pawnshop guitar. Hard on the ears, at least on mine. A lot of elderly
folk, retired I guess, idle away the hours sitting on benches, talking
with each other. One hopes they are contented. It's their look of
stagnation that makes one wonder.*

*From that wonderful book you gave me, under today's date (July
12th), I quote the following passage: "Below are listed some popular
beliefs and superstitions at which the generation born in the Year of
our Lord, 1832, may smile when the now credulous are dead—that
pigs can see the wind—that it is unlucky to pare your nails on
Sunday—to cure foot-corns, cover them with a slice of beef a dwarf
has spit three times upon—a spark in the candle is a sign of a letter
coming—seat a toad on your forehead at sunset to stave off
nightmares."*

*What I like best is the notion that pigs can see the wind. Do you
remember a grade-school friend of mine named Junior Snyder? If
you remember Junior, you'll remember Arabella, his pet pig. Arabella
was white, with ears the color of pink grapefruit, and she used to
stand facing into a breeze, smiling. She was a great smiler. I haven't
thought of Junior or Arabella for years. I'm sure Arabella's long gone.
I wonder what's happened to Junior Snyder.*

More soon, Pa. Morgan.

&

The daily routine was rigorous; bearable for being so.

They learned everything there was to know about a cunning depth-charge weapon called a Hedgehog, and in the waters off the Florida coast, aboard subchasers, practiced and mastered to a second-nature expertness, the Hedgehog's uses.

Evenings were free. "Off" was the lingo word.

By way of recreation, Miami offered movies, bars, nightclubs, the sport (if such could be called) of greyhound races; women. For these diversions, there were takers in plenty. . . . But for some men, in number a sadder plenty, the so-called "free" evenings were gloamings of torment through which drifted desires for pleasures that were far away, in kind sole, and incalculably personal.

Throughout most of July, he spent the evenings in his room, reading and writing letters and attending to the matter of his will, as to which Mr. Selby kept forwarding drafts from his desk in Cleveland: "Dear Morgan, In re Section Four, Clause C, page 8 of my last submission to you, I feel we might better tighten the language to read as follows . . . " "Dear Morgan, As regards your stated wish to provide for your house-keeper, Teresa Carpenter, I would suggest . . . " "Dear Morgan, For the reasons as stated below, I recommend that your bequest to the Hatherton Public Library be distributed in three portions, the first . . . " "Dear Morgan, Further as to your bequest to . . . "

One could drown in the Solon deeps of Mr. Selby's counselings.

&

He formed the habit of taking a walk before going to bed. Which was how, at the beginning of August, he met Lawrence Cuyler and Sidney Aranov, in a late convergence at the front door of the Columbus Hotel, each of them bent on solo perambulations; but, as was normal, they nodded to each other and exchanged a few words that turned willy-nilly into sentences and finally into casual accord: why not work off their boredom by walking together?

At that hap moment their tripod friendship began.

Lawrence was Morgan's age (thirty-three); a New Yorker; a lawyer; married: "Seven weeks ago yesterday," he said—the wedding made possible by delayed orders to report to the SCTC. Morgan asked him where he had gone to law school. Answer: Columbia, with an aforeness of Exeter and Yale. "Speaking of Exeter," Lawrence went on: "I've a friend from those days—Hugh Z. Shurtliff. A relation of yours?"

Morgan said: "He's one of my favorite cousins."

Lawrence laughed: "Middle name, Zachariah. It wasn't until our senior year that he divulged what the Z stood for."

"My family's given to saddling its offspring with unusual names."

Sidney, until then a listener, said: "Zachariah's a Hebrew name. I'm sure you know what it means."

Morgan stopped walking, turned to Sidney, and, in the semi-light of the urban street, sought his eyes: "I'm ashamed to say I *don't* know. Tell me."

"Literally translated it comes out 'Jehovah hath remembered.' In your terms—Christian ones, I mean—Jehovah, of course, is God."

Morgan guffawed: "With whom, on occasion, Hugh's been known to confuse himself. He's always been a bit pontifical. . . . But he's smart. A real brain. He's a rare bird. He's stationed in Washington now, busy at interpreting the Jap codings."

They had recommenced their walk. Sidney said: "That's a heady assignment. How did he get into that line of work?"

Morgan took a moment: "He majored in Asian studies at Princeton. Started to learn Japanese when he was there. Our maternal grandfather spent his adult life as a missionary in Japan, and it's likely Hugh's original interest in Japan was sparked by family stories about him. It's odd, isn't it, how you can know someone all your life and then suddenly come to really *consider* them." Then, switching the conversation back to Lawrence, he asked: "What did the Navy have you doing before you landed here?"

Lawrence summed that he'd served as a gunnery officer on an old "four stacker" destroyer engaged in convoy escort duty between New York and Plymouth, England. Given that bit of information, it was easy for Morgan to ask him if he'd been torpedoed. "No," Lawrence answered: "Amazingly, no. We reached a point where we assumed we would be. I mean, why not? On every run but two that we made, we lost as many ships as a drunk drops dollars at a bar. But our ship was spared. . . . Clue us in about yourself, Sidney."

Sidney was a New Yorker, too. "Well," he qualified, laughing, "in a manner of speaking. *Not* Manhattan. The Bronx." Bronx-born: graduated from public high school, worked his way through Fordham University, after which he'd clerked in a bank by day and gone to Brooklyn Law School at night; "pocketed" his LL.M. degree in June of 1941, immediately took and passed the state bar exam, and: "That being done, I succeeded in convincing my rabbi's daughter I couldn't live without her, and right after we were married—just as we'd agreed I would—I enlisted. For me, until three months ago, it's been the Pacific on a light cruiser operating out of Pearl Harbor." Then, to Morgan: "Now it's your turn."

Morgan gave a vignette account of his schooling and peacetime life, concluding with a brief account of his wartime history to date.

They were near an intersection when he finished, and in the brightness of two powerful street lights, they stopped walking and peered candidly at each other, as if, out of what they had told about themselves, the time had come to add portrait to biography. And then, in a way that irreversibly joined them, somehow they laughed.

. . . It must be told about Sidney that he was a short man, barely of regulation height. "A Sephardic pygmy," he said of himself. But his torso was imposing, a wine vat whose half-sphere frontal measure was wider than his shoulder span. The fit of his shirts was a sartorial nightmare, fine at the shoulders, but across the greater expanse of his chest the cut was too tight, the fabric stretched in a way that put each button under perpetual strain. With the cloth of the shirt pulled like that, so tautly, one could actually see the impulsions of his beating heart, like soft knockings: chung, chung, chung. When he was calm, the chungs happened erratically, occurring in visually uneven spasms, and then the buttons of his shirt danced, wildly: a jig of sorts. (At one such time, Sidney, aware and laughing, said it was his lawyerly ambition to be monetarily successful— "enough"—to one day afford having his shirts made to order.)

"Archival" was the way Morgan came to describe Sidney's mind—an extraordinarily retentive one filled with incidental information he would give voice to at odd moments of kinky relation, and usually in the form of a question. Example: the time he and Morgan were studying a drawing of the Hedgehog's detonating system ("It's a single-track brain") and, without looking up from the drawing, Sidney asked: "Do you know, Morgan, that Hitler was educated by the Jesuits?"

Or, as on one Saturday night when they were drinking together in a bar, they saw a man, a tragic sinister, who had an abnormally large, hairless head an enameller had painted over with red and black and yellow snakes whose tails and bodies encoiled his thick neck and looped around his ill-formed, strutted out ears, up onto the smooth top of his broad pate where their faces were exaggeratedly depicted, orange-eyed, open mouthed, fangs showing; and Sidney, clearly sickened by the sight, said: "Poor bastard." And, looking away: "Aeschylus," he murmured. "Do you know how Aeschylus died?"

The leap made Lawrence laugh. "No."

Morgan said: "Educate us, Sidney."

So there in the bar with its dreary bamboo South Seas motif of mock-Gauguin murals and naked-breasted women, Sidney told how legend has it that an eagle, carrying a tortoise in its claws, mistook Aeschylus's bald head for a rock, and dropped the tortoise onto it, killing instantly, the great Athenian poet. "In 466 B.C.," he concluded in his complete way.

And, another time, at sight of an abundantly dark-haired, pallid-faced beauty with immense imploring eyes, Sidney said: "She's my idea of what Lola Montez must have looked like. You can just see her, can't you? in another era, vamping Austro-Hungarian royals and Muslim agas. . . . When I was fourteen—fifteen maybe—for about a month, I had a real thing about Lola Montez. Read everything I could lay my hands on about her. But my interest began to wane when I found out she was Irish by birth, real name Marie Gilbert. It was the exotic luster of her assumed name that most attracted me. She was only forty-three when she died, God knows of what combination of causes. But she must really have been something to have achieved in her time the reputation of being Europe's 'Great Adventuress,' its 'Unholy Siren.'"

"What were her dates?"

"1818 to 1861," Sidney easily answered. As shown by the way his shirt buttons were dancing, he was wound up: "Mata Hari's another case in point. Of a name overwhelming the imagination, I mean. *She* was German, born Gertrud Zelle. Not exactly a cock-rousing appellation, would you say? But *Mata Hari*. Right away, there's an associative overtone of heterodox sexuality. That she assumed *that* name as an alias to Gertrud Zelle is the answer to *why* she was such a talented spy. Which she was. Very smart. Very well rehearsed. And she was well along in years—in her late thirties—when she was busy extracting all that info from French officers back in 1915, 1917. Obtained usually on the mattress, in ecstasy's full tide. Or maybe just afterwards, by means of somnolent strokings."

You never knew with Sidney what would next be dispensed from the storage-bin of his mind, the endless surprises a part of his charm, part of his worldly melancholy, part of what made him, in lawyerly argument, so persuasive.

❧

In the cramped space of a telephone booth, Morgan had the occasional poignant pleasure of hearing Maud's voice; of listening to her alto accounts of life at home.

Sometimes, he spoke with the twins. Theirs was the awed stutter-and-spate relationship little children have with the phone. Once, he had to appeal to Julia not to shout (she was deafening him) and to his distress she burst into distant tears, asking, through sobs, *how*, if she didn't shout, would he be able to hear her? *"And,"* she wailed, "I have something *important* to tell you."

"But I *will* hear you, sweetheart. Truly I will."

In the background, Maud was helping. ("Softly, Julia. And talk more slowly. Daddy'll hear you, I promise.") So Julia, minding and modulated, though still unsuppressingly excited, moused out her news that yesterday, in the bottom of a Cracker Jack box, she had found a magic ring.

"Julia! How wonderful! Is it beautiful?" He had thought she might try to describe it.

"Yes, it *is*," was the extent of her reply. Then: silence.

"Julia?"

The laughter that came was Maud's. "She's gone, darling. Probably to the hall closet. She's spent most of the day inside it."

"Why?"

"The ring, Morgan. The *magic* ring. It shines in the dark."

"Ah."

❧

All over the world battles were begetting battles.

On September 10, they woke to the news that on the previous day, the Allies had invaded Italy, penetrating her boot at the heel.

In his new atlas, he turned to the map of Italy—something he would

do again and again for twenty months still to come, that being the cruel
length of time the campaign would last—tracking on the map the Allies'
painful, northerly advance; peering, with the aid of a magnifying glass, at
Alps crossed by Hannibal's elephants, recrossed now by caterpillar-
footed tanks; tracing the beds of rivers on whose banks opposing soldiers
were at that moment dying—rivers with ancient, mellifluous names: the
Volturno, the Sangro, the Liri, the Gargliano, the Tiber, the Po, the Arno;
locating the domed pietà cities and towns under current siege: Naples,
Florence, Pisa, Rimini, Bologna, Spezia, Genoa, Mantua, Milan, Verona,
Monfalcone. . . . (*"O! that a man might know / the end of this day's business,
ere it come."*)

On England bombs fell like rain. On Germany bombs fell like rain.

In Russia: an hourly slaughter of soldiers, civilians, children, creatures.

In the Pacific, the fighting was island to island. Some atolls, named in
the newspapers, were unshown on the atlas. And still in the enemy's
grip, the great land-masses of Burma, Malaya, the Dutch East Indies,
the Philippines.

In the Atlantic, with persistent kills of enemy U-boats, the convoy
sea-lanes between North America and Europe were becoming safer.
("Not yet *secure,* gentlemen. But yes, steady on, *safer.*")

In Miami, the hibiscus flowers kept blooming in never-ending abundance.

Morgan. Sidney. Lawrence.

They were each other's entertainment; in gloomy Miami, each other's
light; each other's solace, for in the fullness of their friendship they
sounded in their rambling talks the names of their wives—Maud,
Linda, Pamela—not to be talked *about,* but spoken *of,* in Iliad ways, as
distant inspirations. And by means of shared photographs, each came to
know the face of the others' spouses, and to the degree projected, her
force of attraction. . . . *Someday,* they told each other—someday they
would all really meet.

Each late afternoon, at the moment the boats' prows were turned land-ward, his spirits would begin to rise. Returned to the wharf, the boats moored and all his duties completed, he would set off nearly at a run to cover the ten-block distance between the wharf and the Columbus Hotel, greedy to collect his waiting mail.

Maud's letters came as regularly as dawn; his father's often. Miss Sly sent many notes ("Here is a Peter Arno cartoon I think will amuse you. . . ." "Today I adopted a male kitten, the marmalade runt of a give-away litter. I've never had a cat before. . . ." "The motor of my refrigera-tor has 'given out,' to quote my repairman, himself a tired specimen verging on a similar fate. Impossible to obtain a new one in these wartime days, so Mr. Ward is busy collecting parts from various junk-yard sources. I should hate to have to go back to using the old ice-box, resident in the basement of my house. My refrigerator's problem, emblematic of the times, has unreasonably depressed me. It's silly, I know. So minor a thing.") Each note was similarly concluded: "Yours ever, Zenobia Sly." . . . Letters came from relatives; from Judge Malcolm; from Lillie Ruth and Tessa (cards purchased through their church, the enfolded tidings, prayers); from Doctor Leigh (a now-and-again line scribbled on the run). From Lucy, messages conveyed by a lib-erated pen: accounts of London under siege from the air, of witnessed deeds performed by ordinary people on behalf of ordinary others, by any standard heroic; and Lucy's own confession "of self-satisfaction that in some small way I'm finally doing something useful with my life."

And almost unbelievably, *at last*, a short letter (forwarded by Maud) from the captain—his words inked onto the page in his precise, literal, sincere voice: "Dear Shurtliff, I hope this finds you in good health. I have a new ship, another Liberty. . . ./back in the Pacific/" (here dele-tions by a censor's scissors). "No end in sight to the war in this region. . . ./I've no news to pass on to you from our old group. I most miss the company of yourself and Sarkis. It would do me good to hear from you. Cordially, Rupert Wilkins." With an inexplicably strong sense of urgency, Morgan wrote the captain that night, hesitating only briefly over the salutation: "Sir, dear Rupert . . . It's grand to have your letter in hand. You ask for a rundown of what I've been up to since Durban, so here goes, as best I can. . . ." It was a fairly long letter sent the next day to the given address in San Francisco. As he was writing it, Morgan felt he was speaking to the captain on his ship at sea, a bobbling vessel whose position on an endless spread of ocean was findable only if you were aboard her, and only after making a navigational dusk or dawn shoot of stars, or a noon-time shot of the sun. . . . "I'll write again soon. Sincerely, Morgan Shurtliff."

Equally stirring, and again, *at last,* a letter from Geoffrey in a deliberately small script that filled every inch of the allotted one-page, Red Cross–distributed POW stationery, its tidings selective, ironically cheerful: that he was all right; that he and his fellows were being "well enough" treated; that: "From your father, via mother Red Cross, I've received two books, Chekhov's *Short Stories,* and *A Century of English Essays from Caxton to Belloc,* and from lovely Maud a buffet of tinned foods, greatly appreciated, like the books, by all. I've become a serious chess player. We hold classes: I discourse on the common law; a music theorist instructs us in harmony (I've learned all the key signatures, the intervalic make-up of chords, etc.); a botanist fascinates with lectures on plant life. Under the direction of a would-be actor in our midst, we recently staged a performance of *The Man Who Came to Dinner,* script provided by the R.C. I played a lead role (Maggie Cutler, if you know the play) and we didn't just *read* our lines, we *memorized* them. I created something of a sensation in my tail-hugging towel skirt and low-cleavage blouse (a cut-down shirt), my boobs, à la Lana Turner, fulsome enticements of rolled-up pairs of socks. Got all kinds of randy compliments. From your father's letter, I gather you've had your own ample share of adventure. He abstained from specifics, but given your branch of service, my Einstein mind can guess of what sort. It's all just a matter of moonlight and roses, isn't it." There was a bit more, a shift in tone, as of a reluctance to close. And then the vivid, validatory ending: "Love to you, Morgie. Geoff." It pierced him through. Years, since Geoff had called him "Morgie," and never before with such ability: "*Love* to you. . . ."

On Thursday, October 21, the SCTC captain sought him out and handed him an envelope, official seal embossed on its left-hand corner. Morgan withdrew the enclosed page and read its contents as the captain stood by.

"Congratulations," said the captain.

Morgan shook his extended hand, then saluted: "Thank you, sir."

In such way, he learned he had been promoted, that he was now a full lieutenant; an iota obeyer of a higher rank.

⋖§

"What next?" they asked themselves and each other as November approached, the ending days of the SCTC stint upon them.

Their orders came through on Friday, October 29: Sidney to go to the West Coast, there to board a Buckley class DE, (on which ship, as part of a far-ranging Pacific anti-submarine task force, he would serve for the duration of the war); Lawrence to report forthwith to the gunnery school in Washington, D.C., rumored as being a high-speed, super-tier training course preparatory to battleship duty. (By February 1944, he was in the Pacific, member of a battleship task force that bombarded Kwajalein Atoll at the outset of the invasion of the Marshall Islands; and in 1945, in the last days of the war, in the bombardment of Japan's mainland.)

Morgan's orders: to Boston, to the Boston Navy Yard. Duty: gunnery officer on a spanking new DE, imminently to be launched.

On the evening of the day they received their orders, they went to their customary bar. They were feeling strung—caught between what was nearly over and what was about to begin. They had their own table. It was a windy, rainy night and there was a roof-leak at one end of the bar sufficient to require a crowding at the dry end, more brightly lit than usual on this wet occasion, the greater brightness perhaps the reason for a greater than usual bray of raised voices, tonight entirely male: uniformed men in out of the weather, comfortable with themselves in ways slack, even a bit disreputable. *Louche,* one would have said of the crowd, had they been women. Morgan, searching for cigarettes in a deep pocket of his raincoat, put down on the table his penknife, some small change, the stub of a pencil, and a yellow envelope, producing at last matches and a fresh pack of Camels. He patted the envelope, and Lawrence, guessing, asked: "New pictures?"

"Arrived today."

"Give us a look."

Opulently pleased to oblige, Morgan handed them over, one at a time: a blurred snap of *Caroline* (Maud had written on the back); chasing Ralph over the lawn (Ralph too a blur, hairy-yellow); *Julia,* swinging, hair on end, caught mid-swoop of an earthward drop; the third, last one a clear semblance of the two of them sitting together on the terrace, quiet, their faces beautifully thoughtful, showing that future look he loved so much.

It was this picture Sidney held and looked at for the longest time. Then, relinquishing it, he said: "I *dream* of becoming a father."

․

On the day before he left Miami for Boston, he received from Maud a letter that told of "Ralph's amorous, night-long howlings of desire for Suzy, the Tolbin's pretty young Airedale, just come into her first heat— of Suzy's returned laments of longing for Ralph. We've agreed, the Tolbins and I, to keep Suzy and Ralph leashed until Suzy is, in Mrs. Tolbin's words, back to normal. Being kept apart like that is the way it is for us now, as hard for me as for you. Right now, thinking of you, I could weep, imagining *what* if you were here. . . ." Never before had she written with such erotic boldness. It was the single one of her many letters he destroyed, just as he knew she would never add to her ribboned collection of his wartime letters his active, unequivocal reply—no amazed eyes, chance-voyeurs to their written passion, ever later, to see.

․

Newly commissioned, she was a sophisticated, lethal beauty, her bow sheer as an arrow-shaft, her hull sleek but well hipped. Her skipper's name was Stanley Hodson, "Red" to his officer-familiars, the reason obvious: his hair. He was an Annapolis graduate, the survivor of two torpedoings he didn't at all mind talking about, and with the same panoramic enthusiasm he brought to his descriptions of past sporting events—Davis Cup challenge matches, World Series baseball games, Joe Louis's knockout of Max Schmeling ("that Kraut") back in 1938 (he had *been* there, ringside, cheering for Joe) ETC. He was amusing in a careless, hard-textured, flung kind of way. Narrowly educated, but the narrow lessons well learned: he was a brilliant officer.

Late December, under an overcast sky, they sailed out of Boston into Massachusetts Bay, commence of a "shakedown cruise" that took them up the coast, bowing well out to sea around Gloucester and Cape Ann, northeast past Portsmouth, turning north past Cape Elizabeth, bypassing Portland, into Hussey Sound, keeping in that skinny passage Peaks Island and Great Diamond Island to port, Long Island to starboard, emerging at last into the sheltered waters of Casco Bay. There, pleased with their ship's performance, they let down first anchor.

It was under Red Hodson's command that Morgan served for the rest of the war, performing what Hodson called "necessary, unglamorous tasks": searching constantly for enemy subs in the North Atlantic's near and remote waters; escorting ships ("mothering them") to their rendezvous positions in amassed convoys headed for Europe; in a general way "standing by" throughout the span of time that commenced in the first brutally cold days of 1944, through that year's spring and summer and autumn, into the start of yet another winter, further, into the New Year of 1945, on into another spring, and beyond—into the sunset days of the war's end in the late summer of 1945.

Letters remained the chief means of communication—sporadically received, those written in answer mailed at haphazard intervals from ports put in to for refueling or for the taking on of fresh supplies. As the months passed, Maud wrote more and more about her mother: "Her black moods last longer than ever...." "She stares out the window for hours on end...." "Yesterday, when I went to see her, she never said a word to me. She's lost to me, Morgan. It breaks my heart...." In a letter received in October 1944, Maud reported that a psychiatric nurse was now employed ("a starchy woman in her fifties") who came each evening to the Leighs' house and spent the night in the dressing room adjacent to Mrs. Leigh's bedroom; that widowed Mrs. Corcoran ("pleased to have the extra income") came at noon each day and "companioned" Mrs. Leigh until the night-nurse arrived—the new arrangement put into force "because Lillie Ruth can't cope anymore with Mother's withdrawals." For Morgan, the latter sentence was the most revealing of just how far Mrs. Leigh's derangement must have advanced, that Lillie Ruth, by her patient, sweet persuasions of words and reassuring touch of hand, could no longer disabuse Mrs. Leigh of her secret devils.

. . . "My dear Son—"

. . . Geoff wrote often, his letters received in batches, sorted out by date and read in sequence. None was long and all of them, in their stoicism, strangely gentle.

Received too, at wide intervals, letters from Sidney and Lawrence.

. . . "Dear Mr. Shurtliff . . . Yours ever, Zenobia Sly." Her pithy, staminal notes were as heartening as lark song.

No word from the captain, the lack thereof a source of increasing anxiety. After months of silence, he appealed to Red Hodson: "How can I find out about Rupert Wilkins?" As a survivor of two torpedoings, Hodson understood the nature of the tie that bound Morgan to the captain. Not that he said so. Communion of interior feelings wasn't his style, but taking charge, was. "Leave it to me," he said. "I have a source of info I can tap into." About three weeks went by. And then, on the first day of May, 1944, Red Hodson told him: "I received news this morning about your old captain. His ship was hit—my source doesn't say *when*— off Formosa, all hands lost. I'm sorry, Shurtliff."

᪣

From among those with whom he served on this, his last ship, he formed no lasting friendships. There were three or four men he genuinely liked, but only in daily ways, on daily terms, no one of them ever to be thought of as vital spokes in the wheel of his life.

He had no other great adventures—only existed, confined on the ship with his fellows, ever alert to danger, wearying under the deity lash of Duty and Routine, growing older, feeling Time slipping away, drawing him with it, behind.

(Of this prolonged period, some few years later, he told Sylvia

Phelps—a key, future figure as yet unmet in the narrative of his life—
that had he known back in June of 1943 that there would be two and a
half more years of war to be gotten through—in pure contemplation of
the prospect, out of sheer gloom—he might easily have gone mad.)

There were of course the occurring, great, historic junctures, learned
about at sea via the ship's radio and deeply imagined (written accounts
to be read about days later from, by then, old newspapers):

—on June 6, 1944, the long awaited Allied forces' D-Day invasion of
Europe: beach-head, Normandy—

—on August 25, 1944, the liberation of Paris—

—on October 20, 1944, the landing of U.S. forces on Leyte, the
Philippines; General MacArthur's promised "return"—

—on February 3–11, 1945, the Yalta Conference, held aboard a ship in
the Crimea, during which conference it was agreed between Roosevelt,
Churchill, and Stalin that Russia would enter the war against Japan—

—on February 19, 1945, the landing of U.S. Marines on Iwo Jima—

—on April 1, 1945, the invasion of Okinawa—

—on April 12, 1945, the stunning blow of President Roosevelt's
death; and three days later (they were just inside Monhegan Island, off
Pemaquid Point, the seas kicking up under the force of a squall) they
stood, as many as could in the close space near the radio shack to hear
Arthur Godfrey—his rube voice at moments breaking—tell of the
funeral procession moving down Pennsylvania Avenue on its way to the
White House: "The drums are wrapped in black crepe. They are muffled, as you can hear. And the pace of the musicians—so—*slow*. And
behind them . . . those are Navy boys. And now, just coming past the
Treasury, I can see the horses drawing the caisson . . . and behind it—
the car bearing the man on whose shoulders now falls the terrific burdens and responsibilities that were handled so well by the man whose
body we're paying our last respects to now—God bless him, President
Truman. . . . We return you now to the studio." Among the closely gathered listeners, there was a wordless, dazed shuffling of dispersement, of,
by hand, the brushing away of tears—

—on May 7, the surrender of Germany. V-E Day. End of the war in
Europe. That night, up off Port Clyde, they rode for a while under the

stars close enough to land to see the flames of the victory bonfires and to hear, straining to, the mingled pealings of church-bells rung in celebration. But distance, and the wash of the sea so muted the sound that some men said they couldn't hear the tollings at all; others said they perfectly well could. One man, his hands cupped to his ears, turned to Morgan and uttered the single word: "Beautiful."

—For three months longer—Boredom—vastened after V-E Day by the Atlantic's safeness and the limbo of the half-achieved end to the war, the half-win not yet somehow *experienced:* at the same time, in the Pacific, battles kept occurring, each one reported with an emphatic kind of importance which, when added up, amounted to a series of nerve-wracking, penultimate amens—until—

—*Hiroshima.* On August 6.

For the rest of his life, using the given clue of a current crossword puzzle, he would pencil in ENOLA GAY—the name of the B–29 plane that carried, hazardous (seven tons overweight), and dropped on that unheard-of city, the atom bomb, code-named (as history later taught) LITTLE BOY. At the time, the world was told of a ball of fire that became a cloud, "mushroom" in shape, that attained in the sky a height of forty thousand feet: that the crew of the Enola Gay, fleeing back to the airbase on Tinian in the Marianas, could still see the cloud three hundred and sixty miles away.

—And three days later, August 9, a second bomb (this one code-named FAT MAN) dropped on another unheard-of city: Nagasaki.

—And *then,* on August 14, as the world was told his people wept, the emperor of Japan surrendered his nation into Allied hands.

V-J Day.

The war over. Finished. All.

. . . There on their ship, the vast open sea all around them, the limitless sky overhead—beyond shouting—none of them seemed to know quite what to do. Quite how, after the shouting ceased, to conduct themselves. Some sought solitude. Others stood about in small groups, talking, being in their struck, awed ways comradely, yet the look on their individual faces remarkably blank, their eyes like shining windows, but curtained to interior view.

. . . That night, in the empty silence of his stateroom, he tried for sleep, and failing, fell back on Miss Sly's old incantation: "One good hen, two ducks, three cackling geese, four . . . "—saying the words by rote, but in the end giving up, accepting that sleep would not come. Resigned, becalmed in darkness, he lay then quiet in his berth, thinking about the future: reinventing his life.

✎

Demobilization (at least as rumor understood its arcane workings) operated on a "point" system: of age, marital status, number of children, length of service, ETC.—on which terms and degrees of qualification, Red Hodson told him: "You're a sure bet for early discharge. I'll lay you a ten-dollar wager you'll be mustered out in no more than three months' time."

It was a snail-slow, frittering wait that ended just hours this side of Hodson's prediction.

On Friday, November 12, 1945, in New York, he boarded the same early morning train he had taken at the start of his leave in May of 1943. Two and a half years ago (he thought) as he hesitated at the head of the coach, looking down its length for an unoccupied seat, affronted by the smells associated with confined soldierdom: sweat, cigarette smoke, Wrigley's chewing gum. As before, he was markedly thin, though at that instant of hesitation, he felt oddly heavy. "The tired ox," Saint Jerome said, "treads with a firmer step." As he did then, commencing a slow walk down the aisle to the coach's end, where he sat down next to a middle-aged army NCO whose eyes were closed. "Sorry to disturb you." The man never opened his eyes, just moved his torso, shucked of its overcoat (used as a pillow), closer to the window.

Throughout the journey, mood of spirit, already humbled by war's residuum effects, was further chastened by evidence, visible on all sides, of drabness and dilapidation caused by war's neglect: houses in sore need of paint; uncleaned soot-encrusted facades of public buildings; unreplaced, cracked and broken windows; unrepaired or fallen fences; rusted bridges with rusted railings; an immense, grotesque piece of corroded equipment, looking like a huge praying mantis, abandoned on the rough site of a limestone quarry; and foremost depressing, the coach in which he rode, its floor-covering abraded and gummy, upholstery torn and filthy and stinking, pocked by cigarette burns, the seats' undercoilings sprung, making for the tired traveler a back-breaking ride.

Peals of victory bells having been by now for some time silent, the soldier faces of the car's occupants showed little beyond a classic weariness tinged additionally by the alarms attendant to reversion to civilian status: myriad adjustments to be made: reclamation of personal identity: the reforming of severed relationships with family, spouses, children, lovers, friends, bosses. . . .

. . . Later that afternoon, in the Cleveland Terminal's immense rotunda (again, just as he had before) he stood in place, tall, looking for Maud. They saw each other at the same sudden instant, and as suddenly were in each other's arms, their embrace vehement; swiftly completed. When they separated from it, their eyes were moist, but not raining. Between them, wordlessly reasoned as the ability of their external strength, was sheer relief (*relief,* of all human passions, being the least ambiguous)—that out of the wreckage of war, Fate—upon *them*—had conferred the miraculous gift of a second chance.

For this meeting, she had come alone into Cleveland, her chariot the Harold Teen (showing too its greater age). In it, in the gathering November dusk, they sat in close presence—Morgan driving—skirting the urban shoreline of Lake Erie's gray sea, on, into the country with its remains of harvest: remnant stalks of corn bent earthward in fallow fields, shriveled pumpkins (a few) and shriveled crab apples still clinging to their parent trees; and other yields of autumn, wild: stands of burrs in the wayside ditches, and silvery, feathery tufts of swamp reeds, and bright orange bittersweet, strung like thousands of tiny lanterns through the leafless branches of byroad bushes. By the dashboard lights—glancing whenever he could—he saw Maud's face, its proud beauty uncharacteristically susceptible, only occasionally showing an ascendant vestige of what he always thought of as her *style:* her style of certitude: and in a part of his mind he pondered the fact that *her* life, like his, had been for a long time one of self-abnegation, individual Will, at least on personal terms, not easily assertible during the years of war.

They must have talked during the drive—*must* have—but of what they might have said, he retained no memory, the vivid stead of later recall being the sexual tension between them, at moments extreme—thoroughly suppressed by the foremost mission of "getting home."

HATHERTON. The sign's lettering, gold paint on black wood, showed in the headlights.

Soon, he turned off the highway onto a lesser road, and from it, onto a quiet street arched over by bare-branched elms; at last into their driveway. And for the first time they laughed: Tessa had made of the house an electric celebration: lights blazed from every window. He turned to Maud, his desire to mark the moment with a kiss. Impossible: the front door was so instantly opened, Tessa standing in its frame, waving, two children in white robes slipping past her, shouted at immediately by her to stay right where they were, *not*, in their bedroom slippers, to dare set foot on the damp ground, but Ralph had already bounded down the porch steps, barking, careering toward the car, the marking kiss nipped in the bud.

Out of the car then: long strides over the lawn, shortcutting the flagstone path. "*Tessa.*"

She held him. "You're *back*. Home to stay."

The night's cold air drove them all shivering, immediately indoors: children, dog, Maud, Tessa, himself the last to enter.

The twins were taller. So much taller! As of course they naturally would be, now, at age five and a half. But the photographs of them had failed to prepare him for such a leap of growth, or for their older, judging eyes (it always remained in his mind a moot question how much, *really* if at all, they remembered him) fastened on him in the living room's bright luminance in so fathomless and unforthcoming a way as to cause him to wonder if they were disappointed by what of him they saw: whether, in their afore *idea* of him, he was meant to be (at least in look) somehow more—magical. More storybook-like. Instead of which, a thin, regular man in a dark, wrinkled uniform, seeming a bit to stagger—strange, *strange* he must have seemed to them—lips trembling with emotion and quandary of what name to call each by—Maud to the rescue, seeing him so shaken, whispering in his ear: "Darling . . . Caroline, red slippers—" (the twin in the blue pair, then, Julia).

"Caroline." He stooped and kissed her and ran a smoothing thumb over her forehead's slight frown. Then: "Julia—"

—who smiled at him, a sudden, including radiance: "We go to school," she began.

"Kindeegarden," Caroline muled out the mis-said word.

Still looking at Julia, he mustered up the question: "Do you like it?"

Julia nodded. "There's a boy at school, Edward—" she said the name urgently.

"The Tates' youngest," Maud informed in a quick aside.

"What about Edward, Julia?"

Her answer came in a rush: "He can stand on his head. He's so good at it he could be in a circus if he wanted to."

Maud explained: "Edward's very much admired as a head-stander."

"Ah," he murmured. . . . Edward's was *his* great boyhood accomplishment. . . . (Do it, the Lord commanded: *Show* them.)

"Watch." He heard back the vaunted tone of his spoken imperative, and, *sans façon,* got down on his knees, put his hands flat on the floor, planted his head between them, rocked his body several times forward onto his arms, testing their strength, then gradually, gradually—coins spilling out of his pockets—raised his legs ceilingward—from which achieved, superbly maintained upside-down vantage point, he viewed the twins' amazed faces and heard Maud's sexy gasp of *"Morgan*—I never knew you *could!"* The deed done (Thank you, Lord), he collapsed his body into a ball and rolled over—*twice!*—then sprang with a lithe upward bounce onto his feet and stood, elegantly, calmly erect, gazing at his audience.

Julia pleaded: "Will you do it for Edward? Will you?" Her voice was wild. *"Will* you?"

"Anytime," he told her. "Any old time."

Now he could exit. He said to Maud: "I'm going to wash up a bit—"

"You're fabulous," she replied. "I'll bring you a drink."

వ§

In the hall, at the foot of the stairs, he recalled his dawn departure of two and a half years ago: of how, as a named warrior he had descended the staircase step by step into an absence of unforetellable outcome. Now he ascended the stairs, a returned, private man of domestic heart, hungry to "wife his wife"—beyond which Chaucerian craving, as of the moment and in all the world, for him, no other want existed.

He heard his name spoken.

From where he was standing in the middle of their bedroom he turned and saw her in the doorway, his promised drink in her hand. And for a long moment, they looked at each other.

Maud broke the silence. "You're *real*," she said, exultant. "It won't be more than two hours," she went on, tacitly conspiring: "A little time with the children; a bit of food; *then* . . . No. Don't come near me. *Not yet*." She put his drink on the table, looked at her watch, then back at him. "It's nearly seven. The two hours start now. So hurry down."

What left him speechless was what in her matchless way she had so firmly conveyed to him: that he was to her what she was to him, and that the supremest part of desire resided in the glory of being desired.

▬§

A footnote: years later he was in bed, drugged up, recovering from an operation on his left knee, Julia visiting him in his hospital room, sitting beside him, waking him after a while by a touch to his hand.

He opened his eyes: took in that she was there. "Julia. What a surprise! How lovely to see you. I hope I don't look as awful as I feel."

"You'll be up and around in no time."

"*God*."

She smiled. "You'll never guess what I was thinking just now, sitting here."

"What."

"That I'm probably the only woman on earth whose first really clear memory of her father is of him standing on his head."

▬§

A second footnote: the years of the Second World War remain as a separate epoch in the lives of all who lived through them. Nowadays, once in a while, a gray-haired man or woman will be heard to speak aloud from the soul of those years, and nine times out of ten, what the listener hears, sounds civilized. A slayer of millions was loose in the world (the speaker says) and the slayer had to be slain. And was.

Was the victory worth the cost? (The Listener, probably young and TV-reared, hence [probably], a bit suspicious, might ask.)

Yes. (The Speaker answers.)

On what grounds was the victory worth it? (The Listener persists.)

Of a clear conscience. (The Speaker answers.)

Whose? (The Listener asks.)

Mine! (The Speaker says; then asks of his testing Listener): *Is there any other?*

7 ∽ Shifts of the Shoreline Sands

Mid-November 1947

The church was filled to the limits of its capacity. In his resonant voice, word by word, the Reverend Mr. Halliday advanced the service toward its conclusion: "Into thy hands, O merciful Savior, we commend thy servant, Frances. Acknowledge, we beseech thee, a sheep of thine own fold, a lamb of thine own flock. Receive her into the arms of thy mercy, into the rest of everlasting peace." The *Amen* of the commendation having been said, the six pallbearers took their places beside the coffin. Cued thus, the organist, *vox humana*, began to play Bach's chorale *Ich ruf' zu dir, Herr,* to which minor-key phrases the pallbearers lifted the coffin and began to walk it with conformed footfalls slowly down the aisle.

The congregation stirred, breaking its silence with sighs and muffled coughings and whisperings, the stealthy suppressions suggestive of *night*—transformed in one's imagination as the faint ululations of distant owls, the far barkings of bothered dogs—such smothered sounds as seem Death's worst own, applicable to this funeral's most heart-stopping particular: suicide.

Now the primary mourners moved from the front pews into the center aisle, forming a ritual line behind the coffin, behind Mr. Halliday: Doctor Leigh first, resolute, head held high, marching by his own insistence alone; Maud immediately following, Morgan supporting her; Ansel Shurtliff next, in company with Lucy Blackett, each holding a twin's hand—Caroline and Julia having been deemed old enough, at age seven and a half, to attend their maternal grandmother's funeral ("but not the burial," Maud had determined); then Lillie Ruth on the arm of Maud's cousin, Peter Leigh, followed by Tessa and Dennis; then other Leigh relatives and a small contingent of Shurtliff relations headed by Letitia and Lewis Grant. Last, trooping together down the aisle, a veritable army of Doctor Leigh's professional associates from the Hatherton Hospital and the clinic in Cleveland: fellow surgeons, ad hoc specialists and their disciple interns, nurses, administrative personnel, which parade, after it had passed, freed the remaining congregation to abandon its pews and randomly take to the aisles, center and side.

Outdoors, the November day was not kind. A thin veil of bone-chilling mist hung over the land like a shroud. Facing into the weather, the mourners proceeded from the church to the adjacent cemetery. There, shivering, they came together around the newly dug grave.

At the foot of the grave three men holding shovels stood beside a mound of soil. "If you will, please," Mr. Halliday addressed them. The shortest of the three men touched his hand to his cap. Atop the coffin the first thud fell. Then a second, and a third. "In sure and certain hope, we commit Frances's body to the ground; earth to earth. The Lord lift up his countenance upon her and give her peace. Amen."

"Is it necessary to wait?" Doctor Leigh put the question to Mr. Halliday in a low voice.

Meaning, as Morgan interpreted the inquiry, until the grave was filled. He tightened his grip on Maud's hand: she had so stiffened at her father's question.

"It's as you feel, Doctor Leigh," came Mr. Halliday's reply.

"It will take some time. The weather's very harsh." Doctor Leigh emphasized his words by tugging at his cashmere muffler, pulling it up and out from beneath the collar of his chesterfield coat, arranging it for greater warmth around his neck. "I think it would be best to conclude the ceremony as quickly as possible."

Mr. Halliday said: "If that's your wish." He halted the work of the men with a sign of his hand and turned back to the gathered mourners who, following his lead, recited with him the Lord's Prayer, the murmur of their voices taken by the mist, lost in space. At its conclusion, he opened out his arms and held them, all including: "Almighty God, Father of mercies and giver of all comfort, deal graciously, we pray thee, with all those who mourn, that casting every care on thee, they may know the consolation of thy love; through Jesus Christ our Lord. Amen."

At once, Doctor Leigh turned to Maud and Morgan (flanked by Ansel Shurtliff, Lucy and Lillie Ruth), with the obvious intention of cueing them into step with his own immediate departure.

But Maud, clinging to Morgan, tears in her eyes, announced: "I want to stay."

"It will make for an awkward situation if you do," Doctor Leigh advised her.

A crisis, Morgan's thoughts ran: another crisis of Doctor Leigh's blind creation, its climax blessedly averted by Lillie Ruth, who touched Maud's hand and gently, perfectly told her: "There's all these folks expecting to go to the house, Maudie. Your father wants you with him to receive them." ("Receiving people" had been one of Mrs. Leigh's social phrases.) Lillie Ruth's old voice, heeded by Maud since childhood, influenced her; and Mr. Halliday, who instantly assured her: "I'll of course remain"—and Morgan, desperate for her, knowing her limits, whispered to her, "I'll stay with Mr. Halliday, darling." And Ansel Shurtliff helped by taking her hand from Morgan's clasp and with his other hand reaching out to Lillie Ruth and then, by achieving the attention of Doctor Leigh (busy now at establishing visual contact with his colleagues) with the out-loud statement (tinged, to Morgan's ears, with rare censure): "Whenever you're ready, Douglas."

The Gordian knot having been cut in his favor, Doctor Leigh at once set off, stepping as to fife and drum smartly forward in the direction of the church parking lot, his goal his home with its certain comforts of lit hearth fires, good food and drink. Behind him, Maud, tears pouring down her cheeks, in the clasped company of Ansel Shurtliff and Lillie Ruth and Lucy.

Properly, the others followed. All of them. As is said, like sheep.

Leaving Mr. Halliday and Morgan standing at the head of the grave. Mr. Halliday broke the silence: "Please go ahead now," he told the three men. Thuds of earth fell again on the coffin. Within moments, the men struck the true of a rhythmic, rapid pace. Mr. Halliday turned to Morgan: "It never takes as long as one thinks it will," he said quietly. "You ought to put your hat on, Mr. Shurtliff. It *is* very cold. If I had mine with me, I surely would"—spoken in the practical, situational voice of a military officer who tells a sub to be "at ease."

Morgan did put on his hat, and out of reflex of old habit settled himself into the wartime stance of contingent attention: legs parted in a slight V, arms resting at the sides of his body, eyes forward. In his forward-faced view, gleaming above the nearer, older tombstones, was the relatively new obelisk that marked Judge Malcolm's grave, memories of whom, fleetingly dwelt on now in this day's sad circumstance, filled him with a deeper than ever sense of loss. Beyond Judge Malcolm's grave, importantly placed on a rise of ground, was the turn-of-the-century Van Sinderen mausoleum, beneath which ivy-clad marble portico he and Maud, before they were married, used to sit for hours on a broad seraph-footed bench, talking, talking, locked in each other's arms. Ending his view was the long west side of the church with, rushing upwards, its ruling steeple piercing to shreds the filament veils of the drifting mist. Water, he thought, was Mrs. Leigh's chosen element, this wet day of her funeral an apt conclusion to her death by drowning.

Over the last six months, she had succeeded in fooling all of them, putting on a face of interest in life, declaring, with a burst of a smile, that *yes,* she *would* like to go for a walk or take a drive or come to dinner; going three times with him and Maud into Cleveland to symphony concerts; thrilling Lillie Ruth by playing the piano again (*slow* music; the first movement of Beethoven's "Moonlight" sonata, two or three *lento* preludes of Chopin, some of Mendelssohn's *Songs Without Words*—pieces learned in her youth); and she had taken to reading aloud to Caroline and Julia—*Heidi* and *Black Beauty* and *The Wind in the Willows,* and poems by Longfellow and Whittier—intoning the texts in a voice regained of its strength and velvet allure. She was "irresistibly courteous," Ansel Shurtliff said of her, his own ceremonial manners mirroring hers on those occasional times when he was visiting in Hatherton and would call on her and imbibe with her a late-afternoon glass of sherry.

Throughout these recent months, Morgan had been continually baffled by Doctor Leigh's seeming indifference to his wife's emergence from shadow into sunlight: that he gave no sign of welcoming it; did not rise to greet it; did not partake of it. It was almost as if he begrudged her her reappearance. "The abatement of her mental imbalance." "Her improved state of mind." Such were the words he uttered from the sidelines. A couple of weeks ago, Morgan had seen Mrs. Leigh looking at Doctor Leigh wistfully, as if she were viewing him in a distant context of charm and pleasure. They had been married in the summer of the year he had completed his internship at Massachusetts General Hospital and she had graduated from Smith College. It was odd (as Morgan now thought of it) that he did not know how they had met; in just what way chance had thrown them together. A party at the Boston home of a mutual friend? An introduction made by an acquaintance while on a Sunday walk in Fenway Park? Once upon a time they must have been happy. Maud was sure of it, recounting childhood memories of how lively they had been, how they exuded "fun"; of watching them kiss; of standing in their open bedroom door when she was five or so and seeing the reflection in the cheval mirror of her mother's long thick hair unpinned, loosened down over her shoulders, her father playing with it, gathering it up like soft hay into a bundle and burying his face in it laughing.

How well she had fooled them! To a point where, last June, the latest of a long line of nurses (all despised by her) was dismissed; Mrs. Corcoran, though, retained, but only as a stand-in for Lillie Ruth on Lillie Ruth's days off, and at such times (not infrequent) when Doctor

Leigh, pending dawn surgery at the clinic, stayed overnight in Cleveland.

Ah, her cunning! All summer long she had been fascinated by the swallows that nested in the huge old barn at the rear of the Leigh property, praising the construction of the birds' nests, applauding their dawn-to-dusk energy. She had had Dennis place a wicker chair right in the center of the barn, directly under the criss-cross of beams that sustained the grandeur of its Victorian cupola. "My throne," she called the chair in which she sat for rapt hours watching the swallows. *Hirundo rustica* was their Latin name. "Come with me, Morgan, and see my birds." How many times had he gone with her to the barn? Eighteen? Twenty? "Look how they *dash*"—tracking with her eyes the blue and tan of a fork-tailed streak. "Like comets." Listen to the young ones, she would say. Such a happy racket! She extolled the barn's other allurements: the perpetual hum of bees, the comings and goings of mud-daubers always busy at adding to their mud hives, the sleepy fragrance of old straw and old wood, the nostalgic smell of leather saddlery left hanging in the tackroom. Under her enthroned aegis, Julia and Caroline grew too to love the barn. "A magic place," they called it, using their grandmother's words. If you had to title the story, it would be called *The Summer Weeks of the Barn's Enchantments,* told wonderfully aloud by Frances Leigh. Who could have guessed that her hours spent in the barn involved another story, *un*told, of a plot in the make. *Things,* never mentioned: a cinder block lying on the floor beside the old horse-trough; a long length of rope coiled around a wall-spike; a rusted crowbar leaning aslant in the frame of the north window. And directly behind the barn, near the foot of a sassafras tree, the well: lidded over by a round wooden top fitted at the middle with an iron handle.

In mid-October, all on the morning of the same day, the swallows flew away. Just short of a month later (last Monday, after lunch), Mrs. Leigh went to her room to take her ritual afternoon nap. This was the hour known as "sacred" to her family and friends, when she was never to be disturbed. This was the routine time too for Lillie Ruth—Dennis driving her—to go marketing. Monday, too, was Doctor Leigh's "regular" day at the clinic in Cleveland.

Lillie Ruth and Dennis left the house about two-thirty. They were back by a quarter to four. Lillie Ruth said she had "a feeling" that something wasn't right the minute she and Dennis walked through the back door. She didn't even take off her hat or drop her coat, just went straight up the back stairs to the second floor, down the hall to Mrs. Leigh's room, knocked on the door, got no answer, turned the knob, entered the room's emptiness: saw the piece of paper on the bed. "My time has come," was the message written on it. *"Dennis,"* she had wailed. They went from room to room to room, calling, searching the whole big house, attic to cellar. Closets, too. Nowhere. Outdoors then, running, Lillie Ruth circling the house, calling; Dennis through the garden, running over the lawn's extent, skirting the outside edge of its hedged boundary, then back, the two of them converging from opposite directions at the barn's wide front door, left open by Dennis when he'd taken the car out. The barn silent; empty. *But:* its narrow *back* door open—the well, uncapped—seen beyond. "Call the police," Dennis told Lillie Ruth. . . . No more than ten minutes before Officer Bailey arrived; a bare few more before the ambulance careened into the drive, the fire truck too, sirening, men storming out of the vehicles, running to the back of the barn.

As Officer Bailey put it to Morgan that evening: "The way she did it, Mr. Shurtliff, she couldn't fail."

The crowbar: used as a lever to pry up the well's wooden lid and slide it off to the side. The long line of rope: one end wound around the trunk of the sassafras tree, secured by two knots; a portion of the other end bound and tightly knotted around the ankle of her left leg, the rope's terminus end threaded through the cinder block's open center and knotted a resolute three times. On the well's limestone edging were the scraping marks made when she had shoved the cinder block forward for its advance descent down the well's shaft, herself following a split-second after, the cinder block striking the water, sinking to the well's deep bottom, anchoring her with it in liquid entombment.

"It's nearly done," Mr. Halliday said.

The men were tamping down the soil with the backs of their shovels. The shortest of the trio again touched his hand to his cap: "We'll set in the grass turf tomorrow, Reverend. Anything more for now?"

"Thank you, no." Mr. Halliday spoke to each man: "Much obliged to you Willy, James, Fred." Morgan shook their hands. Then the men, carrying their shovels, went away.

There was one last thing to be done: the laying onto the grave of a cross of white lilies. "Let's do it together," said Mr. Halliday. They stooped and picked it up. The lilies' heavy scent seemed the most the cross weighed. They placed it on the grave. ("She's been lifted up, Morgan, like Elijah and Moses, into the Lord's presence." So Lillie Ruth had told him yesterday.)

In the last few minutes, the mist had thickened into a drizzle. "You must be at least as cold as I am," Mr. Halliday remarked. Warmth and a change into dry clothes would be most welcome, he went on to say. But even damp and chilled as they were, they did not hurry away from the grave, but departed it companionably at a meditative pace. "I'm thankful Lucy Blackett's here," Mr. Halliday said. "Most thankful for Maud's sake. Such a strong friendship, theirs. Sisterly. Very rare." The rhetoric of Mr. Halliday's sermons flowed, but in conversation he tended to speak in jerks or cognitive clumps. "Until yesterday at your house, I'd not seen Lucy for years," he went on. (Since the end of the war, Lucy had been living in New York.) "She's become a great realist. Totally different from the shy illusionist she used to be. I suppose it was her wartime experiences that wrought the change." They were at the point on the gravel path where it forked—one way to the parish house, the other to the church parking lot. "You're all right, Mr. Shurtliff?"

"Oh, yes . . . I was thinking about your word—'illusionist.'"

"*Innocent* might be a better one to describe how Lucy *was*. For that matter—how we *all* once were." His smile was wan, and like his eyes it roved past Morgan toward the cemetery. "Well, we must think about getting on to Doctor Leigh's."

"Yes. I'll see you there in a few minutes."

❧

He entered the Leighs' house to a racket of voices. A white-jacketed caterer's attendant took his coat and told him that Doctor Leigh was in the library: "That way; the second door on your left." The hall was filled with doctoral strangers out from Cleveland. A bald, portly man, emanating sympathy, nabbed him: "You're Douglas's son-in-law, right? I'm—" (his name lost in the buzz around them). "Awfully sorry about Mrs. Leigh. I met her once a long time ago. Yes, I'm at the clinic. Bones and joints."

Lewis Grant gripped Morgan's arm: "Sorry to interrupt, but there's a Mrs. Baxter, Morgan, very befuddled, who says she wants to see you before she goes. She's over there—"

"*Ah.* Thanks, Lewis. She's an old, old friend of Mrs. Leigh's."

"Don't let me keep you," the bones-and-joints man said.

"Thank you for coming," Morgan told him. He crabbed his way to Mrs. Baxter's side.

"Morgan," she said, and instantly began to cry. "I *loved* Frances." She dabbed her eyes, her handkerchief held in a hand crippled by arthritis. "I shouldn't have come, but I wanted to see Maud for a moment. And now I must go. No, really, I *must.* I came in a taxi, but your uncle insists on having Dennis drive me home. Is that all right?"

"It's exactly right. Let me see you to the car." It took some doing, threading her, cane and all, through the crowded hall and down the steps of the front porch. Under the porte-cochere, Dennis was standing beside the car.

Mrs. Baxter greeted him. "Thank you so much, Dennis. I'm such a nuisance. Will you and Maud come to see me soon, Morgan? And bring the children."

"We will, I promise, very soon." He unfolded Mrs. Leigh's old plaid rug and spread it over Mrs. Baxter's knees. "Good-bye." Dennis eased the car forward.

Back in the house, Babs Waring stopped him. "Why haven't you got a drink?"

"I haven't had a chance to get to the source." He was immensely fond of Babs.

"Take this." She thrust the glass she was holding into his hand. "It's bourbon. Just poured. I've had two, so I'm well fortified. I hate funerals. Maud told me she wanted a small service, family and Mrs. Leigh's close friends. Not this horde." She looked around: "This medical mob . . . I doubt the ones from the clinic ever even met Mrs. Leigh." Then, caustically: "Doctor Leigh always manages to get his way, doesn't he? I could have wrung his neck back at the cemetery. Sorry. I'll worry I said that." She shifted gears: "I told Maudie that as soon as the two of you *can,* there's a man I want you to meet."

"Ah." He knew Babs well. "Someone you really like," he stated, smiling.

"Yes. A lot." (Babs's husband, Bob Waring, had been killed in Germany the last winter of the war.) "He's a professor of physics at the University of Chicago. He'll be coming to Cleveland over the Christmas holidays. Maybe then?"

"For sure. You look terrific, Babs. I'm very glad for you."

"I'm awfully glad for myself, Morgan." She peered at him: "You're exhausted, aren't you. I've made a date with Maudie for lunch next Wednesday." She kissed him on the lips: "You'd better circulate."

. . . "Mr. Shurtliff? We've not met before, but Douglas has told me so much about you, I feel I know you. I'm Imogene Truffant. I work in administration at the clinic." She was wearing a black pleated skirt and a pink blouse with a frilled front that emphasized her considerable mammary endowments. Morgan put her age at around forty. "It's too bad about Mrs. Leigh." She lowered her voice: "The *circumstance,* I mean. Douglas is being so heroic, don't you agree? Of course, she's been mental for *so* long, it must almost be a relief to Douglas. . . . This is such a beautiful house," she yammered on, footed beside him as if forever. "This is the first time I've seen it—"

"Lucy," he said, thankful for the sight of her. He attempted an introduction: "Miss Blackett, Miss—"

"We've met," Lucy said, cold as ice. "Your father's looking for you, Morgan."

"Truffant. Imogene Truffant," the woman impressed on Morgan.

"That was a ruse," Lucy told him as they walked away. "Your father's *not* looking for you. I got trapped by that woman earlier on. She's something else. I think she has it in mind to be the second Mrs. Leigh. *"Douglas,"* Lucy cooed, pursing her lips, imitating the way Miss Truffant had said Doctor Leigh's name. "The trick is to keep her away from Maud."

"Where is Maud?"

"In the living room with the real people."

"I need another drink."

They angled their way to a make-shift bar set up by the caterers in a bay-windowed alcove at the end of the hall. From out of the library Doctor Leigh appeared, the boom of his voice urging a trail of his fellows forward toward the bar and the dining room. Bernard Carlin, one of Doctor Leigh's Shaker Club cronies, said: "Here come the healers, Miles Dawson with them. He's in charge of my wife's ulcer. I'm shoving off." Morgan told the bar-attendant that he would pour his own drink, and did. Lucy, viewing the generous splash, murmured: "Easy, love. You've still got a long way to go."

The living room best reflected Mrs. Leigh's younger years. In it were the possessions her family had given her at the time of her marriage, or that had come to her later by inheritance: a fine set of Hepplewhite side chairs; austere portraits of her Puritan ancestors; a splendid pastoral painting by Bibie; her Steinway piano; a gem of an open-fronted Biedermeier cabinet containing her collection of Victorian hand-painted boxes and eccentric porcelain animals (notably an orchestra of antic monkeys). The room's spacious extent was divided into islands of grouped chairs and couches. From the doorway, Morgan scanned the faces of the room's occupants: Peter Leigh, the Howes, the Caspers, Mr. Halliday, Mrs. Blackett (Lucy's mother), Ansel Shurtliff, Lillie Ruth, Letitia and Lewis Grant, two of his cousins (one out from Cleveland, the other come from Cincinnati), Bill Minot (his one-time rival for Maud's hand, Bill still a bachelor, still Maud's favorite tennis partner); the rest of the sizable company composed of what Lucy called "Hatherton's old guard," now grouped in a circle around Maud. Included in the circle were Clara Malcolm (in the widow's black she had kept to since Judge Malcolm's death) and Mrs. Beresford and Fanny Coates (always referred to by Mrs. Leigh as "my dear, dear friend"). It flashed through his mind to wonder what the members of this circle of Mrs. Leigh's intimates would say in answer to Maud's question put to him last Monday night in her first wild grief: "What made her do it, Morgan? What was it that made her do it?" He had not told her his immediate sprung-to-mind answer, which came from Thomas Middleton (that acerbic Jacobean dramatist Geoff Barrows had recently put him on to) who, in his play *The Changeling,* gives to De Flores the famous, double-edged line to say: "Y'are the deed's creature." He had only wordlessly held her in his arms and in the dark stroked her hair and at the spent end of her lamentation, at her vivid request, made love to her, she savagely, and he with her— pagans countervailing Death.

He entered the room, went straight to Maud, kissed her, and stood silently behind her, his hands on her shoulders. Fanny Coates was launched on the sea of a story about going with Mrs. Leigh years ago to an auction at which Mrs. Leigh had somehow managed to twice pur- chase the same pair of Meissen candlesticks. "It was the rampant way she bid that got the auctioneer and his assistant confused beyond redemption. Not to mention the unfortunate man she was bidding *against.* We were all drawn into the muddlement, Frances too, laughing at herself, looking awfully pretty in a brown velvet hat banded with blue flowers. The auctioneer *insisted* on starting the bidding over again from scratch, and we all applauded the second time he banged down his gavel and called out—'Sold, *once,* and at one price, to the lady in the beautiful hat.' Frances was radiant."

Under his hands, Maud's shoulders were level; relaxed. "I'm sure I remember that hat," she said.

"In those days, Frances's hats were her signature," Fanny Coates went on. "I can't think now of the woman's name who made them for her."

"Mrs. Polhemus," Mrs. Beresford shot in.

"Good for you, Ella. Vera Polhemus. She kept a parrot in the back of her shop. A vulgar, noisy bird."

Maud's laughter came, unrestrained, marvelous to hear.

The talk ran on, others joining in, developing as in a fugue the subject of Mrs. Leigh's hats. The group broke up when Fanny Coates announced that she must depart. "If I *can,*" she said. "I'm *stuck*" (in the couch's deep cushions) "like Theseus in the Chair of Forgetfulness." She laughed. Morgan and Bill Minot hoisted her to her feet. She whispered to Morgan, "May I have a private word with you?" Which, in the front hall, standing close to him, she bespoke: "It's about Frances's suicide,

Morgan—" She broke off, opened her purse, withdrew an unsealed envelope and handed it to him. "I've written down my thoughts about it for Maud. It might help her to—*understand*. But you read it first, please. You might think it too much for her to bear." And before he could say a word, she charged on: "Now *please*, please don't dream of seeing me to my car. I can manage perfectly well on my own. It was only getting out of that couch—" She turned from him, went rapidly to the front door, opened it—letting in a whiff of cold dusk air—closed it, and was gone. The envelope fitted perfectly into the breast pocket of his suit coat.

The roisterings coming from the dining room suggested a cocktail party in full swing. In the gentler dignities of the living room, the sound resonated almost as an embarrassment. His aunt, Letitia Grant, said to him: "There's always some note struck at gatherings like this that's out of tune with one's own feelings." Clara Malcolm was kissing Maud good-bye, Mrs. Blackett at her heels. The hands of the mantel clock were joined at 5:25. There was a general stir of departure. From his stand in the dining room, through its wide doorway, Doctor Leigh must have seen the hall filling up with the living room's occupants: must have noticed how coats were claimed, the action of arms finding their way into sleeves and then the arms stretched out to Maud—recipient of final embraces. For he came into the hall, effusive and a bit breathless, like an elder senator of thundery repute who has torn himself from committee in order to greet a visiting body of constituents—or rather to see them off—apologizing for having had so little time to spend with them. He was somewhat overwhelmed, he explained, by the large turn-out of his clinic colleagues. "Impossible to be everywhere at once . . . Good-bye. Most grateful for your support," he kept saying, dry-eyed, shaking hands. "Good-bye." From inside the front door he delivered a last wave to no one in particular, hence to everyone in general.

"We must go too," Morgan told him.

"Is it so late?" he asked, frowning at the sight of Maud and Lucy and Ansel Shurtliff putting on their coats.

"Nearly six."

"Really! I'd no idea."

Maud's voice came clear: "The children and Tessa—" she began.

"Naturally," Doctor Leigh cut her off. "I do wish though you'd stay a bit longer. There are two or three people I'd particularly like you to meet. No? Well, another time." Then, to Lucy and Ansel Shurtliff: "You'll be here another day or two? Splendid. So I'll surely see you."

Maud tried again: "We'll be having dinner at seven. It would be nice if you could join us."

"I doubt I'll be able to—"

"Or drop by later for a nightcap," Morgan interjected, thinking ahead to how empty the large house would be, feeling an impulse of pity for its relic occupant.

A needless concern, as proved by Doctor Leigh's sure reply: "I'm planning to turn in early. *Must* get back to normal. I've a full schedule next week." He kissed Maud and Lucy, each in the same way, a light laying-on of his firm lips to their cheeks. He wrung Ansel Shurtliff's hand; then Morgan's, at the same time saying: "There are some legal matters I'd like to ask you about."

"The weekend," Morgan said.

"Fine. Good night. Good night." Before they were out the door he had turned from them and was on his way back, hurrying, to the dining room.

He thought she was asleep, but in the dark there was the sudden presence of her voice, low but terribly active—like the hum of a high-velocity top spinning on such a muffling surface as a square of linoleum or the cover of a many-paged book—telling him what of the day she remembered as hideous, what enlightening, what inexcusable, what clear, what dim, what shattering: "My father, Morgan . . . I won't ever again be able to kid myself into thinking I like him or can trust him. Not after today. *There,* I've *said* it—" her sigh a desolation, the top beginning to wind down, the murk of her voice now almost a dreamer's as, through a few more rotations still out-loud remembering, she finally dropped over into sleep.

Wednesday evening, 12 November 1947

Dear Maud,

   *I want to keep this letter as brief as possible. It is necessary that I
tell you a bit of personal history. When I was in my late twenties, I
suffered a lengthy period of depression that was called back then "a
nervous collapse." There was no readily seeable cause for it, no reason
I could give then (or now) for it. It simply came on me, a darkness at
noon. The clouds hung over me for several months, then went away.
The nerve specialist into whose care my distraught family had
placed me pronounced me cured, at the same time warning me and
my family that what he called "my proneness toward depression"
would in all likelihood trouble me all my life and be something of a
constant struggle to overcome. I cannot deny the truth of his
prophecy. A great part of my adulthood has been given over to the
struggle, the worst part of which is fear of backsliding into gloom.*
   *The last time I saw your mother (a week ago today), she confided
to me her "terror" that she was lapsing back into isolation. She used
that word, isolation. She said she couldn't stand the thought of
another nurse being brought in to police her, that her idea of living
was not to linger on "crazy." My own experience with such
sufferings credits me the right to say that I understand her preference
to spare herself the prolonged effects of a condition painful beyond
my ability to describe. What she did took courage. I am absolutely
sure that she employed the last of her clarity of mind to leave this
world solely for her own self's sake.*
   *I have no tolerance for anyone who might presume to think
himself good enough or wise enough to pass moral judgment on her
mode of exit.*

Affectionately yours, Fanny Coates

❧

He read the letter the next morning, and over the next few hours pondered the wisdom of giving it to Maud. In the end, he sought Lucy's
advice.

They took an afternoon walk together while Maud rested. At the
edge of the open meadow he handed the letter to Lucy with the question: "Should I give this to Maud?" They stood in place as she read it,
the wind rattling the two pages held in her gloved hands. "Oh," she
murmured, half-way through it, struck; and when she had finished:
"What a shit problem."

It made him laugh—her slinging of the apt profanity, employed for
precisely the purpose it had achieved—of making them *both* laugh, lifting the load of the letter's burden and giving her the lead to ask: "Did
you develop the habit of the four-letter word during the war? To the
point, I mean, where you had to *think* when you got home, *not* to let one
slip out?"

Morgan laughed again: "Sort of. I had a gunner, a guy named
Sutter"—he relished Sutter's name on his tongue again—"who had a
terrific command of obscenities, enough for all of us. He could string
them together the way Cartier strings pearls. One perfectly matched flit
after another."

"I knew an RAF paratrooper in London who could too. He told me
he'd perfected his talent as a youth at Eton. He got himself killed in the
Normandy landings, four-lettering to the end, I'm sure. I've thought a
lot about the war these last three days. It's being back with mother—"
She touched his arm: "Careful—a woodchuck hole."

"Go on with what you were saying."

"About being back with mother, you mean, and thinking about the
war? It's no big revelation, only that it's made me see more clearly than
ever that if it hadn't been for the war I'd still be living with her, still be
playing the role of the dutiful daughter, growing African violets and taking harp lessons and being jealous of my married friends and going quietly mad. . . . Just being under the same roof with her—" Lucy made a
gesture of helplessness. "Oh, Morgan, you know how black and white
her standards are, and about me and the war and men and *sex*"—under-
scored by inflection and with a frown—"my late discovery of it and the

way I've used it, not always wisely. Mother hasn't an inkling of all that. She's still stunned that I'm not living with her; she speaks of my living in New York as a 'phase' I'll get over. And she'd drop dead if she knew about Gerry. Her daughter in a messy affair with a married man? *Unthinkable*."

Lucy's relationship with Gerald Davis was one of the many conditions of surprise of the war's aftermath, long since accepted by him and Maud for what it was: *change:* a familiar shoreline whose sands a hurricane has shifted. . . . They had met in England in 1944 and become lovers: Gerry, an American army lieutenant; married; father of two young children; an architect by profession, his work and home well established in New York before the war, and Gerry, at war's end, returned to life as he had left it; Lucy, to be near him, living now and working (still for the Red Cross) in New York. "How is Gerry?" Morgan asked.

"Hopelessly the same, abetted by me. Unable to split up his home—he adores the kids—both of us sort of settled with things as they are, not pushy about a solution. We always love seeing you when you're in New York."

"I have to be there in a couple of weeks. I talked to Maud a couple of days ago about going with me. She wants to, but it'll depend on Julia and Caroline. It's still a bit early to tell what's going on in their heads and hearts about Mrs. Leigh's death. So far, they seem all right. They keep asking a lot of questions, more or less on the order of the one Caroline asked me this morning—"

"What was it?"

He smiled. "'How much do angels *weigh?*' she wanted to know."

Lucy smiled too: "What did you tell her?"

"The truth. That I didn't know. That I'd never wondered. She seemed awfully pleased that she'd thought of something I hadn't."

"Caroline *would*. They're so different, aren't they, Callie and Julia? I don't know why I assumed that as twins they'd be more alike. But they're night and day."

"Which do you think is which?"

"As if you don't know! Julia's the night. Callie's the day. Completely noon-time." Lucy laughed: "When she grows up, she'll be a really flamboyant woman. Julia's the deep one."

They walked on, in accord, with a companionate ease. And after a moment. "It's great between you and Maud, isn't it." Lucy stated.

"Yes. Very." But because she had sounded so wistful, he humanized his so-positive response with: "Not that the seas of marriage always run smooth." A crow flew over, calling. From an unseen tree a second crow answered the call of the flying one. "Crow talk," he said. Then: "About the letter, Luce. Unless you persuade me to the contrary—"

Her perceptions had always been as sharp as a chef's knife: "But we *agree*," she cut in: "You mustn't give it to Maud. The problem is Fanny Coates."

They exchanged a look of complete understanding. He said: "I think I can find a way not to hurt her."

"It won't be easy. She meant well."

"Maybe just skirt the issue by telling her the time's not right. . . . What are your reasons for withholding it from Maud?"

"Its *tone*." Lucy was fast: "Its all-seeingness. What are yours?"

"The same," he answered. "That it's too definite. *That,* and its kind of—*anger*." He could have gone on, elaborating about the letter's effect on himself: that its certitudes tended to thwart his personal need to question and to wonder, which questions and wonderings, by the very nature of their search, would keep him more closely in touch with a preferred memory of Mrs. Leigh as a beloved exaggeration of his own grapplings with life's everyday devils. He only said: "I'll square it somehow with Fanny Coates. . . . *Look!* There's Ralph"—seen, hell-bent, running toward them: "God, he's been in the creek again. *Down,* boy"—Ralph a wet-haired mess, big paws muddy, mouth opened in a drunk's grin of joy at having met them on the meadow's avenue. *"Down!"*

But Lucy was gleeing with Ralph, petting him, rumpling his ears, exclaiming: "He's such an optimist, Morgan. Such a real, true-blue believer!"

Morgan laughed: "About what I'm not sure, but I certainly know what you mean." And, looking at Lucy, appreciating her: "You're wonderful, Luce."

"Tell it to the Marines," she cocked at him. And, quickly, with a closer emphasis: "Or better still, to Gerry next time you see him." And further, with appeal: "You pray for me, and I'll pray for you. Okay?"

"Okay."

They turned and started back across the meadow, walking slowly arm in arm, Ralph in his bliss cavorting around them.

On Sunday, Ansel Shurtliff returned to his home amidst his orchards, now in winter hibernation. And Lucy went back to New York. And on the next day Caroline and Julia went back to school. And Morgan back to the law, his office now a high juridical aerie in Cleveland's Union Commerce Building: sixteen months ago he had joined the Kissel, Chandler firm. Judge Malcolm had lived just long enough to congratulate him.

On ordinary mornings he left the house for the drive into Cleveland around a quarter to eight, after breakfasting with Maud and Julia and Caroline, after good-byes to them and Tessa and Ralph (handshake of a lifted paw). But on this first Monday morning after Mrs. Leigh's death, the ritual altered: he and Maud said their good-byes in the privacy of his study. "You'll be all right?" he asked her, holding her face between his hands, seeking to read her eyes.

"I've got to be," she answered, shaky, her emotions all on the surface.

"What time is Lillie Ruth coming?" He was counting on Lillie Ruth.

"At ten."

"I'll call you at lunch-time."

They told each other the best words: *I love you.* He picked up his briefcase. "Your gloves," she said. "Don't forget your gloves." And he left her, feeling that he could, for when he kissed her she had mustered up a smile for him.

&

One of the negotiated conditions of his move to Kissel, Chandler had been that he retain his partnership with Judge Malcolm in the Hatherton firm. After Judge Malcolm's death the Hatherton firm, as per agreement, was merged with Kissel, Chandler, and from his Cleveland office Morgan presided over it on a de jure, de facto basis, the on-the-scene running of it left in the hands of a junior partner and two associates. Thus it remained intact, prospering, and still honoring Judge Malcolm's name. About the arrangement, Morgan was not shy to express his pleasure.

Nor was he shy of professional pride at having become a member of the Kissel, Chandler firm.

Roger Chandler, the firm's founder, remained its perpetual surpriser. At sixty-eight years of age, he still gave off a whiff of being something of a boy wonder. He was exuberantly energetic. Always had been. His intelligence, his charm, his legal brilliance were all in place. Always had been. *Plus,* as he said of himself (never when a lady was present), he'd been born *not* with a silver spoon in his mouth, but with a silver horseshoe up his derriere: "Luck is my middle name." Twenty-five years ago, when he had decided to start his own firm, he publicly avouched that it would be "a great one," and went to work to make it so. And succeeded; to such extent that, now, there were adjunct Kissel, Chandler offices in Pittsburgh and New York and Washington, between which offices he regularly (in his words) "rode circuit." He was a terrific litigator. He argued a case the way a brick-layer lays bricks, one solid word at a time, perfectly placed and carefully cemented in the wall of his argument. Over the years it was said of him that he was at least "acquainted" with everyone worth knowing. "Rumor," he said of this charge: "Pure rumor." But at an apropos moment, he would recount to you the circumstance that had provided him the chance to shake Will Rogers's hand and Amelia Earhart's. And one evening, at Henry Luce's home, Chiang Kai-shek's. His "longest brush with *artistic* fame was an after-dinner game of bridge, two of the players yours truly and—don't even bother to guess—Artur Rubinstein." (Over this memory he always particularly smiled.) And there were many unceremonious photographs, such as the one of him sitting with John Foster Dulles on someone's garden bench, both men hatless and coatless and tieless, which informality of dress told a lot about *their* "acquaintanceship." And it was recorded in print that two journalist luminaries of the time—Ed Murrow and John Gunther—referred to him as "my friend." Much, much more could be told about Roger Chandler. But not here; not now. On this November morning,

Morgan felt he had hardly begun to know the man. Geoff Barrows had recently asked him: "What's your sense of him these days?" "Still as something very large." "Such as?" "A many-roomed mansion glimpsed from a distance by a passenger in a speeding car."

Since the firm's beginning, Nicholas ("Nick") Kissel had headed its Trusts and Estates department. In legal jargon, he was what is called a "belt and suspenders lawyer," which is to say very careful; prudent; stubborn about being *sure*. A deep memory and longer than an elephant's. Quiet. He never unsheathed his legal dagger unless driven to, and when he did, watch out. Now seventy years old (and not in the best of health), he was due to retire at the end of this year, 1947, and it was Morgan whom he and Roger Chandler had chosen to take over the T and E department (official date of enthronement January 1, 1948).

On one wall of Nick Kissel's office was a large topographical map of the rich mass of land that lies between Cleveland and Pittsburgh. "America's Ruhr valley," Nick Kissel called it. Or, alternately: "The cradle of America's economic power." He would go on, gonging up the names of John and Andrew and Henry. John D. Rockefeller and Andrew Carnegie and Henry Clay Frick, that is, to mention but three of the original makers of fortunes wrested from the map's depicted terrain. Most of the original "making" group of such vast fortunes as these were now all dead, but their main-tree, many-branched descendants were very much alive and very much in evidence, some of them Kissel, Chandler clients: "Up to you, Morgan, to keep them with the firm." Toward which end, over the last sixteen months, Nick Kissel had spent a great deal of time with Morgan in the study of client files, "backgrounding" him in family histories, confiding to him the individual temperaments of clan members (*and* their in-laws)—*varied* temperaments— that made for such current cases as (in one steep instance) a will contest; in another, a child-custody fight; in another instance, a defamation suit brought by one sibling against another. Endless—the fateful human equations and quagmires that require the law's protection.

By now, Morgan had met and come to know for himself a majority of the firm's T and E clients, a surprising number of whom no longer lived in Cleveland but in New York City. To better serve this latter group, he had sought and gained admittance to practice in New York State, and so these days was often to be found in the Kissel, Chandler New York office: location 120 Broadway—where, from his desk on the thirtieth floor, he had a reach of view that soared like a gull above the tip-end of lower Manhattan out and over the great nautical commotions happening on the harbor waters (commotions that distance made casual), beyond, to the heaven-raised, torch-holding hand of the Statue of Liberty.

. . . "Up to you, Morgan, to keep improving the way the department functions," was one of Nick Kissel's exhortations. Another: "Up to you, Morgan, to bring a new generation of clients to it." "Up to you, Morgan, to keep its reputation shining." ETC. And his obsessive last words: "As long as you stay focused and run scared, you'll do just fine."

In November of 1947, *was* Morgan running scared? You bet. And— as he had recently told Geoff Barrows—"thrilled shitless to be."

❧

Two years before, when he was just home from the war, Maud had remounted her campaign against Julia's calling him by his name. For the campaign he had little heart, and told Maud so. "You won't, though, interfere with *my* efforts?" Maud had asked. No, he had answered, he wouldn't; qualifying: "Let's agree to keep an open mind about it. All right?" They were too immensely happy to quarrel over it. Not that their happiness reconciled their differences, only that, as to their differences, their happiness kept them honest. So, in the daylight, on her own, Maud pushed her cause along, gently, ever gently; persistently. It became something to see, Julia's child's mind from moment to moment working at remembering to call him "Daddy"—but at every instance of her young life that was brilliant, forgetting.

"*Look*, Morgan"—at the breathtaking descent of a falling star.

"Morganmorganmorgan, watch me *do* it!"—on the evening of the day she mastered riding her kid-dinky, two-wheel bike.

"*Caught* you, Morgan"—during a snowy game of Fox-and-Geese, and on the black ice of the frozen pond during a contest of Slide Simon: "Morgan! *Wow!*"

The campaign only lasted about three months. It ended abruptly, in the following way: at breakfast one morning he somehow, by some maladroit move, knocked over his full glass of orange juice and his cup of coffee, himself immediately transfixed by what he had done, and Maud and Caroline immobilized too, just sitting dumbfounded in their chairs (*disgrace*—the judgment in Caroline's wide eyes) silent and staring at the mess of the flooded table and at his shirt splattered of Halloween colors, orange and black, and at the disgusting affair of his drenched pants. Not Julia, though—her arms flung out to him in impulsive sympathy, and her voice too, keening for him: "*Morgan!* Poor, poor dear Morgan."

God, how he loved her!

A few minutes later, after the mess had been dealt with and he was back upstairs changing his clothes, Maud came into their bedroom and all in a hurry threw up her hands and called out: "Morgan, I give up!" When she did this—that is to say, as it was for two seconds actually *happening*—in the way she flung up her hands and in the way her voice sounded, he *saw and heard* Julia. And in that flash of time understood *why* Julia called him "Morgan." Because *Maud* did. Maud: her mother: her example. "I give up—" Maud had said again, this time laughing. "It's fixed in her to call you by your name. I'll never forget it, the way it just— *came out.* 'Morgan. Poor, poor dear Morgan.' Her lovely pity for you."

He stood there in his gartered socks and his Brooks Brothers underwear, and began to speak, stumbling to find the words for his discovery that so much of herself—what *she* was—had found its way into Julia, and that someday Julia might have a daughter who would be in great part: "*you,*" he finished.

As a sensation, this marvelous glimpse of Maud immortal filled his eyes with tears.

&

It had begun to rain.

Of the several knobs on the dashboard panel, which was the one that controlled the windshield wipers? *Ah. That* one.

He was driving his new car. A Buick. He hadn't fully made friends with it yet. Nor it, he thought, with him. But what can you expect of a relationship that's only ten days old? Which was how long he had had the Buick—picked up from the General Motors dealer the Friday before Mrs. Leigh's death.

At war's end, it had taken a while for industry to "tool down" from turning out combat material and "tool up" for turning out products for peacetime use. *Things.* All kinds of things that had worn out or fallen apart and that were considered to be necessities: lawnmowers and toasters and vacuum cleaners and stoves and farm tractors and refrigerators and cars and clocks; and other things that weren't, strictly speaking, necessities, but which were wanted: new radios and new phonographs and new watches and new cameras (all fancier than ever before). Suddenly, or so it seemed, *things* were again on the market, again available, making of everyone a sudden purchaser. "America's new consumerism" was how economists dubbed the mania. Virtually forgotten, the austerities and deprivations of the wartime years. Nowadays when people came together, conversation hinged less and less on memory and more and more on things and future plans. Nationwide, there was a feeling of kick in the air. Like such new-fangled gadgets as electric egg-beaters and electric can-openers, the word—*upbeat*—had been invented.

. . . Maud had a new car too, a Plymouth station wagon, purchased last August. And Miss Sly, finally, a new refrigerator. She had told him about it when they'd met a couple of weeks ago for one of their occasional lunches. "It's completely wonderful, Mr. Shurtliff! The motor purrs like a kitten and the interior's a robin's egg blue. And so *roomy*; the shelves so well organized." She had caught herself at her rapture, and laughed in a way that sent the precariously done-up clump of her hair-bun rocking. "It's ludicrous to be so thrilled by such a thing as a refrigerator! What has happened to me?"

He had looked at her—he always enjoyed looking at her—and laughed with her and told her that in a couple of days he was going to pick up his own new car. This Buick. "How exciting! What color?" "Hunter green." Then he told her that he intended to keep the Harold Teen, put it out to pasture, so to say, and take very good care of it, and let Time make of it a vintage car which, someday, Caroline and Julia might like to lark about in.

. . . Driving along in the November rain, it came to him as a realization that of all the people he knew and was close to, Miss Sly was the one he would be most intimately able to talk to about Mrs. Leigh's life and death. With *her*, there would be (in legal jargon) no conflict of interest, and *from* her, the balm of impersonal aspect.

She was his secret life.

Her name had come up soon after he'd returned home from the war. "I expect to see her from time to time," he had told Maud. Maud had firmly distanced herself: "Just don't tell me when you do, Morgan. I don't want to know." (*Ah*, he had accepted: so be it.)

. . . At some point today, he would telephone her and arrange to have lunch with her next week. He would tell her, then, about Mrs. Leigh, and in that remaining way of hers, she would listen, her eyes on him, but seeing through him, past him, in fixed regard of the great scene: of its *extent*—some of it in sunlight and some of it in the shadow of clouds, and the overhead air alive with imagined swallows in flight.

Yes. What he needed was to have lunch with her: to be seated near her in the tranquil vicinity of her large perspective.

❧

"We will," they told each other when he was first back from the war; when they still couldn't get enough of each other; couldn't, when they were alone and not making love, stop talking about the future and what they intended to do with it, projecting themselves into it, but softly— tossed by bliss and gratification. Plenty of time.

"We really *should*." Spoken at full float about six months later.

"We've *got* to." Said with feet on the ground, about five months after the six months.

"God, we absolutely *must*!" Exploded three months after the five months that had followed the six months. Add it up: over a year. *Ah*, the stages of action, from poetic contemplation to unholy desperation.

"*Must.*" MOVE.

Just glance around, starting with the twins' room—the floor covered wall-to-wall with their jealously guarded possessions, nowhere to walk but on the ceiling. Maud with no quiet, private place to call her own.

His study cyclonic, heaped with books and papers. Tessa's theme: "Don't be in *here*"—meaning her now too small kitchen. Every closet jammed full of everybody's stuff ("Mine!"). How had it come to be that all of them (Ralph included) seemed suddenly to take up so much space, and in ways all-directional, like tomato plants gone rampant in August?

The previous winter, to help them find their new home, they had sought out an elderly real-estate agent named F. Rodney Fuller. "He's odd, extremely odd," a friend told them, "but he knows all the worthwhile properties in the region, and once he gets the scent of what you want, he won't stop until he's dogged it down for you."

So they met with Mr. Fuller. He sat bolt upright in a soft chair in their living room, combing a scraggly goat's beard with the long fingers of a freckled hand, his right eye focused on them, but his left eye its own master, veering off, nearly out of its socket, in a westerly direction. "Tell me your priorities, Mr. and Mrs. Shurtliff," he said in the unestablished voice of a teenage choirboy.

To remain, they told him, in this loved region of the Chagrin River Valley, within a ten-to-twelve-mile radius of Hatherton. The house to be commodious and a good example of whatever architectural style it purported to represent. And land: they must have enough land to roam over and, if possible, either a spring-fed pond or a year-round active creek running through the property. "Is that all too general?" Morgan asked.

"No," Mr. Fuller replied. "It gives me scope. I like scope. . . . Now, about the way I work. I'm not one for dragging my clients here, there, and everywhere to look at places just for the sake of looking. You'll not hear from me until I've found something worthwhile for you to see. It will likely take a while. If you can't be patient—"

"We will be," Morgan assured him.

"What a strange man," Maud said after Mr. Fuller had gone. "Isn't he? Do you think he'll be effective?"

"Yes, to both questions," Morgan said. He didn't add that a part of his confidence in Mr. Fuller lay in the fact that Mr. Fuller hadn't touched on the subject of money, which fact meant to Morgan that Mr. Fuller had found out he didn't have to (not at least as a first inhibiting consideration); that, factored into Mr. Fuller's avowed liking for "scope," was his foreknowledge of Morgan's economic plenty.

Nearly a month went by without a sign from Mr. Fuller other than a one-sentence note whose every written word looked like a spider's web: "I'm investigating two properties I believe might interest you. F. Rodney Fuller." After a further lapse of ten days, just when they were about to wash their hands of him, Mr. Fuller telephoned: "I'd like to show you the two places I wrote you about. Yes, next Saturday is fine. I'll come by in my car at ten sharp. I'll honk. You follow me in your car. Wear over-shoes, please."

The first property had much to recommend it. The house was a rambling Colonial affair set high on a hill amidst five acres of lawn and garden plots and a well-trimmed mature grove of trees. No pond or creek, but from a terrace that flanked the west side of the house, a splendid view of a wide, meandering stretch of the Chagrin River. The house appealed so much that they went through it twice, talking of its many possibilities, pleased by its "glad feel." And they lingered a second time on the terrace, gazing at the ambling river, Mr. Fuller at their side, pulling at his goat's beard, his left eye wandering over the landscape like a free-ranging farm chicken. Finally, he prodded them with: "The other place I want you to see is a mile or so from here."

The tree-lined lane of entry to the second property was marked, eldritch-like, by a pair of Doric columns, each topped by a griffin. ("What's a griffin?" Julia asked that evening when he and Maud were telling her and Caroline about this place. This dream. Morgan answered: "A beast of myth. A fabulous beast with a lion's body and the head and spread wings of an eagle. You'll see," the sound of his voice intense, like Julia's gaze.) At the curved point in the lane where the house sprang into sight, Maud's—"Oh, *Morgan!*"—filled the car. There it was, risen before them, not though in any way lordly or vainglorious— only *fine* in scale, the decorum of its formal facade regulated by the aesthetic symmetries of evenly spaced tall, tall ground-floor windows that implied of generously sized, well-proportioned, high-ceilinged rooms capable of echoing their inhabiter's moods and endeavors and whims and pleasures. *Life,* as it would be lived. . . . Morgan spoke aloud the name that defined its architecture: "Palladian," he said: "Palladian." It rolled on his tongue like a mantra. And then it struck him that, by hearsay, he knew about this place, existent behind its griffined gates: that, in fact, it was something of a regional topic, with qualities of docile legend about it. "I think it's the Ottingen place," he said. And Maud, reminded, said: "Of course!" a bit awed: Ernest Ottingen's name was one that reverberated in Cleveland's history. They remembered reading of his death a couple of months ago; there had been pictures of him in the newspapers, and long commemorative paragraphs detailing his career as an inventor and civil engineer.

In the turnaround in front of the house, Morgan parked his car next to Mr. Fuller's. "Yes," Mr. Fuller confirmed: "Ernest Ottingen's home." Mr. Fuller was filled with information about "Mr. O."—as he continued to refer to Ernest Ottingen. Age, at time of death, ninety-six; a long-time widower; a house-bound invalid for well over a decade; no descendants.

"Who took care of him?" Morgan wanted to know.

"A general factotum named Arthur Eames, with Mr. O. for years," Mr. Fuller answered. "And an elderly couple, very devoted to Mr. O., who acted as cook and gardener. They're all retired now, handsomely provided for by the terms of Mr. O.'s will."

"Who's handling the estate?" was Morgan's next question.

To which Mr. Fuller brightened: "I don't know who the lawyer is, but I *can* tell you that Mr. Eames is the named executor of Mr. O.'s will, along with the Cleveland Trust Company. I went to see Mr. Eames. He's living now outside Elyria. I'd say he's in his eighties, but bright as a diamond. A Victorian gentleman. He was dressed in a black twill suit and a shirt with a celluloid collar!" Mr. Fuller's right eye settled itself on Morgan's face: "I had a strong hunch you and Mrs. Shurtliff would be fetched by this property, and as I've heard there's a considerable list of interested buyers, I thought a visit to Mr. Eames, on your behalf, was appropriate." Before Morgan could rise to this gambit, Mr. Fuller hastened on: "There are twenty acres. It's why I suggested you wear overshoes. You'll want to stroll around the grounds a bit before we go inside, and these January thaws—well, they *do* cause mud." As they set off on their walk, Mr. Fuller gestured over the lawn: "Mr. Eames told me there used to be peacocks."

It was inevitable. A wide, racing brook spilled into a large pond glassed over now by a thin glaze of ice. A tennis court! (*En tout cas*, Maud knew.) A stand of laburnum trees. Willows that shaded a terrace in an instantly imagined summer. And *that* tree? "A weeping silver lime," Mr. Fuller informed: "Rare in this part of the world." A dog cemetery, its location on the rise of a nearby hill; six markers—the earliest date 1910, the most recent 1944—Lear, Ripsy, Solo, Duffy, Daisy, Star. . . . And beyond the extent of the civilized grounds, a surround of meadow and deep woods to wander through for years to come.

With practical eyes they explored the ancillary buildings at the back of the house: a large garage, converted from a one-time stable; an immense south-facing greenhouse ("It could be modified, or better still, replaced by a small one," Morgan said); a tool-shed; an old hennery that shared a common wall with a long-unused stone cowshed ("They ought to come down," Morgan said, but Maud defended the cowshed: "Fixed up a bit, it would make a wonderful getaway place for Caroline and Julia.")

"Shall we see inside the house now?" Mr. Fuller asked.

Ah. From the centrality of an exuberant, two-storied entrance hall, the ground-floor rooms winged out, large and fine, each with a fireplace: living room; dining room; an immense, immensely handsome library with the intimate surprise of an inglenook chimney corner; a sitting room for Maud, completely her own. And—"fundamental"—the kitchen, bright and airy: "It'll have to be redesigned, thoroughly modernized," Maud said of it, "but oh my, the *space!*" And down the hallway, off the kitchen, two private, pretty rooms and bath: "For Tessa." Upstairs, via the sweep of a curved staircase: two grand rooms, "for Caroline, for Julia," connected by a large bathroom; across the broad, pillared hall, two guest rooms: and last, arrived at by an arched, gallery-like corridor, a glorious corner chamber, *theirs*—remote—with an easterly view over the lawn to the framing woods, and from the windows that faced north, a view across garden plots to the pond that on clear, calm nights would mirror, as on a patch of sea, stars and the moon. In this room, Morgan lingered alone, persuaded by its beauty that it was an indicator of the luck of his life.

Mr. Fuller reminded him: "The attic must be seen." And was: huge: a perfect play-arena for the twins and their friends on rainy days and bad stretches of winter weather.

Next, down three flights of an easily negotiated back staircase, to the basement. "Mr. Eames recommends the installation of a new furnace," Mr. Fuller remarked. (To his mounting mental list of new kitchen, the updating of bathrooms, general redecoration, perhaps a small green-house, Morgan added "New furnace.") Mr. Fuller praised the basement: "Dry as a bone," he said, "not a hint of damp. Storage space to burn, and—" he gestured: "*That* door . . . I'll give you the pleasure of opening it, Mr. Shurtliff." He handed Morgan a long-shanked iron key. To the right of the door was a light switch which he flicked on, somewhat dra-matically, just as Morgan turned the key in its lock. The door swung inward to a deep, head-high, cool, redolent cave paneled round with beehive niches for vineyard bottles to rest in. "Lord," Morgan breathed: "What a dream of a wine-cellar." Maud, at his side, said, "Pip will go out of his mind when he sees it."

Back upstairs, they sat on a window bench in the library, Maud, Morgan, Mr. Fuller, in that order, and for the first time Morgan broached the subject of money. "What's the asking price, Mr. Fuller?" The figure, firmly stated, was steep, though not, Morgan thought, unreasonable: the virtues of the house and the extent of land that came with it warranted the sum. "Is it negotiable?"

"I wouldn't think by much," Mr. Fuller answered. "I understand that under the terms of Mr. O.'s will, the proceeds of the sale are to go to Mr. O.'s alma mater."

Ah: decedent loyalty to the campus of youth. "Which is?" Morgan asked.

"Western Reserve University."

Where (possibly) the young Ernest Ottingen, leaning against the trunk of an academic elm, had sketched in a notebook the brainstorm of a first invention (first of many), first patent to follow; and now, these many years later (Morgan's thoughts ran on), the profits from the sale of this house, by testament, to return to the institution that had trained and honed the agilities of his mind: the circle, fidelity's own.

"Morgan?"

He turned to Maud. *Shall we?* he silently asked her. *Shall we pursue this?*

Written in her eyes was an answer that read like the denouement of a racy novel plotted of Sex and Acquisition, for, ciphered in her look, linked inextricably to the buying of this house, was the marital bed. What a glide! He kept gazing at her, into the theater of her eyes, watching as she lowered the curtain on the intimacies of that initial scene, and in an instant raised it again to a stage filled with the presences of everyone she loved, and crowded with props symbolic of everything she believed in, and, over all, hovering in a sort of fanning was, *Time:* circa the rest of their lives.

Mr. Fuller coughed.

Morgan turned to him. "Our children must see it," he said. "Tomorrow's Sunday. They won't be in school. I know it's asking a lot, but—"

"I could meet you here at three," Mr. Fuller said.

"We'll be here on the dot." Morgan smiled his appreciation. Then: "We've a friend, an architect. Desmond Cleary."

"I've heard the name."

"I'd like him to vet the house top to bottom. And I want my father to see it."

"I'll make myself available any time that suits them, Mr. Shurtliff. It ought to be as soon as possible. As I mentioned, there are other buyers, very interested."

"I understand. I'll call them the minute we get home. I'll tell you tomorrow the day and hour I fix with them."

They all stood up. Maud said: "You're being very good to us, Mr. Fuller."

Mr. Fuller's daft left eye shot off, somewhere out of sight, but his sane right eye stayed steady on Maud's face. "My father was a tailor, Mrs. Shurtliff. He used to say that nothing satisfied him more than fitting a suit on a man. I get the same satisfaction from matching up houses to people. Do remind your children to wear overshoes when they come tomorrow." On which disjointed speech, in its way touching, they said good-bye.

The next day Maud took a photograph of Caroline and Julia standing in front of the house. In relation to its tall facade, they were insignificant in height. So Maud told them to raise their hands way up high over their heads. They did, and stretched so, they stood still. Until that moment, they had not been catchable by the camera, racing so fast around and about the outside of the house and exploring it inside, yelling to each other from room to room, peaking around corners, infatuated: who would see what next, first . . . In the picture, taken in the winter sunlight, their eyes shine like silver coins.

On Monday, Desmond Cleary spent the morning in the house. Ansel Shurtliff saw it in the afternoon. Des Cleary's verdict: "It's a rare gem, Morgan. A real opportunity. And it's structurally sound as a dollar. Not a compromise in it." Ansel Shurtliff's cry—"Don't hesitate. *Grab it!*" rang clear as a bell.

Not to go into details: but there *was* a hitch that delayed the closing by some three months. At issue, the property's south boundary line, the disputant the owner of the abutting land. The matter didn't turn litigious, nor did it put the sale at threat, but a new survey had to be made and approved and certified and duly filed, ETC. ETC., all of which took time. So it wasn't until late April that the legal formalities were completed and the house and land, once and for all, *theirs*. Champagne! Then the renovations began. That *list:* new kitchen, all bathrooms updated, new furnace, redecorating, ETC. ETC.; hours spent with architect and contractor; weeks and weeks of labor by workmen—the progress sometimes snail slow, sometimes fast, sometimes arrested because of tardy deliveries of ordered goods; but the long job now virtually finished: December 8th—a mere three weeks away—was the day they were scheduled to move from their old house into what they had come to think of as their "final" home.

"It isn't given to many people to inhabit heaven before they die." That was what Mrs. Leigh had said the last time she went out to the house with him and Maud to see how the renovations were coming along. About a month ago. In the fling of the two-storied entrance hall, descending the staircase, she had stopped mid-way down it and gazed around, smiling, Maud beside her on the same stair, halted, and himself two treads above them. "It isn't given to many people to inhabit heaven before they die." So he had the memory of Maud throwing her arms around Mrs. Leigh and of hearing her say, "Oh Mother, what a beautiful thought," her eyes skimmed over in that sheer way they could with tears, and Mrs. Leigh holding Maud in the clasp of an embrace so tight it looked as if she meant it to last forever.

. . . Morgan drove on, not fast; it was raining harder now. The new Buick's windshield wipers moved back and forth, active and sweeping, but the rain not erasable. That recent day, that moment there on the stairs, Maud fastened in her mother's embrace. No hint that Mrs. Leigh would soon undo it. No forecast of farewell.

෫

His memory made another sudden backward leap: a long one: to 1943, midpoint of the war, to one particular evening of the many he spent in a Miami bar with Sidney Aranov and Lawrence Cuyler. The word "someday" had entered their conversation, meaning some future time when the war would come to an end, a time which, in fulfillment, seemed to them then already ancient. "Someday." No matter how often the word was uttered (and it was uttered very often), its user never followed it up with—"if I survive the war." But the unspoken phrase was always there, hand-in-glove, suffixed to the word.

On the night of this particular memory, Lawrence had been holding forth about what his life was going to be like after the war. How perfect, with Pamela, it was going to be. He had had a lot to drink. So had Sidney. So had Morgan. "Someday. Blue skies. *Years* of blue skies," Lawrence concluded.

"Goethe," Sidney mumbled.

"What? Speak up, professor, I'm sitting in the back row."

"Johann Wolfgang von Goethe," Sidney obliged, assuming the pre-scribed role, leaning on the barroom table as on a lectern: "German poet and philosopher. Trained as a lawyer. Dates 1749–1832. Allow me." He put his right hand in his uniform pocket and brought out a pen and a blank sheet of paper. He screened the paper with his left hand as he printed some words on it. When he was finished, he looked up at

Lawrence and Morgan and said: "Goethe. A literal translation," then handed the paper to them.

WANTED: A DOG THAT NEITHER BARKS NOR BITES, EATS BROKEN GLASS, AND SHITS DIAMONDS.

They nearly gagged, laughing.

Sidney reclaimed the paper, turned it over, wrote another message on its clean side and again handed the paper to Lawrence and Morgan.

WANTED, AT WAR'S END, BY SIDNEY ARANOV: A F—ING ORDINARY DOG.

"That'll be the canine for me," he said. "Metaphorically speaking—an ordinary life; a couple of nice kids; some good lawyering; the chance to grow old with Linda."

Odd, the way things had worked out.

Now, Lawrence and Sidney were both living in New York, both professionally thriving, Lawrence in an old-name law firm (housed in a Wall Street building within easy walking distance of Morgan's New York office), corporate law his specialty; Sidney, a litagator in a young, up-and-coming firm with political connections. At such times as Morgan was in New York, the three of them, their schedules permitting, would hook up for lunch or a late-afternoon drink, coming together in the easy way of their old Miami days. If for some reason they couldn't meet as a trio, Morgan would see Sidney or Lawrence: in whatever combination, the friendships flourished.

(It should be noted that Sidney's professional success was such that he could now afford to have his shirts made to order, which meant no more or less than that they contained enough cloth to adequately accommodate the large span of his vat-like torso. But the very plenitude of cloth produced a new sartorial problem, for, *now*, when he was intellectually or emotionally excited, the action of his heart (always at such times observable) seemed not to beat but instead to blow in puffy gusts that stirred the shirt's fabric in a way suggestive of an untrimmed jib-sail luffing in a light August breeze . . . a sight to see.)

"I dream of becoming a father," Sidney had said in 1943. He and Linda had a son now, David, born a year ago. Morgan had met Linda soon after the war ended, and just as he had somehow been certain he would, had instantly liked her. Subsequently, Maud met her (and Sidney too, of course), and now the four of them were friends. On Maud's occasional trips to New York, they would join ranks, usually for dinner: French, Chinese, Italian, or Indonesian food. They ate geography. Sometimes they went to a concert together or to the theater. (One memorable night, at a midtown cabaret, they heard Mabel Mercer sing. "From This Moment On." "Thank You for the Flowers." "Sunday in Savannah." "By Myself." . . . No one like her, before or since.) But however or wherever they spent the earlier part of the evening, they invariably ended it in the living room of the Aranov's third-floor brownstone apartment, on Seventy-fifth Street, between Lexington and Third avenues. Sidney would pay the baby-sitter and see her out the door, and Linda would bring David from his crib and plant him in Sidney's lap, and Sidney, holding his son and with Linda sitting beside him, would always, literally *always*, turn to Morgan and remind him of "that Goethe evening back in Miami"—employing the memory as a gauge of his and Morgan's post-war marital and paternal happiness—

—by which gauge, Lawrence's post-war life with Pamela had been a disaster. His was the ancient story (in these recent times all too often updated) of the decorated warrior who returns from combat to a wife not the one dreamt of in battle. About Pamela, he had lately told Morgan: "I thought I knew her." He meant—at the time of their marriage, in 1943, smack in the middle of the war. After all, as the "in" children of New York parents of a certain economic and social rank, he and Pamela had been cast together since early childhood, firstly on the kazoo-blowing, paper-hat birthday circuit; secondly, tongue-tied and stiff-kneed, in the de Corcy dancing classes (held November through March on alternate Friday afternoons in the Colony Club ballroom); thirdly, throughout adolescence, at carefully structured parties temporally related to their being home on holiday breaks from their respective boarding-schools; fourthly—fully fledged—when he was at Yale (obsessively dating a string of girls) and Pamela was at Vassar (being obsessively dated by a string of guys), they would bump into each other at football games in New Haven or once in a while at a New York nightclub (down in the Village or up in Harlem) and they would greet each other, casually: "Hello, Pamela." "Hi, Larry." (She was alone in calling him "Larry.") After Yale, and throughout the three years he was at Columbia Law School, their paths did not cross: following her graduation from Vassar, Pamela went to Washington to work in the office of a three-initial government agency (exactly which one Morgan was never told). But with the onset of the war, for whatever reason, she returned to New York and in the autumn of 1942—by which time Lawrence had been in uniform for over a year—they met again. Fatefully. The circumstance: Lawrence, home on a week-end pass, invited to a dinner party given by friends of his parents, Pamela seated next to him at table; and, as he much later told Morgan: "I crashed." Returned to his four-stacker destroyer, he courted Pamela by letter (more accurately, *notes*) written at off-duty moments on a continuum of hazardous convoy-escort voyages to England and back; to England again and back again; again to England and again, back. Which letters Pamela answered, not in like volume or intensity, but enough to encourage him. *Enough*—six months later (in February of 1943), when he was again in New York on a week-end pass, to ask her if they might become engaged. Incredibly, she said yes. And then, only three months later, in late May, just prior to his reporting to the Submarine Chaser Training Course in Miami (by dint of a "delayed-order leave")—strangely and suddenly, like heat lightning, they married: vows exchanged at eleven on a Tuesday morning in the chapel of St. James Episcopal Church, their parents and two Vassar friends of Pamela's in attendance. Followed by a champagne lunch. Followed by a two-night honeymoon. Lawrence's—a bridegroom's— euphoria projected to Morgan and Sidney on that evening in gloomy Miami when the three of then converged at the front door of the Columbus Hotel and took a first walk together and told each other, in a beginning way, their autobiographies.

Whenever Morgan thought about Pamela, it was in terms of the effect she had had on him the one time he met her. . . . The remembered photographs of her which Lawrence had shown to him and Sidney back in Miami had prepared him for the long-legged stunner she in fact *was*: but the photos had not warned of her in-the-flesh animality: that in a social jungle, she was like encountering a leopard, the way she came on, sleek and scented and darkly intelligent. No grasslands languor in her. Add to that lack of languor the stimulus of a conveyed indifference to consequence, and you end up with Morgan's immediate sense of her: as dangerous. That once-ever meeting had taken place in February of 1946. Lawrence, returned from the war a mere four months, already showed signs of a man in emotional chaos. Sidney and Morgan, knowing him as they did, saw him so: nervous and slavishly attentive to Pamela, his humor in short supply.

Pamela spelled it out for him soon thereafter: marriage, she told him, wasn't for her. It kept her from doing the things she wanted to do when she wanted to do them. It prevented her, she said, from being herself. Their marriage, she said, had been a war-time mistake. . . . She told him all this on a Saturday morning. That night, around ten o'clock, Lawrence turned up drunk at Sidney and Linda's apartment. Linda went to bed, leaving Sidney alone with him: Lawrence wild, raving in a drunk's uninhibited, repetitive, unpunctuated way about the wreck of his marriage, about himself, about Pamela: *he* loved *her*—*she* did not love *him*—*men* (he gestured) *"men plural"*—were what she loved, one at a time, to play the gender game with. He ranted on, fluctuating between a weeping, head-in-hands despair and sudden adrenal risings of anger that sent him lurching to his feet. Finally, worn out, with nothing left in him to vent, he sank back on the couch and let Sidney take off his tie and shoes and position him length-wise on the couch for sleep. He was out within seconds. Sidney spread a blanket on the floor and lay down on it, and that way, near him, kept vigil. Around dawn, Lawrence came to, massively disoriented and instantly sick. Sidney, prepared, had a roasting pan as receiver for the heaved-up bile. Then a trip to the bathroom, Sidney acting as a steady crutch, then back to the couch; back on the floor for Sidney. A bit before eight, Linda, fully dressed, emerged from the bedroom. It wouldn't do (she whispered to Sidney) for Lawrence to wake up and to have to face her first thing, there in the small apartment. She'd slip out now and go to her sister's house. She glanced at Lawrence's prone figure: "Try to pin him down for dinner next Thursday night." Sidney nodded and smiled: he loved her belief in the curative powers of food for all ailments, whether of body, soul, or heart. . . . At noon-time, Lawrence came fully around; fully in the grip of what Sidney later described to Morgan as—"an Homeric hangover."

Throughout the afternoon, Sidney looked after him. Got him to quit apologizing; got him to take a shower and to shave. As the first shadows of the early March twilight crept into the room, Lawrence began soberly to talk. It seemed "fantastic" to him to think that at just this time twelve months ago the war was still on, Roosevelt still alive, the atom bomb an undreamt of, undropped thing—himself on a battleship in the Pacific, engaged in ferocious combat, *yet:* yet, in spite of all the horrors that were going on then, he had had *about himself* "a sense of worth," (of) "whole- ness," (of) "hope"; whereas, *now,* he felt "cut down; useless and defeated." His body was slumped dead-weight in his chair, his hands limp in his lap. His eyes, though, were bright and desperate. "Tell me what you think I should do, Sidney."

By dusk-time, Sidney had succeeded in exacting from him the promise that he would seek professional help. It hadn't been easy, per- suading him to take that path. Behind Lawrence's repeated protestations that he—"ought"—to be able, on his own, to pull himself together, "ought," on his own, to prevent himself "from giving up and caving in," Sidney heard, like echoes, the tenets of courage as postulated in the chapel sermons of Lawrence's school-days, wherein Life was analogized to Sport: that as a man, one is judged on the basis of the spirited way one "fights the good fight and gives his all to the playing of the game. . . ."

"I *ought* to be able to—"

"Stop talking that Anglo-Saxon 'ought' stuff," Sidney had finally exploded. "Spare yourself and me any more of it. It's crap, Lawrence. It doesn't apply to what you're up against now. *Look*—: look at it this way: as trained lawyers, we know how to listen to a client's stated legal prob- lem and how to interpret it in terms of a judicious solution. The key word, Caesar, is *trained.* A psychiatrist is trained to interpret *human* problems; trained to understand, *get it?*"

"Maybe."

"Try harder."

"I'll think about what you've said."

"You've just flunked the course. Thinking about it will get you nowhere. If you want to pass the course, you've got to commit to getting the help you need. So will you? Will you put your clean right hand over your dirty left heart and tell me here and now that you *will*?"

Lawrence let out a sound, in part groan, in part sigh. "Okay, okay. I surrender." Then, with a flash of energy that was fresh: "I give you my word I will."

"Eureka! You've just graduated."

On which commendatory note, Lawrence stood up, knotted his tie, put on his suit coat and his overcoat. Sidney walked with him to the elevator. In it, Lawrence kept its door from closing: "*Morgan*—" he said.

Sidney nodded: "I was just thinking about him."

With a tact essential to the equilibrium of their tripod friendship, Lawrence volunteered: "I'll telephone him later this evening; cue him in on what's happened." Then he released his hold on the elevator door and pushed the Down button. The door slid to. Clicked into place. The elevator descended.

Within six weeks, Pamela went to Reno. By early summer, the divorce was (in Lawrence's words) "a done thing."

. . . Shifts of the shoreline sands . . .

These days, fourteen months later, Lawrence seemed to be pretty well recovered. He was still seeing a psychiatrist. He had lost (probably forever) his old air of total ease. He had used to stride into rooms; now he tended to stand in a doorway and look around, peering in, before entering. He was much liked; socially much sought after. But by his own admission, social life, per se, didn't attract him in the "blithe" way it once had. He enjoyed the company of women and had among that sex—"several good friends." It wasn't in the cards, he said, that he would ever marry again. On the other hand, anything was possible. So maybe, at some point, he would. Maybe. "Someday."

❧

The assailing rain—slowing him way down, lengthening the trip into the city, delaying arrival at his office.

After a week away from his desk, and with what would surely be a massive pile-up of work awaiting him, he should logically be regretting the delaying circumstance of the storm. Yet far from regretting it, he welcomed it for its being the prolonging agent of this, his first solitude since Mrs. Leigh's death. . . . It was as if he had two heads, hence two minds, one employed at driving the car, the other (seemingly beyond his power to control it) using up the extended time of this first solitude by taking a kind of synoptic roll-call of the persons he most loved in this world.

Now, present before him: Geoffrey Barrows . . . After five and a half years of war's separation, they had met again; the unforgettable date Friday, January 11, 1946 (at which time Morgan had been home from the war about two months, Geoff nearly six months). They had spoken frequently on the telephone: Hatherton–Philadelphia, Philadelphia–Hatherton: calls of the kind easy between vintage friends. But beyond glossary reassurances of their post-war states of health and mind, they had not attempted to talk about themselves in any way that resembled completeness: there was, they agreed, too much to say, too much that had to be told about the last five years' experiences, too much to tell about what was happening to them now. For such communication as that, they must be together. Thus had come into being this planned, greatly anticipated meeting.

At Geoff's request, they had settled on New York as the place for their reunion. Morgan opted to put up at the Plaza Hotel; Geoff said he would stay at a friend's apartment. In the comfort of a Pullman bedroom, Morgan had made the overnight journey from Cleveland; by ten A.M. he was at the Plaza, settled in a large room windowed above Central Park. Geoff, coming by car from Philadelphia, had promised an "elevenish arrival." At about 10:45, tapped out rhythmically on the room's door, was the identifying knock that went back to their Harvard Law School days: *Da dada da da—DA DA* ("Shave and a haircut—six bits").

"Come in!"

They had had just enough time to sound each other's names before they collided in embrace, following which bodily impact, rocked back from it onto their heels, they looked at each other, laughing, completely amazed at being together again.

Near the room's windows they sat down in the deep comfort of chairs positioned to give a view of the park. There were two pigeons taking temporary shelter on the sill, complaining in throaty tones about the day's weather: typically January, cold and gray and windy. Remoter from the pigeons' voices was the sound of moving traffic and the urgent trill, erratically let, of a doorman's steel whistle blown to summon cabs, and farther away the held pitch of a car's stuck horn, all of which outside auditory pother heightened appreciation of the room as a relatively peaceful, quiet haven.

"God, where to begin?"

Between them, ascendance had never played a role: it would not have occurred to either of them to suppose about his interim story that it was the greater one (though as Morgan would soon learn, Geoff's was surely the more extraordinary).

"You start us off, Morgie," Geoff said.

In the way Geoff said it, Morgan thought he detected an overtone of decided preference that he be the one to begin, which nuance prompted in him an immediate closer scrutiny of his best friend: a tall man of ordered appearance (polished, really) even when he was sitting down, loose and relaxed as he was now, with his long legs stretched out before him, crossed at the ankles; a handsome face; uncommonly blue, discerning eyes; dark, well-groomed hair, seen in this close inspection as beginning to gray, the graying barely noticeable (*until* noticed) and then not as the main indicator of such physical changes as are inevitably wrought by the passage of time, but rather as a complement to some other change, one by far more exceptional (now that Morgan was beginning really to see it) present in the whole expression of the whole face, of high well-being, the charged strike of which, as Morgan fully took it in, caused him to positively exclaim: "You're on top of the world!"

"I am," Geoff immediately said, and exuberantly repeated: "I am!" Then, though, with a sudden augmenting seriousness: "But it's complicated, Morgie."

Ah. Complicated: that potent adjective prized by the imagination as an opener to kingdoms of possibility. Right away—the very instant Geoff said the word—Morgan saw that he wished he could take it back. Why?

For the reason Morgan quickly articulated: "You've just thrown away your chance of getting me to start us off."

Geoff flashed a smile of the kind a girl named Margy Some-thingorother had once described to Morgan as—"Geoffrey's delectable *under* smile"—a half lift of the mouth's corners, made from beneath eyelids lowered in a parody of self-disparagement. "I know," Geoff acknowledged: "Loosen your corset strings, honey." Morgan laughed. Geoff said: "That's what a guy in our camp used to say. Ernest Gustavsen, called 'Gus.' A bomber navigator. He had a raft of fizzy sayings. He claimed he'd gotten them from his mother-in-law. He had one wallet-size snapshot of his wife, one of said mother-in-law, and one of his horse, an old nag named Bubbles." Geoff smiled: "Of the three, Bubbles was the best looking. . . . I hope Gus is happy back home with his trio of femmes. He's from some little town in northern Minnesota. I'll probably never see or hear from him again. But that's true of most everyone in our unit. When it came time for us to disperse—after all those endless months we'd been together—it was weird the way we all mulled around, holding on, handing out our addresses, slapping each other on the back, telling each other we'd for sure stay in touch—knowing as we said it that nine times out of ten, we wouldn't. There was no lie though in our wish to. . . . You know what I'm talking about, Morgie."

"Down to my toes," Morgan answered. He had listened to Geoff, fascinated, attracted more and more to what, *about* him, seemed new: new in the sense that all his interesting qualities of mind and character, familiar from yore, seemed, now, larger in scale; more in the open; more—*offered:* all as evidenced in his greatened ease of self (in the past somewhat inhibited), and in the liberated way he gave utterance to his thoughts—which gains, as Morgan pondered them, he began to define in terms of facility. *Ah.* That was it! Geoff had become—*enabled.* And in the sudden way intuition works, he knew: "You're in love," he stated, abruptly, with a spontaneous effusion of pleasure.

Geoff didn't move a muscle, only sat there low in his chair, eyes as calm as a calm sea, and as tranquilly deep, and his voice the same: "You're wonderful," he said. "You haven't changed. I've been banking on my belief that you wouldn't have."

And with a further advance of intuition, Morgan knew not to say another word; to only listen.

"Along with everything imaginable that a POW camp was, above and beyond all else, it was an obstacle to privacy." (That was Geoff's opening sentence) . . . Everything that took place, took place in the open. That old saying, 'One for all and all for one,' was the key to the sustaining of morale: all of them equal, equally enduring, equally surviving, equally together. One might prefer the company or conversation of X, but the preference was never exercised to a point that excluded Y or Z, adhesion of the group being the thing that most mattered, with private judgments and feelings about those who comprised it, privately held, rarely, rarely overtly shown. It was by means of what Geoff called—"our sanity-keeping activities"—that true individuality spontaneously surfaced: for instance, during the playing of team sports, and of course, most obviously, in the "lectures" delivered on subjects of the lecturer's pre-war field of expertise. And not the least in the sanity-keeping department, the plays they had rehearsed and staged ("I wrote you about the first one we put on, *The Man Who Came to Dinner*, me smooching my way through the role of Maggie Cutler").

So there they all were, *Krigesgefangenen*—POWs—held behind barbed wire, winters and summers, month in and month out.

There were two men in the group whom Geoff singled out and spoke of as "intellectually remarkable." One was the botanist; the other a composer and teacher ("in real life") of music theory—first name "Alan" (Geoff spelled it out), surname "Litt" (also spelled out) . . . Alan Litt . . . a fighter pilot (as Geoff had been). It was Alan Litt who had lectured about music in all its forms: sonatas and symphonies, operas and song-cycles; Alan Litt from whom Geoff had learned "about clefs and scales and key-signatures"—rudiments of an art foreign to him. . . . Geoff went on about Alan Litt: about how, as a POW, he had hoarded blank pieces of paper, and when he'd acquired a few pages, the way he had painstakingly ruled them into a series of music staves, as many as the paper could possibly contain, and how at the noisiest of times, he would sit, "amazingly concentrated," separate from everyone else, doing what— when Geoff asked him—he described to Geoff as "sketching ideas for a string quartet" he had in mind to compose. . . . "There was only one other guy who could seal himself away from the group in something like a similar way—a devout Catholic who prayed on his knees beside his bunk, eyes closed, crucifix in hand, every morning and every night, in full sight of everyone. A ballsy act of humility."

The big, immediate thing Geoff and Alan Litt had in common was a passion for chess. "We were Capablanca and Alekhine," Geoff laughed. "We had a running tournament, the other guys our gallery. I had my claque; Alan had his. But when it came time to bet on a match game, the bettors always favored Alan: he always won." Of those on-going chess bouts, Geoff's summing phrase was: "The effort of trying to best Alan at the game kept me from going crazy." It was necessary, Geoff went on, that he paint as he had such a detailed picture of group life in the camp, and particularly of the chess tournaments with Alan Litt: "As background, Morgie, to what's happened since." To make a long story short: in late April, 1945, word got out—leaked by one of the German guards—that U.S. Army contingents under General Patton were closing in; that most of the guards were shoving off, leaving behind only a skeleton force who would turn over the camp to the Allies when they arrived. Which great event took place soon thereafter. "When the troops moved in and we were released—an insanely glorious moment—we were invited to share dinner in their chow line, and of course we did—ate like wolves—but the food was so different from the stuff we were used to that we suffered, and I do mean *suffered*, gastroenteritis, and had to be treated for a few days in a field hospital. There was a chaplain attached to the hospital who was a great help to us. He spent hours with us, bringing us up to date about the war, campaign sequences and the like, and what was currently happening. The really immense jolt to us was the very recent death of President Roosevelt. . . . We were such blanks, Morgie, so totally out of it that everything he told us sounded like the spin of some kook fabulist making it all up as he went along. . . . I can't imagine what he must have thought of us, hanging on to every word he said, trying to make sense to it, open-mouthed and mystified, like a bunch of idiots listening to Einstein. Weird! . . . Anyhow, when what was left of our insides got to functioning fairly normally again, we were dismissed from the hospital and taken into Munich, and from Munich, flown to Paris. Got there in time to celebrate V-E Day on May eighth. Then off to Cherbourg, and after a fantastic number of physical and psychological tests, put aboard a pre-war British luxury liner and sent home."

It was on the voyage to New York that Geoff and Alan Litt emerged in each other's eyes as *persons*, distinct from their passion for chess, distinct from the group; on the voyage home that they became friends. Slowly. They talked, at first purely on the basis of compared memories referenced in their planes being hit ("Our similarly experienced colossal sensation of disbelief and fear") and of parachuting out, landing in the lap of the enemy: their same fate of ending up alive in the same POW camp. Which experience, as a topic, led to other topics which in turn opened doors—"to interiority, mostly, in the beginning, concerning our professions. What it's like to be a lawyer; what it's like to be a composer: topics that by contrast told a lot about ourselves. I'd never before thought about myself and my background in such detail and so honestly, and certainly never before out-loud—not even with you, Morgie. That's the part, as between *us*, it may be hardest for you to understand."

"Don't underestimate me, Geoff. Go on."

Well, with the voyage ended, the ship tied up to a Hudson River pier, the moment of dispersal at hand, Geoff and Alan had told each other that *they* at least probably would stay in touch. Here's my address and telephone number. Here's mine. Hastily, amid the moment's great confusions, the slips of paper had been exchanged.

Geoff went to Philadelphia, to a homecoming of enormous ("elegantly displayed") parental relief and happiness. (Morgan, knowing Geoff's extremely reserved, patrician parents, thought how perfectly Geoff's phrase suited his own imaginings of what Geoff's homecoming must have been like.) But after the first prodigal days had passed, and the first long evenings of long dinners with gatherings of parental friends—"myself more or less on constant parade, the inaccuracies of the situation began to get to me. . . . Think about it, Morgie. . . . You came back to Maud, to love and sex and all the animations of a life that works for *you*. I came back—Jesus, at my age!—the heir-apparent bachelor son, to my father's house. . . . Within hours of being back, Dad was laying out his plans for my immediate future, that I'd go with him and Mother to Maine for the month of August, the same as we always had, and get in some good sailing, sleep late, get thoroughly rested, then return to Philly in September and replant myself in his law firm. He didn't have to say the rest—it was all implicit—that in time I'd meet some suitable girl to marry, et cetera, et cetera. . . . All of which, if it hadn't been for the war, I probably would have done. *Could* have. No problem, I mean, about my being physically and morally able to. . . . Believe me, Morgie, I don't fault Dad. The presumptions he made about me were all ones I'd set him up for: there I was in the flesh, having volunteered myself, *presented* myself, to be seen by him on the basis of his past sense of me—the war behind me, and me home again, right back, in his mind, to the way I'd been in 1940." Modulations of melancholy and self-disdain had crept into Geoff's voice and he stopped; and in a second: "Hell, I've gotten off track," he said: "Give me a minute."

Morgan used the interval of Geoff's stop to consider Geoff's words about how he "could" have spent his life: could have gone on fulfilling his father's ornamental dreams of the ideal life wished for a mortally idealized son. Almost vehemently, he said: "But you *wouldn't* have, Geoff! You wouldn't have gone on the way you were going. God, the last time we were together—"

"When the twins were christened," Geoff cut in, smiling at the memory.

"Right. *That far back* you told me you had doubts about the path you were on."

"But I'm not sure, *but* for the war, that I'd have had either the sense or the guts to act on my doubts, Morgie, the path, as you call it, that I was on was so exactly the one I'd been brought up to *be* on. And as for the war—to volunteer to serve in it was a part of the ethic of the path I was on. Don't get me wrong: I believed then, and still do, in the war's correctness. I did have the brains to reason that part accurately. I'm only saying that aside from that conviction, volunteering, for me, was as easy as eating cake. It was different for you. For you, it was a real sacrifice, what with being married and having just adopted the twins. I remember we talked about it. . . . And I'll tell you here and now something about myself that applied back then that I *didn't* tell you at the time: that what I most wanted for myself was a taste of danger. I really desired it. I had the idea that if I put myself in the way of danger, something might happen to me big enough to make me feel it, and terrifically. That's how emotionally desperate I was. I'd really begun to wonder if I had it in me to feel deeply about anything, let alone any person."

But there had been all those girls, Morgan reminded him. "You talked about two or three of them with what seemed to me to be a lot of feeling."

Oh, yes, now that Morgan mentioned it, there *had* been all those girls. "Going out with girls—*courting* them," Geoff elaborated, "was one of the things one was expected to do. So I did it." And yes, with at least two girls, there *had* been—"moments." The moments, though, ones of "sensation only." Not—"in heart sustainable." So, when over—"afterwards"—sad. Sad, in that they increased a growing fear, self-accusing, of an inability to love. But that was how it had been *then*. "A millennium change between then and now. *As* I am now, Morgie. Because of Alan."

Ah. Candor, at its greatest, has behind it two possibilities: heat of impending action, or serenity of accomplishment. It was the latter Morgan saw in Geoff's eyes and heard in his voice—that peace was upon him—and that the only part of his story remaining to be told was just how, and when, vis-à-vis Alan Litt, he had reached the milestone.

They sat for a moment, silent, calm; older. Then Geoff picked up with: "A couple of days before we were due to leave for Maine, I got a letter from Alan. Nothing much in it, just to 'report in' was the way he put it, and that if I felt inclined to, he'd like to hear from me. Best wishes. As I said, nothing much. But for me it was light at the end of the tunnel."

Geoff telephoned Alan that evening. The upshot of the call was that they arranged to meet in New York the following Saturday. Not surprisingly, there had been a bit of a scene between Geoff and his father. What about the planned trip to Maine? and so forth. "I oared my way through that set of rapids by promising I'd turn up in Blue Hill no later than the middle of the next week."

So Geoff had gone to New York. Met Alan as arranged. "When I saw him, it was as if the world had reappeared."

Morgan had a flashed memory of his old stateroom aboard the *Stubbins* (lying then at anchor in Aden), of himself sitting on the stateroom's bunk and of Rupert Wilkins sitting in the stateroom's only chair, leaning forward in it, telling of the day he had discovered the sea; of how the captain's face had been emotionally lighted, as Geoff's was lighted now: as love, whatever its found source, irrefutably causes. "When do I get to meet Alan?" he asked.

"Tonight, for dinner. It's all arranged. As I told you earlier, I've banked on my belief that you wouldn't have changed. I've been sure, I mean, that you'd be glad for me."

(A parenthesis: Long years later—in the jaw, jaw, jaw 1990s—Morgan, at age nearly eighty, often thinks of that speedy, fully sophisticated verbal exchange between Geoff and himself, valuing it, still, for its simplicity, and proudly, as being in its faith, quite glorious.)

"When I left Alan after that weekend," Geoff resumed, "I was certain enough of the future of our relationship not to defer telling Dad that I'd made up my mind to leave Philadelphia and set myself up to live and work in New York. You can guess how he took it: as a real scalp. His first approach was to 'reason' with me. He had a paternal duty, he said, to point out to me all I'd be giving up. My settled future in his law firm—those were his words—was his biggest argument, and that to relinquish such an advantage would be ludicrous. That approach was easy for me to handle compared to what followed, when he began behaving like a Christian martyr. What I *hadn't* anticipated was Mother's sympathy to the idea of my making the break. It's one of the few times I've known her to take a position in opposition to Dad's. That did really put him off her *and* me. You know—twice betrayed—son *and* spouse. It was an awful time for the three of us. Really awful. No point in rehashing it. . . . Oh, God, *no*, Morgie. No, I didn't tell them about Alan. They'd never accept it, so why try? But I don't even think about that, particularly right now: there's too much else in the fire at the moment."

Which he went on to reveal: first, that he'd had the luck of finding an apartment a block away from Alan's (Alan's too small to accommodate the two of them). "Both apartments are downtown, on Grove Street; believe it or not, I'll be moving into my place on the first of February." And second: that he had in his pocket three solid job offers, two from good law firms and the third from the Hanover Bank, as a trust officer. ("That's the offer I'm feeling most inclined to take.") He expressed surprise at how quickly, after the interviews, the offers had been made. He put it down to his name: "Geoffrey S. Barrows, *junior* . . . All those interlocking connections with Dad's reputation—"

"Hooey," Morgan cut him off: "Nobody gets hired purely on the basis of his name. You're a well-qualified lawyer with a spectacular war record. You're hot stuff." Then: "Are you hungry? I'm starved. Let's break for lunch."

. . . ("Come at seven," Geoff said when they parted mid-afternoon.)

A tenant roster was mounted on one wall of the building's small outer lobby.

LITT–3D

At the side of the name, encircled in brass, a white ceramic bell. Which Morgan pressed. Six or seven seconds slipped by. Then, flighted down through a voice-tube: "Morgan Shurtliff?"

"Here."

"Grand. Third floor. I'll buzz you in."

He had expected Geoff's voice; Geoff to buzz him in. Instead, Alan. Alan, too, waiting for him when he got off the elevator.

Fully in view at the end of the hall, Geoff, silent, was leaning against an open door, a belly-up black cat in his arms, introduced (in a moment) as—"Cleo."

But first, Alan's handshake and entire, slightly squinted look at Morgan, unsurprised: "Geoffrey's an accurate describer," he said. "Welcome."

Curious, and without benefit of any previous description of Alan, Morgan was the one surprised: by his height, relieved at the shoulders by the merest stoop; by his wide, pale, thin-skinned, tightly stretched brow topped by a black crop of untamable hair (how had he ever managed to comb it in compliance with U.S. Air Force standards?); by his eyes, a deeper brown even than Maud's; by his well-sized, expressive mouth beneath a thin nose (of the kind Trollope often ascribes to rural clerics); by the way all the features of his face actively combined to emphasize his reaction to what was momently being said or done—reactions that immediately *showed* (for you to come to grips with); by his arrestingly male, dense voice, and, when it (soon) came, by his rampant, unarranged, impious, wonderfully infectious laugh.

Geoff, even as Alan and Morgan walked toward him, remained mute: until they were literally upon him. Then he said—"Morgie"—(almost retrospectively, Morgan felt); then smiled and announced, "This is Cleo"; bent and rolled the cat gently out of his arms onto the floor; then rose up, tall.

The three of them then, standing at matched altitudes.

Alan, fastest, was the first to laugh.

In some former year, the common wall between two large rooms had been torn down, creating the huger space of a single five-windowed room. A sixth window had been turned into a door that let onto a fire escape, its long glass panel criss-crossed by a steel trellis. In the daytime, the room would collect the outside light and be brilliant; at this January evening hour, a profusion of lamps lit it: one at the left side of the grand piano's keyboard, three among chairs grouped around a Victorian couch, two on side tables, one on the top of a large desk, one on a four-legged gaming-board inlaid with alternately colored squares on which warrior chessmen were lined up for impending battle; above a round, oak table (set for dining) a three-armed wall sconce—entry into the room an illumination of the mind and will of its lead occupant—sheets of music—manuscript paper on the piano, the staves covered with the musical symbols of compositions-in-progress, more such sheets on the desks; in cabinets and on wall-shelves, volumes of music scores and books and record albums and framed images of immortal composers and photographs of artist-performers—famed, familiar faces—some dead, some living—singers and dancers and instrumentalists and conductors; on a swatch of black velvet, a plaster cast of a left hand (identified for Morgan by Alan as: "Rachmaninoff's *paw!* Look at its flexibility! That span!"); set up in the curve of the piano, two music-stands; on the couch, a metronome residing beside two large-paged, hefty volumes: *32 Sonatas for Pianoforte—Ludwig van Beethoven—Edited by Artur Schnabel* (Morgan read).

You'd have to be blind not to see that what the room was—what it represented—was Alan Litt: that what he did in the room, what, in it, he pursued, was work of a nature that kept him breathing: work that was his very life. Not to be interfered with. Not, at least, for long, and then only at granted times. (Did Geoff know this? That he would never be first?)

Over the course of the evening, Morgan learned that Alan's surname was of Welsh extraction. His parents, dead: killed together instantly, in an automobile accident on the Connecticut Turnpike. At the time the accident occurred, Alan was in California at UCLA studying composition with Arnold Schoenberg. His father had been a doctor; his mother a well-trained violinist ("If she'd wanted to, she could have had a career"). He spoke with obvious pleasure of his sister, Gwen, (his only sibling): "She lives in Princeton, married to an art history professor. They've two boys, age four and six. Exhausting, grand little savages." And with a charming lack of presumption, yet as if he already knew them, he spoke of Maud and Caroline and Julia.

Inevitably, they talked a bit about the war, mostly about the men they had "shared" it with. (Morgan's word.) In the context of considering aloud the war's lingering effects on/in their lives, Alan made the haunting comment: "The one thing I'm sure of about the rest of *my* life is that—as to *hazard*—I've learned all there is to know."

From out of a small kitchen, a good meal had been produced. At dessert-time, Alan brought to the table a terrific array of fruit. "My mania," he said. Then he told Morgan that in about the seventeenth month of being a POW, his craving for fresh fruit had reached a point where it took over his dream life; that night after night, fruit was all he dreamed about. "Nothing else. Just—*fruit.* Erotic dreams about Granny Smith apples peaches papayas sloes strawberries blueberries blackberries raspberries gooseberries plums grapes bananas pineapples honeydew melons apricots mangoes oranges cherries kumquats"—ticking off the fleshy names, his inducing laugh taken up by Morgan and Geoff, Geoff's face criminally alive, and Alan—suddenly—*zoom*—like a hawk on a rabbit—reaching out and seizing Geoff's hand, the same way in an instance of lucid zaniness, Morgan seizes Maud's hand, and the fingers of Alan's and Geoff's hands interlacing as he watched, just as his and Maud's entwined—gripping: not for proof, oh, not for proof: they are way, way, way beyond a need to prove. . . . In the entire evening, it was the single physical gesture that passed between them. What told Morgan the most about the pitch of their relationship—that is, the magnitude of its ardor—was the tremendous command each had of the other's attention. . . . A voracious interest spliced of great animation and great sobriety; sun and shade: blends of engagement reminiscent of himself and Maud in the first heat of their first days as lovers.

. . . And now, nearly two years later, as on this rainy morning Morgan approaches the outskirts of Cleveland—what of Geoff and Alan? Simply: they prosper, individually and together. Geoff has settled into his position as trust officer at the Hanover Bank; he likes the regular hours; he finds the work interesting ("solid in its demands"); he says he's relieved to be out of the "gladiatorial arena" of a law firm. Alan is teaching at Columbia and is "momently" completing the score of a new ballet (commissioned by Martha Graham, premiere scheduled for April '48). About five months ago they moved into an apartment on Washington Square, but Alan maintains the apartment on Grove Street as his separate workplace. . . . Ever since Morgan has known him, Geoff has been an avid admirer of Ralph Waldo Emerson. He reads and re-reads Emerson. Soon after he and Alan moved into the Washington Square apartment, he quoted to Morgan Emerson's line, "Blessed are those who have no talent." Then he said: "I'm coming to understand what the line means, Morgie. In part, it's a comment about being a slave; talent the master. Not a kind master. A whipper. I watch Alan under the lash—" He broke off, frowning, and dropped the subject. But recently, when Morgan was in New York and he and Geoff lunched together and Morgan (indirectly) asked: "How are things going?" Geoff had answered: "Very well. *Very* well. It's taken me longer than it maybe should have, but I've finally, I'm sure *finally*, made peace with Alan's talent. I don't resent it anymore—which I guess is another way of saying I've gotten over being jealous of it." Then he laughed: "Well, you *did* ask. . . . You're transparent, Morgie. . . . Now I'll tell you about that matter at the bank we discussed the last time you were in town."

(A parenthesis: One noon-time about two months ago, Morgan ran into Geoff's father at a Wall Street luncheon club. "Morgan!" "Mr. Barrows, sir." Amidst the white-clothed dining tables and the scurrying waiters, the clatter of dishes and the low, reverberating voices of the all-male diners, Mr. Barrows—his mouth close to Morgan's ear—announced that he was "thoroughly reconciled" to Geoff's move from Philadelphia to New York, "as is Mrs. Barrows." Paroxysmally intent, he whispered on, giving his "theory" of the reason behind Geoff's move to New York ["Geoff's *plight* of motivation," he called it]—the thrust of his argument being that whereas *some* veterans of the war had suffered physical injuries, others had suffered psychological injuries: "Geoff a case in point." Disjointedly, he'd continued: "I don't know if you know that the fellow with whom Geoff is sharing bachelor digs spent time in the same prisoner-of-war camp Geoff was in. We haven't met the fellow. Have you? . . . *Good* to hear that you think well of him. I'll tell that to Mrs. Barrows. . . . *Fine* to see you again, Morgan. Family all well, I hope. . . . Come often to New York, do you? . . . How's your father?"

It seemed an eternity—the length of time it took before Mr. Barrows, still shadow-boxing, finally let him go).

. . . What of Maud in all of this? When he had returned home after that January 1946 reunion with Geoff, when he'd settled down, drink in hand, and told her about Geoff—about the extraordinary turn his life had taken—she was infinitely more interested in Geoff's having "found the courage to leave home" (as she matter-of-factly put it), than in what he'd left home for. Then, with that finite, decided look on her face that always presaged an avowal of strong conviction, she stated: "The sexual part of his relationship with Alan Litt is a private matter between *them*, the same way the sexual part of our relationship is a private matter between *us*."

She was a dream, he thought: a lawyer's dream of what a "peer juror" *ought* to be. That was his first, fast, admiring estimation of what she'd said, any musing about it, though, interrupted: because she was onto another subject—love—running after it at top speed, cheeks reddened by the chase. Love was what most mattered, she kept saying; love the great gift bestowed at last on Geoff. "That's what's important. *That's* what counts," she ended.

. . . Now, to Morgan/Geoff/Alan, Maud is their center. She became so the minute Alan met her. He took to her like a duck to water, (and like a duck to water, she took to him). They have traits and tastes in common: tendencies of impatience; tremendous faith in their (individual) convictions; both like ritual, form, order; each has an antic sense of humor; both despise pretense; each is easily, emotionally stirred—but watch out! each is tough—impassioned, and fervent, yes—but not sentimental. No slop.

Geoff's hugest hold on her heart is Caroline, whose godfather he is. It is a role he takes seriously, Caroline, by his own say, being the closest he'll ever come to having a child of his own. Caroline is thrilled that she is allowed to call him by his name—"Geoffrey"—(sometimes, when she's in a hurry, just—"Geoff"). (Morgan often thinks that in Caroline's mind, and in a way important to her, her "Geoffrey" balances out Julia's "Morgan.")

. . . He's in the city now, stopped by a red light. The light turns yellow, then green, and as he revs the Buick's engine and glides past a delivery van, he thinks what a blessing it is, superb to anticipate, that Geoff and Alan will be coming to Cleveland for a four-day visit between Christmas and New Year's. Soon. Very soon they will pass between the griffin-topped pillars that mark the entrance to his and Maud's and Caroline's and Julia's new home and drive down the poplar-treed lane and be at the house: *be* there; arrived! Imagine the boost: how their presence will counter the residual sorrows of Mrs. Leigh's death.

He sighed when he entered his office. On his desk were two pyramids of mail, and a third, smaller pile, more possible in look. His secretary, Miss Corey, told him she had done her best to separate the letters she thought looked "legal" from the ones she thought looked "personal." "*That* one," she

said, indicating the topmost envelope on the smaller pile, "came a few minutes ago, delivered by a messenger boy." He glanced at the envelope; saw
the distinctively large, looped handwriting. "Thank you, Miss Corey."

He waited while she crossed the room; waited until she had closed his
office door.

Early A.M. November 24, 1947

Dear Mr. Shurtliff,

*From out of what you have from time to time told me about your
mother-in-law, I developed my own set of affections for her, my
own pictures of her. The image of her I hold most dear is the one
derived from your description of her sitting in her barn in company
with your children, watching the comings and goings of the barn's
resident swallows.*

*You may recall that when you first told me of her immense liking
for swallows, I mentioned John Ruskin's name—some vague
memory I had of some words written by him about those birds.
Yesterday (Sunday), I raked through the pages of my Ruskin books
and found the passage. Here it is.*

*"The swallow is an owl that has been trained by the Graces. It is
a bat that loves the morning light. It is the aerial reflection of a
dolphin. It is the tender domestication of a trout."*

*I've been thinking steadily of you since last Wednesday (the 12th)
when I read in the newspaper of Mrs. Leigh's death. As I have a
hunch you will be back in harness this Monday morning, going on
with life, I'm sending you this note to your office. I do hope we can
see each other soon. Will you call me? Do take care of yourself.*

Yours ever,
Zenobia Sly

He held the letter in his left hand, and with his right hand reached, at
once, for the telephone.

8 ✑ Running Through a Decade

1948–1957

On school-days, Caroline and Julia had their evening meal at six o'clock
(Morgan and Maud later, around eight). They were always finished eating by the time Morgan got home from Cleveland (usually by seven),
and they regularly spent what they called "drinking time" with him and
Maud. The four of them would be together, usually in the library, in the
winter-time always before a log fire. The hour had no set procedure to
it, no pattern; it unfolded willy-nilly: a sort of family "show-and-tell"
time. One evening, Julia and Caroline reported that Mrs. Sturgess, their
fourth-grade teacher, had begun the day by rolling down a big wall map
and placing the tip of her long wooden pointer on a far-away country
called India, where, Mrs. Sturgess told the class: "Yesterday, Sunday,
January 30, 1948, a great man died." Caroline said that the next thing
Mrs. Sturgess said was that the man's name would last in time for ever
so long, years and years. Julia, frowning, aiming to be a full and accurate
reporter, cut in with: "Mrs. Sturgess said the man had a 'saintly' charac-

ter, that he spent his life in good ways, *wanting* to." The next thing Mrs. Sturgess did was to hold up a newspaper picture of the man and then the picture was passed around, desk-to-desk, so that they could all have a closer look at it.

Caroline said: "He was bald-headed and he wore glasses and he didn't have many clothes on. You could see his legs. They were very thin, like sticks." Mrs. Sturgess said that the man had been killed by another man, an "impatient" man who didn't agree with what the saintly man thought and felt about a lot of things, so had murdered him. "An awful thing to have done, and for so *silly* a reason, just out of *disagreement.*" (Julia stressed Mrs. Sturgess's words.) Then Mrs. Sturgess went to the blackboard and wrote out in big letters the saintly man's name. Caroline said: "She had us write down the man's name in our copybooks, and then she told us how to *say* his name, and we did, out loud, ten times." Caroline looked at Julia, and Julia nodded, and then, solemnly, in unison, they spoke the man's name: "Ma-hat-ma Gan-dhi." Morgan lowered his eyes, his eyes misted over by tears: these little girls, for the first time in their lives, pondering the sudden lessons of history.

Magical, that first year in their glorious new home. In May the hillside above the pond became a blaze of daffodils, the varieties named in a book Morgan found in an old wooden box tucked away in a remote corner of the attic. On the book's first page was written: "This is the Planting Book kept at my request by my gardener, Everett Dryden. It is a record of his landscaping scheme undertaken for the purpose of enhancing the grounds which surround the house. Many of the flower-sets, particularly those of the tuber kind, were imported from England; their names are listed in the sketches (drawings) of each garden-plot." The message bore the signature: "Ernest Ottingen—1902." And so the varieties of blazing daffodils were identified as Dragon's Fire, Canary, Mary's Hair, Yellow Diamond, Swan's Eye, Sunrise. . . . At dusk, deer often came to drink at the pond. . . . There was an owl that regularly roamed the night-skies, hooting as it hunted. . . . Ralph loved the place. In the morning when Tessa let him out the back door, you'd hear him barking up the new day and see him in all kinds of weather streaking over the lawn, crazy in his joy, crazy in his freedom. You couldn't have

clocked him, he ran so fast. . . . One hot Sunday in August, Morgan saw
a man come out of the woods and stand at the wood's edge, looking at
the house. Morgan accurately took him to be a professional tramp. He
beckoned to the man to come forward, and himself strode across the
lawn toward him. The stranger was elderly. He was "just passing
through," he said: "For old time's sake." He was raggle-taggle in look,
but clean; harmless and entertaining and talkative. He charmed Morgan
into going with him on a walk through the woods, retracing the steps of
what he called "the hobo path." He told Morgan that during the 1930
years of the Great Depression, it was word-of-mouth knowledge in the
hobo underground that if you turned off the main road "right here by
this stand of limpy willows, and took this marked, tree-notched path,
and showed yourself decently at the kitchen door of the Ottingen place,
you'd never be refused a hot meal and something put in a paper bag
handed to you to take away with you." (When they parted, Morgan
slipped the man a sawbuck: "Something for the road.") . . . In November
of 1948, on Election Day, to the amazement of many people, Harry
Truman beat Thomas Dewey in the race for president. And on the same
day, from the library window Morgan saw a flock of wild turkeys marching over the frozen ground, the cocks with their tail-feathers all fanned
out, looking, he said to Maud, "like outraged Republicans." . . . It was by
now a year since Mrs. Leigh's death. With Mrs. Leigh "gone" (as Lillie
Ruth put it), and Dr. Leigh spending less and less time in Hatherton
(more and more in Cleveland), there wasn't all that much for her to do
at the Leighs' old house. Nor for Dennis, either. So in late November,
Lillie Ruth and Dennis began to work nearly full time for Morgan and
Maud. Dennis drove Julia and Caroline the fifteen-or-so miles into
Hatherton to school in the morning and picked them up in the afternoon. Lillie Ruth came out with him every morning (except Sundays)
and spent the day helping Tessa with the cleaning and cooking, the two
of them swathed in their big white duster-aprons, talking and singing as
they worked. Maud said it was lovely to hear them and that it meant the
world to her to have Lillie Ruth's "darling presence" in the house. And
Dennis made himself a wizard around the place, anticipating everybody's needs, bringing in logs for the fireplaces and laying fresh fires,

manning the tractor on winter days, clearing the long lane and the front-door turnaround and the garage area of snowdrifts, polishing the cars, seeing to this and that for Tessa and Lillie Ruth. As Lillie Ruth put it: "With Dennis in charge, what needs to be done, gets done, and *thorough*." . . . Ansel Shurtliff spent the 1948 Christmas with them. He arrived on Christmas Eve afternoon. From their room, Caroline and Julia spotted a car coming down the lane. "It might be Pip," they called out from the top of the stairs. And in a moment: "It *is* Pip"—their whoops bringing everybody, from all directions, into the front hall, Morgan in a rush from the library, flinging open the wide front door to the memorably dashing sight of his father stepping out of the driver's seat of what, on the telephone, he had (darkly, mysteriously) forewarned was his new car. "Pa! *Pa*. My God!" he gasped. The car was a Jaguar, as sleek as its name. "My God," Morgan said again: "Pa!" Ansel Shurtliff, still standing by the car, threw up his hands, boy-like: "There's a chap in Cleveland who's set himself up as a distributor of foreign cars. I passed his place last week and just out of curiosity, I went in to see what he had on hand, and when I saw this"—he bowed his head over the Jaguar's hood—"I couldn't resist it. Simply couldn't, *couldn't*, resist it." He looked young. His voice sounded young. From the front door, Maud called out to him: "*Pip*—you're *sexy*." That, just before she ran to him and threw her arms around his neck and kissed him. Kissed him on the lips. Ansel Shurtliff, when he could, said: "Holy smokes!"—Gary Cooper–like, loose. Handsome. Really handsome. Morgan stroked the Jaguar's fender: "Wow," he said: "Wow!"

⁂

1949. In March, a box-like piece of furniture, big, was carried into the library and "installed" by a pig-nosed, heavyset man dressed in a pair of immaculate, white overalls. "Now this here contraption, Mr. Shurtliff, is your antenna. It controls your reception, and what you want is the best reception you can get, so if you'll just stand by me here with the antenna, I'll show you how to work it for your best results. Now these two steel rods, you want to be sensitive to the way you wing them out so they'll coordinate with your getting yourself your best picture. . . . That's right. . . . Slant that right rod up straighter a mite more. Good . . . I can see you're sensitive to the coordination. It's a knack. Some have it, some don't. You do. Good . . . Call me if you develop a problem. I doubt you will. You've got the best set money can buy." Then the man departed, leaving behind in their lives, to their wonder, television.

South Pacific opened on Broadway, and suddenly everybody was singing "Some Enchanted Evening," and "Younger Than Springtime," and "I'm Gonna Wash That Man Right Outa My Hair" (the twins' favorite).

Toward the year's end (two years after Mrs. Leigh's death), Doctor Leigh turned up at Morgan's office and told Morgan he had a "situation" on his hands. Imogene Truffant. (*Ah.*) "She works in administration at the clinic," Doctor Leigh said. "Some fool from the clinic, I've never found out who, ferried her out to Hatherton for Mrs. Leigh's funeral, then had the gall to take her back to my house after the church service. I mention this because it's possible you met her at that time."

Morgan, silent, nodded. In his mind was a clear image of Imogene Truffant's blowsy presence, a clear memory of how she'd cast a predator's eye on the Leighs' fine house and possessively cooed into his and Lucy Blackett's ears Doctor Leigh's name—"Douglas."

"She's threatening to sue me," Doctor Leigh ploughed on. "A kind of breach-of-promise suit." Well, yes, (he answered Morgan's question), for quite some time prior to Mrs. Leigh's death, he *had* indulged himself with Imogene Truffant, an indulgence he now regretted, but in the cir-cumstance of what he referred to as—"the sexual abstinence forced on me by Mrs. Leigh's long mental illness"—the indulgence seemed to him—"understandable." An error, true: "But man-to-man, Morgan, an understandable error." And what about *after* Mrs. Leigh's death? . . . Well, yes. Afterwards, too, the indulgence had continued: "A habit, Morgan, purely of convenience."

He said that, justifying, sitting there, erect and virile, his complexion, as always, vigorously red, his manner, as always, vigorously confident. Morgan could barely stand to look at him.

"She's said she'll settle for a bit of money. 'Recompense' is the word she uses for what she's after. To my mind, it would be pay for services rendered." Doctor Leigh's smile, vague as it was, was coarse. Then the kicker: "I'd like you to negotiate for me, Morgan. Get her paid off and signed off."

Listening to Doctor Leigh, bearing the brunt of his robust, confident gaze, Morgan thought of Mrs. Leigh, of the torments and confusions and hurts and sorrows of her drowned heart; of the way Doctor Leigh had relegated her to madness. And he thought of Maud, of how, if she knew about this—how, for her beloved mother, she would be wounded. Oh, more than wounded . . . "What sum of money do you have in mind to offer Miss Truffant?"

Well, (Doctor Leigh told him), *she'd* mentioned the sum of fifteen thousand, but that was ridiculous, of course; she'd settle, he was *sure,* for ten thousand. Yes. Ten. He was absolutely sure a solid ten thousand would do the trick.

Morgan said: "I'll offer her twenty-five thousand and hope she'll take it. And I'll draw up some form of document designed to release you from any further claims she might make. The document may or may not stand up to legal scrutiny, and I have no way of guaranteeing you that she'll sign it." (Stunned. Stunned blind was the way Doctor Leigh looked.) "I'll do my best to negotiate for you on those terms."

It was a nightmare, this confrontation with this man esteemed as a skilled doctor, a brilliant surgeon, lauded for his professional dedication, commended for the gratis care he lavished on the sick poor: this man about whom people said that if you lined up all the impoverished folk whose lives he'd saved, the line, men, women, and children, would reach in number to a point that would bore you to count. That was the public reputation of this man, his father-in-law, viewed now, privately, in a disparate light. A nightmare.

In his lap, Doctor Leigh fisted his large hands—hands as red from surgical scourings as his face was red: "What you call your 'terms,' Morgan: why, they're nothing short of absurd. Comical," he sputtered: "Preposterous."

"But they stand," Morgan rebutted. "Unless you agree to them, I can't help you."

Doctor Leigh made a last attempt: "I'd expected a broader sympathy from you, Morgan, a greater man-to-man understanding. And I'd thought that for Maud's sake—"

"*No,*" Morgan warned. He didn't have to say more, the solo word rang so of finality.

The ensuing, hard-eyed awkwardness between them was horrible; and inevitable, Doctor Leigh's compliance to Morgan's terms.

Within a month, Morgan brought the curtain down on Doctor Leigh's "situation." He never met with Imogene Truffant. He did it all by letter, using all the tact he had in him: offered Miss Truffant a twenty-five-thousand-dollar settlement, in return for which she signed a document of agreement that once and for all (as it turned out) brought the matter to a conclusion. In the last communication he received from Miss Truffant, she stated that it was her intention to retire from her position in the administrative offices of the clinic and to move to the drier climate of Arizona, outside of Phoenix, to a place she'd been told was beautiful and good for her asthma. "Paradise Valley" was the name of the place.

(*Ah,* God! What a risible irony!)

About any part of any of this, Maud never knew.

≈§

1950: mid-January. "It had to have been an inside job, Mr. Shurtliff," Dennis said.

"Inside or out, *some job!*" Morgan had laughed.

What inspired this exchange was the robbery by masked men of the Boston Express Office of Brinks, Inc. The haul: 2.8 million dollars; 1.2 million in cash!

The Brinks caper opened the year, and for six months, life rocked along in a fairly usual way. But in June, everything changed: the Korean War erupted, and Americans gasped with disbelief and choked back tears that the nation was at war again, that lives would again be lost on soil in a place so distant, so far far away. And this time, in the minds of many many people, about *this* war, the question arose: *Why? Why are we involved?*

≈§

1951. Early in February, early in the morning, Sidney Aranov telephoned Morgan and Maud: "It's a girl," he crowed: "Judith. Born a bit after midnight. . . . Linda's fine. . . . We're thrilled."

In April, President Truman booted General Douglas MacArthur over the moon, out of sight. "Removed General MacArthur of his Korean command" was the way the radio announcer put it—the general having made the fatal mistake of voicing to a listening world a series of policy statements (self-devised) about the conduct of the Korean War. "*Unauthorized* statements," a feisty Harry S. Truman said. Hence the boot.

People were beginning to talk more and more about a Republican Senator from Wisconsin named Joseph R. McCarthy.

And a book was published that was causing a lot of talk. Title: *The Catcher in the Rye*, by J. D. Salinger.

In late summer, Caroline, having climbed higher in a tree than her friend Billy Humphrey, fell out of the tree and broke her left arm. She was way up high, perched on a limb well above Billy, daring him to join her, when she lost her balance and fell to the ground. It was a heart-stopping, awful accident. Yet she was lucky. She could easily have been killed.

~§

THE HOLLIS ACADEMY
—A School for Day Scholars—
—Founded by Ethan Hollis in 1885—

(So reads the sign at the school's entry-gate).

In September of 1952, Julia and Caroline, now twelve years old, entered the eighth grade of Hollis Academy. To this day, a large portrait of Ethan Hollis hangs in the school's assembly hall. The portrait was painted in 1907, when Mr. Hollis was seventy-two: white hair, sideburns, pince-nez glasses dangling from a black ribbon, a round face, a double chin, lips almost smiling, Platonic blue eyes. In his right hand, Mr. Hollis holds a book against his chest. Missing, is his left arm. It was amputated (at the shoulder) when he was twenty-seven years old (in 1862) after the battle of Fredricksburg, Mr. Hollis having served in the Civil War:

Infantry, Company C, 7th Regiment, Ohio Volunteers (the bronze plaque mounted beneath the portrait informs). In academic circles, Hollis Academy is still held in high repute, still known to be a school "difficult to get into." For Caroline and Julia, possessors of first-rate minds, it was ideal. Caroline's mind was a truly fast one, sometimes dangerously so, tending to gloss. At Hollis, she learned to go slower; to see more. Julia's was a deeper mind. She had fewer fast answers than Caroline; in the classroom, she was rarely the first to raise a hand, not for lack of comprehension, but for reasons of her own private searchings, which searches often caused her to get stuck in a small aspect of the larger whole. You could watch her, frowning, working her way out of her "stuckness," moving her thoughts on. . . . Morgan, ever the fascinated observer of the twins' rapidly developing minds and beings, learned as he watched them something about himself, something that surprised him: a gladness—that he was free to view them without self-reference, the freedom due of course to their not being children of his own blood and genes: not Shurtliffs; not, *as* Shurtliffs to be edited by him—but impersonally viewed and loved and marveled at, in the actual way they actually *were*.

"How fast time flies, Mr. Shurtliff," Miss Sly said to him one noon in October as they lunched together: "It doesn't seem possible that it's been four years since the last presidential election. . . . I fear President Truman will lose to General Eisenhower, not that I'd object so much to having Eisenhower as president, but *that man* he's picked for the position of vice president—I don't like him one little bit. In my opinion he's an opportunist and a sentimentalist, and it's been my experience with human nature that that's a very dangerous combination." The man Miss Sly spoke of was Richard M. Nixon.

As to 1953, four events took place that remained for Morgan forever fresh in memory.

In March, Joseph Stalin died, and Russia passed into Nikita Khrushchev's hands.

In July, at Panmunjom, an armistice was signed that ended the Korean War.

And, wonderfully, two men—a New Zealand–born British mountaineer named Edmund Hillary and a Sherpa guide named Tenzing Norgay—conquered Mount Everest.

And Sidney Aranov took on as a client an actor (a friend of Alan and Geoff), a gifted actor whose name was familiar to theater buffs and movie-goers; "took him on" in August and in October went with him as his legal counsel to official Washington, D.C., and defended him before a legislative body that called itself the House Un-American Activities Committee—a group that for some time had busied itself investigating "Communism in Hollywood." So it was in October that Sidney was pictured in the *New York Times*—seated at his client's side at a table set up in the stately chamber of the House of Representatives; Sidney, facing the committee—the picture taken while he was addressing the committee, faced forward, speaking without notes, eyes wide open, his suit-coat unbuttoned as for a fight, no vest, his shirt, across the span of his chest, a wavy mass of wrinkles. (Morgan, gazing at the picture, felt he could positively see Sidney breathing, in and out, hard, like a boxer). The *New York Times* printed the entire text of Sidney's eloquent speech—a speech, as reported, that drew cheers from many of the gallery spectators (and, as Morgan said to Maud: "from invisible God, *praise*"). *Time* magazine described Sidney as "a modern-day Solon." An apt description of what Sidney, now, in many people's eyes, was considered to be: of what (in Morgan's memory) he had been, ten years ago, in 1943, in gloomy Miami—a Solon in uniform—sitting at a barroom table, musing aloud about what he often referred to as "the case of life," venting his thoughts and feelings, sometimes poetically, sometimes in a ribald way, sometimes satirically, often as a mourner—always as a participant. *Ah:* inherently marvelous Sidney: *updated*.

❧

In February 1954, eight years after they had been divorced, Lawrence and Pamela re-married.

At seven in the evening, in a private reception-cum-dining room at the Pierre Hotel, about thirty celebrants (Maud among them) stood by as the marital tie that had been untied was retied by a state judge.

Drinks and dinner followed the brief civil ceremony. It was an oddly
moving affair, marked by a lot of water-over-the-dam nostalgia; by, on
Lawrence's and Pamela's part, a lot of intelligent humility—the dangers
not lost on them of a second attempt to succeed at what they had so
spectacularly failed at the first time around. Lawrence had never been
able to get Pamela out of his system. As for Pamela, her flings had left
her (in her words) "merely *flung*"—that is to say—*dropped* at a place in
life nowhere in particular. She was now a calmer creature, not by any
means meek, but definitely tamer. During the years since she'd divorced
Lawrence, she'd lived for a while on the West Coast, then for a while in
Denver, then Washington, then Chicago; then about three months ago,
she'd returned to New York, and she and Lawrence met again, this time
at a charity ball—one of those big, splashy, Friday night society "do's"
with balloons strung from the ceiling and large flower arrangements set
in the middle of tables that encircle a ballroom floor, Lester Lanin's
band playing a lot of Cole Porter. Lawrence saw her dancing, unsmiling,
in the arms of a stockbroker whom he vaguely knew: and he'd cut in.
Pamela said: "Larry. *Oh* Larry," in the old hazardous way she'd always
said his name, but with the addition, this time, of that loaded, wistful,
unhinging—*"Oh."* Lawrence danced her off the ballroom floor and they
went together to the cloak-room and retrieved their coats and went out
into the winter night, and Lawrence hailed a cab and they went to his
apartment and made love. (From gleanings supplied to them by
Lawrence, that was the scenario Morgan and Sidney put together about
Lawrence's and Pamela's reunion, the "made love" part of the scenario
strictly their own surmise.) As moving as the re-wedding was, it was also
hilarious. How many weddings have you been to where the groom had
not *one* best man, but *two*—Sidney and Morgan—neither of whom, in
appearance, was at his best: Sidney had conjunctivitis in his left eye, so
was wearing an oversized pair of dark glasses that made him look fraud-
ulent and sinister; Morgan's left ear-lobe, nicked (that morning) by a
barber's scissors, was a protuberance of layered coverings—cotton covered by adhesive tape covered by a rubbery pink substance that was supposed to mask the entire mess so as not to be noticed. Not *noticed*?
Horse-feathers. And how many weddings where the bride's matron of

honor, hugely pregnant, halfway through the wedding feast looked suddenly beyond description alarmed and, in a loud, imperative, white voice—down the long length of the dining table—called out to her husband: "Sam! We've got to go. *Right now.*" (The baby, a boy, the couple's third child was born three hours later at Lenox Hill Hospital.)

వ§

. . . 1954's finest public moment came at the end of the year, on December 2, when, by a vote of 67–22, the United States Senate censured Senator Joseph R. McCarthy. Condemned him. Rendered him useless. Kaput. A great day.

వ§

Enter 1955. During the year's first quarter, life strode along in its customary way. In April, though, a short episode of long consequence took place: a *chance* episode which Morgan (in time) came to believe was fated.

Here is the setting, and this is what happened:

Thursday evening, April 7
City: New York
Place: Carnegie Hall
Occasion: A symphony concert.

The prolonged applause of appreciation for the performance of Brahms's Third Symphony began to subside. Switched on again at full strength, the hall-lights blazed, ceiling to floor, and the audience, blinking, came fully to life, bursting into talk, standing up, collecting its possessions, putting on its coats, commencing to move from seat to aisle—a human herd hoofing its way toward the nearest exit, Morgan and Maud and Caroline and Julia among them, Morgan, as paterfamilias, leading the way up an aisle, fronting a passage for Maud and the twins, glancing back at them every few steps, making sure they were still with him, as close behind as possible. They were about three-quarters of the way up the aisle, moving slowly, Morgan already anticipating the outdoor fresh

air and the short walk down Fifty-seventh Street to the Russian Tea
Room, the twins having been promised an after-concert "supper" there.
He had again just glanced back over his shoulder, had caught in his
glance Maud's smile and Caroline's really beautiful, conscious, extro-
verted, developed fifteen-year-old face, and Julia's face, so differently
beautiful, more tenderly young, lifted ceilingward, secretive in its pleasure, dreamy—"I beg your pardon," he said, drawing back. He had
bumped into a woman, and quite hard: "Please excuse me"—and as the
woman turned toward him: "Miss Sly!" he exclaimed.

"Mr. Shurtliff! My dear." She wrung his hand, laughing: "Imagine!"
(Maud, now, was at his elbow.) "And *Mrs.* Shurtliff," her manner and the
tone of her voice at once more formal: "And these young ladies must be
your daughters," her eyes profoundly set on the twins' faces—the
moment chaotic, people shoving against them, murmuring impatience,
jostling—so that they all moved over to one side, into a row of empty
seats, or rather into three rows, for there was another woman, noticed
now by Morgan and immediately defined by him as Miss Sly's companion at this concert: an arresting woman, elegant, much, much younger
than Miss Sly, younger than himself—who slipped into one row and
waited there, watching; and in the next, second row, Miss Sly, who faced
him and Maud and Julia and Caroline, strung out in that order in the
third row. There was then the action of outstretched hands, Maud's to
Miss Sly's, and the twins' hands forwarded—a fluttering reach—when
Maud introduced them to Miss Sly—and then Miss Sly, remembering
her removed friend, pivoting around toward her, saying her name (completely lost in the din), and her friend's well-mannered instant smile of
acknowledgment and performance of a highly amusing gesture that
pantomimed the social hopelessness of the whole situation: the crowd,
her removed position, the hubbub of voices, *plus*—the separating solidity of Miss Sly's majestic figure, standing there in a planted way,
between all of them.

Morgan, immensely attracted to the woman, returned her smile, his,
like hers, amused; and, still looking at her, her eyes now meeting his, her
smile deepening and aimed right at him (or so he felt, almost as a sensation), the odd thought formed in his mind that between the woman and

himself, a complicity existed, a complicity of understanding which had to do entirely with Miss Sly: that, to the two of *them*, and in *their* eyes—as to the moment's whole scene—they knew that Miss Sly, in her inimitable way, would take charge of it and direct it as she saw fit. . . . *So relax*, was the instruction he took from the woman's sustained smile; under Miss Sly's direction, what *would* be, would *be*.

"—their spring vacation from school," Maud was telling Miss Sly, "and we thought it would be fun to spend a few days of it here in New York."

"Lovely," Miss Sly said: "Lovely, for all of you." (Caroline was studying Miss Sly's face; Julia's eyes were on the large, amber, rhinestone-studded comb stuck through the domed bun of her horse-tail hair.) "A fine concert to my ears, the Brahms a celestial work." Miss Sly's gaze moved from Maud's face back to the twins—a special scrutiny (Morgan thought), like that of a portrait painter who, beyond surface appearance, searches for insight into his subject's intelligence and spirit—

—other aspects of the scene then taking root in his mind: Maud's poise, for instance, which surprised him, given her long-ago expressed aversion—her avowed loathing—of the very idea of his remaining in touch with Miss Sly, virtual years since he had as much as mentioned Miss Sly's name to her. (About the lively continuance of his friendship with Miss Sly, she knew nothing, for it remained a fact that Miss Sly really *was* his secret life.) Yet right now, right at this moment (he was actually witnessing it), Maud was clearly pleased by the chance circumstance of this meeting, palpably enjoying this fleeting opportunity to introduce Caroline and Julia to Miss Sly these fifteen years later: Maud, made secure by the passage of time, carrying off the moment, radiant, flushed with maternal pride.

It was just then that, in contrast to Maud's poise, he became conscious of Miss Sly's lack thereof, intuiting it (he knew her that well); just then that he realized that for her, this meeting was in some way a difficult one: one she would have wished to avoid. His intuition took on additional proof as he saw the eager way she picked up on Caroline's unexpectedly offered next words: "We're going on to the Russian Tea Room," was what Caroline said, sounding adolescently grand and a bit actressy,

Miss Sly lighting on the information: "What a treat! If *I* had the prospect of caviar before me, I'd be positively sprinting toward it! So please, you must all hurry along, not allow me to detain you an instant longer." She looked from Caroline's face to Julia's, to Maud's, to his: "Now, there you go! So nice to see you again, Mrs. Shurtliff, and to meet your children—" shooing them off with such a humorous, lofty, lively sweep of her hand and arm that Maud laughed, and the twins too, murmuring their good-byes as they passed into the aisle and up it, moving easily now that the crowd had thinned, Morgan this time bringing up the rear—not, though, until he'd touched Miss Sly's hand (*her* hand, with a tacit warmth, briefly placed on top of his).

As he passed Miss Sly's waiting, watching friend, a smile flashed between them, rich in accord—*Ah, WE knew, didn't we, that Miss Sly would take charge of the scene and conclude it her way: and isn't she wonderful, strangely wonderful, completely wonderful.* That was the message that passed between them, and so perfectly that he paused, then, there in the aisle, near the woman, just long enough to raise his hand to his forehead and, in a way, to salute her. But something about his gesture, *something,* something perhaps that struck her as being in some way too physical, caused her to suddenly, deeply, femininely blush, and as suddenly, to look terribly shy. That was what remained so vividly in his memory of her: that look of sudden, extreme shyness which had so swiftly overwhelmed the brilliance of her smile.

(It would be four years before he would see her again. Four years before Miss Sly would reintroduce him to her. Sylvia Phelps was her name.)

Out on Fifty-seventh Street, Julia asked him: "That lady, Morgan, the one with the comb in her hair—who is she?"

Julia's question raised in his mind the parenthetical fact that a few weeks before he returned home from the war, it had fallen on Maud's shoulders to tell the twins that they were adopted. She had hoped to delay telling them until he would be with her, but a boy at nursery school, Brian Ashley, had prematurely forced the issue. "Your dad and mom aren't your *real* dad and mom," Brian had hammered into the twins' ears: "I know they aren't," he'd hammered on, "because I heard *my* mom tell *my* dad that they aren't." Ya-ya-ya. Supervising that morning's nursery school play period was nice, astute Miss Baxter, who heard Brian's taunt and had the sense to telephone Maud and tell her what had happened: "I was sure you'd want to know, Mrs. Shurtliff. Caroline seemed quite upset." Then Miss Baxter had laughed: "I guess I ought to tell you too that Julia kicked Brian." Maud said: "You mean *Caroline* kicked him." Miss Baxter said: "No, *Julia* did. It surprised me too, Julia as a kicker. I made light of it—sent Brian off to play with Georgie Fowler. I'm sure the twins will tell you all about the episode." As predicted by Miss Baxter, they did. Or rather, Caroline did, at noon-time, when Maud picked her and Julia up at school. Caroline threw herself onto the car's front seat and at once repeated what Brian had said, and: "What did he mean?" she had asked Maud, and with a greater vehemence, repeated: *"What did he mean?"*

Morgan had never asked Maud to try to reconstruct the exact words she had used to answer Caroline's question, Julia sitting there too, waiting to hear. He had never asked because by the time he returned home from the war, there had been no reason to—the results of her answer were so in place, so fully, wholesomely established: in the twins' five-year-old minds, "adopted" was a marvelous thing to be: *chosen* was the great word: marvelous to have been *chosen:* in all the world and from so many other babies, *chosen* to be loved, loved so much, so much: all along the way, loved so much. That the twins thought so, that they *felt* so, was Maud's achievement, her victory, won on that long-ago day when he was paternally absent, still away at war, when, on her own, she had established love as adoption's base, and so well, so perfectly, that as the twins had grown older and up into a full understanding of what "adopted" *technically* means, the two words they had been overheard to apply about adoption (whenever the topic came up, which it inevitably did every once in the odd while) were "chosen" (they *were*) and "love" (in the present, every unquestioned, ever enduring tense).

("That lady, Morgan, the one with the comb in her hair, who is she?") . . . The four of them were walking close together, arms linked, so Maud heard Julia's question; Caroline, too; and although Julia had put her question to *him,* he knew that Maud would prefer to answer it, to at

least be given the chance to set the tone of an answer. He glanced at
Maud. Her head was turned toward him. He smiled, and she took the
lead, addressing Julia: "She's an old acquaintance," she said. "We met her
years ago, soon after you were born. I haven't seen her since. She hasn't
changed a bit, looks exactly the way she did way back then."

Morgan said: "There's a Latin phrase that best describes her. *Sui
generis*. It means thoroughly unusual—unlike anything or anyone else."

Immediately, Maud said: "It was nice to see her again." She said it in a
firm way that conveyed sincerity, while at the same time implying that
there really wasn't anything more to be said—and anyhow, they were
now under the red awning that marked the entrance to the Russian Tea
Room. Caroline said: "This is so exciting!" Julia stepped aside, and
Caroline too, deferentially, and Maud, smiling, moved forward: the first
of them to go through the revolving door.

. . . Albert Einstein died on the eighteenth of April (a Monday) and
on that same day Ralph fooled around with a porcupine and ended up
the loser. He returned home, howling, from a solo walk in the woods.
Dennis heard him. (Maud was in town attending the Hatherton Library
monthly Board of Trustees meeting.) Later in the day Dennis told her
how Ralph had come running, announcing his troubles by his howls;
how he'd sat down outside the kitchen door "yawping," Dennis said,
"like a baby. His face looked like a dress-maker's pincushion." Dennis
took him to the vet and brought him back about three hours later, "quill
free." But he was an awful sight, pathetic, with his fine muzzle all
swollen out of shape, its whiteness (in age he was by now nearly thirteen
years old) painted over with Mercurochrome and the rims of his blood-
shot eyes phlegmy from the drain-off of his woeful adventure. Julia and
Caroline and Morgan and Maud fussed over him mightily that evening,
petting and hugging him, promising him he'd feel better tomorrow, all
the time, on the television, pictures of Einstein were being shown, and a
running narration going on about his life and work; his genius. (Which
is why, ever since that evening, whenever Morgan thinks of Ralph,
remembering him, he thinks of Einstein. And the other way around:
whenever Einstein's name comes up, he thinks of Ralph.)

. . . Consider for a moment the long reach in everyone's life of what happened down in Montgomery, Alabama, in December of '55: of a seated woman—Rosa Parks was her name—riding on a public bus: of her refusal to give up her seat to a white man: of how her refusal had the effect of opening a pair of stage curtains—old opaque heavy-hanging reeking long-closed drapery pulled apart—revealing at stage center a talented, well-rehearsed other man, ready to speak: Martin Luther King, Junior. (What a name!) And so began the epic drama of the civil rights movement. Soon, throughout the land, a citizen cast of untold thousands would augment the ranks of the initial players.

(*Ah* . . . A last recall about 1955: *Lolita*. Vladimir Nabokov's sprung creation. Oh the number of doomsday folk who whispered the name as if they dared not voice it aloud, as if it were a highly contagious, killer virus.)

ꝶ

Maud dubbed 1956—"Alan Litt's year!" In February, the premiere performance of his first symphony was conducted by Bruno Walter. Sitting with Alan in Carnegie Hall on that memorable evening were Geoff and Alan's sister, Gwen, and Maud and Morgan. The preperformance atmosphere was not lacking in electricity. Luminaries from the music world were present in force. So were the critics.

The symphony's first movement was a tightly wrought, exuberant *Allegro con brio;* the second movement an amiable *Poco allegretto.* In a break from traditional symphonic structure, the third, final movement was a stately *Andante* that began ethereally, *pianissimo,* and built to a climax more intense than loud, and from that sheer extreme receded like a great abating sigh back to *pianissimo.* The cellos sounded the movement's last phrase and held its last note to the end of its aural life.

Silence.

And then the applause began, and gained, and from the podium Bruno Walter waved his arms in the direction of Alan's seat, hailing Alan to rise and come forward, and Alan, quickly, just before he obeyed the command, embraced Geoff, and kissed Gwen and Maud, and by a stretch, clenched Morgan's hand, and then was gone, into the aisle, lithe, moving stageward almost at a run through the applause. (So he never saw the look on Maud's face of awe and admiration, but Morgan did, and in memory, always would.) . . . In March, again in New York (at Town Hall), the Hapsburg Quartet premiered Alan's Third Quartet in G-minor. ("*Mozart's* key, temporarily loaned to me," Alan said.) . . . And in April, Alan was the recipient of the Arthur Haezler Award (given every five years to an American composer), and in April, too, he was awarded the Rattigan Prize (of twenty-five thousand dollars). "Alan's year," Maud said: "All his stars in place!"

ᴥ

. . . Not so for Lucy Blackett. Her long affair with Gerry Davis, begun in war-torn London in 1944, came to an end these twelve years later. In recent months, their meetings had become hasty ones, single hours, seized by Gerry from the demands of his successful career as an architect, and from his family—(his two children, whom he "loved," and his wife, whom he "liked"). He had the capacity for that kind of lethal honesty, and Lucy, for so long a time, the lethal capacity to accept it. Until she woke one morning and, to herself defined what, in Gerry's life, she felt she had come to be: no longer Gerry's companion-lover, but the obliging frail of another woman's husband. That was the way she put it to Maud, blaming only herself for her misery. So she closed the door on their long relationship. Quietly. No scene. And Gerry bowed and went away.

For Lucy, for a harsh while, the void of his departure seemed more than she could bear. Maud saved her. Morgan watched her do it. Again and again she boarded the train to New York, staying with Lucy sometimes for only a day, sometimes for two days, once for nearly a week. "For however long Luce wants me with her, I'll stay": that was Maud's theme, said with variations, over and over.

Slowly, Lucy regained her footing. . . . In late autumn, Maud (just back from yet another trip to New York), told Morgan: "I'm sure she's all right now." Then she began to weep.

Tears of relief, Morgan thought, and said so.

"No," Maud shook her head.

"Then why are you crying?"

"Because," Maud sobbed: "Because I know her. Because I know she'll never look at another man."

๕

. . . "My first glory case," Morgan always (afterwards) called it.

For sixteen months—from September of 1956 to January of 1958—it virtually took over his life.

The crux of the case can be quickly summed:

> > At threat were the interest(s) of two *adopted* (male) children in a long-established family trust valued at millions of dollars.
> > The children had been adopted as infants by the grand-daughter of the grantor (founder) of the trust. > The terms of the trust provided that upon the death of the said grand-daughter, the trust would terminate and the principal be distributed to the said grand-daughter's children: "To her issue, then living, per stirpes," and "if there be no such issue"—the principal would pass to a charity *named* in the trust.

Those were the stated conditions of the trust, the background, so to speak, of the case, the *action* of which commenced at the time of the grand-daughter's death, in February of 1956.

Immediately following the grand-daughter's death, the named charity made its claim in the Surrogate's Court of New York County that at the time the trust was drawn (so many years ago) the phrase—"issue, then living, per stirpes"—would not have applied to adopted children: that, therefore, the principal of the trust should be paid to the charity rather than to the adopted children.

Thus the matter, as a case, came into being.

Now as to the action: in September of 1956, the two adopted children—by now prominent adult men aged thirty-three and thirty-one—retained Morgan to represent and protect their interest(s) in the trust.

At this point, it is necessary to say that the founder (grantor) of the trust had been in his time a famous man of the achieving kind people spoke of, back in those days, as "an all-American Horatio Alger type."

(Hence a great captivator of the public's imagination.) So while he was still alive, he had been the subject of countless newspaper articles and interviews, even of several full-blown biographies, in all of which available material (supplemented by private family papers provided him by his clients) Morgan, for two months, immersed himself for the purpose of *re-creating* the man's personality and character—his attitudes and motivations and habits, his sympathies, his bearings and loyalties in relation to family members and friends, his societal concerns, his *humanity*—which vivid re-creation became a body of evidence sufficient, as Morgan argued it, to persuade the Surrogate's Court that such a man would not—*not*— have excluded adopted children as inheritors of his bounty.

Inevitably, the charity appealed the Surrogate's Court's determination to the Appellate Division of the Supreme Court of the State of New York, before which court Morgan re-argued his case with a skill (again) powerful enough to persuade the Appellate Court to *unanimously* affirm the Surrogate's Court's earlier determination.

In a desperate, last-ditch move, the charity sought leave to appeal the issue to the Court of Appeals of the State of New York. . . .

. . . It is a fact that, except for a murder trial, nothing attracts the public's and the news media's attention faster than a courtroom battle involving immense sums of money. So from that day in September of 1956 when Morgan became one of the key figures in just such a battle, to the day sixteen months later, in January of 1958, when the case was concluded, his name appeared often in print, in press and magazine accounts of the battle's on-going action, and of course, throughout the proceedings, in various law journals. So when he emerged the victor in the case, there was a further, concentrated spate of publicity about him; and so he experienced, and briefly enjoyed, a momentary "fame." ("A fame of the Andy Warhol brand," he would say of it, laughing, twenty years later.)

The brief duration of his "public" fame aside, the case secured his name in the legal world. Carved it, so to say, in stone. *And,* far from incidentally, advanced to greater heights the already stellar reputation of the Kissel, Chandler firm.

Throughout most of 1957, he spent an average of fourteen workdays of every month in New York. *Had* to, because as the case advanced from one phase to the next, each new adversative move required of him that he rethink *his* plea: reposition it; refortify it; in a sense, redecide it. To the solitary hours spent in such review, many additional hours were spent in conference with the two associates engaged in the dig-work of continuous research and in the writing of preliminary drafts of new briefs. So of necessity he became what he called "a long-ride weekly commuter," Cleveland-to-New York and back. Usually, he left Cleveland on Sunday evening, making the overnight journey by Pullman train, then reversing the journey from New York on Wednesday night, arriving back in Cleveland on Thursday morning. Once in a while, if he had to remain in New York on a Thursday, he made the trip by plane. In New York, the place he called "home" was the Stuyvesant Club. There he slept and ate breakfast and at day's end ate dinner and went again early to bed and rose early the next morning and breakfasted and from the club went again to his office. In the physical comforts of good food, good service and a well-appointed bedroom, the Stuyvesant afforded a posh existence. But there the ease ended, snuffed out by the demands of work—demands that made of his life a disciplined, routine affair vaguely reminiscent of his wartime years aboard ship, the oddest resemblance being the sudden way he would at times wake in a dead-of-night sweat, alert, feeling threatened. Such times always coincided with a fresh worry about the case, with running scared in relation to it, as on the *Stubbins,* on a new stretch of new sea that posed new dangers. In an effort to get back to sleep, he would reinvoke Miss Sly's old incantation: One good hen, two ducks, three cackling geese, four—

. . . So of course, one way or another, he would often end up thinking about Miss Sly and himself and of their strangely intimate, formal friendship, and of how he could never quite rid himself of the feeling, *about* their friendship, that it was ordained. Certainly it was a fact that by 1957 they were seeing more of each other than ever before. They met for lunch at least twice a month. Once, (he couldn't afterwards reconstruct just how the moment had come about) they admitted to one another that they "counted" on being together every couple of weeks, that being together "made a difference." They didn't pursue—as a subject—exactly *what* the difference was that being together *made,* and surely never, ever did they speak of their mutual awareness of their ever-increasing closeness.

It never ceased to fascinate him that prior to that 1955 encounter in Carnegie Hall when Miss Sly saw and met the twins as fifteen-year-old girls, she had never permitted him to talk with her about them. By a staying look or gesture, she had steadfastly quashed his attempts. But *after* that encounter, starting immediately thereafter, she had taken the lead in bringing up their names (the first time with an openness that bordered on display), and ever since, and ever more avidly, had retained the lead.

"Tell me," she would say: "*Tell* me"—pinning him in her gaze, her head cocked to one side, the massive bun of her hair, at its pitched angle, threatening to come undone and drop into her soup or onto her salad plate. . . . God knows that in 1957 there was plenty to tell about Caroline and Julia, so much was happening in their lives and in such rapid sequence. . . . This was their senior year at Hollis Academy: the consuming topic of the first four months of 1957 had been *college*. Which one would they enter in the fall? Early on, they had let it be known that they wanted to attend the same college, but wanted to live in separate dormitories. They had applied for admission to three institutions: Radcliffe, Smith (Maud's alma mater) and Bryn Mawr—(and had had the thrill of being accepted by each). During the break of the Hollis spring vacation, he and Maud had taken them to visit the three campuses, after which trip there followed an agonizing week of what Julia and Caroline called—"terminal decision."

"*Tell* me," Miss Sly appealed, leaning toward him across the luncheon table—a picture of suspense. "Bryn Mawr," he said: "They've opted for Bryn Mawr."

"Tell me," she said again in late April, *this* time in appeal for an account of the dinner party organized by Maud (at the twins' behest) in celebration of their seventeenth birthday, all their Hollis classmates in attendance. "Twenty young women," he reported, "all in various stages of bloom!" He'd gone on, narrating how, as one by one the feminine horde had arrived for the party, he had stood with Maud and Julia and Caroline at the foot of the staircase in the festooned hall of their house and greeted each girl and—"as a mere male and father"—been, by each girl, for a moment, "beautifully tolerated," and then, how, with the arrival of the twentieth girl, Caroline had cast upon him a prompter's glance: his cue to disappear. And he had. And gladly: "Because," he laughed, "if I hadn't, I'd have been made deaf for life! What I learned is that when a bunch of seventeen- and eighteen-year-old girls come together as social creatures, they *squeal,* unmercifully, and about *every-thing*." "Their *dresses,*" Miss Sly took over, "and the *entire* way they've gotten themselves up for the party, *hair* and all!" "Exactly." (He didn't, with Miss Sly, say anything about how some of the girls had been shod—in narrow, slick, high-heeled pumps of the sort Sutter had always used to refer to as "Joan Crawford fuck-me shoes." He *had* been more than a little surprised at how sexually advanced [at least in appearance] some of the girls had seemed to him to be.)

"*Tell* me"—three weeks after the occasion of the birthday dinner—about the greater event of the twins' graduation from Hollis Academy—the June evening of the commencement exercises warm enough to warrant keeping the tall windows of the school auditorium open, letting in the fragrance of flowering lilacs. Julia "walked off" with the English Literature Prize; Caroline "capped" an Honorable Mention in Mathematics. From the terribly erect way his father sat throughout the proceedings, Morgan knew what a struggle he was having to control his emotions. Not Maud, though. Her tears had flowed: "Like the Nile." "And *you,* Mr. Shurtliff?" *Ah* . . . Her question made him laugh; his laughter was her answer. Impossible to translate his feelings into words. But he did tell her that when Julia was called forward to receive the English Literature Prize (a handsomely bound collection of Henry James's short stories), her young, solemn dignity as she'd walked across the stage had very nearly undone him.

(Sometimes when they lunched together and had the rare luck of having a few extra minutes to spare, they would linger over their coffee and ruminate outside of Time about nothing much at all, like two very old people about to pass away—a communion of souls. Their friendship had become an entity that capable.)

❦

Money and Morgan.

By the sweat of his lawyer's brow, he earned the money to maintain his family and home to his own standards of accountableness and, by personal inclination, of beauty.

That is an objective statement that could be made about him. It is not a statement he would have made about himself—which isn't to say he was above pride of ability, or was lacking in satisfaction of accomplishment—only that he had been schooled to believe that work is a moral part of what Life is: one of its expectations. The maxim had been drilled into him: "Unless one is incapable of doing so, one earns one's way in life."

Having by chance been born into a circumstance of bed-rock wealth, money was a subject his father, in ethical terms, had obliged him from an early age to think about. He could never forget the day Ansel Shurtliff had sat him down and quoted to him Lord Byron's remark: "Ready money is Aladdin's lamp," then juxtaposed that happy quote with Epicurus' words to the effect that riches don't lessen, only alter, one's troubles. And then how his father had gone on to say that the privilege of having Money carried with it many duties, many societal obligations, after which admonition he had delivered his fierce, valedictory message: that anyone who possesses Money and uses his possession of it as a weapon, or allows his possession of it to bloat his ego into a kingliness out of all proportion to the rest of mankind, "is—to put it in the politest possible terms—an ass." To Morgan's young ears, the way his father intoned the word "ass" came out sounding cold and scornful, beyond redemption, vile.

Given that background conditioning, it was at times almost an embarrassment the way Money kept pursuing him, singling him out, haunting him, hovering near him, over him, depositing willy-nilly into his lap more and more of the cushy green stuff that was the signifier of its omnipresence in his life. Three times during that 1948–1957 decade, Frederick Selby (the Shurtliff family lawyer) summoned him to his office for the purpose of informing him that Money, yet again, had tracked him down and deposited upon him, yet again, more money. The third summoning came in mid-June of 1957. A relative, unknown to Morgan, never met, had died and left him (and three others of his generation) the bulk of a sizable fortune.

"Pa," Morgan telephoned his father: "Who the hell is—*was*—Thurlow Shurtliff?"

Ansel Shurtliff laughed. Then: "I've been expecting this call from you! Fred Selby telephoned me last week to tell me old Thurlow had died. I understand you take very handsomely under the terms of his will."

"Yes. But Pa, I've never heard mention of him! How am I related to him?"

"Well"—his father's laughter came fresh—"he was my second cousin, which I guess makes you his second cousin once removed. And by a very considerable gap in age. Are you sitting down?"

"I am now," Morgan said.

"Because the story of Thurlow's life may surprise you. In our branch of the family, Thurlow's always been more of a legend than a presence, always spoken of as 'a fearless eccentric.' He gained his first fame as a First World War hero, then as a mountain climber. He climbed mountains all over the world—the Matterhorn, Kilimanjaro, peaks in South America. After he satisfied his craze for climbing mountains, he took up ballooning—went every year to France, somewhere near Chartres, to take part in an annual balloon-do that's held there. I have an old, very endearing photograph of him standing in the cab of his balloon, waving to a group of people gawking up at him from the ground. It was taken just as he was commencing one of his aerial ascents. I'll search out the picture and send it to you. You'll be amused by what you can see of the clothes he's wearing. He liked to go about *en travestie*. The one and only time I ever met him, years ago at your cousin Richard Shurtliff's house in Cincinnati, he arrived driving a top-down Pierce-Arrow phaeton. He was gotten up in a mauve-colored hat and a mauve silk scarf and mauve gloves that matched the mauve pleated skirt he was wearing over his pants. I was young enough to be tremendously impressed. . . . Have I rendered you speechless?"

"Not quite." Morgan laughed.

"He was married, by the way, and by all accounts very happily. His wife—they had no children—died about ten years ago. Georgia was her name. I never met her. But Richard Shurtliff once described her to me as looking like a tall, very imposing, ivory-faced Victorian clock of the type you're likely to see in the Great Hall of an English country house— one that chimes on the hour. He also said she had a wonderful sense of humor and a really rare talent for making friends. The next time I see Richard I'll ask him if he has a spare picture of her he might be willing to let you have."

"That would be nice. And I'd much appreciate a look at that picture of Thurlow you mentioned—"

"In the cab of his rising balloon." Ansel Shurtliff laughed again. "I'll hunt it out for you the minute I hang up."

About his unexpected monetary windfall, Morgan next asked: "Why me?"

"Oh, in the end, lacking any children of his own, I think old Thurlow felt the pull of the family name; wanted his means to remain in the family. From what Fred Selby told me, the three other beneficiaries are all in the same cousinly line as yourself, all males and all roughly your age. And Thurlow surely knew that the text of his will would cause a lot of family talk—as it has—and he undoubtedly relished that prospect. . . . You would have liked him, Morgan."

⇜

It was in June too that Lillie Ruth stunned Maud by telling her that on this very Friday, the fourteenth day of the sixth month of 1957, she had "turned" seventy-nine years old; that this time next year, if God wanted her to, she would "become" eighty. She had for so long pretended to youngerness and in appearance and spryness and eagerness worn her pretense so well that no one for a long time had thought to count, to add up the truth, starting with what they all knew: that way back in 1918 when she'd come to work for the Leighs, she had admitted (*then*) to being in age "about forty years old."

"That was *thirty-nine* years ago," Maud mused aloud to Morgan that evening, equating the date in terms of her own age: she had been a four-year-old child when Lillie Ruth entered her life. "I feel foolish, guilty, not to have put it all together," she said, then had gone on to tell him what Lillie Ruth had talked about after confessing her real age: how, seated together on the couch in Maud's sitting room, holding each other's hands, they had exchanged memories of Maud's mother, and then how Lillie Ruth ("looking suddenly tired") had revealed to Maud what she called "her greatest *want*," which was to live out her last years "under the same roof" with Maud (so too of course with him)—not just be driven out by Dennis of a morning to the house, then driven back in the afternoon to her own place (a square-fronted, three-room abode set down on an area of land referred to by older Hathertonians as "the Negro district.") "I've grown timid to be alone at night, Maudie," were Lillie Ruth's final words; her ultimate confession.

It was plain to them what to do: all that extra unused space adjacent to and level with Tessa's rooms (no stairs involved) must be renovated and made fine for Lillie Ruth ("Lovely and *appropriate*," Maud projected), toward which end Morgan telephoned his architect the next morning and told him to look at the space and submit, as soon as possible, a sitting room, bedroom, and bath design of what would be Lillie Ruth's future home.

"Ready money is Aladdin's lamp": the sentence came back to him a couple of weeks later when he and Maud showed Lillie Ruth the architect's drawings. Unforgettable, the way she clapped her hands together and praised Jesus and flung herself into Maud's arms. *Ah:* sheer magic, being able to honor her by providing her her "greatest want."

The architect found a builder. The renovation would begin in a month's time. "We'll have you moved in by October," Morgan told her. In the quiet, June-sunlit library, Lillie Ruth again struck her hands together. A second thunder-clap of joy.

⋟

. . . By July, what he sorely needed was a vacation. "The case," alas, precluded the possibility. "But just you wait," he kept telling Maud: "The instant the case is settled, we'll be off, my love, to distant lands"—waxing poetic with her about their plan-in-the-make to board an ocean liner and sail away to Europe: "The instant the case is settled." The phrase became a prayer of anticipation they chanted to each other all that summer.

All that summer of the discovery, by young men, of Caroline and Julia.

Beginning in about the third week in June (just as Lillie Ruth had long ago predicted they would) boys began to turn up and buzz around the twins in numbers like flies. They drove between the griffin gate-posts and came down the lane in all makes and types of cars, remnant jalopies, station wagons, convertibles, chamois-shined sedans; one stripling piloted a sassy new jeep. Some of the youths were the privileged sons of family friends and acquaintances, which nicety of social connection did not necessarily mean that such *known* young men posed any less a threat (in Morgan's and Maud's eyes) than did the young men whose faces and names were new to them—youths whom the twins had met at dances, or beside the country club swimming pool, or at sailboat races at the Eagle Lake Club, or wherever else on a sunny afternoon the young crowd found itself, here and there, to be. Most of the youths were the twins' age, newly graduated from private day schools or eastern prep schools, due to start college in the fall. And as opposite as north is to south, as down is to up, cold to hot, black to white, they behaved one way with Caroline, the other way with Julia. It was fascinating to see. Around Caroline, they postured and made themselves vivid—showing off their speed and stamina on the tennis court, making tricky dives into swimming pools—competing hard for Caroline's attention. Around Julia, they behaved more like friends than rivals. (Early on in the summer Lillie Ruth said: "It's Julia's *unity* that gentles them." Ansel Shurtliff said: "Julia's an aesthetic creature. If I were a lad, I'd be awed by her." Maud said: "Boys mirror her shyness.")

There was one youth who was older than all the others—Mitchell Talmadge, called "Mitch." He had already completed his freshman year at Princeton. He was dark eyed and dark haired and slim hipped. Developed. Morgan titled him—"The Sophisticate"—and by the time July rolled around, he and Maud knew that Mitch had gained a special hold on Caroline's imagination. They knew he had from the way Caroline acted whenever Mitch was due to play tennis with her or to take her sailing or to carry her off to a movie or an evening party. A few minutes before Mitch was expected, Caroline would become either abnormally animated or abnormally placid. ("Wired, or in a trance," was the way Maud put it). One Sunday afternoon she positioned herself at the top of the long curved staircase and stayed there until Mitch had been admitted through the front door into the hall. Then, from above, over the stair-railing, she called down to him—"Mitch." And then, slowly, she began to descend the stairs. She was wearing a short-skirted tennis dress. At the bottom of the staircase Mitch stood, his face raised to her, the fingers of his right hand wrapped around a newel post, gripping it. His eyes never left her. Morgan, from his paternal stand in the library doorway, watched Mitch watch her, and for a moment—remembering what it was like to be a sexually revved-up young man of nineteen years—he almost felt sorry for Mitch. *Almost.*

He and Maud were in complete agreement that, as to boys, Caroline was the twin to worry about. In June, Maud had vouched: "She has it in her to be *led.*" In July, after witnessing that staircase scene, Morgan vouched: "She has it in her to *lead.*" Maud said: "I know. I'm going to speak to her about that. . . . No, Morgan, you shouldn't be there when I do. It's too *female* a topic. . . . Leave it to me. . . . *I'll* instruct; *you* be the guard-dog." They both laughed then, looking and looking at each other: balanced.

That summer, with Morgan away so much of the time in New York, Ansel Shurtliff spent many days with Maud. She would telephone him (he always waited to be *asked*) and he would leave his home, leave the burgeoning acres of his beloved orchards to go to her. (Toward the end of June, he wrote her a note: "How *tremendous* it is, my dear Maud, at my age, to be made to feel both wanted *and* useful. I am a fortunate man! *Pip.*") He told Morgan that the summer had for him "a throwback feel" to the war years when he and Maud had stood sentry-duty together. "But that was then," he had mused on, "and this is *now*, and where, oh where has the time gone? . . . Caroline and Julia, grown up! All of a sudden!" And then he smiled: "It amuses me, the *grand* paternal effect I have on the young crowd—particularly on the lads—when you're not here. How they kowtow to me: Shurtliff the Elder *authorized* by Shurtliff the Younger to occupy the Imperial Throne of Espial while Shurtliff the Younger is absent. I love the power!" He grinned: "But what I love even more is the look of amazement on the lads' faces when they see me getting in or out of my new Jaguar" (which second such car, dark red, he had recently purchased). "How they do stare! I tell you, Morgan: when *your* time rolls around as the grand-father of grown-up grand-children, *if you can,* be in possession of a 'Jag,' because, in the eyes of a bunch of lads, it's the equivalent—for *clout*—of Merlin's wand." He said it gaily, the sun on his white hair as he strolled with Morgan over the lawn. "But now," he said, "*you* talk, son. I want to hear the latest news of your case. And did you see Geoff and Alan on your last trip to New York? Maud told me they're coming for a visit in August. I'd like to see them when they're here. And what's Sidney up to these days?"

Morgan never got the chance to answer.

"Morgan! Pip!" Julia's voice.

Morgan and his father stopped walking; turned around. The call had come from way over *there*, across the broad sweep of lawn, from the direction of the pond.

"Morgan . . . Pip . . . *Wait.*"

And then Julia came running toward them; waving, smiling. As she came on, Morgan—the years tumbling backwards—saw her for a flash as a child again whom he would catch in his arms and swing up over his head. But running forward, getting closer, she regained in his eyes the actuality of what she was now—"Grown up, all of a sudden"—just as his father had said.

"Morgan, Pip." And, near: "If you're not being private, may I join you?"

Morgan took her hand (he *could* do *that*). Then suddenly he thought of Henry James: a pictorial impression of those grandly eloquent out-door scenes in James's novels: a summer day—a carpet of grass—a long vista—three people strolling together into the future of the story.

It must be noted that Julia and Caroline did not idle away the whole of that summer. There was a limit, they said, to the amount of time one could spend "just lollygagging around, being frivolous."

They enrolled in two Hollis Academy Summer School courses: Advanced Oral and Written French, and Prose and Poetry of the American Civil War. For five weeks, from early July into August, Monday through Friday, nine A.M. to noon, they were in the classroom. Each course required a hefty amount of homework. Julia established a work/play schedule and rarely broke from it. Caroline was flexibility itself. "Mood" was her declared time-piece: "I'm in the mood to study." Or: "I'll study later; right now I'm in the mood to play." Exactly which mood she would be in largely depended on what the young crowd was going to be doing on a given afternoon or evening, and on whether or not Mitch would be a participant. (One day, Morgan overheard her tell Julia that she wasn't "in the mood" to do whatever it was Julia had suggested might be fun, and Julia, in a rare display of sisterly irritation, exploded: "Callie! Just say 'yes' or 'no.' Give up that mood talk. It's so high horse. So Greta Garbo!" Morgan wondered: would there be a quarrel? No. Only a silence, sensed as thick, punctuated perhaps by a glare from Caroline. Marvelously, Julia's outburst had its effect: from that day on, Caroline trashed—"mood.")

❧

Early in August, Mitch vanished from the scene.

For the bulk of the week, Morgan had been in New York, but as usual, he was back home for the weekend. And as usual, on Saturday, cars came and went, bearing, in varying numbers, members of the young crowd. Some stayed just long enough to say they'd be back later. Others remained and played tennis or simply flopped down under a shade tree and talked. Some walked in the woods. Some took off their shoes and waded in the creek like kids, the girls holding up their skirts, the lads attending them, making sure they didn't lose their footing. Some sought the creek's upstream pool, there to be entertained by frogs and crayfish and turtles, armored beetles and Jesus spiders, red-winged blackbirds, a chance bittern fishing in the shallows. Seen at a glance from the house, and devoid of sound, the several pictures of the young crowd's activities were distant enough to seem to be timeless, dream-like. And for a while, for an hour or so, that was the way it would be. But then, after a while, one group would become restless and pull itself together and collect its scattered possessions—shoes and socks and purses, tennis rackets and a hat or two—and recross the lawn to their cars, and drive away. And in a little while, another group would arrive. *Who now?* the ones who had remained would ask.

Of Mitch, always heretofore a conspicuous presence, Morgan, on this Saturday, saw no sign. "What's become of him?" he asked Maud that evening.

"I've been waiting for a quiet time to tell you," she said. "As of last Wednesday evening, he's a thing of the past."

"Oh? What happened?"

"I'm not sure. It's something of a mystery. . . . He picked up Callie after lunch on Wednesday to take her sailing, and you know me: just before they drove off, I asked my usual question, 'What time can I expect you back?'—and Callie said five-thirty, that she wanted to get started on her homework before dinner. She repeated it, five-thirty at the very latest. A few minutes after they left, Bruce Wilson arrived in his car to take Julia—you'll never guess to do *what.*"

Morgan smiled: "I'm afraid to try."

"Bruce's springer spaniel, Pansy's her name, had had six puppies, and Bruce wanted Julia to see them right away."

"You're right, I'd never have guessed. . . . So we've got Caroline off sailing with Mitch, and Julia off puppying with Bruce, and what about you, sweet? How did you spend the afternoon?"

"Errands." Maud made a face. "I went into town and did a pile-up of niggling errands. *Enthralling.* I got back shortly before six. Callie hadn't returned, but I didn't think to worry. Not then. Julia and Bruce were on the terrace. They asked me to join them, and I did. They told me all about the puppies. Julia was ecstatic about them. I do like Bruce. He's intelligent. Peaceful, too." She smiled: "He sits still! The Wylie boy came by the other day and I was a wreck after spending five minutes with him. It was like being with someone having a fit—one hand scratching his head, the other twisting a shirt button, both legs—he was sitting beside me—both legs jigging up and down a mile a minute." She stopped; then: "I guess what I want to emphasize about Julia's and

Bruce's company is how adult it was, how pleasant it was for me just to be with them, drinking lemonade, feeling the day cool down—it had been so hot. It was lovely. So lovely that I didn't realize how late it was. I was really startled when Bruce looked at his watch and said it was nearly seven, that he'd have to hurry along or he'd be late getting home for dinner. And of course, right away I thought of Callie. . . . While Julia was seeing Bruce out, I called the Eagle Lake Club. The steward told me Callie and Mitch had left the club about a quarter to five. It only takes about half an hour to get from there to here, and, oh Morgan, I thought of an auto accident—*something*—something serious enough to prevent Callie from following our rule about calling home; checking in. But I kept my head. I talked it over with Julia and Tessa, and we agreed to wait until eight before we did anything—alerted the police or called Mitch's parents. Tessa kept up the line that whatever had happened to Callie and Mitch would turn out to be no more than general silliness. She urged Julia and me to go ahead with dinner—by now it was well past seven—so Julia and I went into the dining room—"

Morgan imagined them in the large, fine room, not sitting at the long table used for dinner parties, but at the more intimate round table set up by the double bank of high north windows, three places laid, flowers, the beauty of ritual order, Ralph lying as usual in a mannerly way near Maud's chair, night descending, fireflies, like earthly stars, beginning to light the outside darkness, napkins unfolded: the strain: Caroline unaccounted for.

"—and we'd no more than sat down," Maud was saying, "than Julia started in again, telling me not to worry, Tessa chiming in as she served us, and it annoyed me, and I told them that if Callie and Mitch weren't in any difficulty, if they really were all right, then their thoughtlessness was inexcusable, and I meant to have it out with them—especially with Callie—the minute they returned. Julia waited until Tessa left the room and then, Morgan, she took my hand and looked at me so deeply, right into my eyes, and asked me, *begged* me not to confront Callie when she returned, to let *her* see Callie first—"

"How exactly did she put it?" Morgan interrupted.

"Oh—'Please, Mother, please let me handle this with Callie; please, let me go to the door when she comes, please.' Over and over. She wouldn't let go. I don't remember saying a word, but I must have nodded—done something she took for consent, because she thanked me and let go of my hand and began to eat her dinner. I was so damned upset. . . . Anyhow, at about ten to eight—I'd just finished composing in my head what I was going to say to the police—Ralph got to his feet and headed for the front hall and Julia said he'd heard a car; that it would be Callie and Mitch. "I'll see to it, Mother," she told me—completely in command, Morgan, and as if by right. That was what was so impressive about her, what made me let her have her way—that she made me feel she had the greater *right* to cope with the situation than I had. And then I realized *why:* the *twin* element: the mirroring way she and Callie come together when they're jubilant or when there's trouble—how each one *becomes* the other—and that I shouldn't, *mustn't* interfere with it. Does that sound crazy?"

"No. No, Maud." He would have liked to have said more: liked to have told her that he thought her intuition marvelous: that after all these years of knowing her, she could still amaze him by her courage to act on her intuitions. But she was speaking again: "I did go into the hall, over to the front window by the library door. Julia was standing with Ralph under the portico. All the outdoor lights were on, so I could see everything. And in a few seconds, Mitch's car rounded the bend in the lane, coming on really fast. It made me furious, the speed. He pulled up into the turnaround—stopped just long enough for Callie to open the car door and get out. Believe me: no one's ever exited a car faster or slammed the door harder than Callie did. And then Mitch drove off. Not a word. Just drove away. And Callie ran to Julia. I only had a glimpse of her, but enough to see that she was terribly angry and that she looked—unarranged. Sort of messy. She said something to Julia, I couldn't hear what, and then the two of them came through the front door—they didn't see me—and bolted up the stairs, down the hall to Callie's room. Tessa came to me, relieved, like I was. Then she went back to the kitchen and I went into the library and poured a drink and—"

"Waited." Morgan finished the sentence for her. "How long?"

"It seemed like years. About twenty minutes."

"And?"

"Julia finally joined me. She told me Callie would be down in a few minutes. She was darling, Morgan. She kissed me and thanked me and she said everything was all right, honestly all right, she could promise me it was. Beyond that, she didn't say anything, and I didn't ask. . . . Then Callie appeared, looking very tidy. She'd changed her dress. She'd clearly been crying and she was serious. Head-to-toe *serious*. She said she wanted to apologize for what had happened, for worrying me, that she was truly sorry, and then her eyes filled with tears and she said, 'I want you to know I haven't done anything to disgrace us.'"

Tears, now, were in Maud's eyes.

In Morgan's. It was the inclusiveness of "us" that did it. In the fullness of his own feelings he sat, wordless, loving Caroline, lost in thought about what it all meant—meant to Caroline: how little there was left for him and Maud, parentally, to do. Finally, looking at Maud, he asked: "Is there anything else I ought to know?"

"Not that I can think of," Maud answered, her eyes still brimming. "Callie and I hugged each other, and then she said she must apologize to Tessa too, and she went to the pantry, and Tessa, bless her heart, came back with her from the pantry to Julia and me and kind of roped us all together and made us go into the dining room and eat something." Maud gestured—a shooing motion of her hand: "Now you know everything I know. Oh—except that at bedtime, when Callie kissed me good night, she said 'I'm finished with Mitch.' That was all she said about him."

Ah. He and Maud didn't speculate about what, maybe, had happened; it would have been feckless to do so. They shared unspoken images, born of experience and old memories, of (undoubtedly) some young, urgent, intense experimental physicalness—what used to be called "heavy necking"—Caroline's refusal, in the end, to go all the way. They did believe she *had* refused.

The next day, Morgan let Caroline know that he knew all about last Wednesday night's episode. He wasn't lofty about it; he didn't have to be because Caroline told him she was sure he *would* know, and that she was glad he knew, that she had learned a lesson from it, and that most of all she was very disgusted with herself for being such a "dunce" about

Mitch. She never volunteered any particulars about what had happened—about why Mitch was a thing of the past—and Julia, who surely knew precisely why, never, out of twinship loyalty, dropped a hint.

For Morgan and Maud, Mitch's disappearance from the scene comprised the summer's mystery.

"Grandfather Leigh," was the way Julia and Caroline addressed their maternal grandfather.

"Doctor Leigh," Morgan formally called him. That, or—"Sir."

"Father," Maud honored him.

He continued to fly in and out of their lives like a large bird, a heron or a hawk or some other important aerial specimen sighted usually through binoculars, on the wing. At least once a month he would come for lunch or dinner. He had a maddening way of arriving somewhat in advance of the hour he was due, thereby shortening the length of time he could, "in conscience," stay. Nothing much had changed about him in the ten years since Mrs. Leigh's death. At age seventy-three, he still was meticulously tailored; still wore jaunty polka-dot bow ties; still spoke in a boomy, authoritative voice, always confident of what he was saying; was still healthy, robust and vigorous; was still going strong as an influential physician and surgeon. His hands were as steady as ever. A good while back he had sold the Hatherton house (Morgan had salvaged the beautiful vine-and-leaf-carved library mantel and had it installed in Maud's sitting room) and bought, in Cleveland, a commodious apartment in a newly erected, arrestingly "modern" building fronted on Lake Erie. He kept a Finnish manservant named Tauno, a fiftyish general factotum, and he led a remarkably active social life. Morgan and Maud were continually surprised at how often they encountered him at concerts, at the theater, occasionally at a dinner party given by a mutual friend. He was known for being a "regular" at large functions of a civic kind: fund-raisers for this or that "Cause," and at benefit affairs on behalf of the clinic, the art museum, the Cleveland Symphony, etc. Men of his age, men of the genial, clubby sort, liked him. So did widows of his age, and some younger women—jolly ones with Rubenesque complexions and figures—whom he escorted here and there, always with a broad, fair-weather kind of style.

His fondness of Caroline and Julia was not to be doubted, nor was the genuiness of his interest in them and in what was currently happening to them. But he never had the time to give to such details of their lives as required patience or that held the threat of involving him in extended ways that might possibly mean changing or rearranging his prescribed plans. *His* agenda (he would have you know) was a fixed thing that *mattered:* one not easily altered. So his relationship to them (and theirs to him), however well presented and nicely framed, was limited; lacking in depth and color. Still, he did maintain a position in their lives, which position, for its understood symbolic value, meant something to him, and to them.

As much as he had it in him to love, he loved Maud. And Maud, in her honoring way, loved him. They were not close. For Maud, the ghost of her mother always stood between them. They were extremely careful with one another, careful about what they said to each other, and how they said it. The sadness of their circumspection lent to their relationship a serious, almost desperate strength—gave it a certain finite reality, affirmed by their common blood and by memories that dated back to the time when Doctor Leigh was a young father and Maud a child— resonant memories that were uncomplex and innocent and optimistic. (Seeing them together now, Morgan would often marvel at the versatility of love, at how much a thing of a thousand aspects love is.)

For himself, Morgan would have preferred the vitality of an active aversion to Doctor Leigh rather than what he did feel about him, which was only a dry and lifeless toleration. Between him and Doctor Leigh, manners were their means of getting along—their chariot of transport on the dusty in-law road.

⋅◈⋅

The last two weeks of August and the first week of September were given over to "preparations" (Tessa's word) for Julia's and Caroline's departure for college. *Clothes* were Maud's and the twins' consuming concern. They talked clothes around the clock. Dresses and skirts and blouses and sweaters and coats and all the attendant trappings of scarves and shoes and gloves, etc. Again and again they went into Cleveland to shop. ("They're obsessed," Morgan told his father. "I'm out of it! I don't exist. Clothes are all.")

But when it came to the matter of choosing which "things" they would take away with them, Julia and Caroline consulted him. Drew him in. Which small, cherished objects from their rooms here at home did he think would best adorn their dormitory rooms? And from a pile of photographs, which did he think was the best image of Maud? Of himself? Of the house? Of Ralph? And: that snapshot of Lillie Ruth and Tessa and Dennis: could he have it copied? On and on. Small decisions of huge heart.

On their last full day at home, he could only stand at the open doors of their rooms, looking in at them as they folded up and packed into their initialed suitcases their clothes and their different collections of "things." And then the rising of the next morning's sun. A clear, brilliant Sunday: the day of their departure—Maud to accompany them on the train trip to Philadelphia ("going along," she had explained to others, "to help them settle into their college rooms").

In the afternoon, he drove them into Cleveland, walked with them through the vast, crowded terminal (two redcaps following, bearing their luggage), handed them aboard the waiting train, into the plush of a Pullman car drawing room; held Caroline in a tight embrace, then Julia, who, with her kiss, spoke his name, "Morgan," and let out into his ear a soft sob. *"Write,"* he told her, trying to smile. Maud next in his arms: "I'll see you Thursday," she said to him, her voice uncharacteristically thin from the emotion of this parting's meaning: this line drawn down the middle of their lives. Then the porter's urgent voice telling him he must go.

He drove out of the city, attaining at last the quieter country roads, dusk darkening the gold of the September fields, the night's first mysteries gathering in the wayside woodlands, a part of him weeping; back, alone, to the house he loved, empty now—and hushed; and spilling out from every corner of its many tall rooms a near-decade's cornucopia of memories: unrepeatable achievements and irreversible mistakes which willingly (or not) he and Maud and Julia and Caroline together had made happen.

He turned on lights, poured a drink, ate a sandwich, lit a fire in the library and sat before it, reimagining his life, the war, the torpedoing and the unnameable luck of his survival, reviewing the multitude of his subsequent blessings. He let Ralph out, late, to pee, and heard the hoot of an owl, and surveyed the sky, checking the stars' formations, and then, as in a timeless narrative, man and dog went back into the house and side by side, tired, climbed the stairs and went to bed.

Maud would be back on Thursday. He fell asleep thinking of her, missing her, finally, the most.

Sometime around the beginning of October they moved Lillie Ruth into what she called "the bliss" of her new home. "For good and all, we're with each other," she told Maud: "Together, under the same roof." When it had come time to "decorate" the rooms (Lillie Ruth's word again), Maud had consulted her at every step. Curtains, rugs, furniture. ("It must all be to Lillie Ruth's liking," had been Maud's dictum.) From her small house, by way of wordly goods, Lillie Ruth brought very little: her Bible, her clothes, her Sunday hats (some dating back to Mrs. Leigh's time), and one solid chair, wooden-armed and wooden-backed, its frayed cushions replaced by new ones covered in the same floral fabric she and Maud had chosen for the curtains that adorned the windows of: "my parlor"—which proud word she applied to the room where she would sit on future occasions with the few "outside folk" who mattered to her: those of her time who were still flourishing: her Baptist minister and some of the older singers in her church choir (in which she still sang). "Deep River." "We are climbing Jacob's ladder / Soldiers of the Cross." "My savior Lord / Be with me." Spirituals that had long inspired her.

In Morgan's eyes, hers was a joyful faith of immense possibility, modestly aspired to—one whose bright, mortal impulse he had experienced, even fancied he understood. In the last four or five years, he had become less and less able to stomach religion of the melancholy pulpity kind that offers windy, cunning answers to eternal riddles, answers which, in their narrowness, seemed often (to him) to exclude the potential for different answers; and worse: that robbed conjecture of frolic.

Lillie Ruth's presence in their home augmented the pleasure he took from the house itself: heightened its rooms in feel to a sweeter measure than ever. He couldn't tell whose delight was the greater: his, or Maud's, or Lillie Ruth's.

8

Before they went away, he had imagined the letters Julia and Caroline would write home to him and Maud.

The letters would be long ones, filled with interesting information and fascinating observations and amusing anecdotes about every aspect of their lives' new circumstance. Page by page, the letters would reveal the individual states of their minds and hearts.

What a fantasy!

Letters? Oh, no time for the writing of *letters* (they separately declared). But *notes*, yes: "Whenever possible." (Whenever possible turned out to be not often.)

Ah, though: the telephone! They *did*, frequently, call home. Julia's voice. Caroline's. A few minutes then of voluminous talk, after which, with the 'phone put back in its cradle, he and Maud would review what they had just been told, what words they had just heard, by which clues they would come to a few conclusions about how each twin was "adjusting" to college life: how fitting in and getting on, keeping up; staying afloat. And then they would smile or frown or sigh a sigh of satisfaction or confusion, depending on the way it seemed to them the plot ("My dear Watson; my dear Holmes") was momently thickening.

(. . . It was a fine, frosty, moonlit night in early November. They were returning home at a late hour from a dinner party. The driving was easy. They had gone for several miles without speaking: one of those calm, wedded silences he deeply loved—gently broken when Maud, in the voice of a dreamer who wakes to the surprise of *being* awake, said: "I was so sure I'd miss them terribly. *Terribly*."

[Caroline and Julia, he knew she meant.] "And you don't?" he asked.

"*No.* Oh, I do think of them a lot, but not in the hourly way I'd imagined I would. What about you?"

"Ah, Maud. My love! I too was sure I'd miss them terribly."

"And you don't," she stated.

Verbatim, he told her: "*No.* Oh, I do think of them a lot, but not in the hourly way I'd imagined I would."

"Stop the car," she said.

He did.

"Kiss me," she said.

He did.

And it was then, in the shared experience of surprise at how their parental suppositions had betrayed them, that he told her, laughing, about the fabulous letters he had imagined Julia and Caroline would write home.)

❧

A few informing words engraved on stiff white cards summed the complex, decade-long story of his professional life:

KISSEL AND CHANDLER
HEREBY ANNOUNCES THAT
THE FIRM NAME WILL CHANGE:
EFFECTIVE JANUARY 1, 1958
THE FIRM
WILL BE KNOWN
AS
KISSEL, CHANDLER, SHURTLIFF & COLT

The announcements, many in number, were mailed from the Cleveland office on the last Monday of November. There followed many verbal and written congratulations, all sunshine, and for a while, grand to bask in.

❧

In mid-December, Caroline and Julia came home for the Christmas/ New Year's holidays.

Early in the morning, at the Cleveland Terminal, he and Maud stood together, peering through a set of barrier windows that provided a steamy downward view onto the depot tracks where newly arrived trains were stopped. It was like watching the opening action of a movie. They both saw the twins at the same time: "There they are!"

Rollicky was the way Caroline and Julia looked, and lit, stepping down from the open door of a tail-end Pullman car onto the long train-side platform, the porter handing them their suitcases (Morgan watched them decide not to wait for a redcap), then starting to walk forward, chummy, side-by-side, coming on, getting gradually closer, veering a bit to the left as they approached the ramp that led upwards into the termi-nal's rotunda, and, as they mounted the ramp, attempting to run, laugh-ing because they couldn't—run—burdened as they were by their suit-cases and what seemed (to him) to be a mind-boggling number of smaller bags slung on straps from their shoulders. "Callie's cut her hair!" he heard Maud say. Julia's, though, was longer than ever, a fair cascade smoothed back from her face and held at the nape of her neck by a wide amber clip. The clip made him think of Miss Sly, which thought occu-pied him, in a sense, emotionally, detaining him—Maud had left his side. Being tall, he was able to see her standing in a crowd—over there—at the top of the ramp, her arms opened out to Caroline and Julia, who were now just entering the rotunda. The flash of Julia's amber hair-clip again caught his eye. But now—he immediately noticed—the clip was askew, dangling down at a slant in her hair. Its clasp had come undone. And then the clip fell—he saw it fall—onto the terminal's tiled floor, and he moved swiftly forward, head down, intent, swiftly to retrieve it before it would be stepped on and crushed, there were so many people moving erratically around. So it was from a bent position, and belatedly, that he stood up to kiss Caroline, then Julia, and then to hand to Julia, to her surprise, her amber hair-clip—

—all in a second remembering himself as a fourteen-year-old boy, shaking, as, on stage, faced toward the filled assembly hall of his boarding school, he recited from memory a poem of Browning's. "Memorabilia" was the poem's title. . . . It was weird, really weird, there in the noisy, bustling terminal, the way the poem sprang so completely to mind. . . .

In the car, driving home, Caroline and Julia and Maud talked and talked, skipping from subject to subject, a kind of spirited verbal hop-scotch. And all the time, dominant above their voices, the poem stayed steady in his mind. And when they were out of the city, out in the country, he stopped the car at a spot he deemed safe and shifted his torso around toward the back seat, toward Julia and Caroline (Maud at his side) and, urgently—really in order to rid himself of the poem—appealed to them: "Indulge me! Allow me to test my memory by reciting a poem to you." And as they looked at him, smiling, he announced (just as he had years ago, in his school's assembly-hall): "'Memorabilia,' by Robert Browning:

> Ah, did you once see Shelley plain,
>   And did he stop to speak to you
> And did you speak to him again?
>   How strange it seems and new!
>
> But you were living before that,
>   And also you are living after;
> And the memory I started at—
>   My starting moves your laughter.
>
> I crossed a moor, with a name of its own
>   And a certain use in the world no doubt,
> Yet a hand's-breadth of it shines alone
>   'Mid the blank miles round about:
>
> For there I picked up on the heather
>   And there I put inside my breast
> A moulted feather, an eagle-feather!
>   Well, I forget the rest."

He recited each verse easily, not once hesitating. Stunned himself a bit thereby, then fell silent, joining Maud and Julia and Caroline in their silence: an intimate silence, eccentric to the four of them, familiar and tranquil and trusting. No need, therefore, for him to explain the *why* of his compulsion to recite the poem aloud to them (the "why" anyhow too prodigiously complicated, even for his own understanding). And after a moment he said: "Thank you, ladies," and laughed with them and ran his thumb over Maud's cheek, then looked again at Julia and Caroline: "It's terrific, the four of us, together again," he said. He turned in his seat and started the car, Maud and Julia and Caroline talking again, himself now a participant, all of them animated and excited, speeding down the stretch of road that ran parallel to the banks of the ice-rimmed Chagrin River, anticipating the sight, soon, of the marking griffin-gates of their home-lane: entry into the making of new memories.

(*Ah!* that amber hair-clip, picked up like that eagle's feather! About almost everything else of that morning of the twins' return—"Well, I forget the rest.")

ew

Amid the seasonal decorations of hung mistletoe and scarlet-berried holly and fragrant pine boughs brought in from the woods and ferny ropes of evergreens wound around the staircase banister; amid, in a sky of a million stars, the single liturgically brilliant one on which the Magi trained their eyes for guidance to the stable wherein lay the Babe, imagined each year newborn; amid, between families and friends, the house-to-house, place-to-place travels (great personal seekings); amid all the feasting and earthly plenty of Christmas and of New Year's toasts and high resolutions and elegiac rememberings of bygone days: amid all these multifarious distractions, Morgan's and Maud's attention dwelt most on Julia and Caroline.

They couldn't help comparing the Julia and Caroline of Now with the Julia and Caroline of Yore—Yore being so recent a time as last summer, though in relation to how much each twin had changed during the intervening three and a half months, last summer seemed to belong to the distant past—all the contrasting qualities that had previously distinguished them were now so fully particularized, so greatly enlarged. Morgan was sure that, now, a stranger meeting them for the first time would not at once take them to be twins, but instead as two strongly resembling sisters who had been closely conceived, born eleven or so months apart. Oh, with each other they were as perceptive and as intimately capable as ever, but the old interacting alchemy of their twinship no longer inextricably combined them: each had become her own mistress.

Each was conscious of this great change, and each, in her distinct way, attributed the coming about of the change to their residing at college in separate dormitories. Caroline lauded the arrangement—all but raised the flag over the success of it: "By living apart, we're individually known and individually regarded. I'm me, and Julia's Julia. It's perfect!" Julia spoke of the arrangement in a way far more personal: "By being on my own, I'm finding out a lot about myself, some of it sort of strange to get used to."

Each had made her own set of friends. By description, Caroline's set sounded older than Julia's set; older, not so much in age as in the Serpent sense: whether by instinct or by rehearsal, Caroline simply knew a whole lot more about the world's workings than Julia did, which knowledge showed most in her humor—in the fast way she picked up double-meaning possibilities (quizzical lift of her eyebrows, a gambit smile, then her laughter, proportionately, disarmingly decorous, but still definitely on target). She was faster than ever, too, at protesting what she considered to be a spoken or written fallacy. ("Ah, but Callie! Be *gentler*," Morgan advised her: "Adversative keenness is stimulating, but if it's so mordantly expressed, you'll never persuade us to your side.") She *was* vivid! And in a way catching. In her presence, people of all ages seemed to become more alive: it was as though by being near her, some smoldering ember in themselves took on fresh fire. She was equipped, (Morgan thought) to move mountains. (With a bit of luck, and if, *if* she learned discretion, she just might, someday, really *might* move mountains.)

Discretion was Julia's inborn gift. Julia: still soft, still actually innocent, but (and the proviso of that "but" was enormous) in imagination so talented that, while being still a resident of Eden, she could intuit, could *feel* the contrasting, impending atmospherics of life outside the Garden. This talent had the effect of causing her to seem at times . . . sad. Not in the gloomy sense. Her capacity for pleasure was too rich to allow for anything as cheap as gloom. In the awed sense—*sad;* made sober by her young discovery about life that as marvelous as it is, and thrilling, it is also a very problematic affair, often unsafe and as often distorting: a hall of mirrors. . . . She was a keen, accurate observer and a terrific listener. And like all people who are more interested in others than in themselves, she was everybody's confidante. Well, to a degree: discernment being also her gift, she knew the difference between what was important to hear, to lend mind or sympathy to or to rejoice over, as against what was a waste of time to listen to. Yet even with the backing of that innate discernment, the fact remained that when she *was* drawn in, it was all the way and with a strong tendency for keeps. (And in some future time, drawn in by passion for some as yet unmet love—well, that would be the moment when Fate would declare itself: when Fate might rule.) . . . One Sunday afternoon, she and Morgan took a walk together and she told him: "I want to be a writer." "I'm not surprised," he said. Then, quickly, she said: "I won't mind if you tell Mother, but please, Morgan, don't tell anyone else, not even Pip." He said: "It's a difficult, wonderful thing to want to be. I'm flattered you've told me. I'll leave it to you to tell Maud in your own time; she'd like best to hear it from you. . . . Does Callie know?" he risked to ask. Julia shook her head: "No." (It was then, due to the final tone of her answer, that he took in the real extent of how far apart she and Caroline had come to be.)

During the holidays, there were of course whole intervals of time that resembled—except for the weather—last summer's days. The young crowd, as nomadic as ever, came and went and came again and again went away, but now, when they stayed, they skated on the iced-over pond or carried on sexual flirtations by hurling softly formed snowballs at each other. One day they made a big snowman of the W. C. Fields type, complete with a cigar between his sculpted, red-painted lips and on his head, somebody's father's cast-off top hat. And next to W. C. Fields, they made a snow-woman: Mae West (the size of whose breasts Maud made them modify, plus removing the stuck-on tits: two purple plums). Sometimes, driven indoors by the cold, they would all sit around on the floor before a blazing fire and talk and talk, or put on records and dance; once in a while, after a peppery choosing-up of sides, they would play very sophisticated games of Who Am I? or of Dumb Crambo. There were whole hours when the tiled area of the front hall looked like the floor of a badly run sports emporium that specializes in arctic footwear, there would be so many pairs of kicked-off boots and over-shoes lying around in melted-snow puddles.

Caroline was enormously popular—a siren in the lads' eyes—hotly sought after as a date for nighttime parties and dances. Julia went to fewer parties ("As many as I want to go to," she said), usually with her friend Bruce Wilson, who was serious and peculiarly confident. Morgan and Maud's old rule about midnight's being the hour to be home from evening parties was extended to one A.M.: NO LATER THAN! They were most always in bed, often awake, always chaste, awaiting Julia's knock on their bedroom door and her softly spoken: "I'm back"—(often earlier than the deadline hour), and for Caroline's knock (rarely earlier—three times almost dangerously later) and her similar, reporting words.

Over the holidays Doctor Leigh, ever on the fly, put in a few vigorous appearances. Ansel Shurtliff came for Christmas and stayed on to wel-come in the New Year, for which event Geoff and Alan arrived from New York on December 30, bringing with them late Christmas pre-sents, distributed—festively—to one and all that evening after dinner. Alan handed Morgan an old, thin, leather-bound, worn, but still intact book: "I found it in a secondhand bookshop down in the Village. It's a queer little production."

Morgan, extremely curious, opened the book to its first page and read out loud its title: "*A Digest of Celtic Names*, Compiled by Ian MacNaghten, Esq.; Privately Printed—1909."

"Turn to page twelve," Alan said.

On page twelve, marked in the margin by a filled-in circle of faded India ink, he saw his name: *MÔR-GĂN [Welsh]: A dweller on the sea.*

He read it to himself, and sat there, silent, hugely surprised: until that moment, he had had no knowledge that his given name was Welsh in origin, let alone, what, in Welsh, it meant.

He heard his father's voice, his laughter: "You look dumbfounded, Morgan! We're all panting to know what you've found on page twelve."

He passed the book, opened to the stated page, to Ansel Shurtliff. "Did you know this, Pa?"

It took only a second for his father to read the words, first to himself, next in a struck voice aloud to the others, then to exclaim: "I had no idea! None whatsoever"—and, turning to Alan, addressing him: "It was my wife's father's first name. That's how we came to pass it on to"—he turned back to Morgan—"to *you*. I'm certain that neither your mother nor her father had any inkling of the name's being Welsh, or of its meaning in that language. They'd have told me if they'd known. They both reveled in all such out-of-the way lore. . . . Why Alan, how you have enlightened us!"

Everybody was active now, talking, passing the book around, hand-to-hand. Morgan, though, was in a world of thoughts completely his own. *Morgan: a dweller on the sea.* The words suggested perpetual brine, perpetual drift: a loner's existence devoid of witnesses. It surprised him how much within himself he denied that definition of his name. A dweller on the sea? Ah, no! Not this Morgan. Define *this* Morgan as a dweller on the land, in his way a deeply-rooted tree: *proof* (it comforted him to think) that in one's given name there is no destiny.

. . . On New Year's Eve, they all went into Cleveland for Lewis and Letitia Grant's annual party, Maud, Julia, and Alan in Morgan's car; Caroline and Geoff with Ansel Shurtliff in his "Jag." All their lives, Caroline and Julia had heard about this party; this was the first time they were going to it, Letitia Grant having pronounced them old enough now to attend. "Why are you so excited about this particular party?" Maud asked. "Because," Julia explained, "because, *finally,* Callie and I'll see what it's really like. We've imagined it for so long, since we were little. We used to spend hours talking about it and pretending we were at it, dressed up like princesses, surrounded by princes—everything gorgeous—fabulous clusters of flowers hanging by pure gold ropes from the ceiling and chiffon-veiled pink lights—that was Callie's idea—and the air scented with a foreign, awfully exotic perfume, Arabian, we thought!" Caroline, in on these nursery remembrances, said: "We're prepared, on *those* terms, to be disappointed." Maud laughed: "On those terms, you're bound to be."

Still, it was a grand party; on its own terms, memorable. At midnight, as he always did, Lewis Grant led the company in a first toast to the New Year: "To 1958." (When he did that, Morgan looked at Maud. She understood that his gaze went far beyond 1958, that it kept faith with what, earlier in the evening, they had told each about the last ten years—the decade just ended: that it had been the best, the happiest of their lives: "So look at me at midnight, won't you. Look at me, so we can toast together the next ten years.")

They got home around two-thirty. As they were getting out of their coats, Maud announced: "Breakfast at noon."

Ansel Shurtliff said: "I promise you won't see me one minute before."

Morgan turned to Geoff and Alan: "Let's have a brandy."

"Let's do that."

"Are ladies not welcome?" Caroline asked.

"Certainly *not*," Maud told her.

"Come on, Callie," Julia said.

(Good night, loves. Good night. Sleep well. Bless all. Good night.)

What did they talk about over their brandies? Nothing monumental. They were too pleasantly spent, too relaxed for such exertions. Oh, inevitably, the New Year's mythic power drew from them some out-loud personal concerns: Morgan's, about his case (the New York State Court of Appeals ruling expected in January); Geoff's "hope" that the position he'd put in for as president of the Balfour Foundation would come through; Alan's simply spoken wish "for a quiet year, good for work." And they touched on the matter of their ages: in 1958, each of them would "chalk up" forty-seven years. "God, we're pushing fifty," Geoff said. Alan checked him: "Don't complain. Think of the times during the war when you doubted you'd live through the next day. We're damn lucky to be pushing fifty."

"I'm going to fall asleep right here in this chair."

"Don't."

They stood up. Turned out the lights. Went into the front hall and side-by-side, mock soldierly, mounted the stairs.

"Sweet dreams."

They laughed.

"Shh . . ."

9 ∞ Soaring

Monday, January 13, 1958

In Cleveland, the morning sky was gray. Lake Erie was gray. A cold, misty rain enshrouded the city. "Gloomy," Morgan's secretary said of the day, sighing as she entered his office. He was sitting at his desk. Miss Corey took her usual chair opposite him. After checking, as she always did, that her knees were covered by her skirt, she uncapped her pen and opened her shorthand pad. The phone on his desk rang. Miss Corey reached out and picked it up. "It's Mr. Buchanan calling from the New York office," she reported. (*Ah,* John Buchanan.) Miss Corey handed him the phone.

"John. How are you?"

"Fine, thanks. I have splendid news for you, Morgan. It came through a few minutes ago."

"Dare I guess?"

"Dare indeed." Quickly then, John Buchanan told him that in the matter of his long, hard-fought case, the New York State Court of

Appeals had at last rendered its decision. "It's your win, Morgan. Yours all the way. Your crown to wear."

"*John!*"—Morgan all but yelled.

"Before you start to explode in earnest, let me say I've already air-mailed a copy of the court's order to you. You should have it by Wednesday. Thursday for sure. You're due to be here next week, right? So I'll save my congratulations until I see you. . . . Do I have your permission, as of now, to spread the good news among our colleagues?"

"Please do. And thanks, John. Many thanks."

"My pleasure."

He hung up the phone. Miss Corey again took up her pen and shorthand pad. "Not now, Miss Corey." He told her to go down the hall, please, to George Colt's office: "Find out if he's free, and if he is, tell him I'd like to see him as soon as possible." All in a usual voice. It wasn't until she was out of the room, until he was alone, that belief overwhelmed him. Belief, as in the fact of a mountain risen to view. The actuality of its existence. That it was, in truth, *there*. There, as in conclusion: that the conflict was over; ended. Ended by the court's decision, which decision concretely favored his two clients: made of them victors: sealed, forever, their victory. Abruptly, and completely, he began to shake. From sheer relief, sheer elation, to shake. *Walk,* he told himself. Stand up and walk around the room—

"What's up, Morgan?"

George Colt was standing in the doorway. George Colt, as in Kissel, Chandler, Shurtliff & Colt.

"George! You startled me."

"You look slammed."

"I am. There's terrific news."

"Is it what I think it is?"

"Yes. *Yes.*"

"Stop talking like Molly Bloom. Spell it out for me."

The spelling out didn't take long. And the minute George Colt left him, creaming off almost at a run "to tell the others," Morgan did the next vital thing: telephoned his clients. Two separate, exultant long-distance calls.

That done, *then,* his Cleveland colleagues, led by George Colt, converged upon him. Lawyers' glee. Nothing quite like it! By mid-afternoon, armed with the court's by now publicly released ruling, newspaper and magazine reporters began to surface (at which moment the clock began ticking off the seconds of what, years later, reminiscing about his first "glory" case, Morgan would dub "my fifteen minutes of fame").

For the next few days—without apology—he heaped the full magnitude of his winner's euphoria on his family and his closest friends. With Maud, for a couple of nights, all he was good for was fucking. That, and in the dark, afterwards, not quite completely exhausted, talking with her about their long-promised, long anticipated trip to Europe, soon to be embarked on! For he had, *had,* in the wild midst of his euphoria, called the New York office of the Cunard Line and secured their passage. On Tuesday, February 25, they would sail from New York; have the fine pleasures of the Atlantic crossing ("God, the freedom!"); have four days in London, then on to Paris; from Paris to Avallon and Vézelay (Vézelay, vividly remembered as the favorite place of his fifteenth summer when his father had taken him to Europe on what, back then, was called "The Grand Tour"); then back to England, to Southampton, there to reboard ship for the return voyage, docking in New York on Wednesday, March 26; then the train trip to Cleveland: *home*—in time to receive Julia and Caroline, whose spring vacation from college would commence on Saturday, March 29. All the dates in place. Fixed. ("O, wonderful, wonderful, and most wonderful, wonderful! and yet again wonderful! and after that out of all whooping." To Maud he quoted his favorite Shakespeare line.) They lay in the dark, talking in each other's arms: *This is what we'll do. This is the way it will be.*

(Before they had gone to bed, it had begun to snow. They had stood at a window and watched the huge flakes fall. It was one of those rare, windless January blizzards, the snowflakes softly dropping, the lawn, as far as they could see, all white. "A bride's new sheet," Maud said, leaning against him. "Listen. Listen to the silence.")

10 ~ Suddenly

These things never happened, but are always.

—SALLUST (CAIUS SALLUSTIUS CRISPUS,
86 B.C.–C. 34 B.C.), *OF GODS AND OF THE WORLD*

Their plan was to leave Cleveland (by train) for New York on Friday evening. In New York, over the week-end and on Monday, they would have the fun of seeing Geoff and Alan, Lucy Blackett, Sidney and Linda, Lawrence and Pamela. On Tuesday, they would board ship and sail away.

Yesterday, he had had a farewell lunch with Miss Sly. When they parted, Miss Sly had said: "I know you'll have a glorious time, Mr. Shurtliff. I'll be thinking of you and Mrs. Shurtliff in all those wonderful places. Call me the minute you get back." In their warm, ceremonial way, they embraced. "Good-bye." "Good-bye." After he left her, he'd gone back to his office, said a final round of good-byes there, sat for a moment at his desk for what would be the last time in a long time—the surface of his desk clean, no papers on it; nothing left to be attended to. This is what it's like to be care-free, he had thought. Then he had picked up his briefcase and swung off, out of his office, down the corridor, passing other open office doors, waving as he was waved to all the way to the elevator. Out of sight. DOWN, thanks to Mr. Otis, to the building's ground floor.

Driving home, he turned on the car radio. Frank Sinatra: "So while there's music and moonlight and love and romance / Let's face the music and dance." Ta ta-tatata-ta ta. Then some swing: Big Band versions of "Tuxedo Junction" and "Celery Stalks at Midnight." Old war-time stuff. Boogie: "Beat Me, Daddy, Eight to the Bar." He turned off the radio. He didn't need it. He had, after all, his own repertoire to sing to himself. He drove fast, eager to be home, eager to be with Maud, eager to see his father, who was coming to spend the night. ("I want a last evening with you and Maud before you leave," Ansel Shurtliff had said.) He arrived home, incredibly happy; announced his arrival with a ballpark yell when he entered the house. Maud and his father were already ensconced in the library. *Ah*, the warmth of a blazing hearth fire. Maud's kiss. His father's bear-hug. Drinks. "I've just told Pip that I'm virtually packed," Maud said. Morgan said: "By this time tomorrow night I'll be packed, too. God, I'm excited. Exorbitantly excited."

She died alone. The next morning. In their bedroom. Dropped onto the floor close to their bed.

Morgan had gotten up at seven-thirty. Maud had opened her eyes just long enough to say she wanted to sleep a while more. She was tired, she said. She'd been racing about so much, she said: "Getting ready." For their trip . . . "Wake me if I'm not downstairs by nine," she said. She'd smiled and turned in the bed onto her side. Closed her eyes. He had showered, shaved, dressed. She was asleep when he left their room. His father was already at the table in the dining room. "Nothing like one of Tessa's breakfasts," Ansel Shurtliff greeted him. They read the papers, talked. The February morning had just begun to come on bright. Morgan looked at his watch: "It's almost nine-thirty! I told Maud I'd wake her at nine."

When he found her—close on to nine-thirty, dropped like that onto the floor close to their bed—by Dr. Forbes's calculation, she'd been dead about an hour. From down the private hallway that led to their bedroom, and with the door of their room closed, and the house so large, if she had cried out, she wouldn't have been heard. "But if you had been with her, there wouldn't have been anything you could have done for her," Dr. Forbes said. "It was a massive hemorrhage, a massive black-out, Morgan. In such cases, death occurs in seconds. A moment or two and it's all over. She would hardly have had time to know what was happening to her." (Yet, *had* she said his name? Breathed it at the last, hoping?)

One draws on memory's examples to make it through such a time. Morgan thought of the captain: of how he had behaved in the first hours after the *Stubbins* was torpedoed: of his iron will, his insistence on surviving—on surviving survival, that is: how he had conducted himself in a way that had obliged those of the crew left living to care that they were alive. Strange, that he thought of the captain before he thought of his father: his father, sitting right there beside him. His father, who had sustained the death of *his* wife—the words on her tombstone now remembered: *Caroline Cunningham Shurtliff / Born—28 March 1887 / Died Age 36—3 April 1923 / Beloved Wife of Ansel Osborne Shurtliff / Mother of Morgan Cunningham Shurtliff.*

"You must think about Julia and Caroline," his father said.

He must telephone Bryn Mawr's dean. No. First—Lucy Blackett. Lucy would go from New York to Philadelphia to be with Julia and Caroline; she would accompany them on the plane trip to Cleveland: they shouldn't be alone on the flight home. Call Lucy. No. First call the airline: get the plane schedule, secure the tickets, then call Lucy; then the dean—the unmet dean, experienced in such matters as this. When Morgan spoke with her, he heard experience in her voice. She would go herself, she told him, and get Julia and Caroline from their classes and break the news to them (she would *have* to tell them what had happened, she said); then she would bring them back to her office and then she would call Morgan, and then it would be his turn to speak with them. *His* turn: not long in coming. Beyond confirming the terrible truth, he told them that Lucy was on her way to them, that she would come home with them on the plane—everything was arranged; Pip and Dennis would meet them at the airport; he wished he could meet them himself, but he couldn't: there was too much that had to be seen to here at home. "By nightfall, though, we'll be together," he told them.

Next, with his father, he drew up a list of people who must be told as

soon as possible. Doctor Leigh's name headed Morgan's list. Doctor
Leigh would be asked to notify other Leigh relations—excepting Peter
Leigh (Maud's favorite cousin; Julia's godfather). Morgan to call Peter;
then the minister; then George Colt, who would tell the firm's partners;
then Mary Berridge (ask Mary to tell Ann Goodyear and Jane Garth
and Sally Myers (Maud's "tennis pals"). Ansel Shurtliff would call
Letitia and Lewis Grant and Shurtliff cousins in Cleveland, Cincinnati,
Pittsburgh, and New York. . . . A secondary list was begun and set aside.
Mustn't put the cart before the horse: a death notice should be written
out next, and was: Morgan dictated it over the phone to Miss Corey
(who, in turn, dictated it to the proper editors of the designated newspapers). Then back to the secondary list.

Those few names that didn't require being written down kept spring-
ing to mind: Geoff, Alan, Sidney, Lawrence, Miss Sly.

In the kitchen, Lillie Ruth and Tessa were grieving. Not that you
could hear them weeping: only that you knew they were. They had
begun to prepare lunch, to plan dinner. To stay strong (Lillie Ruth had
earlier said), folks would have to eat.

The day went on without cadence. At two-thirty, the minister arrived.
The Reverend Mr. Daniels. A thin, dark-haired man with deep-set eyes
and large, expressive hands. He limped into the library. One of his legs
was shorter than the other. A terrible limp: a war injury. He was still
spoken of as the "new" Presbyterian minister (the Reverend Mr.
Halliday having retired three years ago: gone to live with his unmarried
sister in Bangor, Maine). Maud had grown fond of Mr. Daniels. . . .
When Morgan had spoken with Mr. Daniels in the morning, they had
fixed Monday as the day when the funeral would be. No, Morgan said
now, she was not going to be cremated. In body whole, in a coffin, she
would be buried in the Leigh family plot. Near her mother. Soon after
her mother died, Maud had said that that was what she would someday
want. Someday. Some distant day, transiently (when she'd said it), imagined. That was all Morgan had to go on. But she *had* said it. So that was
how it would be. Which psalms to be spoken? Which hymns sung? To
those questions, Morgan replied that he must await Julia's and Caroline's
coming: that they would want to help choose which psalms, which

hymns. A eulogy? No. Only the simple service; the simple ritual words Maud had known by heart.

Later in the afternoon, after his father and Dennis had left for the airport, Morgan telephoned Miss Sly at her Tilden-Herne office. Her secretary asked: "Who's calling, please?" He gave his name. He was all right until he heard Miss Sly's voice: "Mr. Shurtliff! What a pleasing dividend to yesterday's lunch." "Miss Sly—" he said, then stopped. Something (his tone? his immediate silence?) warned her: "Something's happened," she said: "Take your time, Mr. Shurtliff." He managed finally to tell her. "Oh," she gasped: "*Oh.*" And in a moment: "Don't try to talk. . . . I'd go to you this minute, but that wouldn't be appropriate, would it? We'll have to wait a few days to see each other—as soon as *you* can, whenever you can, for as long as you can. . . . Don't try to talk. . . . We'll talk next week when we're together. I'll hang up now. My dearest love to you, Mr. Shurtliff." Then the click of disconnection, merciful.

Around five, Doctor Leigh and Peter Leigh arrived. Doctor Leigh was dry-eyed. "If it had to be," he said, "at least thank God it was fast." Dry-eyed, but his usually ruddy face was drained of color and he moved slowly, his vigor all gone. He said he must have a word with Lillie Ruth, and left the room. Peter Leigh asked: "Is there anything I can do for you, Morgan?" "Come for a quick walk with me," Morgan said: "I've got to have a breath of fresh air."

Julia and Caroline and Lucy arrived about seven-thirty. Lucy and Ansel Shurtliff joined Doctor Leigh and Peter Leigh in the library. Morgan took Julia and Caroline into Maud's sitting room. There, Caroline slumped into a chair, put her head in her hands and began to sob. Julia, in his arms, still in her coat, asked him: "What will we do, Morgan? What will we do without her?" He held her, praying: praying that an answer to her question be given him—some word or celestial sign: something they could cling to in the void. None came.

In a bit, Julia said she wanted to see Lillie Ruth and Tessa. Caroline said: "Wait for me." She stood up and wiped her eyes and took Julia's hand and they left the room, together like that, holding hands. Morgan called out after them, "Ask Lucy to come here, please."

Lucy's face, when she entered the room, had heartbreak written all over it. "Morgan." "Lucy." There was a period at the end of their spoken names. "Lucy," he said, swallowing, this time with a comma after her name: "I don't know how to start to thank you." Lucy cut him off: "You can start by shutting up," she flared, bright and desperate. Then, standing there before him, her hands trembling, she began a bit to rant: "Keep me busy. That's all I ask. I'll do anything, anything to make time pass." She looked wild; her voice was low; furious: "Why Maud? *Maudie,* of all people, with the world full of creeps and fools no one would miss." She ranted on: "I don't believe in anything anymore. Just in effort. That's all I believe in. Effort. All I ask of you is to keep me busy. *Use me.*" She was in a thousand pieces. "Lucy—" They stood there, clasped together, holding each other up. "Lucy." "Morgan." Period. Period.

In a few minutes, all of them came together again. They ate, a sort of buffet supper, plates in their laps, sitting in a circle: Morgan, Julia, Ansel Shurtliff, Lucy, Peter Leigh, Caroline (the fingers of her left hand lost in the thick of Ralph's fur), Doctor Leigh—all of them engaged in a conspiracy of cheerfulness. They talked, non-stop, about anything other than what they were all thinking about. They didn't look at each other— that would have been too risky—just past each other, at a painting or at an object, or out the bank of windows, into the night. At about ten o'clock, Doctor Leigh told Peter that they must go: the drive into Cleveland could take longer than usual, he said: there would likely be February fog. He kissed Julia and Caroline; shook Ansel Shurtliff's hand. "Remember me to your mother," he said to Lucy. In the front hall, as if he was concluding a doctoral house call, he handed Morgan an envelope: "Sleeping pills," he said: "Nembutal. Take two before you go to bed. I'll come back tomorrow." All in a dry-as-dust voice. "I'll see you tomorrow too, Morgan," Peter said, trailing Doctor Leigh out the door.

It had been arranged that Dennis would drive Lucy into Hatherton to her mother's house. Dennis was waiting in the car at the front portico. Lucy kissed Julia and Caroline, then Ansel Shurtliff and Morgan. "You're my family," she told them. She was calm now; sweet. "I'll be back first thing in the morning." Then she turned and left them.

SHURTLIFF—Maud (née Leigh). Suddenly, at age 43, on
Thursday, February 20, 1958. She is survived by her husband,
Morgan, by her daughters, Caroline and Julia, by her father, Dr.
Douglas Leigh, by her father-in-law, Ansel Shurtliff, and by a
host of friends. Funeral service and interment Monday, February
24 at 3:00 P.M., First Presbyterian Church, Hatherton, Ohio.

(The above, as printed in the obituary pages of *The Cleveland Plain
Dealer, The New York Times, The Cincinnati Enquirer, The Pittsburgh
Press, The Hatherton Record*, Friday, February 21, 1958)

SHURTLIFF—Maud. The Headmaster, the Board of Trustees
and the Faculty of Hollis Academy acknowledge with deep sadness the death of Maud Shurtliff, one of Hollis's most valued and
generous Trustees. To her husband, Morgan Shurtliff, and her
daughters, Caroline and Julia Shurtliff, and to her many friends,
we offer our most sincere sympathies.

Gerald Lamont
Headmaster, Hollis Academy
(From *The Cleveland Plain Dealer*, Saturday, February 22, 1958)

SHURTLIFF—Maud (Leigh). The Members of the Medical
Board of the Hatherton Hospital note with sorrow the sudden
passing of Maud Leigh Shurtliff, dedicated patron of the
Hatherton Hospital and daughter of our esteemed colleague, Dr.
Douglas Leigh. To the members of the Shurtliff family and to Dr.
Leigh we offer our heartfelt condolences.

Albert Brooke, M.D.
President, Medical Board
Hatherton Hospital
(From *The Hatherton Record*, Saturday, February 22, 1958)

In one of the Cleveland papers there was a long obituary, part fact, part
blown-up fairy tale. It gave the cause of her sudden death: "a cerebral
hemorrhage." It stated that she died—"at home." It told whose daughter
she was. It informed that in June of 1937, she married Morgan
Cunningham Shurtliff. (It coupled the Shurtliff name with the Taft
name—the coupling expanded upon in a skewed statement to the effect
that in Ohio civic, cultural, political, and industrial circles, both names
were "synonymous with leadership"; Morgan was described as "a lawyer
of national repute.") It listed those "institutions" which had most
"gained" from Maud Shurtliff's "devoted interest and support." It said
she had "two college-age daughters, Caroline and Julia." There was a picture, culled from the paper's files. Below the picture was the caption:
"Mrs. Morgan Shurtliff at the March 1956 gala benefit for the Cleveland
Orchestra."

Some society reporter who didn't know the first thing about her had
written the article.

≈§

On Saturday afternoon, Geoff and Alan arrived. With Geoff, when they
were alone, Morgan finally broke down. What freed him to weep was
Geoff's calling him—"Morgie." The tender way Geoff said it had the
surprise of rediscovery—as of something tangible—an object, refound in
the drawer of an old bureau or closer, in an old coat pocket—a mislaid
object, all but forgotten, not particularly missed until refound, then

instantly radiant because it had lasted and was uncomplicated and was again in hand. "Morgie."

On Sunday, in the early evening, Sidney and Linda and Lawrence arrived. Now, everyone was there. (Even Pamela, who wasn't. She had written a note to Morgan; Lawrence gave it to him. "Dear Morgan, Forgive me for not coming. Funerals aren't my thing. Something about them makes me misbehave. About Maud's slipping out of our lives, I don't know what to say. No words of mine can cover the loss. Love, Pam." Her note, so typical of her, made her seem to be there. He re-read it the next morning. Its very toughness, like a cane handed to a cripple, helped support him.)

&

You can imagine for yourself the funeral, the filled church, the collected grief, the long line of people who walked behind the shoulder-born coffin to the cemetery and who stood, heads bowed, as the last words were said, graveside. And you can imagine for yourself the large gathering at the house afterwards, after the funeral: who was there and some of what was said. You don't have to be told. In your own way, from your own experience, you know all about endings.

Of course, about Endings, as a *Theme*—the possible variations are infinite in number. But you know that, too.

&

On Tuesday, Geoff and Alan and Lawrence and Linda and Sidney returned to New York. Sidney, especially hard to part from. Of them all, of everyone, only Sidney had talked with him about death. They had sat down on a couch, no one else in the room, and Sidney, in his impulsive, uninhibited way, looking up as if toward it, had said the slab word—*death*—squinting (he wasn't wearing his glasses), the thick brows of his heavily lidded eyes nearly touching as he peered forward, trying for himself in the immediate dimly lit circumstance to—beyond feeling it—*see* it. Finally, as if by the aid of some light cast unexpectedly upon it, sighing, he spoke of it as: "Beyond immensity, immense . . . impossible to do battle with . . . one of Nature's unreckonable surprises . . . retaliation of any kind out of the question." Then he had quoted those ancient words of Sallust's—"These things never happened, but are always"— then had put a hand on Morgan's arm and let it stay there, resting. As in surrender.

On Wednesday, Lucy too returned to New York.

On Thursday, Julia and Caroline went back to college. Last Tuesday, the day after the funeral, he had asked them if they wanted to go back, if they felt equal to going back. Might they want to take the rest of the semester off? A sort of leave of absence . . . He had thought he *must* ask them. But they were ahead of him. Between themselves they had already considered the question; had already decided they would go back. "We'll be all right," Caroline said. "We have each other." Julia said: "We're sure it's what Mother would want us to do." And too (they reminded him), it was only a month or so before their spring vacation would begin: they would be home again that soon. Morgan said: "And between now and then, I'll go to New York. We'll have a weekend together in New York." . . . Oh, they were light-years ahead of him. It was their youth and energy and curiosity that made them brave. . . . What his experience couldn't keep him from doing was seeing them, at moments, as a pair of naive possums attempting to cross a high-speed parkway at evening rush hour. Julia especially. On her own, she might have decided to remain at home, *might* have—in the spirit of one of those young women in a dark Brontë novel whose tribute to the dead was to withdraw for a while from the world. . . . But no: about Julia that was a wrong idea, wrong because it was only one aspect of the whole picture—the one that showed at unbidden moments when awe and fright at what had happened could be seen on her face and in her eyes—moments *he* read into and saw as a reflection of his own awe and fright, as warnings of his own possible collapse. He admonished himself not to sell Julia short: even were she on her own, he must believe, must trust, that she would have correctly decided to go back to college. . . . He was the one frantic; the one who had to invent for himself the semblance of a reason to go on. "In June," he said to Julia and Caroline, "we'll go to Europe. The three of us. We'll plan the trip over your spring break. Will you," he asked, desperate, "*will* you go to Europe with me in June?" They nodded, tears in their eyes, sitting solemnly, very still, giving their silent answer: *Yes*. . . . Oh, in pure courage, however come by, they were light-years ahead of him.

On Friday, Ansel Shurtliff went home.

These departures were like a Ten Little Indians countdown: now, he was the only one left.

What he couldn't get over was how—with Maud's heart stopped—his own kept on beating, insisting that he pay attention to the fact that it was. Going on. Beating.

On Saturday, in the morning, after a terrible night (heavy, sweaty, drugged sleep), he telephoned Miss Sly. It was the first time he had ever called her at home; the first time he had ever spoken with her on a week-end day; the first time he would propose to her that they meet not at noon-time for lunch, but in the evening, for dinner.

"Every time the phone has rung, I've hoped it would be you," she said.

He put to her his thought that if, if by chance she was free—tonight—he would drive into Cleveland and: would she have an early dinner with him?

"I would like very much to, Mr. Shurtliff."

He named a restaurant, one they had never been to before. "We can meet there, or I'll pick you up at your house, whichever—"

"I know exactly where the restaurant is. It's an easy hop from my house. I'll meet you there."

"At seven," he said.

"I'll be waiting."

In his heart, he instantly felt that this was the start of something altogether new between him and Miss Sly—some indescribable *nearer* connection (even) more exceptional than had existed between them, before. Why was he so certain that if he had a future at all, Miss Sly, better than anyone else, could reveal it to him?

11 ∽ Eclipse

Eclipse: from the Greek word *ekleipsis*. Literal meaning: abandonment; cessation.

E—clipse (i-'klips): *n* 1.a. The partial or complete obscuring, relative to a designated observer, of one celestial body by another. b. The period of time during which such an obscuring occurs.

2. Any temporary or permanent dimming or cutting off of light. (Definition as given in *The American Heritage Dictionary of the English Language*)

The eclipse of Maud's death—which is to say its darkness—lasted about a year.

One of that year's worst moments occurred a couple of weeks after she died. *Worst*, as in inane; as in ignominious. He struck a man. A fool named Bryce Richardson. One is supposed to ignore fools, especially fools one barely knows; fools of the merest acquaintanceship. It happened at the Union Club, in the washroom, midafternoon of a Thursday. He was alone in the washroom, standing before a mirror that ran the length of the wall above the wash-basins—re-knotting his tie—when Bryce Richardson walked in. "Why, hello there, Morgan," Bryce Richardson greeted him, sounding—familiar. "Hello, Bryce," Morgan returned. That should have been all. But Bryce Richardson said: "I've been in Florida for a month. Only got back yesterday. I ran into Jack Thorpe this morning— you know Jack Thorpe, don't you?—and he told me about your wife's death." Period. Bryce Richardson took up a position two wash-basins down from Morgan's, turned on the water faucet, ran his hands through the flow, turned off the faucet and began to dry his hands. Then, in the mirror, he looked at Morgan. "You never know," he said. In the mirror, Morgan met Bryce Richardson's eyes. A glance. Then Bryce Richardson, with his Florida tan, still gazing at Morgan in the mirror, smug in his pin-striped suit and crested gold cuff-links, in a rubbing, clubby voice, said: "It's a rough deal. . . . But the way I look at it, when a guy's rich, he can stand anything. Right?" Morgan took the two steps toward him and swung at him. Struck him on the chin. Then drew back, appalled by what he had done, but wordless of apology. Bryce Richardson—his tanned face doused a sudden crimson—drew back too, and all in a second, feigning a Christ-like restraint, squared his shoulders: "I ought to report you to the membership committee," he said. Morgan turned from him, loathing him, and went away, down the corridor to the cloak-room, where he retrieved his overcoat and briefcase and continued on through the club's lobby, out its front door, onto the city street, into the cold daylight of the March afternoon that was for him then a gathered darkness, walking along, thinking maybe he was slipping into madness, striking a fool like Richardson, feeling as he walked on more and more at odds with the world, more hopeless, more desperate, walking now faster in the daylit darkness, stumbling: no clarity in sight.

❧

In the first days after her death, a lot of people offered him a lot of advice about how to "handle" his "loss." These offerings didn't come from his family or from close friends, but from such well-meaning folk as comprised the benign, limited, contactual relationships of his ordinary, everyday life—older, open-eyed men and women whose own experiences with death emboldened them to speak: Dave, the local garage mechanic (himself a widower); Miss Kenny, the postmistress; Mr. Eldon, the pharmacist; Mrs. Dawson, his dentist's nurse; Felix, his Cleveland barber; Joe, who shined his shoes; on and on. "Take my advice" was the standard opener. Sometimes when he felt terribly tired (he often did) he would jiggle the loose change in his pocket, would pretend to be in a hurry, but they would hold him: "Take my advice," they would repeat, madly, humanly compelled to give it.

—"*Socialize*. Don't be by yourself."

—"Get a pair of kittens. They'll divert you, the way they play."

—"Learn something new, like a language. Do you know French? Well, then Spanish maybe. What's important is the mental effort."

—"Fix a routine for yourself and force yourself to stick to it."

—"My brother took up crocheting after his wife passed away. He says it calmed him. He made a lap-throw for our sister. It's a show-piece, it's so fine. I don't see you crocheting, Mr. Shurtliff, but there's other kinds of hand-work you could do, like wood carving. Anything of a soothing nature to pick up at bad times."

Foolish advice. In the extreme, foolish. Yet often, the eyes of the person giving the foolish advice would be aglisten with tears. Or was it, often, through the sprung watery veiling in his own eyes that he imagined their tears? No. Because he so often *felt* the presence of their tears. Like ghosts, tears don't always have to be seen to be believed.

❧

All through March and April, Ralph looked for Maud to return from wherever she'd gone to do whatever it was she did when she wasn't at home. This was the longest she had ever stayed away. But she would be back. He maintained a faith that she would return. Every time he heard a car come down the lane, he rose to his feet, ears cocked, tail up. *This* time, surely. At such moments of hope, his eyes would appear to widen and fill with a mix of remonstrance (Where the Hell had she been?) and joy that she was anyhow back, so he would forgive her. But then, when he was again disappointed, he would lower his tail and ears and sink again back down onto the rug; settle down, sighing, to more waiting. His arthritis had worsened since she'd absented herself. He couldn't hustle about as he used to; couldn't, anymore, run. His knee joints were swollen; his legs were shaky. Sometimes he ate lying down. He went outdoors only when he had to, to do those two things decent dogs don't do in the house. He had his pride.

You know his history. That he was an injured stray found in a roadside ditch back in 1943, his age therefore a thing of estimation. But by that spring of 1958, he was for sure a deep sixteen; more likely seventeen. Now, crippled and in pain, he waited for Maud to return, confident that when she did, she would work on him some magic that would do away with whatever it was that was keeping him a rag, keeping him from running, keeping him quiet, keeping the house quiet too and the people in it, no one of them running around much either these days.

Morgan knew him: knew him for the soul he was: knew that these were some of the things going through his dog's mind—things that he hoped over and livened to whenever he heard a car come down the lane. Surely *this* time . . .

The vet, a tender, realistic man, told Morgan the time had come. Morgan said it must happen at home, in the library, Ralph's favorite room, over by the west windows that afforded the broadest view across the lawn. Put Ralph's blanket there. Next Saturday—the first Saturday in May—would be the day it would happen. In the morning.

Ralph was surprised to see the vet *here*. Usually, he met him *there*, in that other place, with its peculiar smells and the despised presence, often, of cats. So, though he didn't make the effort of rising to his feet when the vet showed up in the library, he did wag his tail (something he never did in the circumstance of that other place); wagged it harder when the vet stooped to pat him. But stayed lying down, warm in the morning sun. . . . They talked for a moment, Morgan and the vet. Then Morgan sat down on the floor. He said, "*Ralph*. Ralph, boy," and reached out his hand, took a front paw and held it. Ralph nosed his hand.

It was over in a matter of seconds.

Ralph lay then, dead, looking, if you only glanced, asleep.

Earlier that morning, Dennis had helped Morgan dig a grave in the dog cemetery up on the brow of the hill where the daffodils would soon be blooming. There, in the company of those other beloved, gone canines—Lear, Ripsy, Solo, Duffy, Daisy, Star—now, a new stone marker:

RALPH
1943–May 3, 1958

"In all my life, it was the hardest thing I have ever had to do," Morgan wrote Julia and Caroline that night.

❧

The soon-to-come trip to Europe with Julia and Caroline created the problem of finding a responsible man who would be a capable protector of Lillie Ruth and Tessa and act too as a general guard of the house and grounds. Someone who would be there night and day. Dennis solved the problem. "My cousin Willis, Mr. Shurtliff. He's the answer. He's just been retired as night-watchman at the Ralston plant, not on account of his age, he's only fifty-seven, the Ralston people wanted him to stay on, but Willis, well, his kids are grown and moved on, and Willis's wife, she died a dozen or more years ago, and Willis just a little while back took it into his head to look for new work, said he was tired of the same routine he's kept to for so long," Dennis ran on, non-stop. "Lillie Ruth and Tessa know all about Wills. He's one of our church, and the Ralston people if you ask them will give Willis as good a recommendation as the gold Pullman watch and chain they gave him when he retired."

Willis Cob. Called "Wills." By mid-May, Wills was settled in the quarters over the garage that had once, long ago, housed a chauffeur. During the daytime he worked around the place with Dennis. At day's end, when Dennis went to his own home, Wills took over. Lillie Ruth said: "Don't you worry about anything's going wrong here while you're away, Morgan. Wills'll see to everything just fine." The inexactness of her word—"everything"—was an evasion: she knew Morgan wouldn't hear of her thanking him directly for providing a night-time guardian for herself and Tessa. She put her hand on his arm, light as a dropped autumn leaf, her old eyes regarding him, brimming. It was one of the many times he sat with her, both of them often silent, remembering Maud.

❧

The Cunard liner was huge and beautiful.

To Caroline and Julia he praised the ship as a noble, proud survivor of World War II. All during the war years (he told them) she had crossed and recrossed the Atlantic in conditions hazardous beyond words—

thousands and thousands of soldiers aboard her. He personalized her, posing the possibility that she was the very ship that had borne Geoff and Alan home to the States after their release from the POW camp. . . . And then he spoke of the war's end and of how she had spent months and months in dry dock being refitted and refurbished as a luxury liner: made again a majesty of the sea. "And what a queen she is!"

Their suite (in first class) consisted of Julia's and Caroline's stateroom, his stateroom, and a sitting room. These quarters opened onto a private deck. Caroline said it was as if they were royalty, the way the staff took care of them. Such is the Cunard tradition, Morgan replied, then went on to say that the standard of service was as fine today as it had been thirty-two years ago when he was fifteen and Pip had taken him to Europe on another Cunard liner.

Inevitably, and almost immediately, Caroline discovered the crowd of college students traveling in cabin and tourist classes (Cunard's strict designations), and it was to those regions of the ship she wended her way in the afternoons. Usually Julia went with her. He encouraged these hours spent with their contemporaries. When they returned from these escapes they regaled him with stories about the people they had met. There was the happy coincidence of finding a just-graduated Bryn Mawr girl (this trip a graduation present from her grand-parents), and believe it or not, a pair of "twin guys—Yalies," who were, in Caroline's words, "fantastic fun." And there were two girls ("English lit majors, University of Michigan") whose company Julia especially enjoyed; and others. As they told him about these new friends, they would glance at each other: coded messages not always readily (by him) translatable. . . . A thought formed in his mind—of connection—between the lively nature of these escapes and the fact that they took place in that part of the ship he remembered from his seafaring wartime life as being a ship's most actual realm, where one was close to the rhythmic workings of the ship's engines, where one could "feel her pulse" (as Sarkis used to say), where the sea's lappings against her side were audible, all of which sensations were barely realizable in the elevated remove of first class.

The Atlantic stayed smooth for this June crossing.

Julia and Caroline loved dressing, formally, for dinner each night. He listened to them talking and laughing as they readied themselves to go with him to the splendid dining room. When they emerged from their stateroom in their long dresses, they always looked particularly lovely, charmed and charming. He would hold out his hands to them and, thinking of Maud, he would embrace them. One evening there was a dance, a "gala," and a worldly, unattached, middle-aged Norwegian man swept Caroline onto the dance-floor, not once but five times. The ship's photographer took a picture of them—dipping—to music that encouraged knee bends and slides and close flirtation, not quite a tango. Julia danced with a reticent, well-spoken youth from Richmond, Virginia (traveling with his parents). She and the young man looked soft, gliding over the floor, talking as they danced; smiling. The young man's left hand stayed light and shy in the middle of her back, just above her waist. Held in the Norwegian's commanding grip, Caroline looked avid. Maud's word—*wired*—sprang to mind (*Ah,* Callie).

High life on the high seas.

But then there were those other times when the three of them sat quietly together on their private deck in the sea-hazy sunlight, times when Maud was present in their minds, times when they would speak of her. Those were the times when he felt about Julia and Caroline that they were his self-appointed protectors, that on this voyage they were not in his keeping, but that he was in theirs: that they were saving him.

. . . A week in and around London; then Stratford; then Stonehenge on an afternoon of dramatic weather—purple-black clouds and rain that seemed to turn green as it neared the ground; Salisbury (the rise and glory of the cathedral); three more days spent rambling in the English countryside. Then to France: Paris, where for a couple of afternoons and evenings Caroline and Julia linked up again (by prior arrangement) with the shipboard college crowd, augmented by fresh faces. Then by car to Chartres and Orléans and Avallon (Vézelay bypassed as having been too promised to Maud); then, via circuitous roads bordered by poplar trees, back to Paris for the plane-hop to Venice. After Venice, in slow stages, again by car, to Florence; from Florence to Rome, and from Rome to Cherbourg for the return voyage to New York.

The trip filled most of the summer.

... "Would you like to read this, Morgan?" Julia asked him in mid-August, when they were back home. "This," handed to him, turned out to be a kind of diary-notebook, her record of the trip: *A Journey, Sea, Land, and Air.* "Why, Julia!" he said, deeply pleased: *"Yes."* He read it that evening, every word, surprised by the pictorial and atmospheric accuracy of her descriptions of the places and things that had especially captivated her, surprised most by the emotional range of her responses to certain of the trip's random happenings: her account, for instance, of how she had "desperately bargained" for a finely wrought nineteenth-century silver salamander "spotted" in the window of a side-street antique store in Avallon, the salamander described as being "about six inches long; raised head; large, slanted, slightly protruding eyes; a long mouth receding into the neckless beginnings of its slim body; splayed-out feet, the toes delicate but gripping and inquisitive, like little fingers; a long diminishing tail curling back on itself at the end ... The instant I saw it, I knew I wanted it, not only because I like salamanders and this one looked so *real*, but because of my faith in the myth about salamanders that they can withstand the trial of being put in fire and come out alive. I wanted it as a symbol, to have for myself, for future inspiration. The man in the antique shop stated the very lowest figure he would sell it at, still too steep a price for me to pay from the available money allotted me for purchases on this trip, but Morgan advanced me the difference against my next month's allowance, so I was able to get it. The man in the shop gave me a padded draw-string bag to keep it in, 'safe, during your travels' he told me in English. As I write, the salamander is in front of me, out of its bag, lying on the dark wood of the desk in Callie's and my hotel room here in Avallon. The way its body shines reminds me of the day Mother and I saw a salamander sunning itself on a rock in the middle of our creek. I was six, maybe seven. We sat on the creek-bank watching it for what seemed to me a long time. It was while we were watching it that Mother told me that flames couldn't harm it, not flames from the God-made sun, or flames from man-made fires." (He read these sentences and for a moment was blind, unable to read on until after he cleared the tears from his eyes.)

Caroline told everyone, everyone, that from beginning to end, the trip had been "fabulous"; beyond her wildest dreams, *"fabulous."* To a special few people she showed the picture of herself dancing in the infatuated arms of the worldly middle-aged Norwegian. His name (she informed the special few) was Niels. Niels Somethingorother. On the last day aboard ship, he had slipped his card into the side-pocket of her purse, but somewhere along the way she had lost it.

᠅

(Before they left for Europe, he'd given Miss Sly an itinerary of the trip and the addresses of the hotels where they would be staying. She had fixed him in her strictest gaze: "You *will* honestly keep me posted about how you are, how you're bearing up without Mrs. Shurtliff. You will, won't you." Thus she opened the way to a correspondence more intimate and in assembly greater than had been amassed between them during the years of the war. City by city, her letters awaited him at the check-in desks of the named hotels. "Dear Mr. Shurtliff—" He wrote her frequently. Cards and letters. "Dear Miss Sly—" Never, ever, did she address him by his first name; unthinkable that he would ever call her "Zenobia." They cared for each other in a way too unusual for such usual familiarity. Yet it was as he had known it would be—this heightened, more flexible, more assuming relationship that had set in between them since Maud's death. At sea, on the day before they were due to arrive in New York, he sent her a cable: "If you can, save next Wednesday for lunch. Will telephone to verify. As ever, Morgan Shurtliff." And so, that following Wednesday, they met, and with their strange ardor, embraced. And, in their usual restaurant, after they were seated, she peered at him for a whole moment, deeply, with the large eyes of a wise lioness gazing from a high position over a large tract of land, reading the terrain, reading *him:* and then she said: "I can tell. . . . You're still aching. Oh, my dear Mr. Shurtliff.")

᠅

Julia and Caroline had two short weeks at home before they went back to college. They opted to go by plane, so he parted from them at the airport. He stood amidst a crowd on an outdoor deck and watched the plane zoom down the runway and rise from the ground. By the time he got to his car, it was well aloft; in another couple of minutes, it had disappeared into a flock of clouds. He thought that from now on, the plane would be the way to go; *speed,* now, the great impulse; the great thing. No more the train, that old, important, earthbound prolonger of expectation. Think how the train had once been hailed! How Victorians, saluting the wonder of it, had dubbed it "The Iron Horse." Hail now the plane, celestial, way up there, ripping through the clouds, still ascending. Angels of Heaven, beware!

❦

In October, on a week-end visit, his father spoke out: "You're drinking far too much these days."

"Don't censure me," Morgan warned.

Dinner was long over. They were in the library, Ansel Shurtliff sitting in a straight-backed chair, Morgan in a wing-chair, sunk in it, staring into the fire, morose, face flushed, forehead damp.

"It wasn't my intention to censure you, but as you've used the word, I assume you'd prefer to be honestly 'censured' than silently pitied, by me or anyone else."

What a barb! "I'm going to bed."

"It *is* late. I'll see you at breakfast."

He was aware of the graceless way he rose from his chair, aware that as he crossed the room he veered a bit, right to left, and furious when he stumbled on the library's threshold floorboard. "Shit," he murmured, not caring that the crude expletive reached his father's ears; his father sitting there, observing his sloppy exit.

He woke with a headache. He put himself through the drill of a cold shower. He shaved with an unsteady hand. But his memory of the night before was intact: that clash with his father; his father's sticking barb. He was late getting downstairs for breakfast. "I'm sorry about last night," he said to his father.

"Have your breakfast, son. We've got all day to talk. Or shall we start now?"

"Why not?" It came out hard-spoken, airy and defensive.

His father turned on him a candid look tinged a bit with the mystical (a look known to Morgan as a presager of paternal reminiscence). "All right . . . I'll start off by telling you what happened to me after your mother died." (Of all possible openings, he had not expected this one.) "All things considered, I think I behaved fairly well in the first months after she died. There were so many things to be dealt with, so many honorings owed to the dead, and of course, first and foremost, there was *you,* a twelve-year-old boy in piteous distress, hurting in your young way as much as I was hurting in my older way. The effort of attending to all such immediate matters sustained me for a while. Kept me on track. Gave me a sense of purpose. But then, about six months down the road, and more or less unexpectedly, I hit trouble. Trouble in the form of myself . . . I ran into myself coming down the road from the opposite direction and I saw myself in disarray, without much hope of a future of much value. I can't think of a better way to say it. . . . It was the endless erratics of adjustment to life without your mother that had finally gotten to me. Most of all, I felt unmanned. Unvirile. That's when I hit bottom, which is where I think you are now, at the nadir of your grief. But I kept plodding on, doing what I thought were all the right things, trying not to think about myself. Not *facing* myself, I mean . . . You'll never guess who freed me. Your Aunt Letitia! She sat me down one day and lectured me on what she called 'The Art of Being Selfish.' Fancy Letitia doing that! She told me to stop being 'noble.' She said if I didn't begin to take an interest in myself, no one would give a hang about me, not even the people I thought I was being noble *for.* Oh, she was mean, the way she lit into me." Here, Ansel Shurtliff laughed: "You know the way she dresses up for every occasion. . . . Well, for the delivery of her lecture to me she'd gotten herself up in a red dress, that big diamond brooch she'd inherited pinned on her bosom. She looked like one of the Roman Furies—that blood-red dress and that dazzling brooch underscoring every word she said, plus the way she kept shaking her finger in my face, telling me off. . . . Your egg's gotten cold. . . . I think I've made my point, except to say that in my opinion, for what it's worth to you, the time's come for you to make some root and branch changes in your life. . . . Shouldn't you ask Tessa to boil you another egg?"

That was the Saturday morning start of what, afterwards, he thought of as "the crisis week-end," perpetrated by his father.

On Sunday afternoon, just before he stepped into his Jaguar for the drive to his home, Ansel Shurtliff made his final speech: "Don't make the mistake of living in the past, Morgan. It's a futile, fatal thing to do. Let Maud go, loved as she will always be.... And now I'm going—I hope not entirely to your immense relief."

Then that handshake. The Jag's engine's purr. A last glance.

"Good-bye until soon, Pa."

ॐ

KISSEL, CHANDLER, SHURTLIFF & COLT

Before Maud died, back in early February, Morgan had told George Colt he thought the time was "ripe" for making the New York office a more "important" part of the Kissel, Chandler practice. The Cleveland office, long established and high in repute, was zinging along on greased tracks. Ditto the Pittsburgh branch. "But I've got this idea, George, that we ought to expand the New York office—turn it into a real contender, equal to the best of existing New York firms."

George Colt listened hard to Morgan's idea, then rocked back in his chair and looked for a long moment out the window, smiling, as if the stone facade of the building across the avenue were a pleasing, living sight—a great, green, unfolding, unfenced field—his smile sort of dreamy. Morgan knew what, about his idea, was floating through George Colt's mind: that it was very ambitious, very, for the reason of its unprecedented reach, very daring.

("Bear in mind," Morgan would tell a later generation of lawyers, "this was back in 1958. Back when law firms were still small in size, referred to within the profession as 'shops.' Back to a time when, within the unit of a given firm, partner relationships were close pacts of balanced trust, deemed, like marriages, almost sacred." He would go on to say that the Kissel, Chandler firm, back in 1958, was ranked as being large, consisting as it did of twenty-five lawyers, ten of whom were partners, fifteen of whom were associates. "Minuscule by today's standards," he would add, elaborating further that it wasn't until sometime in the 1970s— with the proliferation of government agencies and statutory regulations and ever-changing tax policies (as plaguing to individual citizens as to corporations)—that law firms began to become the huge behemoths they are today, with hundreds of partners and hundreds of associates and subsidiary offices scattered all over the world).

Finally, George Colt withdrew his gaze from the building's facade across the avenue. He looked now at Morgan. Then, still smiling, though not in his previous dreamy way, he verbally served up *his* idea of Morgan's idea. He said that it was "dicey," but worthy of consideration; a matter to be put before the firm's entire partnership. "You'd be the one to front it, Morgan. You've got the clout, what with your recent big win and all."

"Ah George, bless you! That's exactly what I'd hoped you'd say."

"It'd be a big undertaking. You'd have to spend most of your time in New York; keep on being a long-distance commuter. How would that sit with Maud?"

"So well that, pending approval of the idea, she's begun to talk about our getting a small apartment in New York. A snuggery, just for the two of us. And why not? With Julia and Caroline off at college, she's free to spend time away from home. She has close friends in New York—"

"So for both of you, it would be okay," George Colt cut in—

"Better than just okay," Morgan shot back.

"Grand . . . We'll put it to the others at the next partners' meeting. We ought all to be in accord: that way, if the project fails it'll be on all our shoulders."

"It won't fail."

"It damn well better not!"

. . . But then everything changed. Maud died. And Morgan shelved the idea. Couldn't rise to the challenge of it. Not until now, nearly eight months later, in the wake of that crisis week-end perpetrated by his father. Now—as a possible salvation—he took up the idea again.

George Colt's response? "I knew you would, Morgan, given time. I've already talked it over with the others. We're all for it."

So, starting in November, he began (on paper) to give body to his idea, to plot its course and ready it for launching—a chanceful sink-or-float *thing*, maybe personally murderous. His nights to come would be sleepless, but a sleeplessness wholly different from the aching, despairing wakefulness of sorrow. Now his pride was involved. (That line of

Shakespeare's: ". . . he might yet recover, and prove an ass." *His* recovery, were it to come at all, to be proved—*not*—an ass).

❧

There was the mounting dread of the first Christmas without Maud.

Again, Letitia Grant took up the cudgel, this time on Julia's and Caroline's behalf. She would make it her business, she said, to see that they didn't spend their Christmas holidays grieving for their mother. Maud, she said, would roll in her grave at the very thought of such prolonged mourning. "They'll have had their eyes glued in books since last September, Morgan. They'll have earned some fun. And they are eighteen! Maud had it in mind to give a Christmas dance in their honor. . . . Oh, I agree! A big affair would be inappropriate. But a pretty, spanky, reasonably small tea-dance would be perfectly seemly. Leave it to me."

At the Grants' house, on Saturday, December 20, in a winterized, barber-pole-striped tent set up off the living room, amid potted greenery and flowers galore, the young crowd danced. So did their parents; so did their white-haired parents' parents, Doctor Leigh and Ansel Shurtliff among them. Trust Letitia to have hired a terrific band—not a blaring one, but plenty lively: what Caroline called "romantic hip."

He danced four times, first with Julia, then with Caroline, then, as everyone looked on, with both of them, encircling them with his arms, somehow waltzing, honoring them that way, that they were eighteen, "debs," being formally "brought out" (Letitia's words). Last of all, as everyone took to the floor, he danced with Letitia. He remained of course at the party; stayed on until it ended, but only as a paternal, viewing presence, docked on the sidelines, not faking the pleasure he took in the affair, but not lost in it either. Somewhere in between. Between felicity and sorrow.

Geoff had come from New York for this occasion of the twins' "debut." He said it wasn't to be missed, Caroline being his goddaughter and Julia his next, best-loved girl. He brought them presents: matched Tiffany sapphire bar-pins: "commemorative tokens." In the swell of laughter and movement and music, as the party neared its peak, he sidled up to Morgan: "Are you all right, Morgie?" he asked, knowing.

"I think so, Geoff."

They stood together, watching the action. "That lorn maiden," Geoff said after a bit, nodding in the direction of a limp-haired, sad-faced, unattended girl.

"Helen Mayhew," Morgan supplied her name.

"She needs some seeing to," Geoff said. "I'll give her a whirl."

"A bloody saint is what you are."

Geoff laughed. "Hardly. Just a well brought-up ex-Philadelphian." Then: "Hang on, Morgie."

With which words, Geoff left him. He saw the gentle way Geoff touched Helen Mayhew's arm, then took her by the hand and led her onto the dance floor. The band was playing "That Old Black Magic." (Look, Maud. Look how Geoff is succeeding at giving Godfrey Mayhew's daughter a good time. Look at her smile! Ah, Maud.)

◦◦

With a seeming usualness, the dreaded holidays passed. Even the weather behaved in a seasonably usual way, producing two snowstorms, gale winds, cold days and colder nights. The telephone rang a lot, and the front doorbell. Caroline and Julia (Caroline more than Julia) went to parties. Their friends (all home from different colleges for the holidays) came by during the day to hike in the woods or to skate on the pond's black ice (the males played raucous games of hockey) or just to sit around indoors, talking and laughing—Caroline's crowd noisy, confident, demonstrative; Julia's smaller group quieter, far less overtly excitable. (Bruce Wilson, now in his junior year at Columbia, and more than ever intellectually serious, came often, *very* often, Morgan noted, to see Julia, bringing his springer spaniel, Pansy, with him. "I hope you don't mind Pansy, Mr. Shurtliff," Bruce said. "*Mind*, Bruce? It's wonderful having a dog in the house again. Pansy's welcome anytime.") This differently geared mix of friends came together too on several evenings that began with dinner and ended late; more talk, more laughter, all (as Morgan heard it) as usual. He kept telling himself that it was the resiliency of Caroline's and Julia's youth that enabled them to be— *usual*. As if Maud were still alive. For this ability, for them, he was thankful. . . . But on the day they returned to college, an episode took place that made a lie of his assumptions about their easy-seeming, all-as-usual behavior. It happened at the airport as the three of them waited together for the flight to be called. Not a long wait. *All passengers traveling on Flight 303 to Philadelphia should now proceed to gate five.* "Gate five is *that* way," Morgan said, starting to herd them—

Abruptly, Caroline grabbed one of his arms and one of Julia's: *"Wait,"* she said, holding them in place: "There's something I want to say."

"What." Julia demanded.

"That we've made it through," Caroline began, fiercely, her lips, though, trembling: "There were times when I was afraid we wouldn't"— tears were in her eyes now—"when I thought we wouldn't be able to."

And Julia, ardent—an instant twin such as he had not seen her for some while to be—said: "But we *did*. The three of us. Somehow we made it through."

He looked at them, unable to speak. They had one face, one selfsame, sorrow-riddled, victorious face.

All passengers . . . The second announcement came, imperative.

He was a statue.

They kissed him and picked up their hand luggage and turned from him and commenced walking toward gate five.

He watched them go; watched them go. Until he came alive, and able to—finally able to—he called after them: "I'll see you in New York soon. I'll arrange it."

They heard and looked over their shoulders back at him and smiled, then moved on, almost running forward.

It took him a considerable time—he was still that struck, still within himself that humbled—to simply proceed.

From the airport he went into the city, to his office. He would work at his desk for the rest of the day. He was taking Miss Sly to dinner that evening. It would be their first meeting in this New Year of 1959.

~§

In early January he was officially installed as the head of the New York branch of Kissel, Chandler, Shurtliff & Colt. (*Branch* was his orchardist father's word.)

Later in the month, after a careful search, he bought an apartment in a building located at the corner of Fifth Avenue and Seventy-third Street. It was of considerable size, consisting of a long, gallery-like entrance hall, living room, dining room, library, four bedrooms, kitchen, and maid's room. In the first week in February, a decorator (recommended by Lucy Blackett) went to work, supervising painters, measuring windows for curtaining, ETC. ETC. In his spare time, he began to furnish the apartment, aided by Julia and Caroline when they came to New York for stray weekends away from college. "Our New York home," Julia said of the apartment. Caroline, employing her favorite adjective, said: "Fabulous! It's going to be fabulous!"

To his very great surprise, the thought kept occurring to him that at some future time (and most certainly if the venture of the New York office proved successful) he would give up the glorious house he and Maud had committed to back in 1947, eleven years ago, now ghostly. He shared this thought with no one.

Friday, February 20, 1959

A year to the day of Maud's death.

For this day, he returned to Hatherton.

Camellias are my favorite flowers, Maud always said. . . . A long time ago, with Dennis's help, she had planted six camellia bushes at one end of the old greenhouse. Warmly bedded and well tended, the bushes had flourished. Annually, beginning in early February, the bushes bloomed, the flowers white and cool. *Beautiful. So beautiful.* He got up early in the morning and went to the greenhouse and clipped from the bushes a few of the flowers and, still in the near-dark of the barely-born day, drove to the cemetery. There, he laid the flowers on her grave. Overhead, through filaments of gauzy gray clouds, the sun was struggling to show itself. He stayed beside the grave, looking up at the sky, watching the sun's attempt, witnessing its determination. And all at once—astonishing—it parted the clouds and blazed, a scheming, golden orb, and he thought that right before his eyes, all in a second, a whole year had passed. That the eclipse was over.

Light, then.

A force of nature!

Part Two ∽

1 ∞ Prologue

It is mid-April, the spring of 1959.

At the end of this workday, he is taking a walk in Central Park. On one of the park's small, man-made lakes a pair of ducks are swimming, creating vees on the water's surface. He stops walking and stands still, watching them. He sings a song to himself. *Flow gently, sweet Afton, among thy green braes.* It was one of the songs he sang as a boy in school, in the fifth grade. . . . He hasn't thought of the song for years. Why now does he remember it, singing it to himself? In the lake there are no reeds growing, no meander of water as with a stream's flow. It is the presence of the swimming ducks that reminds him of the absence of reeds and that the lake's water is contained. Yet there the ducks are, happily swimming, not looking at all compromised. . . . Then a man comes along. Like himself, the man is dressed in a suit and tie, out for a walk at the end of the day, wearing a hat. A well-groomed yellow Labrador retriever trots at the man's side. The dog sees the ducks and begins to bark and leap, straining at its leash. The ducks flap their wings and paddle forward, skimming along, all commotion, half in and half out of the water, then rise up quacking into the air and fly away. The man smiles at Morgan; Morgan returns his smile. Man and dog walk on. But Morgan lingers, not minding that the ducks are gone. . . . Now the farther scene engages him—the rise of the hill on the other side of the lake, glimpses of the tops of buildings crowned by clouds pinkened by the setting sun. He stands there, greatly taken by the scene, conscious that his enjoyment of it is due in large part to his anticipation of the evening soon to come. He looks at his watch. Time to go. *Don't be later than six,* Ann had said. He strides off, liking the feel of being in a hurry.

≈§

Ann Montgomery.

He met her about a month ago at a dinner party given by Pamela and Lawrence. When Pam invited him to the party, she described it as "a duty party, Morgan—people we don't often see but owe an evening to. I need an extra man. Will you do me the favor of coming?" At table, seated on his right, was Ann Montgomery. By the time dinner was over he knew he would end the night with her, making love to her. She paved the way, she told him so many certain facts about herself: that she'd been twice married and twice divorced, that what she'd never do was marry again, that she really liked being single, going to parties alone, getting to know new people. "On my own terms," she'd quickly added, laughing. She and Pamela had been in the same class at Vassar. "Vassar's our connection," Ann said: "We meet a couple of times a year, usually over the matter of fund-raising." The last time they'd met, Ann had paid for lunch: "It's sweet of Pam to have me to dinner in return for a mere lunch." She had asked him if he was married. He had answered with a simple no. She talked on, luring him with her chatter, her independence, her shady humor. Her laughter was infectious, a sort of musical hum. There seemed to be no rancor in her. All through dinner she kept glancing at his hands. When the party was over, he offered to take her home. In the taxi, curbside at her apartment building, when she asked him if he would like to "bed" her, he said yes, looking right at her, yes he would.

It was the first time since Maud's death. A turning point.

Ann works for a publishing firm, Grosset & Dunlap, editing reference books. She has short, straight dark hair, hazel eyes, a small nose with chiseled nostrils, a generous mouth, a rangy, well-hipped body and smallish breasts. In one corner of her large bedroom there is an exercise bike. She keeps a record of how many in-place miles she pedals every day. She is an erotic sophisticate, though not in any ways unknown to him: just terribly skilled. Sometimes she asks him for more, *more*, mewing the word. At such times, afterwards, she looks old (which she's not; she's only forty-one or -two) and turns her face away from him as if, in her spent state, he mustn't see her. But she recovers quickly; all she needs is a moment. Always, always she tells him he is wonderful, that he is wonderfully good at it. He repeats what she has said, turning it on herself: she too is wonderfully good at it. From the beginning she let him know he is not her only resource; that there are two others. "Old friends," she calls them. She is not curious about his past or present life. (By now, she knows his wife died more than a year ago; he has, though, never spoken Maud's name to her.) About her own life, he mirrors her incuriosity. What they do tell each other is that they like each other, and that their affair (if that's what it is), exactly as it is, is fine: that for both of them, just as it is, it couldn't be better.

∾

Almost immediately, the people closest to him in heart and mind saw the difference in him and in their individual ways, spoke of it.

His father used the word "potent": "I'm pleased to see you looking your old potent self again," he said. The broad, secular way he said it caused Morgan almost to shy: because of the flashed revelation about his father that after *his* wife's death (Morgan's mother's death), in time and clandestinely, there had been someone with whom he too had formed a sexual liaison; someone who had made him, again, a "potent" man. Who? Who could it have been? he instantly wondered. . . . From the summer he turned thirteen (by which time his mother had been dead over a year), he retained a memory of standing at a window in his Aunt Letitia's house, watching his father play a spirited game of croquet with a lady. Now he remembered his father's laughter, how his father and the lady had laughed together—that his father was laughing at all!—that something the lady said, something she kept saying, kept making his father laugh. Other than the fact that she made his father laugh, he hadn't a least memory of the distant lady. But now he wondered: had *she* been the one? . . . He would never know; could never ask, standing there now beside his father, adultly reassessing his remark.

Geoff, savvy, said: "You've rejoined the world."

Miss Sly said: "You've recovered. Amen." That was all she said.

Sidney said: "I'll quote you a line. 'His tunes were frozen up in his horn, and come out now by thawing.'"

Morgan laughed: "Who the hell said that?"

Sidney, the eternal educator, answered: "A German named Rudolph Rapse, born in 1737, died in 1794."

"I've never heard of him."

"It's a line from one of his books, *The Travels of Baron Munchausen.* I'll give you a copy. It's very amusing." Then, lawyer-like: "Am I correct in thinking that the quote applies?"

"You're correct."

"I'm glad for you, Morgan. So's Linda."

"God, Sidney, is it so obvious?"

"Yeah." Sidney laughed: "Yeah, it is."

Next to Geoff, Sidney remains his closest friend. Of all his contemporaries, Morgan feels about Sidney's life that it is the most anchored, the most complete, personally and professionally. He sees Sidney often. Their meetings easily occur: Sidney and Linda have long since moved from their small post-war brownstone apartment and live now in a sprawling, book-lined apartment on East Seventieth Street, just a few blocks away from Morgan's apartment. With Sidney, he often takes an end-of-the-day walk. Sometimes Sidney's and Linda's two children— David, now thirteen years old, and Judith, eight—come along on these walks, accompanied by the family dog, a blue-eyed Dalmatian whose name (not surprisingly) is Goethe. Once in a while, Linda joins them, but only once in a while. Usually she remains at home, cooking, firmly fixed in her belief that food, as prepared by her and only by her, will keep Nature's troubles, indigestion to earthquake, at bay.

She won't consider employing someone to help her with the cooking. She must do it all, and all by herself. Often, when Morgan and Sidney hook up for a walk, Sidney will hand Morgan a message she has scrawled on a piece of kitchen note-paper: "I'll be disappointed if you don't come back with S. for dinner." Or some other differently worded invitation: "I'm counting on you to help eat up what I'm concocting. I've doubled the recipe, so you *have* to come." Morgan is devoted to her. How could he not be? In heart, she is one of the world's great women.

Lawrence too saw the difference in him. But he didn't directly speak of it. He commented instead on Morgan's new suit and on the more colorful neckties he's wearing these days. . . . Over the last five years, since Lawrence and Pamela re-married, Lawrence has become more and more "abstract" (Morgan's word). Sidney puts it another way: "He's out of touch with himself," Sidney says. Morgan thinks the cause of Lawrence's abstractness is that he's given himself completely over to Pamela, that Pamela consumes him. Sidney rebuts that the same thing could be said about Pamela: that Lawrence consumes her. "It's an interchangeable obsession." What worries Sidney and Morgan about this interchangeable obsession is that it seems to be based so much on regret: regret about the years lost between the time Pamela and Lawrence divorced and the time they re-married. Those lost years are the reason they are childless. That they have no children is a subject they can't put to rest. The lack haunts them. "My fault," Pamela will say, harking back to the hurly-burly years she wasted, the years when she "could" have been having babies, when she and Lawrence "should" have been rearing a family. "No, it's not your fault, Pam," Lawrence regularly counters, "it's just the way things happened," absolving her of blame, excusing them both, nurturing that way their mutual regret, keeping it alive. . . . What's interesting is how they compensate for their childless state. Pamela spends three days a week as a teacher's aide at a big public school up in Harlem, helping slow children to read and write; Lawrence is now the president of the board of directors of a long-established, privately funded foster-care agency ("The Shepherd's Home" is its sentimental, Victorian name) for children from families broken apart by poverty or sickness or addictive vices. Every so often he says he'd like to "quit the law" and devote himself full time to making the Shepherd's Home a model for other institutions of its kind. He could easily afford to quit the law; he has a handsome income from monies inherited from his grand-father. But he goes on, not quitting. The sorry truth is that his career as a lawyer is in no way distinguished, its mediocrity due (too) to those five years spent in the wake of his and Pamela's divorce—unfocused years of missed chances and flubbed opportunities that put him out of step with his contemporaries and caused him, within the profession, to lose rank. Blown years he's never been able to make up for. In his firm, he is a lower-echelon partner, regarded as a post-war casualty. Yet his professional life, dim and routine and ordinary as it is, appears to mean a lot to him. "The attraction of the predictable" is how Sidney sums the mystery. More deeply, Sidney thinks Lawrence is terrified of making any major change in his life. "I think he sees change as disaster," Sidney further says. "Maybe, more than anything, it's his fear of change that's behind his abstractness." Whatever: the fact remains that the only time Lawrence's air of abstractness disappears is when he talks with Sidney and Morgan about the war. That's when he sits up straight in a chair, eyes slightly narrowed, the expression on his face keen and eager and again potential as he brings up, like a thirsty man bringing up water from a well, incidents, scenes, stories from the war years, romancing his accounts; building on them. From those remote 1943 limbo months he and Morgan and Sidney spent in Miami, he remembers the names of streets, the names of bars they frequented—details such as Morgan and Sidney have long since forgotten. . . . *O the brotherhood of those strange times,* Sidney poetically says, smiling, one of his hands on Lawrence's arm, the other on Morgan's arm. Thus, on the basis of the bond forged between them in those by-gone times, their tripod friendship continues.

꿏

Soon after Morgan met Ann Montgomery, he took Lucy Blackett (as he very often does) to dinner. They had a drink at Lucy's apartment before going on to a downtown restaurant. In the cab on the way to the restaurant, Lucy remarked: "It's been ages since I've seen you so—*relaxed.*"

Ah. . . . From her remark, he took its two key words—*ages* (under-

stood as the length of time that has passed since Maud's death), and—
relaxed (inflected by Lucy in a way insinuative of carnal abatement). By
which tonal nuance, he knew that Lucy knew. Normally, he would have
laughed and told her straight out that he knew she knew. That's the
usual way their friendship works. And anyhow, between him and Lucy
there are no secrets. But in this instance, he decided to remain silent,
certain that she would soon abandon insinuation and honestly address
the subject: honestly, *as* a subject, nail it. He preferred that she be the
one to do so.

Since the day three years ago when Lucy ended her affair with Gerry
Davis, her life, as far as men are concerned, has been a blank. After she
had recovered from her near breakdown sorrow at losing Gerry, Maud,
sibyl-like, had predicted that Lucy would never look at another man.
Not, at least, sexually. And she hasn't. . . . Her history with men had
been one of late discovery and tardy emergence: at age nearly thirty she
had still been a virgin. Once, a long time ago, in an almost clinical way,
she had reviewed with Morgan her cosseted girlhood spent under her
mother's puritanical eye, which rigid scrutiny had caused in her the gender shyness that had all but ruined the younger years of her life. She had
spoken of her residual amazement that she had found the courage to go
behind her mother's back and to volunteer, in 1941, for overseas duty in
the Red Cross, thereby freeing herself from her mother's proprietorial
gaze. (She had reviewed too the irony of the fact that whereas World
War II had liberated *her*, World War I had made of her mother an early,
bitter, wintry widow; Lucy, three years old when her father was killed in
France in 1917.) . . . In late 1943, from blitz-torn London, Lucy had
written a letter to Maud in which she revealed that she had been
deflowered by an RAF pilot. About her deflowerer, she had given no
details. Whether he was older or younger than she, how she had met
him, if, after losing her virginity to him, she ever saw him again remain
to this day (at least to Morgan) a mystery. She has never, though, made a
secret of the fact that subsequent to her deflowering, she led an
extremely active sex life. It wasn't until after she met and fell in love with
Gerry Davis that she stopped her marathon couplings (candidly self-
described as "promiscuous") and settled down to that single relationship

with Gerry, committing herself whole-heartedly to it until, by her own doing, the affair had ended.

She did not at once pursue the matter of her remark made in the taxi. She let it rest until after they were seated in the restaurant, until after they had studied the menu and decided what they would eat, until after he had given their order to the waiter; put it off further, still wearing her glasses, looking around the restaurant, looking at the other diners until, at last, in complete control of the moment, splendid in her confidence, she took off her glasses and, naked-eyed, gazing at him, stated: "You've found a skirt."

How she nailed the subject, reverting to that jaunty WW II phrase used by soldiers with soldiers, perfectly conveyed her understanding of its character: as purely sexual; no motivation of love in it.

"Ah, Luce," he said: "You do see everything."

Spontaneously, they joined hands, the gesture natural between them, natural to their long friendship, to their indestructible bond of Maud; natural too that they would sit like that for a moment, quietly, in a removed corner of a public place, silently facing each other, bridging time, seeing themselves through each other's eyes—what they know about each other, what they've been through separately and together, the condition of their lives now, mid-point of life itself: how they individually manage. He sees Lucy as unique in her mastery over repinings for happinesses that were never fully hers in the past and that she knows will never occur for her in the future; unique in her imagination of what *isn't* hers, but of what does exist for others, pitfalls and passions and possibilities, sightings of which never cease to excite her. The prodigious way she attends upon these sightings, the way she woos them to her and engages in their existence is what keeps her amusing and feisty and stylish and warm—qualities now freshly displayed: "About this skirt, Morgan, let me tell you my sense of her. She's—well—*bedroomish* by nature. But not a nympho. She's unmarried, probably divorced. No kids. Not a burning intellect, but plenty bright. . . . It's not anything that will last."

"You're right on all counts."

"But it's a breakthrough for you. You couldn't have stayed celibate forever. You're not the celibate type."

"What's the celibate type?"

"*Stoics.*" Lucy spat out the word. "I hate stoics. The way they settle into being resigned to fate but still stay hopeful. The Job theme. Or a variation on the Job theme. I've never admired Job." She caught on, suddenly, to how wound up she was, and dismissed her tirade with: "Anyhow, thanks to the found skirt, you're safe from all that. It's a debt you owe her."

"I know."

"Just don't fall into the trap of making it an eternal debt."

"I won't."

"Now I'm going to shut up."

She made him laugh. "You're sure you're finished?"

"I'm sure."

The waiter came, bearing their food. They moved on to other topics. Lucy reiterated her satisfaction with her recent promotion at the Red Cross, a professional elevation by no means inconsiderable. In turn, Morgan spoke of his work, much on his mind: he would be going to Cleveland next week for the purpose of bringing the firm's partnership up to tick on the venture of the New York office: "A promising report," he told Lucy. "Cause for cautious celebration." Then, somewhat anxiously, he talked about Julia and Caroline—of what a large adjustment it will be for them to be spending the bulk of the fast-approaching summer in New York instead of in Cleveland.

"You're worrying unnecessarily," Lucy said. "It'll be a real adventure for them. They're thrilled with their plans."

Plans fully in place. Julia is already enrolled in a summer-school course at Columbia: subject: *The American Novel in the Twentieth Century;* Caroline's wish for a "worthwhile" part-time summer job has been granted by Geoff (ascended, a few months ago, to the presidency of the Balfour Foundation). Under Geoff's direction, she will be researching grant applications pertinent to urban environmental problems (the environment her current "big interest"). Reflective of her quixotic temperament, her interests have a way of changing from month to month, a tendency worrisome to Morgan. In the past year, her avowed "big interests" have been psychology, political science, and anthropology, in that order. Now, the environment. "That's some scattering," Morgan said. "I hope it's not indicative of deeper confusions. Do you think I give her too much leeway, Luce?"

Lucy smiled: "If you didn't give it to her, she'd take it anyhow. I think she slipped in the environment as one of her interests in order to cinch the Balfour job. Geoff thinks so too, but as he says, it shows she made it her business to find out that one of the Balfour major concerns has to do with environmental problems. Her curiosity's a plus."

"I have a hard time keeping up with her these days—"

"She seems perfectly normal to me," Lucy cut in. "I think she's doing exactly the same thing most of her friends are doing—looking around. Surveying the scene. Why hurry her? Julia's an altogether different story. . . . Alan and Geoff had me to dinner last week—didn't I tell you about it? Maybe I'm losing my mind—"

"Tell me now."

"I meant to tell you because Alan talked quite a bit about Julia—"

"Oh?"

"Mostly about her writing. He was fascinating. He said she reminds him of himself when he was nineteen—that in the same way he knew for sure he was going to be a composer, damn all else, she knows she's going to be a writer. He said that that kind of certainty, when it's backed by talent, is the be-all and end-all of self-knowledge."

"Alan's one of Julia's heroes. *Living* heroes—"

"Mine, too!" Lucy exclaimed. "Do you know what he's up to now?"

"The last time I saw him he mentioned that he's working on an opera—"

"That's it! He's working on an opera! But he won't give a hint about the story. I tried and tried to wangle it out of him, but he wouldn't budge an inch."

Ten years ago, when Lucy and Alan first met, who would ever have guessed they would become friends? Militating against the possibility, their thoroughly different backgrounds and the vast disparity between Alan's formidable talent and Lucy's plainer endowments. So what was it that attracted them to each other in the first instance and that binds them today? Foremost is their love of speculation. (In Geoff's words: "They'll *consider* anything.") Anything. Who's to say that the Kentucky

Derby won't someday be won by a mule? That the lines in the palms of our individual hands don't hold the secret to our future destinies? That swans aren't adulterous? That somewhere in the skies there's not another world populated by Whatevers who don't look like us but who know more about us than we know about ourselves? Which last speculation invariably leads them to their mutual, unshakable belief in UFOs. When they talk with each other about UFOs they look like a pair of religious zealots experiencing a transport of faith. They collect and codify newspaper and magazine accounts of people who have seen UFOs, in whose backyards UFOs have landed. Their most recent UFO thrill is the "sworn" statement of a commercial airline pilot to the effect that his plane was "tracked" by a UFO on a night flight between Boston and Bermuda, the plane's instrument panel "blacked out" for nearly half an hour, during which time the plane was "guided" by the UFO—"lit up like an ocean liner, huge and blindingly beautiful, silvering the heavens for miles around."

"Wow!" Morgan said in response to Lucy's telling of this most recent marvel.

"You're irreverent," Lucy told him.

Morgan laughed. "What would you like for dessert?"

"Crème brûlée."

"I hope they have it."

"They do. I saw it listed on the menu."

❧

Wednesday night, May 13, 1959

He had spent the evening with Ann. They had had their time in bed. Afterwards, Ann had rustled up some food—scrambled eggs and toast, Stilton cheese and fruit with a glass of port for dessert. He'd left her around eleven. He'd walked home.

When he entered his apartment, the telephone was ringing, any call at that late hour always somewhat alarming, at the very least, disconcerting. He ran down the hall into the library, switched on the ceiling light and picked up the phone. "Hello—"

"Morgan—"

George Colt's voice. "George. I just walked in the door this instant."

"So I gather. I've been trying to reach you all evening."

"What's up?"

George Colt cleared his throat. "Sad tidings, Morgan. Roger Chandler died this afternoon. Collapsed in his office. Tom Gervase and Willard Blair were with him when it happened. As you know, Roger's been working with them on the Seidiman-Kinkaid merger. According to Tom, Roger was holding forth, sharp as ever, when he began to choke—a violent spasm, kind of a whole-body seizure. Willard ran off to call a doctor. Tom tried to help Roger, but wasn't able to. Not a damn thing really to be done. Nothing. By the time Willard got back to Roger's office, Roger was all but gone. . . . Morgan?"

"Sorry, George. It's difficult to take in—"

George Colt went on, supplying a few more details, all more or less easily imaginable about any mid-afternoon death in such an unlikely place as a law office—one word following another, like beasts of burden moving along in single file, orderly, obedient to a difficult task: "The funeral could be as early as Saturday, as late as Monday, depending on aspects of organization. It's bound to be something of a state occasion. Natalie's taken hold." (Natalie Chandler Sears, Roger's oldest daughter, a methodical, vigorous woman in her mid-fifties; Roger's wife long dead.) "I spoke with her at length earlier this evening. She seemed to be bearing up very well, hard as it is at any age to lose a parent. She has it in mind for the Governor to give the eulogy. He likely will. She wants you or me to speak—'to represent the firm' was the way she put it."

"If that were to be done at all, Nick should do it."

"My thought too, but I can't see it happening. He's physically too infirm. I think it'd strain him beyond reason."

"Does he know Roger's died?"

"Not yet. Natalie asked me to call Noland. As you know, she can't stand Noland—" (Noland Kissel, Nicholas Kissel's black-sheep son; the father-son relationship for many years a notoriously uneasy one.) "Have you reached Noland?"

"Yes. He was decency itself. He pleaded against telling Nick tonight—

said he was sure it would be best to wait until morning. He's very protective of Nick these days. Odd the way things work out, isn't it—Noland, I mean, being protective of Nick."

Morgan said: "I'll get to Cleveland sometime tomorrow, George, with luck on that noon-time flight I usually take."

"Call me in the morning when you know your schedule. I'll meet whatever plane you're on."

Morgan replaced the phone in its cradle.

Alone in the library—the room itself and the apartment still relatively new to him, in feel still somewhat strange—he looked above the desk at the wall on which he had hung several informal photographs of friends. There, in one of the photographs, faced into the light of a summer day, eighty-year-old Roger Chandler was seen sitting on the top step of a fence stile, a meadow stretching off behind him, gleam of a pond's water in the distance, image of the resting man a part of the landscape's finality. On the bottom of the photograph, written in pen strokes as fine as a spider's thread, Roger Chandler had quoted from *Hamlet:* "Those friends thou hast . . . Grapple them to thy soul with hoops of steel."

He crossed the room and opened one of its windows, letting in a needed stir of fresh air. He looked down on the cars going by on Fifth Avenue. On the park side of the avenue, seated on a municipal bench, a man and a woman were locked in each other's arms, kissing; kissing. . . . He turned around; turned back to the photograph of Roger Chandler. From the height at which the photograph was hung, Roger Chandler's eyes gazed out through the photo's covering glass, out through the room's open window, out into the extremes of space. *Ultima Thule:* Recalled from a long-ago Latin class, the two words sprang to mind, accompanied by an image of the Latin master, Mr. Scudder, (clad in a worn, elbow-patched tweed jacket and unpressed gray flannels) writing the words on the school-room blackboard, then verbally defining them: "Thule is the place thought of by ancients as the northernmost part of the livable world, hence the Latin phrase, *ultima Thule,* by literal translation, *farthest* Thule; by implication either a very remote, near-mythical *region,* or, in terms of human aspiration, as an ideal *goal.*" . . . *Ultima Thule:* the site-aim, perhaps, of Roger Chandler's gaze.

On the municipal bench, the man and woman continued to kiss.

By evening of the next day, the fact of Roger Chandler's death was nationally known, his life and career written about in newspapers and verbally aired on the radio and pictured, a bit, on television. The funeral was on Monday. Filling the church were people from all walks of life, modest to mighty, each with his or her private memories of Roger Chandler: memories of when and where they had met him and of how he had illuminated or influenced or even entirely altered the course of their lives. He was that capable kind of Zeus-like man. . . . Among the mighty at the funeral were Dean Acheson and Adlai Stevenson; and Michael Andress (sent to represent President Eisenhower); and Ed Murrow and John Gunther; state and federal judges; a flock of ideologically mixed ecclesiastics. The Governor delivered the eulogy. Neither Morgan nor George Colt spoke, both of them, pre-funeral, being in accord that Natalie's idea of having one of them speak ("to represent the firm") showed what George Colt called "a delicate lapse of judgment." They didn't of course put it that way to Natalie. Instead, they spoke with her about "protocol": of the propriety of allowing the Governor full and solitary sway. To their immense relief, she took the bait, hook, line, and sinker.

A final particular about the funeral: conspicuously placed at the head of the church's center aisle was a well-worn, straight-backed leather chair. Residing in the middle of the chair's seat was an urn, obelisk in shape: container of the decedent's ashes. At the gathering after the funeral, old, enfeebled Nicholas Kissel said to Morgan: "I liked Natalie's touch of having Roger's desk-chair on display." Then, with a blue-veined trembling hand raised to brush away the tears in his eyes: "It was the urn occupying it I couldn't bear the sight of."

For a week, the bronze naming plates riven into the entrance doors of the Kissel, Chandler, Shurtliff & Colt law offices (in Cleveland, Pittsburgh, and New York) remained draped in black ribbon.

From May 14 to May 28, Morgan stayed in Cleveland. He spent the greater part of this lengthy stay working with George Colt on the foremost problem created by Roger Chandler's death—namely, the reassigning of Roger Chandler's clients and on-going cases to others of the firm's partnership, which changes of representation altered the rank of some partners, necessitating thereby a realignment of share in the firm's income, etc. etc. Inevitably, other problems arose, some complex, some mundane, all, though, in solution, time consuming.

Each day was a binge-day of intense work and of catching up on the doings of people he loved and had seen little of in the last four and a half months: his father, Miss Sly, Letitia and Lewis Grant, Peter Leigh, Lillie Ruth, Mrs. Malcolm (Judge Malcolm's widow, now ancient, by her own laughing say: "Older than Methuselah's cat."); and others of long-standing, affectionate social relationship (seen as a group at an evening party given by Charlie and Louise Blair); and one other— Doctor Leigh.

Throughout this stay, he reverted (*regressed* was the more accurate word, albeit bitter) to his old routine of leaving the Hatherton house early every morning, driving into Cleveland to his office, and at the late end of each day (usually very late) driving back to the house. Each time he returned to it his hatred of entering it deepened. The very thought of walking through its front door into the hushed gloom of its empty rooms filled him with dread: for there the fact was that now, except for Dennis's and Wills's daily, checking walk-throughs of its tall rooms, and Lillie Ruth's and Tessa's weekly cleanings and dustings, it knew no life, so had become, in feel, an elaborate tomb. Increasingly, he feared the affects of its enshrined memories on his sanity, even that the power of its memories might somehow kill him. Unable to bear the mischief solitudes of his and Maud's old bedroom, he slept in one of its guest rooms.

In the last couple of months, amid the professional satisfactions and personal pleasures of his New York life, the thought of parting from the house had occasionally occurred to him, always though in a fleeting, almost fugitive, and certainly undeveloped, unurgent way. But now, at this time of this protracted stay, the truth came clear to him that the house had nothing to do with his current life and still less with any

future life he desired to make for himself. This truth—now fully understood—comprised his ultimate estrangement from it.

Now he knew he would sell it. The knowledge toughened in him a
privacy of intent. About his decision to sell it, he dismissed as intrusive
the idea of seeking a second "objective opinion." By himself, he had
anguished over his decision *enough,* and at a cost too emotionally dear to
repeat.

At the right moment, he would simply announce his decision: declare
it as irrevocable.

(A parenthesis: When he was eight years old, his father had taken
him to what had been advertised in the county newspaper as 'A
Homing-Pigeon Race Meet.' The event had been terribly slow in getting under way—a long, long couple of hours milling around in a dusty,
stubbly field under the noon-time heat of a blazing August sun, looking
at caged pigeons and listening to the owner of each pigeon yammer on
about his pigeon's champion qualities—width of its wingspan, strength
of its wings, its swiftness in flight, its infallible sense of direction—the
point of each owner's brag being that *his* pigeon was the one best qualified to set the speed record for getting back to its home roost, in short,
to win the race: take the prize. The sun was awfully hot. The men who
owned the pigeons seemed a cookie-cutter lot, clumped together, sweaty
and purple-faced, standing in the hot sun, gabbing on and on about
their pigeons. The only men who weren't standing were the four "officials." They were sitting down on canvas camp-chairs under the shade of
a makeshift awning, passing back and forth between themselves sheets
of paper, endlessly, importantly studying what was written on each
sheet, the sun getting hotter and hotter. . . . Finally, finally some action.
One of the officials—a square-shouldered, heavyset man in a red shirt,
lumbered to his feet and mounted a wooden box. He flapped out the
white fabric of a rolled-up pennant: signal that the race was about to
start. The pigeons' owners, stop-watches in hand, bent to their pigeon's
cages. Attend the white pennant. . . . The word *ready* was at last yelled
out, followed at once by the slipping sound of cage-locks being
unbolted. A breath. The red-shirted official lowered the flag. *Then:* then
a noise instant and awing as the released birds took to the air, spearing it

like arrows shot sunward, rising higher and higher, traveling—compassed on their homeward paths, all of them arced suddenly out of sight, gone from view at the horizon's rim, *gone!*—Morgan's eyes, though, still raised to where they had been, searching. Someone, not his father, nudged him: "You'll go blind, boy, looking into the sun like that." The stranger's words were his last clear memory. Because then he fainted. . . . When he came to, his father was kneeling on the ground beside him, murmuring his name, blurred and floaty, over and over: "*Morgan,* Morgan, *Morgan.*" Little by little, everything righted itself. He drank water from a tin cup held to his lips by his father's hand. He heard someone say: "Too much excitement for the lad." And someone else: "Too much sun." Then his father lifted him up and cradled him close in his arms and carried him all the way across the field to where the car was parked. "I'll roll down all the windows and we'll get going. Cool you off. I'm so sorry, Morgan. I feel such a fool." "I'm all right, Pa. Really I am. It wasn't the sun. It was the birds. The way they took off! The way they *went!* They were *spectacular!*" (It thrilled him to use the big word: it matched his feeling about the birds, that *they* were thrilling.) "Not worth fainting for, though," his father said. "But Pa, they *were* spectacular!" "Sit back, son. I'm going to drive fast. I want to get you home as quickly as possible. What you need is some cool tea with a lot of sugar in it. Here we go." Like the arrowed pigeons, Morgan thought. Oh the way they'd shot skyward out of their cages: that spectacular *lift!*)

He owed to Lillie Ruth the first utterance of his decision to sell the house: because of her granted "heart's wish" to live out her days in it. He intended to provide for her another home—a comfortable, agreeable place within walking distance of her church and close enough to Hatherton's town-center so that she could shop and go, whenever she wanted to, to what she still called "moving picture shows" (her favorite worldly entertainment). She was now in her eighty-second year; she should not live alone. Her new home must be large enough to accommodate a companion. He was certain that, given time, this could all be achieved. Still, he could not quite imagine rendering upon her the blow that she was to be removed from the home that had been created for her. But at some point he must do it; the sooner the better. Not yet, though—still not quite able to imagine doing it—suffering the thought, wearying.

Lord, the liberating surprises that in life occur! As on the Saturday after Roger Chandler's funeral.

. . . He had spent the morning in the library, working on a brief. Lillie Ruth brought him lunch on a tray. "There's something I need to tell you, Morgan," she said. "If you have time this afternoon, come and see me." He surely would, he told her. Three o'clock? Yes . . . At three sharp, he put aside his work and went from the library's relative haven into the front hall, center of the large house, of its beauty—middle of its immense and heartbreaking, terrible, unbearable quiet—on, through the darkened dining room (curtains drawn across the tall bank of its easterly windows), through the lifeless order of the butler's pantry, through the kitchen (even the kitchen quiet this afternoon; Tessa off for the day), on, further, down the length of the back corridor.

She heard his approaching footsteps. "Morgan—" she called out.

As she always did, she made a little ceremony of welcoming him into this room she called her "parlor." And there were daffodils in a glass bowl (Canary, Swan's Eye, Dragon's Fire, Sunrise. . .). In chairs drawn close together, they seated themselves, combined, immediately, by the ineradicable atmosphere of that other time of Maud alive. Usually, they tended to speak of that other time, not to dwell on it, but briefly to think aloud of it before moving on to current subjects. But not today. Between them, today, it felt not the thing to do—to hark back—the feeling (as he experienced it) so strong that it silenced him, as it seemed for a moment to silence Lillie Ruth until, of the two of them, she found the voice to say: "We don't belong here anymore, Morgan. We know in ourselves why."

Instantly he told her: "I'm going to sell the house."

She didn't as much as blink, only touched his hand and said: "There's no reason left in the world for you to hang on to it."

Remember, after the long, hot affliction of waiting around, the way the end had suddenly come? The pigeons released from their cages, going up sunward like shot arrows, higher and higher—elevated—arced away in the sky all at once at the horizon's rim—*escaped!* Remember?

Amazing—that he did not faint at Lillie Ruth's feet, her words were of a magnitude that freeing to him to hear.

He tore on: "I've been thinking about where you'll live. I want—"

She stopped him: "It's all settled, Morgan, where I'll live."

"Settled?" he exclaimed: "In what way, *settled*?"

She reached out and picked up from off the top of an adjacent table an envelope—and handed it to him: "For you to see, Morgan."

For him to see . . . He drew out from the unsealed envelope a couple of pages of stiff paper—a legal document, to which was attached a short, typewritten note. The note bore no salutation—only the recent date— *11 May 1959*—followed by a two-sentence text: *This is a deed made out in your name, to the house you indicated to me you would like to own. I have purchased it for you.*

Then the windy, big-as-life penned signature: *Douglas Leigh.*

"Now don't look like that, Morgan. That's the look Callie gets on her face when she's been crossed."

"How did this happen, Lillie Ruth?"

She started off by reminding him of Doctor Leigh's habit of visiting her—

—which erratic visits had begun soon after Maud's death. To Morgan, Doctor Leigh had defined the visits as "doctoral calls" he felt "obliged" to make on Lillie Ruth: "Given her age and all, it makes sense for me to keep tabs on her health," he had regularly said (or words to that effect). Much as Morgan disliked his father-in-law, he had credited him this pedigree of loyalty to Lillie Ruth, while at the same time believing that the truer reason for his calls on her was that Maud's death had havocked him in ways he couldn't handle on his proud own—Lillie Ruth the more actual physician, sitting with him, assuaging the pain of his sorrow by means of her simple-hearted human goodness and near providential patience.

What Morgan learned now from Lillie Ruth was that since last January (at which time Morgan had virtually residenced himself in New York), Doctor Leigh had been coming to see her more and more frequently; as often as once a week. . . . Here, in her narrative, Lillie Ruth told Morgan that early in April, she had asked her church minister,

Pastor Eldon, to help her look for some other place she could move to. "I knew you'd understand, Morgan, how it doesn't feel right anymore, living here without Maudie, you in New York and Callie and Julia grown up and away too, and I knew if I did find another place, you'd help me get it."

Morgan nodded. "Tell me about the property."

The fine thing was that as Lillie Ruth described it, the property fitted his idea of what he had had in mind to look for, *for* her. It was in a decent neighborhood, near her church, near town (on Linden Street in the block between Forster Street and Gidden Street). The house was a one-story stucco "bungalow"; it had a front porch and "a nice little garden-patch of a backyard." As she spoke, she looked intensely at him, and he at her, seeing her back through time, through the many years he had known her, and then forward again to this moment. She was leaning toward him in her chair, her hair cloudy white, her face deeply wrinkled, the pupils of her eyes dimmed a bit by age, but her mind clear as fresh water: that wonderful word—*sane:* she had so brilliantly thought through her continuance.

Having finished describing the house, she went on: "I hadn't a notion Pastor Eldon and I would find a place as soon as we did. It got me a little ahead of myself. I can tell you the date we found it—April the twenty-ninth. That same day, late in the afternoon, Doctor Leigh came by the way he does, I never know when it'll be. I was sitting right where I am now, going over everything in my mind, crying a little bit, feeling betwixt and between, and he caught me at it. What was the matter with me, he wanted to know. You know how he can be, Morgan, how he can wear on. I felt awkward. . . . Right or wrong, he got it out of me about staying on here and he straight out asked me if I wanted to move, and I told him the truth. Where was I thinking I'd move to, he asked me, and I told him about the place Pastor Eldon and I had found that morning. He asked a lot of questions about the place, where it was and the size and did I really, really like it, and then he asked me about you, Morgan—if you knew about it, and I told him you didn't but I was going to telephone you in New York and tell you. He said I shouldn't do that, I should wait and tell you face-to-face the next time you were here.

He said he doubted the property would sell in the meantime, that I shouldn't feel rushed about getting it. I knew you'd be coming soon, the way you do every month . . . but Mr. Chandler's dying, his funeral and all—"

"Back up, Lillie Ruth. Tell me how it came to be that Doctor Leigh bought the property—"

"Oh he just went and did it, Morgan, all on his own. I didn't know a thing about it until he came to see me a week ago last Tuesday—the day before your Mr. Chandler died. That's when he gave me the envelope and explained to me what he'd done. He didn't give me a minute to say anything. He only put on his hat and walked out the door. He hasn't been back since. I was so flabbergasted I didn't know for a while what to think or how to feel—"

"How do you feel about it now?"

"That's what I want to talk over with you, Morgan. I've thought and thought about it—"

"And?"

She waited a second, then raised her right arm, bent at the elbow, the palm of her hand showing—a pulpit gesture: "I think he did it for Mrs. Leigh. After all the time that's gone by since she died, he's been talking about her lately. I guess it's on his mind, her drowning herself and him so bent on his own life he didn't see well enough how troubled she was. Getting older like he is, Judgment Day staring him in the face, I reckon he's scared." She paused, then preached: "Where I'll live, Morgan—we should let it stay settled the way he's settled it. Just let it be."

Her complete understanding of Doctor Leigh's motive and the veracity of her simple description of it, formed the base of an argument he could not refute (pissed though he personally was by his father-in-law's chicane method of atoning). He said: "We'll let it be." Then: "I'll telephone Doctor Leigh and make a date to see him. If he doesn't volunteer to tell me he's bought the property for you, I'll have to bring it up. I need your permission to do that. May I?"

"Yes. And I'd like you to tell him for me that I'm grateful to him. I'll tell him myself the next time he comes out, but I'll rest easier if he knows it in the meantime."

"I'll tell him," he said, his mind racing (his pulse too), thinking of all the other people who must be told (and as soon as possible) of his decision to sell the house, feeling the pressure of the speeded up necessity to do so—the sudden necessity just one of the several consequences resulting from Doctor Leigh's precipitously interposed act of buying the property for Lillie Ruth. He stated aloud the names of the first two people on his list: Tessa and Dennis. "They're very much on my mind," he said. "I'll tell them next week I'm going to sell the house."

She responded at once: "It won't surprise them. They know how it is for you, that with Maudie gone you can't be happy here anymore."

(He dared not comment on her concluding words.) What he strove to do next was to lead her, gently, into the matter of his conviction that she should not live alone. "I'm especially concerned about Tessa," he said: "About where she'll live—"

"Oh, I know where she'd most *like* to live—"

"Where?"

"With me. Live with *me*."

He was as fast as a bass snapping at dawn bait: "And would *you* like her to live with you?"

"More than anything."

"It's *done!*" he said. "I promise you I'll arrange it."

She had a way of showing jubilation better than anyone else he knew. She gave him a smile, brilliant as sunlight—then praised the Lord.

He did, then, project a bit of a time-plan: "It'll be mid-August when we clear out the house. Julia and Callie'll be free then for a couple of weeks before they go back to college. They have to have a say about a lot of things—which of their possessions they'll want sent on to the New York apartment, what should go into storage. It'll be a huge task for them *and* for me." He all but sighed: "God, I dread to think of it."

"We'll all put our hands to it, Morgan. Don't you worry, it'll all work out." Then, out of context, almost child-like, she said: "I haven't felt so peaceful for a long time."

(He hadn't reached her point of peace—yet. But she did make him feel that someday he might.) He made no secret of looking at his watch.

"I'm sorry to say I must go, Lillie Ruth. I'm meeting a friend for dinner in Cleveland. What time is Tessa due back?" (He was reluctant to leave her without company in the house.)

"She fixed it with Dennis to have him drive her out from Hatherton at six. They'll be on time. And Wills is here, in the garage. I'll be fine. You run along."

"I want to change my clothes—spruce myself up a bit. . . . Don't get up, Lillie Ruth." He bent to her; kissed her cheek; thanked her; received from her again the pact of her marvelous smile.

. . . And who was the unnamed person he was on his way to meet in Cleveland? For whom he was risking arrest by driving at a speed well in excess of the legal limit? Of course: Miss Sly.

Since January they had seen each other only four times. Communication between meetings had been by telephone. At least once a week he had called her, New York to Cleveland, or she had called him, Cleveland to New York, short, bridging calls prompted by love, a love no more or less strange than any love. (As it existed between him and Miss Sly, Love went under the alias of "Friendship.")

He arrived at the restaurant a bit ahead of the appointed hour and waited for her in the glass-domed atrium-like foyer, pacing back and forth, the day's earlier revelations still working on him in opposing ways—muscle, relief, absurd ire, degrees of wonder—his first glimpse of her at the restaurant's front door an instant ballast. He hurried toward her. "Mr. Shurtliff!"—she sang out in advance of their embrace.

"Miss Sly."

Seated at an alcove table, drinks in hand, they touched glasses, and she said it was wonderful—"Being together in the flesh. Now we can talk about all the matters we won't have broached with each other over the 'phone."

This opening was not her usual one. Usually, she led off with an imperative "*Tell* me"—after which pilot command she would name the subject she was most eager to hear, from *him*, about. Her opening tonight begged (he felt) a reversal: *his* turn to tell *her* to tell *him* (about *what* he did not know to name). "Tell *me*," he said.

She took his point, and smiled over it, then put to him an imperative opposite of "*Tell* me." "*Ask* me," she said, "what I hope I've finally made up my mind to do."

The oddness of her request stimulated him to state the question in full: "What is it you hope you've finally made up your mind to do?"

He expected an entertaining answer, a breezy kind of *tale* about some long-held, endearingly capricious whim she was at last going to satisfy. He sat back, prepared to be amused. So it startled him to see how intense and serious she suddenly became (troubled, he thought). "What?" he prodded, this time gently.

"Retire," she said, very, very quietly, then at once enlarged the word to its fullest personal and professional extent: "Relinquish my position as head of the Tilden-Herne Adoption Agency."

He was silent—surprised to silence—and she went on: "I've wanted to talk with you about this, but it seemed too difficult on the phone—impossible, really—I've been in such turmoil trying to right with myself the idea of *voluntary* retirement—it goes so against the grain of how I was schooled to think about life—the ethic that one keeps at one's chosen work as long as one effectively and honorably *can*—any other way of behaving, self-indulgent. But I'm getting on toward seventy and I'm yearning to do some things *just for myself*—read more than I can now, and get back to my easel—take some drawing lessons at the Art Institute—*travel*—"(her list was written in her eyes' appeal, in her voice's ardor)—"and there's the press of time—my growing feeling that if I delay much longer, the chances are I never—"

He couldn't let her finish. He reached across the table and gripped her wrist: "You don't have to justify," he said.

Her body, her whole presence, went *still*—the way a large, alerted animal can go suddenly still, frozen in place. Until she blinked. "Repeat that," she said.

"You don't have to justify."

"Oh my dear Mr. Shurtliff, how you *have* saved me! I dread to think of the spectacle I'd have made of myself next Tuesday, ranting on as I have with you, projecting guilt, virtually *apologizing* for my desire to step down—"

"Whoa!" he reined her in: "You're going too fast. What happens next Tuesday?"

She threw up her hands. "How stupid of me! I should have thought to tell you straight off that the Tilden-Herne board of directors meets next Tuesday, and I've imposed on myself that date as a then-or-never deadline for informing them—"

"Be prepared," he cut in. "They'll do their damnedest to dissuade you."

"Well, they won't succeed," she replied. "I'm decided. I *want* out, and I am going to *get* out."

She was completely herself again: Miss Zenobia Sly, grandly in charge.

"Oh, I won't just march away—won't leave the agency in the lurch. I'll give the board ample time to find and install a successor. But I swear to you they'll not succeed in getting me off the track of my intention to retire."

He took a moment—the lawyer—thinking how to frame some final words of support—affronting words (outside the established etiquette of their relationship) that might remain with her should she begin to weaken. "Hell," he said in a low, physical tone, "just *tell*'em. Just *tell*'em, baby."

She delighted him. She—she laughed. A cascade of vivid laughter. "I *will*," she exclaimed in a voice that rang of *Eureka!* "I *must*, because I see that if I *don't*, you will cease to respect me *enough* to address me ever again as 'baby.'"

It would linger with him how he marveled afresh, then, at their relation: would it always increase, he wondered, as over the years it steadily had, and in a way external to their nourishment of it, as if—all by itself—it existed *for* them?

"What time on Tuesday does your board meet?"

"Two o'clock."

"Call me when the meeting's over. I'll be in my office, very eager to hear about it."

"I will *want* to call you, and I *shall*."

It was as in a play, the interposing action then of the waiter appearing and placing before them their meal's first course (fresh asparagus soup). And after the waiter left them, after they had tasted the soup and remarked upon it ("Delicious"), Miss Sly said: "Now about *you*, Mr. Shurtliff . . . You look very tired. It's been a misery for you, Roger Chandler's death—the double injury of losing both a beloved friend *and* your firm's most senior partner. I can't help worrying about you."

She said this in the practical way of a presiding shepherd. His perpetual sense of her as being somehow something akin to a shepherd was heightened by a visual illusion. . . . Caught in a beam of light from a ceiling chandelier, the rounded top of the eternal amber comb that held in place the huge bun of her done-up hair glowed—the arched effect over the top of her head a halo: an illusion it heartened him to consider. Because it set him up to confide to her that, hard as the blow of Roger Chandler's death had been, the truer reason for his tiredness was differently sourced. "It has to do with my Hatherton house," he said. And he told her then of his recently-come-by realization that he must part from the house. Briefly, he summed the *why*. He was lawyerly, meticulous, about not confusing his personal why with the house itself: so intrinsically glorious; so beautiful. Of his fear of the memories contained in its high rooms, he made no mention. Yet, subversively, the memories crowded upon him and seized him, and for a dangerous moment—like a swimmer overwhelmed by the force of an immense, sudden sea-swell— he went under, lost his breath, struggled, regained the air, inhaled—and rapidly stated: "It is my plan to sell it."

"We will hope to a well-wedded couple with growing children," she instantly said, aware of his distress, involved in it, thinking (he understood) to abet his recovery by an image of the house's continuance in keeping with his own brilliantly happy years in it.

"And a dog," he said.

"Or a cat," she replied. Then gave up her attempt to help him. "Somehow one finds the strength to do these heartbreaking, necessary things. And one should always endeavor to practice what one preaches. Your need, your *private* need to sell the house requires of you—" She paused, then tossed at him (he saw the coming word, aimed in its noun form), "—no *justification*."

"*Baby,*" he quietly said.

"Exactly."

They faced each other, whole: a pair of equilibrists.

And then, after a moment, he said: "I spent a somewhat extraordinary hour with Lillie Ruth this afternoon."

"Tell me."

He structured his telling as an episode in an on-going story. It was easy to do because she was thoroughly familiar with all the story's characters—Lillie Ruth, Doctor Leigh, dead Mrs. Leigh, Tessa; he had for years so often spoken of them to her, and in many contexts. He began by confessing his long-sustained dread of informing Lillie Ruth of his decision to sell the house, then gave his account of how Lillie Ruth in her prescient way had taken the lead by telling him—"We don't belong here anymore, Morgan," with which words "*She freed me!*" he said now to Miss Sly, cadencing the wonder with an outward and upward lift of his hands, as of something marvelous let go into the air. "You see what I mean—"

"Yes. Yes I do, Mr. Shurtliff. Go on."

So he did, and completely. . . . As regards Doctor Leigh's role in the story, her remarkable memory served to make her a contributor to the narrative. She cited the year—"1947"—and recalled the details of that year's summer when Mrs. Leigh had sat day after day in the Leighs' grand, cupola-crowned Victorian barn watching the swallows dart up into the geometric forest of the barn's high rafters, bidding others to join her at her sweet, innocent vigil—Lillie Ruth singing, walking across the carpet of grass that lay between the Leighs' fine house and the barn, carrying trays, serving up iced tea and lemonade to the gallery of bird-watchers, everyone thrilled by Mrs. Leigh's summer-long happiness—*everyone except Doctor Leigh:* Mrs. Leigh sitting there, plotting with herself her suicide—

"*Of course!*" Miss Sly exclaimed: "Lillie Ruth's intuition of why Doctor Leigh has purchased a future abode for her is as accurate as accurate can be! And she and you, Mr. Shurtliff, are right not to protest his having done so." Then, in a quieter voice: "It's astonishing, isn't it, how our past actions catch up with us, how we can't outrun them no matter how hard we try."

All this verbal terrain had taken a while to cover. They were now nearly finished with the meal's main course (perfectly cooked roast of lamb; pink). Mortality and memory and homely philosophy aside, they were carnivores. He put down his fork. In much the same way he liked to look for a myriad time at a familiar, long-admired tract of land, he liked simply to look at her, first at certain parts of her face, the sensitive mouth, slightly beaky nose, rounded chin, high, decisive forehead, valleyed eyes that could be blue, could be gray-blue, could be blue-green; then to contemplate the entire visage: permanent to him. "As of this evening, only you and Lillie Ruth know I'm going to sell the house. Now though, now that I'm free to, I'll inform others. Julia and Caroline"—he lingered over their names—"I can't tell *them* until they're back in New York with me, out of college for the summer. They've got their final exams to get through. I must wait—" He perhaps looked (as he felt) suddenly burdened again, suddenly chaotic—

—for she interrupted him with the diverting remark: "I thought of them on their recent birthday, their nineteenth—"

"Which we've yet to celebrate," he cut in, glad for the shift. "They've requested and I've promised them a party with our New York friends and an assortment of their college mates. Caroline's the gala girl," he smiled. "She'll organize the party."

"You have a birthday soon, Mr. Shurtliff—"

(Ah, she did remember everything.) "Yes; I'll be forty-eight in June." Then, directly: "I don't know the month of your birthday."

"September," she said. "I'll be seventy in September. . . . Oh, I am so eager to be shed of my Tilden-Herne responsibilities! And I warn you, when I am, I expect to go often to New York—"

"Where I'll entertain you royally any and every time you're there."

"I shall count on you to," she replied. Then, with her chin rested in the palm of her right hand and her eyes full on him: "You've *become* a New Yorker. It's written all over you—that you've found peace there."

"*Is* it?" he laughed. "Well, I have. I'm tremendously excited about my work there, and I like living there. It's endlessly surprising."

"And you're well settled in your apartment?"

"Almost," he answered. "I desperately need to find a cook-house-keeper. I'd just begun to contact some domestic employment agencies a couple of weeks ago. Before Roger died. I'll pick up those contacts the minute I get back. I hope, *hope* to find someone and have her moved in and functioning by the time Julia and Caroline arrive—"

"*No!*" She fairly leapt at him: "No, Mr. Shurtliff. That's wrong of you to do on your own. You must involve your daughters in your search for a housekeeper. Let them sit in on the interviews. Allow them a voice. You must, must include them in the making of their new home."

She said all this with terrific speed and heat. She had never before, with him, been so—*personal*.

But Lord! How *what* she had said did strike him!

"You *do* understand, don't you, Mr. Shurtliff?" she insisted.

"Perfectly. And I assure you I will do it."

At once, she visibly relaxed, and at once (he would never forget it) came nearer than she ever would, as regards their relationship, to self-reference: "With *you*," she said, "I have always been able to say what I feel."

"As I have with you," he immediately replied.

This exchange comprised between them a certain tranquil joy (peculiarly, afterwards, to him, haunting). (Many years later, when he was an old man, one of his regrets was that he did not tell her then and there simply that he loved her, but had, instead, then, only made that formal, combining pronouncement—"As I have with you.")

Over dessert they talked a bit about national affairs, most particularly about a senator—John Fitzgerald Kennedy, "the agreeable son of a very determined father" (Miss Sly's words). "Jack," the senator was becoming known as. . . . It was after ten when he walked her to the lighted lot where she had parked her car. "Stick to your guns on Tuesday," he said, "and call me the minute the action is over."

"I will, on both charges. . . . When do you return to New York?"

"On Thursday. But I'll be back here in a couple of weeks. We'll arrange a time to meet."

He unlocked the car door and held it open for her, then returned the key-ring to her. They embraced. She gathered up her skirt, got into the car, then said: "My goodness, I almost forgot! I brought you something." From her ample purse, she took out some pages. "It's a recently published short story, written by a friend. I cut it out of the magazine it was printed in. Don't have it on your mind to return it. I have another copy. It's an odd story. Interesting, I think. . . . Good night, my dear Mr. Shurtliff. Thank you for dinner. It was lovely in every way."

She drove off. As he next did, going out of the city on the road that rimmed Lake Erie, its waters calm in the calm May night, going on into the dark countryside; deeper on. In the three coming months, how many times would he go—*back*—to the Hatherton house? *Ah*, not many. Twenty? Twenty-five? He made a bet with himself: twenty-five at the most. Start counting, beginning Now.

✑

. . . Later, nearing midnight, lying on a guest room bed in the ghostly silence of the ghostly house, too curious not to and anyhow not able to sleep, he started to read the story she had given him (published, he was careful to note, in the March (1959) issue of *The Alexandrian Review*, a magazine he had not before heard of; nor had he, before, heard of the story's author: S. K. P. Dobson).

THE STEEPLECHASE

> It is reported that occasionally in the mid-to-late 1800s, in England, Scotland, Wales, and Ireland, two men in love with the same woman would mount their horses and, using a distant church-steeple as their goal, race toward it, as if it were the woman. By agreement, the man who lost the race would cease his courtship of the woman.

That was the story's first paragraph.

The story's three personae had no baptismal names. There was the one Man, and the other Man, and there was the Woman.

By artful suggestion, the story's Author seduced the story's Reader into a web-like belief that both the story's men were of the same social rank, both of the same mature age, both fair-featured, both worldly, and both—to the story's Woman—in her eyes and as, in the obliquities of her erotic imagination she appraised them—equally inflaming.

The steeplechase of this story commenced at cockcrow of a cold, hoar-frosty day in mid-April of a long-ago year. The two men met on the hill-top of a wild moor remote from village and folk. Each was the only witness of the other's arrival at this place. In the cold dawn air the horses' and the men's breathings were little white tragedies of exhaled clouds, continuously being formed, and by evaporation, continuously vanishing.

Visible in the eastern distance, fixed against the sky, was the church-steeple.

(A risen phallus, it occurred to the story's Reader to think.)

Astride their horses, the men positioned themselves side by side. There passed between them a glance, a swift eyeing of insane resolve similar to hatred. Then they nodded, each to the other, and at the same instant bolted forward, away, whipping their horses over a cruelly long course of gorse-mounded, rock-studded fields, spurring them to leap ditches and scabrous fences and dense and thorny hedges, foxes and rab-bits and game birds and woken ground-larks fleeing before them—

Elsewhere (ever historically elsewhere) was the story's Woman. In a large, richly furnished, heavily curtained room, she lay alone on a bed, naked and self-absorbed. When the story's Reader entered the room, the story's Author caused the Reader to smell, inspissated in the room's air, the fetch of an aphrodisiac odor—

Did the Woman, lying there—*so*—on the bed, know to anticipate the approaching noise of the horses' hoofbeats? Yes. And did she hear the curses the two men hurled at each other as, lashing and lashing their panting steeds, they drew nigh? Yes, she did. And did the sound of their voices excite her? Ah, yes. The extreme, though, happened as the men rode by, as—riding by—they let upon her their separately tongued, sep-arate cries of desire that twice multiplied the pleasure she was giving herself, twice complicating it, making it more and ever more exquisite—

—all as the violent men rode by and were gone; of their erethismic cries and of the horses' hoofbeats naught an echo—

—while in the by-now late night, alone and carnal on yet another bed elsewhere, the story's Reader (cleped Morgan Shurtliff) masturbated, completing thereby for the story's Author the Woman's climax—

—but not the story.

He finished reading the story, afterwards.

One of the horses refused a jump and threw its rider. Dead then, the one Man. The Woman—on learning of the death of *that* Man—began at once to love him. Of all the men in all the world, he became the one man she would have chosen. Wracked by phantasies of what might have been (?) a great happiness (?) she went mad. At the dawn hour of a later, bitterly cold winter morning, an old female servant found her naked on the bed, frozen to death. The story's other Man—reject of the story's Woman—spent himself out in drunkenness and low debauchery and died at a sooner-than-later time, *when* seemed not to matter.

The End

. . . But there is no such thing as an end to any story. . . . To suggest otherwise (Morgan mused) was only this story's Author's way of dismissing the story's Reader; which musing (a kind of personal reality) prompted him to look at the alarm clock's face. 1:22 A.M.—the new day (as he found himself in it) already more than an hour old. Sensible of the need to sleep, he switched off the bedside light and closed his eyes, only to remain awake, still in the story's thrall, still immersed in its drama and psychological commotions. But then, after an indefinite while, and rather abruptly, his thoughts (if such involuntary wildings as were going on in his head could be called) shifted from the story to the story's author— S. K. P. Dobson: a nom de plume (he decided) . . . an invented name to hide behind . . . all those obscuring, genderless initials . . . but the author surely a woman . . . how old? . . . where domiciled? . . . what like? . . . which conjecturings, after a further indefinite while, were dispelled by the sudden appearance—a vivid image—of the story's agent: Miss Sly.

—"I brought you something," she had said (handing him the something). "It's a recently published short story, written by a friend. . . . It's an odd story. Interesting, I think—" she had gone on blandly to say—

—*blandly*, about such an entrapping fiction of human folly and human delusion, in its creation so achieved, by its author's talent so successfully (at least upon himself) so successfully *sprung* as to have caused him to participate in the story's action . . . thinking now of the peculiarity of his having masturbated in the middle of his reading of the story . . . wondering now at the somehow way the story's author had transferred (trans-ported) him onto one of the story's pages, leaving it to the story's *next* reader to figure out how he got there, the story's next reader surely by the author's deft hand similarly translocated . . . verging now on the very edge of sleep—irrationally ensnarled in that old apothegm: When we think a thing, the thing we think is not the thing we think we think, but only the thing we think we think we think—

"You look like shit" was George Colt's Monday morning greeting to him, in the office, a very few hours later.

"Ah, gracious George, tread lightly," Morgan intoned. "Rejoice that I'm here at all to companion you through the swamp of work that lies this day before us."

George laughed. "Reduced to bad poetry, are you? You must have had a helluva week-end." Then, quickly serious, with what Morgan knew to be genuine affection and concern: "You *are* all right, Morgan? Essentially, I mean."

"Not to worry, George. I had a tiring week-end, but a worthwhile one. I'll tell you about it over lunch—"

—at which time—hungry and self-possessed after a forenoon of hard work—without prelude, he said to George Colt: "As a result of some good things that happened over the week-end, I'm finally in the clear to go ahead with my plan to sell my Hatherton house."

"Morgan!"

"Are you that surprised, George?"

"Only for a second, Morgan. . . . I'm not ultimately surprised. I certainly see why you'd *want* to."

"So you see why I'm going to."

They knew each other so well they could have been old men. But they weren't old. Only old enough to understand that between *them,* any further words on the subject were unnecessary.

வ§

After lunch, he called Doctor Leigh's office. "You're in luck, Mr. Shurtliff," the nurse told him. "The doctor's just walked through the door. Hold on, please—"

Then Doctor Leigh's full-throated baritone: "Morgan—you've caught me in the nick of time. I'm just in from the clinic. I've a patient waiting, so I mustn't indulge myself, lingering on the 'phone. You know how it is—if you get behind with one appointment, you get behind with the rest of the day's appointments. Good to hear your voice." (So far Morgan had not uttered a word.) "I've had it in mind to ring you, but I've been so busy this week hosting a group of visiting medics from Spain of all places—an interesting group, I must say. But we mustn't go on chatting—"

Morgan shot in with: "I had a long talk with Lillie Ruth yesterday, and I need to see you. What about tomorrow morning?"

"Tomorrow's out. So's Wednesday. Wednesday is Spain's last day. Thursday morning?"

"Too late. I go back to New York on Thursday. Why don't I drop by your office later this afternoon?"

"I could only give you a few minutes, Morgan. I'm due at a black-tie dinner at seven-thirty."

God, the energy of the man! "I'll take the few minutes. What time?"

"Will five-thirty suit you?"

"Yes, I'll see you then."

At five-thirty sharp, Doctor Leigh opened the door of his private office. "Well, well, Morgan. Come in. Things going well for you, are they? You look a bit tired, but all busy people look tired at the end of a busy day, including myself, I suppose. Do you think I look tired? Do sit down." (Doctor Leigh, of course, did not look tired.) "Now about Lillie Ruth. Did she tell you—"

"Everything," Morgan said. "She's immensely touched by your gift to her of the house. She asked me to tell you as much."

"All things considered, buying the place for her seemed to me to be the Christian thing to do." (Morgan hated Doctor Leigh's broad-broom sweep of "all things considered" and the piousness of "the Christian thing to do.") "You ought to have a look at the place, Morgan."

"I will, of course. I haven't had a chance yet. Lillie Ruth gave me a happy description of it." (Doctor Leigh's eyes were on his wrist-watch.) "Houses are a large part of today's topic," Morgan went on. "I'm going to sell mine."

"Are you indeed? It'll go fast, I'm sure, being the splendid property it is." Doctor Leigh said this in a voice as flat as a mill pond. But then, with a slight inflection of interest: "When did you decide to sell it?"

"I've been thinking about it for some time, but only recently concluded that I must. Really only a few days ago."

"It's a pity I didn't know," Doctor Leigh said. "We might have gotten together on the buying of Lillie Ruth's house."

"So we might have," Morgan replied. "My reason for pushing to see you today has to do with my monetary concerns for Lillie Ruth's future—with Dennis's too—because of course my selling of my house means that they'll both be retiring, and I want to tell you *directly* that it's my intention to purchase annuities that will provide them with an income for the rest of their lives."

"Well, speaking man-to-man, Morgan, I've always assumed that in some form or other, you'd see to that matter, especially as they've been in your full-time service for the last eleven or so years, has it been? How time does fly! Have you informed them of your intentions?"

"Not yet. I expect to tomorrow. As I think I told you, I go back to New York on Thursday."

"When will you next be in these parts?"

"In a couple of weeks. Perhaps then we can arrange to see each other in a more leisurely way. But right now, there's one more thing, very important to me to ask you about—the mantel you allowed me to have removed from the library of *your* Hatherton house at the time you sold the house—that I had installed in Maud's sitting room—" Whether it was the mention of Maud's name or mention of the mantel, Morgan would never for certain know, but some tinge of softness showed suddenly on Doctor Leigh's face. "I hope you will let me keep it. If you do, I'll have it sent to New York—"

"Do you have a working fireplace in your apartment?"

"Yes. In the living room."

"Then by all means, you should keep it. I'm pleased that you want to. It's an extraordinarily handsome thing. Beautifully carved. I remember bringing in an ivy leaf one day and comparing it to the carved ones. The duplications were wonderful. Charming flowers, too—the blooms imitated in fine detail."

For the thousandth time, Morgan marveled at the man, sitting stiffly there in his pristinely white doctor's robe, his neck encased in the iron hold of a cruelly starched shirt collar, his tie tightly knotted, his eyes suddenly misted over—talking of the mantel's carved ivy leaves and flowers, but shying clear of any out-loud recall of Maud or Mrs. Leigh: of, when they were alive, *their* often avowed admiration and love of the chimney-piece. . . . "I do thank you," Morgan said. "And now I must let you go. You mentioned that you have a dinner engagement—"

"For the Spaniards," Doctor Leigh said, rising from his chair, extending his hand. "Tell Lillie Ruth I'll likely get out for a visit with her next week-end."

"She'll be pleased to see you. Thank you again, sir."

"Good-bye, Morgan. Take care of yourself."

There at the end, Doctor Leigh smiled.

"Mr. Shurtliff—"

"Miss Sly." This was Tuesday, late afternoon of the next day, Miss Sly on the telephone, keeping her promise to call him at the conclusion of the Tilden-Herne board of trustees meeting. "How did it go?"

"Very, very well. I might even say spectacularly." She laughed. "They made such a fuss when I told them of my wish to retire—raised so many objections—all very flattering to me, quite overwhelming really." She sounded breathless.

"But you held firm—"

"I did indeed. And I stressed that I want out by next January. I'm going to meet with some of the board members next week to work out the details. I couldn't be more thrilled."

"You sound so," Morgan said. "We'll have a private celebration in a couple of weeks. I'll call you from New York to set a date. It's wonderful, Miss Sly."

"Wonderful for *me*. You were such a help to me, Mr. Shurtliff; such a *brace*—" She broke off. Morgan heard a background voice speaking to her; and in a moment: "That was my secretary reminding me that I have an appointment with my dentist at five. Such a let-down after my triumph—"

"Before you go, let me quickly tell you that I read 'The Steeplechase'—"

"Did you!" she burst out: "And did you like it?"

"'Like' is hardly the word. I think it's remarkable."

"Oh, I *am* so glad," she crowed. "I think so too, but I'm so prejudiced by my regard for its author—I've known her all her life—that I hardly dare to trust my judgment. . . . But forgive me. I shall be late at the dentist's if I don't leave this minute—"

"Run!" Morgan said. *"Congratulations."*

"Thank you, my dear, thank you. Call me soon."

He hung up. He imagined her picking up her purse, hurrying out of her office, the bun of her done-up hair rocking in rhythm with her free gait. And when he let that image go, he focused briefly on what, willynilly, she had confirmed for him: that the author of "The Steeplechase"—S. K. P. Dobson—was a woman.

❧

That evening he had dinner with his father at the Union Club.

In the club's lounge—a large, high-ceilinged, congenially formal room—a lively crowd of pre-dinner drinkers was gathered. Half the room's length away, he spotted his father enthroned in one of a pair of high-backed leather chairs. Ansel Shurtliff raised his hand and waved, but remained in place. Morgan hurried to him. *"Pa."*

"Forgive me for staying pat, son, but I didn't dare risk losing these chairs. What a horde! Not overly noisy though. . . . As you see, I presumed you'd have your usual bourbon."

Atop a square, knee-high oak table was the enticing clutter of a glass of bourbon, a glass of sherry, a silver bucket and a pair of ice-tongs. Morgan sat down and took from the bucket three ice-cubes and dropped them into the bourbon. He handed the glass of sherry to his father, then picked up his own glass and, meeting his father's eyes, anxious to make his announcement, itchy to have it done, said: "I've decided to sell the Hatherton house, Pa."

No more than a second passed. "So you've come to it at last!"

In all his imaginings of what his father might say, this intense, prompt, conclusive statement had not been conceived. It quite marvelously startled him, and he was just at the point of remarking on it when he saw on his father's face the look he knew as a presager of something further to be said. He waited—

Not for long: "If it hadn't been for my orchards, Morgan—my apple trees—I'd have sold my house after your mother died. But you lack such a binding reason for keeping yours. Sell it, son, and God-speed."

It was a full blessing, one beyond words welcome, but again, Morgan had no chance to speak, his father rushed on so: "As regards the practical side of your move, I'd be glad to put you in touch with old Ambrose Hawes. Do you remember him? He's still in the antique-auction business, and his eye for the rare is as keen as ever. He'd be able to advise you about how best to dispose of some of your larger possessions—that fifteen-foot-long dining table, for instance, and that front-hall, baronial bench—things like that, all worthy of regard, ultimate nuisances though that they are. . . . But there'll be plenty of time to think about all such matters. Now let's have our drinks and dinner. . . . Bring me up to date on your New York doings."

For Morgan, these words were a perfect release.

Later, in the grip of his father's good-night embrace, Morgan said: "Thank you as always, Pa. You're as good as a week's vacation."

Ansel Shurtliff laughed. "Keep your eyes on the long view, Morgan. Perspective! The long view . . . And one final admonition: don't drive too fast."

. . . Forty minutes later, on a clear stretch of road, still a few miles from Hatherton—the night air cool, the stars above the open field so bright they seemed to be dancing, he heard himself singing—caught himself doing it—driving along, not too fast, singing!

⁓

On Wednesday, mid-afternoon, he met with Lillie Ruth and Tessa and Dennis. He gave each of them a formal document that explained how, in their retirement, they would be separately provided for. He named mid-June as the time the house would "officially" be put on the market, and the end of August as the deadline time for it to be emptied of all its contents. "Come September," he said, "we'll leave it."

They were in the library, seated closely together, four motley humans: Lillie Ruth, light-skinned (she had once told him she was "born of a blood mix"); himself, white; Dennis, black as wet tar; Tessa—her brown complexion spotted by a few berry-sized, milky "blotches" (Lillie Ruth's word): Lillie Ruth, eighty-two; Dennis, seventy-three; Tessa, fifty-five; himself, soon to be forty-eight. Collectively, they were two-hundred-fifty-eight years old: four distinct minds and souls speaking in one language about the fortunate chance that had brought them in the first instance together; talking, interchangeably, about what had been and what was and what would be: still together.

(A parenthetical epilogue to that afternoon: distant years later, in the 1990s [when he was as old as Lillie Ruth was now], someone, not herein to be named, accused him of "idealizing" this foursome relationship and he told that person: "Discover for yourself who your friends are.")

On that same Wednesday, after dinner, he sought out Wills in Wills's quarters over the garage. Wills would stay on as caretaker of the house until it was sold. He told Wills the amount of money—"a bonus"—Wills in due course would receive. Wills had huge hands. He took Morgan's right hand and clamped it between his two huge ones and pumped Morgan's whole arm up and down, up and down. *"Wills!"* Morgan laughed, nearly yelling. Wills said: "It'll be money for me when my rocking-chair days come on me. Hear me, Mr. Shurtliff? Money for my rocking-chair days!"

After he left Wills, he telephoned Ann Montgomery. "Yes," she said: "Yes, Morgan Shurtliff, I'm expecting you tomorrow night at seven." (She often, undressed, addressed him by his full name, sort of purring it. Then she would laugh, as she did now: that soft, shivering, physical laugh.)

The next day, at noon, he boarded the plane for the flight to New York. Up there in the sky, he took out of his briefcase a leather-bound calendar-notebook and a red pencil. He opened the notebook to today's page and drew a circle around the date—Thursday, May 28, 1959—by which self-coded means, as much on the notebook's page as in his celebratory sense of it, he decorated the date.

2 ✍ That Singular Summer, into Autumn

All noise and radiance, on the first Thursday in June, Caroline and Julia arrived from college. Trailing them through the apartment's front door, pushing a baggage trolley, was Lester, one of the building's elevator operators. Caroline watched as Lester removed from the trolley a mound of various-sized suitcases and a rope-tied box of books and two canvas bags exploding at the seams with what Julia called "vital stuff." After the trolley was emptied and Lester departed, Morgan stood—a kissed, embraced father—looking at his daughters' brilliant faces, feeling their summer excitement, seeing them happy—*previous* to what he must soon tell them: that they were to be parted from their Hatherton home.

Of course he didn't tell them on the day of their arrival. He put it off until the next day's late afternoon. "There is something we must talk over. I'll be in the living room." Those were the words by which, brief moments ago, he had separately summoned them. So it was in the living room he awaited them. It was a fine, well-proportioned room with four wide, tall windows giving on to a high view of Central Park. A room (he thought) of great potential. In time it would contain the large dark-red-and-deep-blue Herati-patterned Bidjar carpet and some of the paintings and furniture now in the living room of the Hatherton house. In time too, the oak-carved ivy-and-floral Leigh mantel would replace the severe black marble chimney-piece—

"Here we are, Morgan," Julia said.

He had been so engrossed in imagining how the room would be changed, he had not heard their quiet approach down the hall.

Julia joined him on the couch; Caroline sat cross-legged on the floor, facing them.

Nothing for him then but to proceed. "I'm going to sell the Hatherton house," he bluntly stated. "I must, because—"

Julia interrupted. "Mother's death," she murmured.

Caroline nodded. "I love the house," she said. "I'll always love it, but without Mother, I don't like being in it."

They had stated the case for relinquishment so fleetly, with such adult directness, that it left him with nothing to say. And he had been for so long prepared to say so much! Or, more accurately, he had expected to *have* to say so much that now, with his words all taken from him, he sat mute, almost dumb, staring off, until, after a moment, they stirred, as if prodding him, so that he did then look at them, and, looking, saw how *they* were looking at *him*—keenly: expectantly. *Lead us,* their eyes said. *Let the relinquishment begin.*

"I have a plan," he said.

He named August 15 as the date they would leave New York and go to Hatherton and clear out from the house all of their possessions—

—(leaving the house empty of all but their memories of it)—

—which unspoken thought simultaneously, palpably seized them, placing them in each other's sight suddenly on the extreme edge of emotional breakdown—

He would not allow it. "We mustn't," he said. "We'll say no more about the move this evening. Now, *now* let's talk about the rest of the summer."

Enthusiastically, they took hold of the subject, and so well, so earnestly that it engaged them for a considerable length of time—for so long in fact that when it did occur to him to consult his watch, he let out a whistle of surprise and exclaimed: "It's almost seven! We're to meet Geoff and Alan and Lucy for dinner at quarter to eight."

"Oh! You should have told us sooner!" Caroline said. "I must change my dress. Are we going to a restaurant?"

"Yes. *Giovanni's*—"

"Bliss!" she yipped, and ran out of the room.

Julia remained with him. Just for a bit longer. "I must change too, Morgan."

"So must I. . . . Thank you, Julia."

Still, after she left him, he stayed on the couch, resting, breathing in and out, in and out, in and out, like a long-distance runner who's just crossed, just now, the finish line.

ᴥᵹ

Together (ah, Miss Sly) they interviewed a small parade of prospective cook-housekeepers. They chose Elsa Althaus. She was Austrian (from a village near Vienna); a Roman Catholic. She had come to America after the war, in 1948. She was in her mid-fifties. Her hair was gray and straight and cut short. She was quite tall, on the plump side of bony, and plainly countenanced. Her eyes, large and blue-gray and heavily lashed, were her best physical feature. She had a clear, dulcet voice and a generous smile. She brought to her interview one letter of reference from her former employer of ten years (Mrs. D. S. Bouvier, languishing now in an Upper East Side nursing home—"Dying from old-age ills," Elsa told them, crossing herself). In the letter, Mrs. Bouvier lauded Elsa's character and her organizational and culinary skills. All of which praises, within a couple of weeks after she moved in, Elsa proved true. "Miss *Car*-oline." "Miss *Chew*-lia." "*Mister* Shurtliff." (She intoned the *Mister* in a royal way.) When she cooked, she kept the kitchen radio tuned to one station: WQXR. "To the great music. At WQXR, they know the great composers," she said. "Mozart, Schubert, Beethoven *und so weiter*." (For her cooking and taste in music, Alan Litt thought her "divine.")

ᴥᵹ

Julia declared herself "thrilled" by her course of study at Columbia. . . . Remember her Hatherton friend Bruce Wilson, owner of the springer spaniel named Pansy? Bruce was a senior now at Columbia, majoring in philosophy. His interest in Julia was as great as ever. There was another young man in thrall to Julia: Alex Winston. Alex was also a senior at Columbia ("pre-med"). Morgan knew Alex's father, a banker.

Alex vied with Bruce for Julia's free time. Both of them came often (separately) to dinner. Alex took Julia to movies, sometimes to a "night-spot"—the Blue Angel or the Rainbow Room, or to a currently "in" downtown "jazz-joint." Bruce didn't have that kind of money to spend. He and Julia went to museums and took long walks in Central Park and sat of an evening in the living room, talking, talking, talking, sometimes reading aloud to each other. When it got late, time for Bruce to go, he and Julia would embrace and kiss each other lightly, unurgently on the lips.

⋞

Under Geoff's aegis, Caroline went to work at the Balfour Foundation, researching and writing reports about proposals submitted to the foundation by organizations seeking funds for various environmental projects. She was one of four summer "apprentices." At Balfour's offices on West Fifty-fifth Street just off Fifth Avenue, she occupied "a dinky cell, just big enough to hold a desk, a waste-paper basket, and me." Geoff was a tough taskmaster. He rejected her first report. It lacked clarity and focus, he told her: "Re-think it and rewrite it." She got huffy. She went so far as to accuse Geoff of being harder on her than on the other apprentices. Geoff's retort: "I adore you, Callie, but not in the office." (It was from Geoff, not from Caroline, that Morgan heard about this confrontation.) Caroline submitted a second report. Geoff thought it an improvement over the first report, though still "too sprawled," then went over it with her idea by idea, paragraph by paragraph, showing her how to cause her conclusions to cohere. Her third try—"Hit the mark"—and Geoff (good godfather that he was), in celebration of her achievement, took her to lunch at "21." After that, there was no stopping her. By the time July rolled around, Geoff told Morgan: "She's settled in. She's terrific. . . . A word of warning, though, about a guy named Seth Ferrison.

He's my summer mistake. And he's got the hots for Callie. Don't let him in your door, Morgie."

"He's already entered. I've met him. He came home with Callie day before yesterday. He likes bourbon—"

"He's a white-shoe smoothie. Don't give him an inch."

"I won't, but Callie might. . . . Maybe not. We'll hope not. Anyhow, he's got plenty of competition. I like to think there's safety in numbers."

"She's such a beauty."

"'Beauty is as beauty does.' Sex is the demon."

Geoff laughed. "So what's new?"

~§

Sex. The demon Sex . . . Sometime in late June, Ann Montgomery told him she feared she was becoming too fond of him. "I haven't any sense that you're similarly affected, Morgan." It would have been easier for him if she hadn't sounded so wistful. She pronounced sentence on them: "We shouldn't see each other so often. Maybe once in a while." He liked her enough not to see her again. . . . He had, that summer, four other single-purposed lays, all four instigated by the women. That was what most surprised him: *their* instincts, at the instant they met him, of his readiness. That, and the number of women who would have had him, and the number he would not consider having (young, conspicuously excitable women, or disillusioned wives out to revenge a lapsed husband). But of older, fully fledged divorced or otherwise unattached women, there were plenty who kept offering themselves. He met them at "drop-in" cocktail parties given by the spouses of lawyers he knew, and at other large social affairs he felt obliged from time to time to attend. One of the four lays he met at a noisy gathering sponsored by the United States Trust Company; or had it been the Fiduciary Trust Company? (He couldn't, by summer's end, remember which.) Beyond a reciprocally sought satiation, the four women meant nothing to him, nor, he was sure, did he mean anything to them. They merged in his mind, forgettable in their transiency. He didn't go so far as to label these flings *sins,* but neither did he like himself the better for them. He realized then, about himself, that only in the exchanges made in a sworn conjugal bed would he ever again achieve anything resembling the finer shades of sexual joy. A chilling realization: he doubted that such chance would ever, again, come his way.

Work became the intimate that most sustained him. His high-stakes gamble on his ability to successfully expand the New York Kissel, Chandler office had begun to pay off. He had sought and attracted new clients, three of whom were Croesus-rich and bore, therefore, the usual familial and psychological and legal problems great wealth imposes on its possessors. Such clients are the mainstay of a trust-and-estates practice. Establishing a corporate department was the next challenge incumbent upon him to accomplish, toward which end (back in April) he had let it be known to his New York colleagues that he was on the look-out for someone to head such a department. A friend at Davis Polk Wardwell Sunderland & Kiendl told him about a man named William Hallet. "He's a very talented corporate lawyer, Morgan, and a very persuasive business getter." So why had Hallet not ascended to a partnership? "Well, he's a bit of a maverick. A bit hard to control." "Is he tamable?" "I think yes—by the right person. You'll have to decide that for yourself. But if you think you can tame him, you should fix your terms and go for him. I happen to know there are other firms interested in him." Morgan got hold of Hallet's credentials: Exeter; University of Chicago; Columbia LL.B., Law Review, Kent Scholar; served as a Marine in World War II (Pacific arena), decorated for valor; forty-four years old; married; two children. He met with Hallet, two long sessions: "If you think that, under my supervision, you can conduct your enthusiasms in a way that matches in delicacy your legal talents, I'll take you on as an associate. And if you measure up, I can promise you a partnership *sooner* than later. Believe me, with the other firms you're considering, it'll be later." (Maybe) it was the "sooner" inducement that swung Hallet to accept his offer. . . . In the Cleveland office, his choice of Hallet raised some eyebrows. So George Colt came to New York and met Hallet and sided with Morgan in Hallet's favor: "Let's do it, Morgan. Let's bet on him." Tamed, Hallet was fine. In fact, excellent. In further fact, superb. Morgan, in a continuance of gratitude that upon the venture of the New York office the sun kept shining, the sky not falling, worked harder; harder.

On a hot Saturday afternoon he was standing on the Tiffany corner of Fifth Avenue and Fifty-seventh Street, waiting for the light to change.

"Mr. Shurtliff. *Sir*."

That voice! An unbelievable, indescribable instant. As if sixteen years hadn't gone by. Before he turned, he said, "Sutter," then, face-to, repeated: "Sutter—"

—displaced: both of them displaced, staring incredulously at each other, not there on the corner of Fifth and Fifty-seventh, but on the *Stubbins,* checking the guns . . . in the lifeboat after the torpedoing . . . being rescued . . . saved . . . near-gone survivors set ashore in alien Durban, South Africa, yet there they were in the racket of New York traffic, being jostled by passers-by: the light had twice changed.

"Let's have a drink."

"Where?" Sutter asked, as if there could be no refuge for their kind.

"I know a place on Fifty-eighth. It's quiet. We can talk."

They fell into step, elbow-to-elbow; walked, not speaking; walked the short distance to Fifty-eighth Street: a small restaurant there, with a dark little bar attached to it. From out of the bright sunlight, they entered the dark bar; sat down in a booth—

"What'll you have?"

"A double Scotch. No ice."

"Two," Morgan told the waiter.

Some awkwardness then—rank, after all this time, still strangely in effect, and their clothes a chasm between them of prosperity and luck-lessness, Sutter eyeing the pristine coolness of Morgan's seersucker suit, himself perspiring in soiled, dun-colored gabardine, yet the tremendous emotionality of connection—

The waiter returned with their drinks. They touched glasses and began to talk.

Sutter wanted to know: "After we all split up, did you stay in touch with the captain?"

Enough, (Morgan said) to find out that the captain had died in the Pacific, off Formosa; another torpedoing: all hands lost.

"Shit," Sutter oathed. He wanted to know: "What about the others of our crew? Have you ever heard from any of them? Ever run into any of them?"

Morgan shook his head.

Sutter wanted to know: "*Our* torpedoing. Do you ever dream about it? The Owl's dying in the lifeboat? Putting him over the side like he was shark bait? Do you ever dream about it?"

"Occasionally. When I'm anxious about something. The dreams take different forms. They're not always specific, I mean."

"Yeah."

They went on talking for about fifteen minutes, not once smiling. That was the hardest part: that they could find nothing to smile over. Sutter had put on weight. He had a damaged man's look of permanent fatigue, of a terrible solitariness, of being able to fall densely asleep in odd places, at odd hours. Morgan risked: "What's keeping you busy these days?"

"Shipping. I'm with a Greek-owned shipping firm. Lots of travel. Different countries. Different ports. I'm just up from Panama. Got here yesterday; on to Boston tomorrow." (For a minute he sounded like the old Sutter, wide-open; but fast, then, to say no more about himself.) "What about you, Mr. Shurtliff?"

"I'm still lawyering," Morgan said. "Will you have another drink?"

"Better not," Sutter answered. "I've got an appointment downtown with the guy in charge of our New York docks." (He was clearly restive. He wanted to go. He reached for his wallet.)

"Let me get this round," Morgan said. "When you're next in New York, give me a ring, will you? I'm listed in the 'phone book, home and office."

They knew they'd never see each other again.

Out on the hot street, they shook hands. Then—all of a sudden— Sutter struck an attitude, went gorgeous: "Fuck 'em all but six, and save *them* for pallbearers. Right, Mr. Shurtliff?"

Morgan laughed. "Right."

Sutter turned west, toward Sixth Avenue; Morgan turned east, toward Fifth, reeling a little from the hastily downed, extremely unaccustomed mid-afternoon double Scotch.

On one of their rambles in Central Park, Julia and Bruce found a half-starved kitten. They were walking on a path that took them by a set of rocks. They heard the faint meowing and traced the sound to the opening of a small cave in the heap of scree. Bruce reached in and brought out the little cat. He handed it to Julia. Julia (later) told Morgan that when she took it, it didn't move, didn't meow again: "It only *sighed*," she said. Except for two brown patches on its right flank, it was white; short haired. It had blue eyes. Bruce thought it was a female. Morgan came home from the office to its presence, to Elsa and Julia and Caroline and Bruce hovering over the box they'd put the kitten in, the bottom of the box carpeted with a clean kitchen towel. "Ve keep it, Mr. Shurtliff," Elsa said. "I know of cats. It vill be no trouble and a nice companion." Julia appealed: "Please, Morgan—" He gave a qualified consent: a vet must see it first thing in the morning. If the vet thought the kitten had a chance—yes—they would keep it. Bruce stayed for dinner. What to name the kitten? Bruce came up with Hannah. But what if the kitten turned out to be a male? "Then Hannibal," Bruce said. . . . A vet was seen: Hannah would apply (the vet said) and not to worry: "She'll be fine." (Three days later, Morgan called Miss Sly. "We have a cat," he told her, "named Hannah." "Oh, I *am* so pleased—for all of you," Miss Sly said.)

❧

"Bliss"—was the word Caroline kept using about life in New York. That, and—"inspired."

❧

He bought a Mercedes of a color variously described as "maroon," "chestnut brown," "deep red"—anyhow, marvelous looking. He enthused to Geoff: "It clings to the road like a lover." He garaged it on Seventy-fifth Street between Park and Lexington.

"*Wheels!*" Julia said. "Now that we've got wheels, we can go anywhere." Which is what, on weekends, they did, exploring parts of Connecticut, the Hudson Highlands, the Hamptons. Elsa packed picnics for them, or they ate at inns, or had Sunday lunch at the country homes of friends.

He began to think about acquiring a week-end house. Would it be by the sea? Or would it be an inland place, with woods and a creek? Think about it.

❝

Lillie Ruth and Tessa and Dennis had begun to dismantle the Hatherton house. . . . In mid-July, when he went back to Cleveland for the monthly partners' meeting, the curtains in the downstairs rooms had been taken down and layered in tissue paper and packed into boxes. Through the high, naked windows the summer light streamed in on rolled-up rugs and on covered furniture clustered in the middle of the big rooms.

He took his father's advice and met with old, rotund Ambrose Hawes, the "legendary" antique dealer. Dwarfed in height by the tall, denuded windows, he went from room to room with Mr. Hawes, deciding what of each room's furnishings he would keep and what would be put up for auction. He liked Mr. Hawes; trusted him. He worried only about fire: no sooner did Mr. Hawes extinguish one cigarette than he lit another. Two stiff fingers of his left hand were nicotine-yellow, like old ivory.

The house was now "officially" on the market. An agent named Arthur Griffeth was in charge of selling it.

One evening, Morgan worked in the library, packing the books he wanted in New York: books that went way back in his life: boyhood tales; his first Latin primer, and the Latin text of *Commentarii* (Caesar's dry, solipsistic account of the first seven years of the Gallic War, studied and frowned over in Mr. Scudder's class); the oil-and-salt-water-damaged Bible he'd kept with him in the lifeboat; Joyce's *Ulysses*; retrieved from a top shelf, no title on its cover; the copy of *Fanny Hill* (purchased when he was in law school from a shady backstreet Boston dealer); the volumes of *The Landed Gentry* (bought in Durban, South Africa); and the *Everyday Book* (published in 1832) that his father had given him in 1943, half-way through the war. Dickens's novels, and those of Trollope. All of Conrad. Shakespeare's tragedies and comedies.

Little by little the house and its ancillary buildings were being emp-

tied out. In the garage was the old Chevrolet convertible: the Harold
Teen. (If the Harold Teen could talk, many of its stories would have to
do with kissing, with X-rated love made on its leather-covered front
seat—passion that couldn't wait for the marital bed. If the Harold Teen
could talk, some of its stories would be about Caroline and Julia, for, in
it, they had learned to drive—Julia, once, nearly ditching it.) In the way
a good man takes care of an old, long-serving mare, Dennis had continued to take care of the Harold Teen. Once in a while, on a fair day, he
took it for a run on the country roads. "Would you like to have it,
Dennis?" "Like to have it, Mr. Shurtliff? Lord, I surely would."
"Consider it yours. I'll see to the paper-work."

Of the house's myriad entities, what remained undisturbed were its
terrace trees, its garden, its tennis court, its bedded brook, its pond, its
long Jamesian stretch of lawn; and, up on the hill, the granite headstones
in the dog cemetery—1910 to 1958—Lear, Ripsy, Solo, Duffy, Daisy,
Star. Ralph.

🦢

"How much longer do you think you'll be, Callie?"

"Ten minutes at the most."

Fifteen minutes later: "How much longer, Callie?"

"A sec more—"

Ten minutes later: "*Caroline: HANG UP.*"

There were four 'phones in the apartment: one in the big walk-in
closet off the front hall, one in the library, one in Morgan's bedroom,
one in the kitchen. The four 'phones were interconnected, listed in the
phone book under *Shurtliff, M: RE*gent 7–3513.

"How much longer, Callie?" he would ask. Or Julia would ask. Or
Elsa: "Excuse me, Miss *Car*-oline, but for the grocery delivery I must
call Gristede's." *How much longer, Callie?* Finally, shots were fired: commence of the Telephone War. Caroline stated her terms for a Peace
Agreement: "In *my* bedroom, my *own* phone, listed under *my* name." So
be it. But at the time he agreed to the peace settlement, he hadn't reck-
oned on the profligate way Caroline would use her "own" 'phone. The
first month's bill was a whopper.

"An accounting error," Caroline grandly said of the bill when Morgan showed it to her.

He handed her the bill's second page on which were listed the calls she'd made to scattered friends in Minneapolis, Cleveland, Nantucket, New Orleans. "The frequency of the calls, Callie, and the length of time you talked—those three calls to New Orleans, each one over an hour—"

"I promise I'll do better next month," Caroline said.

He laughed. "Hold it, babe! What do you mean by 'better'? Do you have friends in Mexico City? In New Zealand? Afghanistan? What may I expect in the way of 'better'?"

After that, Caroline's telephone habits shifted to the right side of "better."

❧

Geoff met some guy on a bus and began to spend time with him—Alan absent at a music festival in Italy, Geoff restless.

"Restless" was Geoff's word.

Geoff talked about the guy. Morgan listened. He heard about the guy's good looks and about how amusing he was and how "understanding." But nothing concrete, such as how the guy earned a living, or how old he was: just Geoff's uncharacteristically arch, infatuated abstractions, the most insidious, the most insistently harped on, the guy's "understanding."

"You're not listening," Geoff said.

"No . . . What I'm doing is sitting here trying to figure out what's behind your big-deal need to go on with me about the guy."

Geoff, with an elaborate, superior politeness, said: "Let's drop it. I shouldn't have told you. I thought you'd understand."

That word again. "Since when has being 'understood' been so important to you? Are you talking about Alan?"

Geoff bristled: "No. I am *not* talking about Alan."

"So what's with this guy's—'understanding?'"

"I asked you to drop it."

"I can't. I'm too fond of Alan. . . . If Maud were alive and I told you I was flirting with some beauty on the side, you'd slaughter me."

Geoff put down his glass; stood up, said: "I'm going."

Three days later, Geoff telephoned. He volunteered to mention the guy again. In the past tense. "He was an aberrance, Morgie."

Morgan laughed. "An aberrance . . . I'm an expert on aberrances. I had my last fling with one a week or so ago. What are you doing tonight?"

"Nothing."

"Come to dinner. At seven."

"I'll be there."

Alan was soon back from Italy. Geoff's and Alan's domestic life resumed as usual.

~§

June and July had vanished. Flown away.

August next, and already half-gone. On its seventh day—a Friday—Caroline concluded her summer apprenticeship at the Balfour Foundation. On its thirteenth day, Julia attended her last class at Columbia.

Now it was Saturday, August 15, the scheduled date to depart New York for Hatherton.

At breakfast, Caroline said: "So far, it's been a perfect summer." Julia agreed. Morgan prayed that their declared "perfect summer" would not be ruined by the task of moving out of the Hatherton house.

Good-bye, Elsa. Good-bye, Hannah. Back soon.

They went by car. They took turns driving. They talked. They sang. They played their favorite game, "Who Am I?" They dozed. They spent the night at a pretty inn called *The Blue Bottle*. They made of the two-day trip a lark.

~§

The task of moving occupied them for eleven days. Of all their labors, clearing out the attic was the hardest. Something about the attic itself, (perhaps) its very apartness from the rest of the house, which remove gave it the feel of a place stranded in Time. Its air was filmy; it smelled drowsy; all the heat of August seemed collected in it. They opened its unscreened windows. Bees flew in and droned above their heads, high up in the vaulted beams where spiders lived in woven palaces. Scattered

about on the floor were what, at first view, looked like an endless number of old trunks and unlabeled boxes. Against one wall there were three
shoulder-high filing-cabinets, and off in a corner, a steel safe. Gazing at
these marooned receptacles, they knowingly sighed: inside each one, in
the form of *things,* the past resided. He glanced at Julia; at Caroline. He
said: "Let's get to it" (resolutely, in a voice that forbade mourning). . . . . Once in a while, one of them exclaimed over something. Julia's:
"*Look* at this"; Caroline's: "Look at *this!*" His own eruption: "My
God!"—when he brought out from a trunk the linen jacket supplied him
(after the torpedoing) by the English padre who ran the Seamen's
Mission in Durban, South Africa (the jacket, smelling of lavender, carefully folded, stored away—so—by Maud). There were boxes and boxes
filled with nursery play-things: dolls and dolls' clothes, and frayed, lop-
eared stuffed animals whose eyes were beads, whose noses were buttons;
and Halloween masks and costumes; a miniature tea service; picture
books; figurines of knights and princesses and ballet dancers; jigsaw
puzzles; board games. On and on. On and on. In their hands, Julia and
Caroline held again these things of childhood, marveling at the forgotten, at the outlived. But no! Not outlived: for into new boxes, they
repacked some of the things: "For the daughters we'll someday have,"
(they said). Morgan heard them say it.

It took two days to clear out the attic.

(He didn't open the safe. He knew exactly what it contained: his and
Maud's impassioned, violently restrained courtship love-letters, ribboned together, and their war-time letters; and, in one cardboard file,
their marriage certificates (church and state); and in a second cardboard
file, all the legal documents pertaining to the adoption of Julia and
Caroline; and in a third cardboard file, folded between an ecclesiastically
embossed rectangle of soft white leather, the attestations of their christening: *Julia Leigh Shurtliff; Caroline Cunningham Shurtliff.* And somewhere in the safe, Mrs. Leigh's suicide note, "*My time has come*"—the
note sealed in a blue envelope and locked away in the safe by Maud
twelve years ago. Recently, he had asked his father: "Will you keep the
safe in your house, Pa? Keep it there for me? I can't bear the thought of
its going into storage." "I'll put it in your mother's dressing-room

closet," Ansel Shurtliff had replied. "That's where it will be, son, anytime you want it.")

Promptly, every afternoon at four-thirty, they left the house and drove to Shaker Heights, to Letitia and Lewis Grant's large, patrician home. Back in July, Letitia had collared Morgan and delivered upon him a lengthy, emotionally charged speech. "As you've decided to sell your Hatherton house, Morgan, you must consent to my and Lewis's wish that you and Caroline and Julia make our home your *Cleveland* home. Make it your Cleveland *address*. . . . No, we'll hear no words to the contrary. . . . Oh, my dear Morgan, you see how it is with Lewis and me, biffing about at our advanced age in this huge, fully-staffed house, which I pray to God we'll finish out our lives in, but so *many* rooms, especially so many bedrooms—ten—*count them!*—ten bedrooms all crying out to be used. We don't give those lovely week-long house parties anymore for the lugubrious reason that most of our friends prefer dying in their own beds—we're all so *old*! But that's all beside the point. . . . You're to have one of the guest suites, and Julia and Caroline those two adjoining rooms overlooking the rose garden. Your father knows of this plan and hopes with Lewis and me that you'll agree to it." She was extraordinary. So was Lewis. Facing both of them, looking into their eyes, Morgan had simply said: "Yes, Aunt Letitia. Yes, Lewis. *Thank you.*"

That was how it came to be that each afternoon he and Julia and Caroline went to the Grants' house, now their Cleveland address— quickly known to Julia's and Caroline's former school friends. Now it was here that the young crowd (no longer *so* young) flocked in the evenings. They came for dinner, two or three at a time, or they arrived in bunches, trooping in and lingering for a few minutes before going off to other named diversions. Morgan's friends came for dinner too, and Doctor Leigh, importantly, as Julia and Caroline's maternal grand-father; and easily, elegantly, with his orchardist tranquillity, Ansel Shurtliff came often for overnight visits. The formal order, the harmony, the pleasurable interplay of these evenings chez Grant canceled out the complexities and emotional strains of the days spent in the Hatherton house—each day checked off on the calendar by Morgan: a crawling countdown.

And then (in retrospect quite suddenly), there were no more days to be checked off. On the morning of August 27, an immense van (empty but for eight men) rumbled down the tree-lined lane and snorted to a stop at the house's front door. Six hours later the van departed the house, slower than it had come, the van so loaded, the men so tired.

◆

(It seems strange that he and Julia and Caroline would remember so clearly and in such minute detail those days they spent moving out of the Hatherton house—the sheer labor, the controversies, the laughs, the often tearful moments—but that they couldn't, afterwards, agree about what it had been "like" to undo the years they had spent in the house. "Unreal" was their closest in-common word. "Unreal," they would say, then lapse into silence, each silently lost in a personal reflection of the word's meaning. Yet the fact of completion—the reality of the unreality that by mid-afternoon on that Thursday, August 27, 1959, nothing of themselves was left in the house. No thing. Nothing.)

◆

He couldn't wait to get to the office the next morning.

Each day of the eleven days occupied in moving, he and George Colt had conferred by phone. Each day, George Colt had assured him that all was well in the Kissel, Chandler world. Still, he couldn't wait to prove it to himself.

"Morgan—"

"George! Come in, come in—"

The famous Colt saunter, then, into Morgan's office, and the ritual handshake. "I bet you feel like dancing," George Colt said.

"More like going to church and falling on my knees to thank God it's over. That old rubric about the hell of moving doesn't half begin to state the case. But it *is* over, George. *Done.*"

"I've always held to the view that anybody who has survived a move has a right to crow about it. I'll listen if you want to let forth. Not for long though. There are a couple of pending matters you're going to be pleased to know about. They're exciting. Really exciting."

He listened closely to George Colt's account of the "pending matters." They *were* exciting. *Really* exciting. By noon-time, the move had receded so far in his consciousness as to seem distant, like something that had been completed quite a while ago: certainly much, much longer ago than just yesterday.

🦢

He had lunch with Miss Sly.

"The move is behind you, my dear Mr. Shurtliff!" By which exuberant words, with open arms, she greeted him.

She was the fair sky after the clouds. She was celebration. She shone, like the sun, even over the matter of what she would have for lunch: "The lobster salad or the crab cakes! What a wrenching decision! I'm always so hungry when I'm happy. The crab cakes, please. Are you starved too?"

"Yes," he smiled. "Yes, I am—" enjoying the distinctive sound of her alto voice and the very sight of that extraordinary, head-topping, done-up dome of her hair.

He had brought three photographs of Hannah to show to her. Hannah teasing a ball with her front paws. Hannah asleep. Hannah making an upward leap toward a toy mouse suspended at the end of a string.

"Oh, she *is* charming," Miss Sly said. "May I keep this picture of her leaping?"

"Yes. I'm touched you want it."

She kept looking at the picture. "I like to sketch cats at play. I don't claim to draw well, though I *am* improving. I used to stew over every pencil stroke, but no more. I'm learning to be fast, to let the strokes *occur*—'in the spirit of the perceived action'—is the way my new teacher says it."

"Ah! You've a new teacher."

"Mr. Bancroft. I enrolled in his class at the Art Institute about a month ago. I'm so thrilled to be studying again I hardly dare speak of it for fear I'll wake up and find it's a dream. . . . I *have*, you see, truly begun to withdraw from Tilden-Herne. And you watch me! Come January, when I'm fully retired, I shall *really* improve as a sketcher of cats. . . . But I mustn't ramble on, though when I'm with you, I always *do* ramble on. It's because you oblige me by giving an impression of patience. And you're not by nature patient. You're *impatient*. As impatient as I am. It's a virtue we share."

"Impatience isn't usually regarded as a virtue."

"It's allowing it to show that makes of impatience a fault."

The twist of her reasoning made him laugh. "Would you ever consider giving me one of your sketches of a cat at play?"

She fairly blushed. "I might. When I'm improved."

"I'll keep asking."

"I'll count on you to keep asking." She put the picture in the side pocket of her commodious purse. Then she said: "You were so concerned about the move's possibly harsh effects on your daughters. Are your anxieties in that regard laid to rest?"

Over the course of the summer, he had kept her informed of Julia's and Caroline's different pursuits and of their repeatedly expressed happiness of their life in New York; so it was on the solidity of that known base that he structured an answer to her question. "As it's turned out, my anxieties appear to have been excessive; more, I think, applicable to myself than to them. I don't mean to imply that the move was easy for them, only to say that they managed it with surprising style. Maybe *grace* is the better word." He smiled; or almost smiled. "They're stunningly grown up. Much more than I'd realized. And they are marvelously *individual;* individually equipped; individually confident." He did, then, truly smile. "I'm beyond words proud of them."

"Justly so," she said. She was looking at him very hard. "But you seem troubled."

"Less troubled than humbled," he countered. "The fact is, I'm having a bit of a problem adjusting to the magnitude of their adultness. They're independent of each other, and certainly independent of me—" He halted. Then: "I feel side-lined: as a *father,* I mean."

"That's a very ancient, very universal feeling," she said, "and very appropriate. But you know that."

"Yes, I do—"

"—and I have no doubt you'll accommodate to their maturity very well." She leaned then, as if seeking closer contact, toward him across the table. "Forgive me, Mr. Shurtliff, if I appear too presumptuous in saying that I think what you're really struggling with is the move's effect on *you*—that it's freshened in you a consciousness of your *singleness,* your *single* loneliness."

Two things checked him for a moment: first was the amount of comfort he took from her comprehension of his truer condition (about which, on his own, he would never have spoken); and second (and more) was the arresting precision of her word—*singleness.*

"Mr. Shurtliff?"

"I was wondering what I'd do without you," he said.

"Oh my dear, thank you. For a moment, I was afraid I'd terribly overstepped myself."

"Never." He might have (but did not) attempt to tell her that her insight released him to be, *with her,* tacitly, honestly himself. "You relax me," was what he did say (which remark, as they both understood it, closed the subject).

He asked her then: "Have you chosen the person who will succeed you at Tilden-Herne?"

"We've narrowed the field down to two candidates. They're both well qualified. I'm hoping the board of trustees will . . . "

And so they talked on. . . . They parted, after their lunch, in their usual way, with a strong embrace. "When do you and your daughters return to New York?"

"Day after tomorrow."

"Call me," she said. "I'll want to know you're safely home."

"I will. And remember: I want one of your sketches."

"You inspire me." She laughed. "Good-bye, Mr. Shurtliff, until *soon.*"

"It will be soon. Good-bye, Miss Sly."

He handed her into a waiting taxi; then he hailed a taxi for himself, and went back to his office.

‏ਝ

Saturday, August 29

"Everyone who matters is here," Lillie Ruth said.

Every one (Morgan thought). Julia, Caroline, Dennis and his wife Louisa, Ansel Shurtliff, Letitia and Lewis Grant, Doctor Leigh, Pastor and Mrs. Eldon, all gathered in the living room of Lillie Ruth's and Tessa's new home—the room a near duplication of Lillie Ruth's "parlor" in the Hatherton house: same curtains (recut and sewn to fit the smaller windows), same couch, same chairs, same timeless photographs displayed on the same tables, flowers arranged in the same remembered vases. It was mid-afternoon of a blue sky day. They talked about the past and about the future and were happy. For this party, Doctor Leigh had surprised them all by deviating from his usual drill of arriving well in advance of a party's due hour, then of leaving almost at once, pleading "the call of duty," or whatever: anyhow creating confusion. On this occasion, he showed up some twenty minutes late and settled himself somewhat theatrically in a chair, where he (amazingly) remained. Sitting so, large and vigorous, he made a speech (interrupting all conversation)—a kind of toast, raising high his glass of iced tea, treating it like a filled glass of champagne: "To everyone here," he bawled out, picking up Lillie Ruth's words, "everyone—my grand-daughters in the springtime of their lives—my son-in-law in the prime of life—I won't touch on the ages of the rest of us—no need to because what's important is that we're all sailing on, young and old,"—looking from face to face as at a fleet of royal vessels, himself the King's admiral (as if, Morgan thought, as in Longfellow's poem, they were each a "Ship of State")—"that's the great thing to do—to sail on—sail on—"

"Amen!" Pastor Eldon flashed: *"Amen."* By which churchly code, everyone was freed to resume their conversations—

... "We'll be back for a three-day visit between Christmas and the New Year," Julia was saying to Lillie Ruth.

"And between now and then, you'd better write plenty of letters to Tessa and me," Lillie Ruth said. "You hear me, Julia? Callie?"

The happy chatter continued. More reminiscence, more gathered pleasure—until about an hour later, Letitia stood up and said good heavens, *her* group would have to leave or they'd be late for dinner. She herded her group—Lewis and Ansel Shurtliff and Julia and Caroline and Morgan—and made a comedy of spanking them out the front door, everyone laughing at the way she did it. No time for prolonged good-byes. No chance for tears to collect in anyone's eyes.

❧

Morgan was driving. Julia was sitting beside him on the Mercedes's front seat; Caroline was in the back seat. They were on the last leg of the trip home to New York. "We'll be there in a couple of hours," he said.

"It's the last day of August," Julia mused.

"Summer's end—" he said.

"—and so swift in passing," Julia said.

They fell silent. One of those soft, contemplative silences people sink into when they've been traveling for several hours. Even Caroline, silent; though, when he glanced in the rear-view mirror, he saw that she was busy pushing a pencil around on a sheet of tablet paper; frowning. And about fifteen miles down the road later, she said: "Listen to this! I've done the arithmetic—"

"What arithmetic?"

"*Listen!* You *have* to listen. . . . June plus July plus August equals three months, which particular three months add up to ninety-two days. Are you with me? Okay . . . *those* ninety-two *days* are equal to two thousand two hundred eight *hours*. Two thousand two hundred eight *hours* are equal to one hundred thirty-two thousand four hundred eighty *minutes*—and those one hundred thirty-two thousand four hundred eighty *minutes* are equal to seven million nine hundred forty-eight thousand eight hundred *seconds*. How about *that*!"

"All those *seconds*—nearly eight million—sound like forever," Julia said.

"Oh, Julia, you're crazy!" Caroline scowled: "Three months is what sounds like *forever*."

"It all depends on whether you're looking ahead or looking back," Julia replied.

He tended to agree with Julia, but withheld comment, needing to concentrate on the road, on—as they steadily neared the city—the increase of traffic. . . . Now, Caroline and Julia were occupied in drawing up and comparing separate lists of what they had to do and of what, in the matter of clothes, they had to buy before they returned to college. "I can't believe we've only got a week to do it all in," Caroline said.

Julia agreed: "I can't believe it either."

He drove on. And then, in a fast-gone while—

—*Hello, Elsa! Hello, Hannah! Hello, hello! It's wonderful to be home. Wonderful.*

◦§

On Tuesday, September 8, Julia and Caroline departed for college.

"Now is only you and Hannah and myself," Elsa said to him. "To keep me busy, and you not to miss Miss *Car*-oline and Miss *Chew*-lia too much, you must invite many people for dinners, *Mister* Shurtliff."

"I will, Elsa. Thank you. I will."

◦§

In mid-September, the Hatherton house was sold to a couple named Trask: Bernard and Emily Trask: parents of a boy, Otto, age seven, and a girl, Antonia, age four.

. . . Morgan had stipulated that he wanted the house to pass into the keeping of just such a family as the Trasks appeared to be. There had been other prospective buyers hot to acquire the house, but of them all, only the Trasks had young children, and only the Trasks (as reported by Morgan's agent) had taken touching notice of the dog cemetery: had stood and read aloud the names commemorated on each headstone— the while their children, Otto and Antonia, with their two Jack Russell terriers, ran free, here and there and back, over the lawn.

3 ✑ Adjacent Destinies

*He had come to Cleveland from New York for the monthly partners meet-*ing, held usually on the second Wednesday of every month; this month, however, an exception: the meeting had taken place yesterday, Tuesday, October 13, 1959. He had arrived on Monday in the late afternoon and gone straight from the airport to the Grants' house. There, after a pleas-ant dinner with Letitia and Lewis, he pleaded the need to retire early. "Tomorrow's going to be a non-stop day," he told them, evoking Roger Chandler's old phrase. Letitia said: "I assumed it would be. I've told Maisie you'll want an early breakfast." (Maisie was the Grants' longtime cook.) Lewis and Letitia walked him up the stairs and down the hall to what were now established in their home as his rooms. "Good night, Morgan darling," Letitia said. In tone and lift, her voice was her dead sister's voice: his mother's voice. "Thank you, Aunt Letitia." He kissed her, then shook Lewis's hand. "Thank you," he said again. As always, they gestured his thanks away.

He slept like a rock, arose at six-thirty and was in his office by eight.

Most of the morning was spent with an elderly, physically feeble but still mentally keen client who voiced an "imperative need" to revise his will. (He had seven grand-children, all male, all young adults, four "promising," three "regrettably irresponsible," distribution of wealth the issue, and by what means? Outright inheritance for the "promising" four? Controlled trusts for the "irresponsible" three?) Then a conference lunch with George Colt. Finally, at three-thirty, the partners meeting, longer than usual, dusk by the time it ended. Then back to the Grants' for dinner, after which (with apologies to Letitia and Lewis) more desk-work, then bed (late), and another early rise, another intense work morning at the office.

Now it was Wednesday afternoon and he was at the airport, waiting to board the plane for the return trip to New York. He was sitting down, idling away the minutes in observation of the variety of human scenes taking place around him—airports, theaters of a sort, audience and players one and the same, revealing themselves in all conditions of pleasure, anxiety, regret, ennui, even anger: that middle-aged couple standing over there, obviously miserable, turning away from each other, then facing each other again, something gone bitterly wrong between them, yet they could not separate, the plot of their problem now audible: "You lied to me," the woman was heard to say—"*Lied* to me"—beginning to cry; the man flushed and desperate—

To be privy to their distress was wrong. He looked away—

—and saw, coming down the terminal's long middle aisle, Miss Sly, and, with her, a woman—instantly recognized, instantly placed: that Carnegie Hall concert he and Maud and Julia and Caroline had attended more than four years ago: that moment when, as they were leaving the hall, they had encountered Miss Sly in the company of this woman—the chaotic, crowded, complicated encounter vividly recalled, and in so replete a way that he sat over it, reliving it, thinking on it in relation to all that had happened—*since:* wondering at the remarkableness of reencountering Miss Sly and the woman here in this other crowded public place this long time later.

They—Miss Sly and the woman—had by now advanced so far as to be at the airline's check-in counter. There, into the hands of an attendant, the woman put her ticket and her suitcase. The attendant weighed the suitcase, tagged it, placed it on the luggage belt, looked again at the woman's ticket, stamped it, and, with a nod and commercial smile, handed it back to her. Having been "cleared" for the flight, she rejoined Miss Sly.

He had watched all this as it had occurred, fascinated by the woman: by the quiet beauty of her intelligent face, her tallness, her calm bearing, which calmness above all else impressed and strangely touched him, causing him to wonder what had so distinctly formed it, what it was composed of, what it would take to shatter it. He put her age as younger than his own, perhaps by as much as a decade.

He stood up then, and made his way to Miss Sly's side. He put his hand on her arm. She turned, all sharp surprise: she had not seen him coming. "Mr. Shurtliff!" she exclaimed. "Miss Sly," he said. He kissed her lightly on her left cheek. Then he turned and met the woman's eyes, resting, blue, full on him. She smiled—a swift, positive smile. He was sure she remembered him. He looked at her for a longer than usual couple of seconds—

—the lingerance broken by Miss Sly, who, with a ceremonial politeness to the point of stiffness, said: "I recall the former time the three of us met as being so hectic I wasn't able to properly introduce you. Miss Phelps, Mr. Shurtliff. Mr. Shurtliff, Miss Phelps."

Added to her extreme formality (in itself daunting) was a tight-lipped coldness of a kind denying. The combination stunned him. He could not account for it except to think that his voluntary act of publicly seeking her out when she was in someone else's company and greeting her with so intimate a thing as a kiss, had offended her strict professional scruple that their friendship be always privately conducted. The other possibility was that he had intruded at a critical moment on some matter of personal importance to her and Miss Phelps. He thought of all this, and felt it in a second, and, as quickly, decided to withdraw. He bowed, and took a step away, backward—

—but Miss Phelps, then, extended her hand: "Hello, *again*," she said.

Her emphatic underscoring of the word—"again"—confirmed his conviction that she remembered him. He took her hand and shook it and said: "Yes; *again*," then added her name: "Miss Phelps."

Her smile freshened. "I remember your wife and daughters too," she said, "—especially your one daughter's excitement about going on to the Russian Tea Room for supper after the concert."

"You've an amazing memory," he said. "That was Caroline. She's so grown up now that I doubt she'd be similarly excited, though in her defense, I have to say she remains a great devotee of the Russian Tea Room, as does my other daughter, Julia." He was conscious that he was perhaps being too exact, too extending, but because Miss Phelps kept smiling and because her smile conveyed interest—and, having accounted for Caroline and Julia, a wish to tell her about Maud seized him—a compulsion—acted on almost before he knew it: "My wife died some while ago," he said.

"Oh," she said; struck. "*Oh*—"

By stepping forward, Miss Sly interposed herself between him and Miss Phelps, virtually blocking them from further contact, and, with her eyes concentrated on him, said: "When we last spoke on the 'phone, Mr. Shurtliff, you told me you'd be in Cleveland this week for your monthly partners meeting and that it would be a whirlwind trip. I incorrectly assumed you'd come on Tuesday and return to New York on Thursday as you usually do."

The absolute specifics of this lengthy awkward speech, with its implication that he had not been quite straight with her, caused in him more than a little distress. In the fine trust of their long relationship, they had never before become postured in such a mutually demeaning way: he, to *explain;* she, to be explained *to.* But what other course was there *than* to explain? "The date of the meeting was changed," he said, "and it's been even more of a whirlwind trip than I'd anticipated. No chance at all to call you—"

"Oh," she broke in, "I didn't mean—you mustn't think—" Her face mirrored his own distress. "It's seeing you here and so unexpectedly that's unhinged me. Airports are—" She fumbled, then concluded "—so disorienting."

"Yes," he said, "they are."

All passengers holding tickets on Flight Thirty-two to New York should now begin to board the plane.

The broadcast announcement saved them.

He took her hand. "I'll call you very soon," he said.

"Please do," she said. "And please excuse me, Mr. Shurtliff, for being so—so *distracted*."

"Don't give it a thought," he said.

He turned to Miss Phelps; lowered his head; raised it; a sort of bow. Then he strode off.

His assigned seat on the plane was on the starboard side, forward, in the second row next to the window. The day was fair, the flight flawless. The plane landed at LaGuardia ten minutes ahead of schedule. When it came to a full stop, he stood up and faced aft, looking for her. She was seven rows back. She saw him, and waved, and stayed where she was. Other passengers trailed past her.

"Hello, yet again."

He would always wonder at his lack of surprise that she (had) waited for him. And equally unsurprised that she so easily accepted his presence directly behind her as they proceeded down the plane's narrow aisle toward its rear exit, and that when they got to the exit, she allowed him to go before her so that he might hand her down the steps of the steep steel staircase, aircraft to ground, and that once on the ground they continued on together to where they would reclaim their suitcases. All in silence. Until, arrived at the flight's designated luggage belt, he put to her his first question: "Do you live in New York or are you just visiting?"

"Oh, I'm a long-time New Yorker."

"I'm on my way to becoming one." And, as they waited for their suitcases to turn up on the moving belt, he asked his second question: "Is someone meeting you?"

"No."

"Then let's go into town in the same cab."

"That might inconvenience you—"

"That's not possible—"

"I live on East End Avenue between Seventy-ninth and Eightieth Streets. Where do you live?"

"On Fifth Avenue, at Seventy-third Street . . . Ah, there's my suitcase."

"And there's mine. . . . *Don't*. You've your own to carry. *And* your briefcase."

"None of them are heavy."

In the close confinement of the taxi's back seat, she sat in a calm of her own making (or so he described it to himself). She seemed miles away. They were in the crawling thick of rush-hour traffic. "I hope you're not in a hurry," he said. "Once we cross the Triborough Bridge, I think the traffic will clear a bit."

"Zee told me you're a lawyer."

"Yes, I am. Zee? Miss Sly you mean—"

"Yes."

"You've known her a long time?"

She glanced at him, and smiled. "All my life. She's my godmother. I've always called her 'Zee.'"

"You couldn't have managed 'Zenobia' when you were a child."

"Then, *or* now," she laughed. "'Zenobia' is such a formidable name. *Too* unusual really."

"There's not very much that's usual about her."

"No," she said. "No, there isn't."

She looked again out the cab's window at the farther view of the urban landscape. Finally he said: "After she introduced us, she didn't seem quite herself."

"'Unhinged.' Wasn't that her word? What I believe is that she wanted to pay equal attention to both of us and that she sort of went to pieces when she found she couldn't. As you undoubtedly know, there's no one on earth who's better intentioned than she is. . . . There's my river."

The East River, seen now below them as they traversed the long high span of the Triborough Bridge and moved, faster then, onto the East Side Drive, the dark river now off to their left, bordering the road. He wondered if she had used the river as a means of not talking further about Miss Sly. "Do you have a view of the river from your apartment?" he asked.

"Yes. It's a great distraction. I like to watch the boats, and I like the rhythm of the tidal changes. . . . *Your* view must be of Central Park. That would be a distraction too."

"We ought to tell the driver your exact address."

Which was 25 East End Avenue.

They were soon there. He got out of the cab; she quickly followed. The doorman came running.

"Welcome back, Miss Phelps."

"Thank you, Roy."

The cabbie opened the taxi's trunk. Her suitcase was on top of his. It was as the cabbie lifted it out—then—that he noticed, goldenly etched in the leather above the suitcase's handle, the three initials *S.K.P.* And then, facing her, ignoring the cabbie's and the doorman's presence, then—having in his mind put it all together—*then*, that he hazarded: "'The Steeplechase.'"

She showed immense surprise. "Zee!" she said. "She gave you a copy!"

"It's a terrific story," he said, conscious of a rush of color reddening his cheeks. Then, of a sudden, still looking at her: "Who's Dobson?"

"A fiction," she answered.

"I was afraid he might be a husband."

"No."

The doorman had walked away with her suitcase into the building. The cabbie had reseated himself, waiting, inside the taxi—

She said: "Thank you for the ride—"

"If I were to call you, would you have dinner with me?"

"Yes, Mr. Shurtliff, I would."

"Morgan," he supplied.

"Sylvia," she offered. "Good-bye."

"Good-bye."

Thus it began.

❧

For two days he kept himself from calling her. Until Saturday afternoon. When she answered the phone, her voice sounded remote. He identified himself and immediately said: "I fear I'm interrupting your work."

"You are, but it's a welcome interruption."

"I won't let it become a lengthy one. When may we meet for dinner?"

"My date book's in the other room. Hang on." And in a moment: "I'm back, date book and all. Back in the real world. When the phone rang, I was interrogating a story character, trying to get him to confide his first name to me. Do you like your first name?"

(What an odd turn.) "Yes, I think so," he said. "Yes."

"I wish I liked mine more than I do. I wouldn't have chosen it for myself—"

"It seems a fine name to me. What's your problem with it?"

"Its *sound*. It sounds misty, undecided, not—"

His laughter checked her. "This is one of the most unexpected conversations I've ever had."

"But innocent," she said. (The qualifier even more unexpected, he thought.) "I'm free next Friday evening."

Almost a week away. He had hoped it would be sooner, but did not say so. "That's perfect. I'll pick you up at seven, if that's all right."

"Friday at seven. Thank you, Morgan. Good-bye until then."

"Good-bye, Sylvia."

ے

Monday, October 19, 1959

Dear Miss Sly,

Only to report that all is well here and to tell you that I look forward to seeing you in mid-November, at which time you might give me a sketch of Hannah? I'll call you well in advance of the time I'll be in Cleveland. I think of you and, as always, I miss you.

M.S.

No mention of their encounter at the airport five days ago. No mention of Sylvia Phelps. Just a short note of the usual kind he regularly wrote to her.

ے

A raw bitter night leaning toward winter. Rain. A gale wind.

He would always remember the date: Friday, October 23, 1959.

When the cab stopped in front of her building, he saw her standing just inside the building's glass double-door. *"Wait,"* he told the driver. "We'll be going on from here to the Plaza Hotel."

He was out of the cab in an instant.

They met half-way under the strung length of the building's awning, the rain pelting down on the overhead canvas—he with his hat off, held in his left hand, she with the wind ballooning out her black cape, revealing its crimson lining, her hair blown too, covering half her face. "I love this kind of wild weather" was the first thing she said. Then: "Hello again, Morgan."

"Hello again, Sylvia."

Quick then, into the cab.

"Where are you taking me?" she asked. "Is my hair a mess?"

"To the Edwardian Room at the Plaza. No, your hair's not a mess." It had fallen back in place—her hair—thick and softly straight, and in the cab's dim interior light, bronze-hued, framing her face.

"It's one of my favorite places."

"I'm glad."

From East End Avenue, the cabbie crossed on Seventy-ninth Street to Fifth Avenue. On one side of the avenue were the lighted cliff-fronts of apartment buildings. Stretching off on the avenue's other side was Central Park. In the wind, the branches of the park's great trees were bending and twisting. Torn from the tree's limbs, the last of the autumn leaves were flying in all directions. As they neared Seventy-third Street he said: "This is my neighborhood," and, "There's my building."

"How high up are you?"

"The twelfth floor."

"Way up above the trees," she murmured.

"Yes."

Their table in the Edwardian Room was next to the parkside windows. Outside, outdoors, the weather continued to riot. But inside, indoors, conditions were velvet. Conversation between them was easy. One of them would talk, the other would listen. Shot arrow, receiving target. Then a reversal. She fascinated: her fast, supple mind, her free and rich imagination that could give lyrical birth to angels or in a switch cause dragons, spitting fire, to appear. All through dinner he was aware of adventure, of a personal excitement that made him within himself, to himself, feel *new*, like a first-time traveler. . . . There was for him only one yore disturbing moment. It happened as they were finishing dessert. All in an instant, the weather dramatically worsened. The rain turned spate; the wind flung it solid against the window. Wham. Wham. The window (seemed) to quake, its great pane of glass to tremble; to go on trembling. She put down her spoon and placed her hand on the window, flat against it, articulate, and held it there. . . . It must have been the sight of her feminine hand, the sight of it as she held it like that, volunteered against the weather's violence, that brought back the fracturing memory of being in the shell of the lifeboat tossed by the storm that had conjured Death and caused the captain's steadying hands on the tiller to blister and to bleed—*this* memory that sent his hand at once toward hers, at once to draw her hand away from the window, to protect it—but the gesture just in time arrested, his hand not quite on hers: "It'll get cold," he said, husky.

She removed it from the window.

A brief silence then between them, dispelled by her with: "When we leave here, I'd enjoy giving you a nightcap at my house. If that appeals."

"It does. Very much. The problem will be to get a cab."

"Oh, we will," she calmly replied.

The door to her apartment, when unlocked, swung back into a lighted entry hall (darkness beyond) with a closet on the left (she hung up his coat and her cape) and on the right another door, slightly ajar, pointed out by her with the Britishly identifying word: "A 'loo.' I'll turn on some lights in the living room. I'll see you presently."

He entered the living room a few moments later, attracted to its location (at the end of the entry hall) by the promised lamplight. She was there before him, waiting, standing by the room's eastern bank of windows. He looked first at her, then around, and again around, prolonging an appreciative take of the whole room; then said of it: "Wonderful."

Books lined its north wall, floor to ceiling. Mid-point of this wall was a deep, multi-pillowed couch, a tall lamp beside it; draped over the couch's back, a colorful, embroidered Kashmir shawl, and in front of the couch, a large, square, japanned table, books and a collection of glimpsed objects atop it. The long span of the room's south wall was broken by two doors. One of the doors was open, exposing a lighted corridor leading to—what other wonders? Seen through the half-closed other door, a small pantry (kitchen beyond it). Between the two doors was a handsome dining table set about with four matched Adam chairs. In the rest of the room's space were inviting groupings of padded stools and small, nested tables and comfortable other chairs. An aesthetically ordered, peaceful, peaceful room. Still in a large way taking it in, he said again: "Wonderful." At her beckoning, he walked forward to the bank of windows and stood beside her, close, and looked then down—down through the rain-drenched rays of esplanade lights onto the river—onto its turbulent roilings of white-capped waves, the tide running contrary to the wind, so spray erupting in spouts up, the gunning rain though strafing the spouts back—looking with her down on the tempest's wildings—

"—but I promised you a drink," she said, and turned away.

By which spoken words she concluded a sentence whose unspoken beginning he did not trust himself to guess.

"Brandy? Scotch? Bourbon?"

"Scotch, please," he said. "No ice. A splash of tap water."

"While I'm getting it, here's something that will interest you."

From a near-by table she picked up and handed him a framed photograph, quite large, of a group of girls standing erectly, importantly, on the steps of a solemn building, six girls on the bottom step, five on the middle step, four on the top step—all dressed alike in turn-of-the-century ankle-length black skirts and high-collared, long-sleeved white blouses. All were shod in black shoes. Each held a bouquet of flowers (springtime blooms, he thought). He went to the couch and sat down and by the tall lamp's stronger light, studied the picture: the maidens' faces. In the front row, Miss Sly! Young, proud Zenobia, with waist-long hair and a young earnest brow and young earnest eyes staring straight out of the picture, straight into the future—

Sylvia then, standing over him: "You did find her—" and, to his nod: "It's an affecting picture, isn't it. All those yesteryear girls." She put his drink on the table, then seated herself beside him on the couch. "*That* girl"—pointing to the girl whose left arm touched Miss Sly's right arm—"is—*was* my mother at age seventeen, the same age as Zee." The photograph's year (she next told him) was 1907; June, its month. A graduation photograph: the girls "products" of—Miss Choate's School for Cultivated Presbyterian Females. (She smiled when she stated the school's full name.) Over the two years her mother and Miss Sly attended Miss Choate's school—"being finished"—they became friends. "*Dear* friends," she said, employing the tender word of the photograph's bygone era. "My mother was an only child and so was Zee, so their friendship was of a sisterly kind. That magnitude of affinity. Zee was with my mother when she died. Which says it all, doesn't it. . . . My mother died four years ago. January seventeenth, 1955, to be precise. She'd been ailing for a while, but she kept from me that she was direly ill. I'd spent Christmas with her. Zee was there too—"

"Where was there?"

"Cincinnati. That's where my mother lived the last ten years of her life. It's an interesting city."

"I agree," he said. "I know it fairly well because I have cousins there." Then: "Did your mother ever live with you *here*? In this apartment, I mean. I ask because it has such a long-time lived-in feel to it."

"I think it must be the old furniture—all inherited—that gives it that feel, because I've only had the place for three years. I bought it after my mother died, with some of the money she left me. That's the irony, that by dying she provided me with a whole different life than the one I'd led for years—teaching English literature at a private school here in New York. The money made it possible for me to move from a tiny apartment to this one, and to quit teaching and begin *really* to write. To have the necessary *time* to write. That's how I've come to be, to the extent I *am*, S. K. P. Dobson." (She smiled. A slight, swift smile.) "I'm talking a lot. . . . It's the storm, I guess."

"The storm and my curiosity," he said. "If I ask too many questions, or wrong ones, I'm sure you'll balk."

She laughed. "You're right. I'm very capable of balking."

What else, that first evening, either by means of his questions or her profferings, did he learn about her?

—That her mother's maiden name was Keith (baptismal name, Ella), hence the K. in S. K. P. Dobson. (In his mind, Dobson was parenthetical.)

—That her father, Edgar Niles Phelps, had died in 1943 at age fifty-four—that he'd been an investment banker—

—That (and her face lit up when she told him—*this*): that two months ago she had completed "three novella-length tales" —that the tales — "will be *out*, Morgan, *published* in about nine months' time. I signed the publisher's contract two weeks ago. I'm still over the moon with joy."

"God, that's wonderful!" he exclaimed. "Wonderful. I can't wait to read the stories."

"I'll give you one to take home with you. As thanks for this evening. I'll get it now." She stood up. "Would you like to see my study?"

"Yes. Yes."

She led him through the southern wall's fully open door down the lighted corridor (past a peripherally glimpsed bedroom) to a three-windowed corner room atmosphered, like a scholar's carrel, of a sequestered seriousness and patience. Residing on a hip-high, double-backed, lion-clawed pedestal were two venerable dictionaries. Against the room's only blank wall (shelves of books its other walls) was an immense rectangular desk, its surface covered with a strew of sharpened pencils and paper clips and erasers a pushed-back typewriter a feather duster a carved wooden tortoise pages of lined foolscap paper containing handwritten words words words—"It's the hugest desk I've ever seen," he said. "Like an acre of prime land."

"It was my father's."

"I know I know I'm overusing the word, but it's all wonderful, the room, the desk, the books, the privacy, everything—*you. You're* wonderful."

She visibly shied, and in a low, sharply dissenting voice said: "If only I were."

In his own way sensitive, he felt put at a distance, as if he'd been too raptorial, too—*sudden*. But sudden was the state he was in: his plight the mischief that he had so suddenly not been able to not display it. He retreated into silence until, after a period of time that in terms of all he was thinking and feeling was not long, she said: "One has about one's own life so many regrets to account for. That's what I meant when I said—'If only I *were* wonderful.'"

Another unclockable moment.

Then she took a few steps forward and opened one of the desk's drawers and withdrew a manuscript and handed it to him. "It's a strange tale. I hope you like it, Morgan."

They returned to the living room and stood again for a moment (this one clockably terminate) by the windows.

"It's stopped raining. . . . The next time we meet, *I'll* ask all the questions."

"I'll call you tomorrow to fix a date. I hope you'll let the next time be soon." He said this quietly, with a certain internal anxiousness, aware that she had an established life: friends, plans, a work routine, commitments. "It's late. I must go."

In the hall, when he put on his overcoat, he slipped the pages of the story (thick, loosely folded) into the coat's deep, interior breast pocket. "Where no last drop of rain can reach it," he said. He took her extended hand. "Good night. Good night, Sylvia."

"Good night, Morgan." And then: "We'll talk tomorrow."

To his ears, those words sounded of a marvelous yield. He looked at his watch. "It's ten past midnight—"

"Today, then," she said.

In the building's lobby, the doorman said: "I'll try whistling for a cab, sir."

"Thanks, but don't trouble yourself. I want to walk for a bit."

He pulled down the brim of his hat and turned up the collar of his coat and pushed off, left, to Seventy-ninth Street; then he turned right, faced into the wind, treading the same route the cabbie had driven over at the evening's beginning, walking the long blocks away: East End Avenue to First Avenue to Second Avenue to Third Avenue, Lexington next behind him, then Park, forward to Madison—walking in a condition of sober inebriation, wind and distance no matter—

He was, of course—and he knew it—already marked by love for her.

. . . The long trek was a physical release and sufficiently tiring to send him straight to bed when he got home. Well, almost straight to bed. He went first into the library and put the story she'd given him on his desk and smoothed out its pages, the number of which, on examination, surprised him. Fifty-four single-spaced typewritten pages. Enough pages, when folded (as he had carried them in his overcoat pocket) to have stopped a late-night miscreant's knife from a frontal penetration of his heart. Curiosity drove him to read the story's title and its first paragraph.

A NIGHT AT DSIATZDAVO

-One-

In the autumn of the fiftieth year of the nineteenth century, Count Alexandre Rodzanski was returning with his wife from his country estate in Litzbark to his winter residence in Warsaw when, because of the Countess's acute fatigue, he was forced, with his entire retinue, to stay for two days' time at the inn in the remote municipality of Dsiatzdavo.

He disciplined himself not to read on. *Wait,* he told himself.

Hannah followed him into his bedroom. She had formed the habit of sleeping at night on his bed, curled in a ball beside him. He liked having her there; liked her living presence. She slept soundly through what remained of the night; he slept fitfully; shallowly. The alarm clock rang as usual at seven-fifteen. He got up and showered and shaved and dressed. At eight, as usual, Elsa served him breakfast. As he ate, he skimmed the pages of the *New York Times.* His mind was on the story: the novella, described by Sylvia as "a strange tale." By noon, he had finished reading it. . . . The genesis of its action was a peasant uprising (revolt) in the 1850s, in the Polish province of Krajovoitz. Its lead characters: the Count Rodzanski; Nicholas Simienski (mayor of Dsiatzdavo), and the mayor's wife, Madame Simienski; a youth, Maarko—the story's tragic hero.

After lunch, he dialed her number.

"Hello," she said.

He disguised his voice (or tried to). "Can you hear me? Can you hear me? I'm—"

"Is this Morgan?" she quietly, very quietly asked.

"Can you hear me? I'm desperate to reach S. K. P. Dobson. I'm calling prior to the invention of the telephone—calling from a village in Poland, pronounced I think Dee-zee-atz-davo—"

"*Morgan,*" she stopped him.

"Sylvia. When may I see you? To tell you of my enjoyment and admiration of the story. *When?*"

They secured the date: Saturday evening, October 31. "A week from today," he repeated. "Here at my home, at seven, for dinner."

"I'll be there," she said. "I'd be there even if you hadn't read the story, even if you didn't like it."

He hung up, euphoric.

✑

He went through the week terribly conscious of the symptoms (all internally experienced) of weightlessness and float and dream. He wondered at himself, a forty-eight-year-old man, that he was sensationed so. Externally, he functioned effectively, lawyering at pitch, with energy to burn and both feet on the ground (yet all the time, at all moments, feeling—*secret*).

He spent one evening with Geoff, sounding out Geoff's thoughts about a new case that had come his way the previous week. The case involved a malpractice claim against a famous psychiatric hospital. At issue was the hospital's sloppy care of a prominent scientist (an astrophysicist) who had entered the hospital as a patient for treatment of a depression so profound he had twice attempted suicide. When the scientist had been admitted to the hospital, it was understood that he would be under constant surveillance: under what the hospital's presiding chief had called "an around-the-clock suicide watch." But the hospital's doctors and nurses had been fatally lax: ten days after the scientist entered the named hospital, he was found dead in his room: by means of the sturdy laces taken from the two pairs of shoes he had brought with him to the hospital, he had hung himself. It was the scientist's widow, left with two young children to rear and educate, who wished to file against the hospital a suit for wrongful death. . . . When

Morgan finished summing up the facts of the case, Geoff's first words were: "*Lord,* what a tragedy." Then: "If you take it on, Morgie, and if it goes to trial, it'll make news. Big news. More legal fame for you, boy. . . . And you were the guy who once upon a time was going to practice rural law in a quiet county-seat town in Ohio. Remember?"

"Vaguely." Morgan laughed.

"You *are* going to take the case, aren't you?"

"Yes I am—going to—take the case."

. . . That was the week, too, when the severe black marble mantel was removed from the living room and the Leigh mantel installed in its place. The task took two men three days to accomplish. He arrived home from the office on Wednesday evening and was greeted by Elsa: "*Mister* Shurtliff, they have finished! Go see!" He didn't even put down his briefcase. He strode ahead of her, hurrying to the mantel existentially myriad of fern and flowers and ivy and memory all entwined, seen not through tears, but boldly, for what it was: *connection.* And beautiful. Beautiful.

. . . On Friday he received from Miss Sly a letter in response to his October 19 note to her.

> *My dear Mr. Shurtliff,*
>
> *It's lovely to anticipate being with you in mid-November.*
> *I've made several sketches of Hannah, one of which I'm quite proud of. But with the hope of amusing you, I'll show ALL of the drawings to you.*
> *I've been concerned about our meeting at the airport. I think I must have seemed to you quite addle-brained. Please put down my admitted confusion to the surprise of seeing you in such a restless, unsociable milieu. I've been spoiled by the quiet, ever pleasant circumstances of our accustomed meetings, such as the one I look forward to in November. Interim blessings to you.*
>
> *As ever,*
> *Zenobia Sly*

Between them, Sylvia's name remained conspicuously unwritten.

✍

Saturday evening: October 31

"Sylvia—"

"Hello, Morgan." And, "Good evening," this latter greeting to Elsa.

For Elsa was there too. It would not have occurred to Elsa to be otherwise than in the front hall when a guest arrived, to show herself ready to attend upon the guest. To suggest that she spare herself the effort of this self-imposed "duty" would have offended her.

He introduced them, Elsa, to Miss Phelps, and, true to the old adage that a good master is the slave of a good servant, he did what Elsa would have him do: he handed her Miss Phelps's coat. She took it, hung in the hall closet, then dismissed herself and returned to the kitchen. End of that ritual.

Now they were alone—though briefly, for Hannah came meowing down the hall. "A cat!" Sylvia exclaimed, stooping to pet. "What a gorgeous little creature."

"Hannah," he informed.

"May I hold you, Hannah?"

"You can try," he spoke for Hannah.

Hannah then, belly-up in Sylvia's arms. "How old is she?"

"Five months, give or take a bit. We're not sure."

"Where did you get her?"

"That's a story—"

"I want to hear it."

"In a minute," he smiled. "Come." He touched her elbow and guided her toward the library.

. . . "A *real* library," she said. "How fine!"

He mixed her prescribed drink: bourbon on ice with a bit of soda. He had Scotch, neat. They sat down opposite each other, the space of a small table between them. Hannah had wriggled out of Sylvia's arms and was acting cat: idling about, rubbing against chair legs, being snobbish, ignoring the humans.

Sylvia's dress was a mossy shade of green that influenced the color of her eyes, made them more gray than blue, and in the white field of her gaze, more immense. She was looking at him in a pending way, waiting, he supposed, to hear Hannah's story. But he couldn't seem to organize his thoughts, there seemed suddenly so much to say—Hannah only a fractional part of it.

Perhaps she interpreted his silence as a sign that she should be the first to speak, for she did, then, and definitely: "I hope you remember my telling you that at our next meeting, I'd ply *you* with questions—"

"I have some left-over ones to put to you," he countered.

"We might be up all night, asking and answering."

"It's possible."

"Let's begin again," she said. "Where did you get Hannah?"

Which, for him, meant beginning with Julia and Julia's friend, Bruce Wilson: of how Julia and Bruce found Hannah last July while they were walking in Central Park; of their hearing a kitten's pathetic cries and their tracing the sound to a set of rocks—the small cave where Hannah was cowering—and of Bruce's nervy act of reaching into the cave and bringing Hannah out, and of Julia's later words: 'When Bruce handed her to me, when I held her, she didn't move, didn't meow again—only *sighed*.' He stopped; smiled: "The rest is obvious."

"A story with a happy ending," Sylvia said. "One thing leads to another, in this instance Hannah to your daughter Julia. I wondered if your daughters, Julia and—"

"Caroline," he reminded.

"—if they would be here tonight."

"Ah," he breathed, freshly conscious of their ignorance about most every aspect of one another's lives, but eager to fill the gaps, wanting to, to bring her closer: "They're away at college, in their junior year at Bryn Mawr. They're not the adolescent girls you met at Carnegie Hall four years ago."

"Four years ago." She put her hand to her forehead. "I hadn't dated that meeting as being that long ago." And: "What tremendous changes for them, for you, since then."

He wondered if these last words were an antenna reference to Maud; to Maud's death. But what he said was: "Tremendous changes for you too . . . yet here we are."

"Here indeed. 'Blow, bugle, blow, set the wild echoes flying.'" Her voice was soft. And, after a moment: "Before we go any further, I've a sort of confession to make to you. It's to do with your surname."

"My surname—"

"Yes. I got to thinking this past week about the geographical oddity of re-meeting you in Cleveland. And then I recalled your saying that you have cousins living in Cincinnati. And then, late but logically, it dawned on me that you're not just any garden variety of Shurtliff, but one of *them*—an Ohio Shurtliff, and—"

"God, is that all?"

"Stop laughing. Hear me out. . . . The basis of my confession is a strong memory of hearing my father talk about a Shurtliff with whom he worked. Oscar Shurtliff—"

"Old Oscar! The banker," he interrupted. "Did your father think well of him?"

She smiled. "So well that whenever he said Oscar Shurtliff's name, it was with the same praise-be, doxology voice he'd say Glore Forgan. To my father, Glore Forgan was a mighty name because it was the investment firm he was associated with." Her smile deepened: "Personally, I've always thought Glore Forgan sounded like a name Grimm might have dreamt up for a fairy-story about a fast-eyed Norwegian troll."

She made him laugh. "*Two* fast-eyed Norwegian trolls, as I'm sure you know. J. Russel Forgan and Charles Glore. A pair of naturals. *Big* trolls in the money world. But those two aside, I have to tell you it gives me great pleasure to think that your father and one of my relatives were friends."

"In the dim past," she mused again in that soft voice. "Anyhow, Morgan, that's my confession—that I finally located you in the firmament of Ohio Shurtliffs."

His laughter came fresh. "In the Ohio Shurtliff clan—it's so large—there are some of our number who are awfully earthbound."

She feigned a nonsense grandeur: "Be assured, sir, that in my view, you are among the elevated Ohio Shurtliffs."

"Ah, ma'am: those are kind words."

"But now, Morgan, as I've told you about my parents, tell me about yours. Are they still among the living?"

"My father's marvelously extant. My mother died when I was twelve."

"Twelve's a terrible age to be half-orphaned. A nowhere time of life." Then: "Do you have brothers? Sisters?"

"No. Do you?"

"No."

He got up and busied himself replenishing their drinks, and while he was standing, removed from a nearby bookshelf a framed photograph. She reached for it. "I'm no good with a camera, but this will give you a hint of Caroline and Julia as they look now."

In the snapshot, they were sitting, sunstruck, on the trunk of a tree that had fallen at the base of a waterfall, Julia in profile staring at the cascading water, Caroline alert and poised, posing for the focused camera. He had taken the picture last summer on one of their week-end picnics in the Hudson Valley. Sylvia looked hard at the picture. "They *are* beautiful. The one facing the camera—"

"That's Caroline."

"—comes across as particularly vivid. Is Julia shy?"

"In a sense, yes. She's an observer. Caroline's a brilliant participant. . . . But here: I'd like you to see this picture too."

Again, she held out her hand to receive the second photograph, and after a first fast look, spontaneously said: "What an elegant guy." And after a longer look, amended: "Elegant *man.* And how you do resemble him. Is he your father?"

"Yes. And thank you. I'll take as a compliment any resemblance to him you'll grant me."

"Is it a recent picture of him?"

"Yes."

"What does he do? His profession, I mean."

To which question, he gave a long-way-around answer, starting with Ansel Shurtliff's temperament, his serene, quiet nature, and from there went on to say that he was an avid reader of history and a collector of old books storied of the eternal plights and losses and ambitions and achievements of long-deceased people whose lives are prophesies of everybody's life of whatever era—that while he astutely performed all his responsibilities to family and fortune—he would, if asked what he did with his own life, what his major occupation was, he would reply: "I'm an orchardist." And then he described to her his father's acres and acres of apple trees that bloomed in the springtime over the land like a great, fragrant, white, descended cloud, the sight so beatific as to be, in his father's word—"Elysian." He had never talked about his father to anyone in quite this way; he was somewhat surprised at the approach he had taken in answering her question, and he said as much to her now, then further surprised himself by the more personal statement: "Between him and me, there's a remarkable lack of Freudian frenzy— not that the usual father-son psychometrics don't exist in our relation- ship: they do, but not in a way that's ever divided us."

"That's a definition of love," she said.

"I agree."

"Love—as a morality—makes me think of my current preoccupation with the Seven Deadly Sins—Pride Lechery Envy Anger Covetousness Gluttony Sloth." She reeled them off, bang bang bang. "Which do you think is the most destructive?"

He looked at her, delighted. This was what it was like to be with her—these sudden coercive shifts of conversational weather—like being caught in an unseasonable act of Nature: a thunderstorm in January. "God," he smiled, "I've never been asked that question. . . . But Envy, I *think,* though I guess what I really think is that no sin is singular. One sin loads into another, I mean—Envy into Covetousness, Gluttony into Sloth, Pride into Anger—"

"But don't you agree that any single one of the seven sins could wreck a person's life if it becomes an obsession?"

"Put that way, yes. Any obsession is lethal—"

The sound of approaching footsteps interrupted. Elsa, then, standing in the library's doorway: "Dinner, *Mister* Shurtliff."

During dinner, he told her again of his admiration for *A Night at Dsiatzdavo.* He spoke in some detail of the pathos of the story's hero and heroine; and then he spoke of the style of the writing: that, to him, as a reader, the style produced the illusion of being a fine translation of a story authored in the first instance by a Pole or a Russian.

"Oh Morgan, you're this writer's dream of a good reader. I worked so

hard to get that *feel* of translation. You encourage me to believe I succeeded. . . . I'm working on another strange tale, this one laid in China
in the 1870s—"

"Can you tell me about it?"

"I'll tell you a bit."

The "bit": Two crease-faced Chinese women grown old together at the
task of raising silkworms—tending the charcoal fires that evenly heated
the lofts where the silkworms' reed cages were housed—perpetually providing the black caterpillars with fresh green mulberry leaves—the caterpillars spinning their cocoons, spinning, spinning—and after the cocoons
were spun, the two old women harvesting the cocoons, then putting the
cocoons in ovens and perfectly baking them, killing thereby the chrysalis
inside (the smell of freshly baked cocoons a repulsive stench)—all this
torturous labor performed in order to keep one old opium-smoking local
Yuanling merchant, Lin Mung, supplied with the golden thread. Day
after day after day, as the two old women toiled, they recounted to each
other the dreams each had dreamt the previous night: the twist: that as
they daily recounted their previous night's dreams, they spoke word for
word in unison, because the dreams they dreamt were the same dreams:
always exactly the same dreams. "I won't tell you the tale at the heart of
each of their dreams," Sylvia said. "I'll make you wait to read it."

"I'll wait," he said. And: "After we finish dinner, there's something I
want you to see. It bears a relationship to the dedication of the old
Chinese women." He stated what the something was: the living room
mantel. He supposed it was her vivid account of the the old women's
laborings that made him think of the mantel and of how its anonymous
creator must have spent his strength and eyesight carving the mantel's
lilies and leaves. "I won't attempt to describe it. It has to be seen." He
did, though, tell her of the mantel's Leigh origin—the mantel having
been the visual wonder in the library of the house Maud had been raised
in, which house had been built in the 1870s, which date fostered the calculation that the mantel was at least three-quarters of a century old. So
Maud's name had come up, and Sylvia's interposed question—"When
did she die, Morgan?"—and his answer, delivered in a way, in a tone,
final: "Nearly two years ago."

Then they talked of other things.

At dinner's end, Sylvia thanked Elsa—"for the feast." Elsa responded with one of her shy smiles and the royal collective: "We hope you will come often to dinner." Sylvia said, "I will."

In the living room, she stood before the mantel and for some while simply silently looked at it. Then, still silent, she extended her right hand and traced with a finger one of the ivy vines that ran across the mantel's entire width, the stem parent to a profusion of singularly sized, singularly veined leaves. When, where her tracery stopped, where the tendril-vine curled away and was lost to sight (by visual intimation behind the mantel's front), she asserted, "It's alive"—then, with a kind of transfixed melancholy—"but nothing known about its creator, where or when he was born, where or when he died."

His instant reaction to what she'd said was a wish to be in whole included by her in her melancholy. But, search as he quickly did, he could find nothing in her words, nothing in her inflection that might license him to tell her of this wish, which lack of empowerment, coupled with a fear of crowding her (she might flee) prompted him to behave and speak in a way consonant with the ordinary: "Let's honor its creator by having a fire. It'll be the first since the mantel's installation in this room—an inauguration of sorts."

She stood by as he displaced the fire-screen and opened the chimney flue (slight shower of soot) and applied a lit match to rolled-up wads of newspaper that were nested beneath thin splits of pine kindling. Licks of flame then as the kindling took, igniting in turn the logs that bridged the andirons. Against the spray of sparks, he returned the fire-screen to its guarding place. "I must wash," he said, looking at his soot-soiled hand. "Shall I show you—so you'll know?" Together, they went into the front hall and from there down the bedroom hall: "To Julia's room," he said. "It's a more interesting room than the guest room." He turned on the room's overhead light and opened the bathroom door; then he left her and continued down the hall to his own room.

When she rejoined him in the living room, she said: "I couldn't resist looking in Julia's bookcase. I assume the books are hers—"

"They are."

"She's a highly developed reader. James and Faulkner and Turgenev and and and . . . all of Willa Cather's novels."

He decided to tell her: "Julia wants to be a writer."

"Besides wanting to be, do you know if she *aches* to be?"

"I'm afraid so," he smiled. "I think she has the necessary stamina."

"May the gods bless and keep her."

"If you don't mind, I'd like to send her a copy of *A Night at Dsiatzdavo*."

"Mind? I'm proud you want to."

She declined his offer of an after-dinner drink. He poured a brandy for himself. They sat close enough to the fire to receive its cheer but removed enough from its blaze to not be overly warmed. Hannah deigned to lie in Sylvia's lap and to purr, and from slit-eyes to closed eyes, to finally sleep. "Lovely to be before a fire with a contented cat on one's lap." She told of Tillie, her childhood cat. "Tillie was six years old when I was born; I was eleven when she died. Her death was my introduction to finality. We got another cat—Vera. Vera was sweet, and she lived a long time, but it's Tillie I really remember." He said it was a new experience for him, having a cat as a pet. Dogs had always been his animal companions. Dogs. The last dog, Ralph. He described Ralph, which memory led to a description of Ralph's burial place in the dog cemetery of the recently relinquished Hatherton house. . . . Sitting autobiographically there, watching the logs burn to embers, they talked on, asking and answering, filling the gaps. No great revelations, but finding out, little by little. And there were some fine silences too, silences that felt natural and open, the last one, late in the evening—the expression on her face again so meditative—he broke with the intimate question: "What are you thinking about?"

She looked from the fire at him and met not so much his gaze, but the reach of its attitude. She must have felt its reach—she so conveyed that she had, first by a suddenness of flushed cheeks, next by a proud show of greater calm, as if she had been challenged and wouldn't expose herself as a coward. She did though, then, hesitate, but in a mitigating way which bolstered his masculine intuition that he'd gained an edge, a certain advantage. Quickly, not to lose it, he repeated his question, but this time in the more ardent, more accusing past tense: "What *were* you thinking about?"

"Chance," she answered, hard. "Specifically—what Joseph Conrad said about the strange originality of the way Chance works."

"And?" he forced.

"And about us. About our re-meeting at the Cleveland airport."

Over these words, for the first time he touched her: bent forward and cupped her chin in his hand and ran his thumb over her cheek, and put a period on her spoken name. "Sylvia."

She said: "We won't rush."

"No. I promise we won't rush. I'll leave it to you to set the pace."

That ticking clock . . . She looked from his face to the clock's face. "It's after eleven. I've got to go, Morgan. You should know about me that I'm a compulsive early riser. I'm not happy with myself if I'm not bathed and breakfasted and at work by eight A.M. at the latest."

"When is the best time to call you?"

"Noon. Or late afternoon. Those are probably the best times for you too."

"Will you break your work routine and go with me a week from tomorrow—Sunday—to the country? We could leave around one; that would give you the morning to work. Up near Garrison, on the Hudson River—you like big rivers—there's an excellent inn. Very good food. We could take a mountain walk, then have an early evening dinner. I'd have you back by nine. Will you?"

"That's a very enticing invitation—"

"So?"

"Yes," she said.

"Now I'll take you home."

"You needn't. Just put me in a cab."

"I won't just put you in a cab. I'll take you home."

"I won't fight."

"Good. Let's go."

In the cab, pledged not to rush, they sat apart. Her calm was now of a kind august, like a fate. He was calm too—because of his belief in her: that now she understood the *aboutness* of his seriousness: that its syntax was love.

He left her at her building's door.

"Good night, Morgan."

"Good night, Sylvia."

❧

The interim week passed. He worked hard and well.

Sidney and Linda and Lawrence and Pamela came for dinner Tuesday night.

Wednesday evening, Julia and Caroline called from Bryn Mawr. Caroline was a verbal postcard. There was a ceiling leak in her dormitory room. She'd been assigned another room while the culprit pipe was being fixed and the ceiling replastered. An "angelic" Haverford guy had helped her move all her stuff to the second room. Must go now. Masses of reading to do. Good-bye. . . . "Everything's normal with me, Morgan," Julia laughed. She asked how he was, and Elsa and Hannah. She said she was looking forward to the long up-coming Thanksgiving weekend. "May I invite Bruce for Thanksgiving dinner, Morgan?" "Of course, of course. Bruce is always welcome." Then she too signed off: "Good night, Morgan. A big hug to you." "Good night, dear Julia."

He telephoned Letitia and Lewis Grant to confirm that he would arrive in Cleveland the following Monday. Letitia, imperious as usual, informed him: "Your father's coming for dinner on Monday, Morgan. He'll spend the night, so we'll have a leisurely evening with him."

"Perfect," he said.

Early Wednesday morning, he called Miss Sly at her office. "It's telepathy, Mr. Shurtliff. I was just thinking to telephone you this very minute." He posed his question: "May we meet for lunch next Tuesday at twelve-thirty at our usual restaurant?" She answered at once: "Yes. I'm eager to see you. . . . Good-bye for now, Mr. Shurtliff." No politesse of brief chit-chat. He figured he had caught her at a busy moment.

He spent Friday evening with Geoff and Alan.

On Saturday he sent a bouquet of yellow freesia to Sylvia. *Tomorrow, at one o'clock sharp. M.* That was the message he wrote on the card that accompanied the blooms.

ᐱᢒ

This was tomorrow, Sunday, November 8; a nippy but brilliantly sunny day, ideal for an outing in the country.

"Hello, Morgan. Thank you for the beautiful flowers."

"Hello, Sylvia." Her gray coat was collared and cuffed with Astrakhan fur. And she was shod in a pair of knee-high leather boots. "You look like a Russian countess." And she carried a small, suede tote bag. "What's in the bag?"

"Essentials," she said. "A hairbrush and comb, a pencil, a notebook, and a pair of proper shoes to wear at dinner."

Out of the city, driving fast, headed north to the Hudson Highlands, he told her where they were going to walk. "Opposite West Point," he said, "on a remnant of the Sloan estate that includes a mountain called the South Redoubt. I represent one of the Sloan family heirs and have an anytime permission to hike the land." (Always, since, whenever he thinks about the walk they took and about the dinner they ate at the inn, his thoughts come to rest on Sylvia's conclusive words spoken as they drove back to the city: "This has been our day of unreckonable discovery.")

They scrambled up the steep earth-ramp of an old bridle path to a high narrow ridge of scrubby flatland very near the top of the South Redoubt mountain. Having achieved the ridge, they could go no further: the barrier of a cliff loomed in front of them. Panting a bit, they turned full around and gazed over the great scene before them. Color was the blue sky and the greens of conifers: pine and spruce and fir. The rest of the vast landscape—the wintry leafless forests and solemn fields and shallow marshes—looked unpainted. Far below, bedded in the valley, the Hudson River flowed, mighty, gleaming in the sun. On its distant opposite shore, West Point's military buildings were small. A hawk soared into view. By such a bird, the ancient Greeks were awed, Sylvia said, breaking the silence, her eyes on the hawk. To sight a raptor in flight was believed fortunate: an omen of good things to come for the beholder. Could one wish on the hawk the same way one wishes on a new moon? The hawk flew lower, beneath them, searching the valley's fields for prey. Oh, to be able to do that! To soar in the welkin and then descend and halt in the air and hover as the hawk was hovering now, its wings extended, motionless, its tail feathers a russet fan in the sunlight (how long could it remain perched like that in the air?), until it did then move its wings in rapid spurts, up and down, up and down, gaining speed, attaining altitude, soaring again above them. "Wish on it."

It was as they retraced their steps on the old bridle path, back down the mountain's long slope, that he told her: "I'm going to Cleveland tomorrow."

"When will you be back?"

"On Thursday."

"Will you see Zee while you're there?"

He smiled. "*Your* Zee; *my* Miss Sly," he said. "And yes, I'm going to see her. It's all arranged. We're meeting for lunch on Tuesday. I'd like your permission to tell her about us—"

"That we've become friends, you mean," she cut in. "But you don't need my permission. I've already told her. You make me wonder if I should have asked *your* permission—"

"No, no. I'm boundlessly glad you told her. I'm only surprised she didn't mention to me that you had. . . . When did you tell her?"

"A week ago today. The day after I had dinner at your house." She stopped walking and turned to him. "What I need to know is what it is between you and Zee that makes me feel left out. *What is it?*"

How could he, then, have laughed? Yet he did, helplessly, over the magnitude of her question, laugh! "Well may you ask!" Laughing, standing there, tall, he attempted, by means of flamboyance, to explain his laughter. "Our relationship—Zenobia Sly's and mine—is so complex, so strange, so eccentrically marvelous, so thoroughly improbable, so peculiarly divine—"

"I'm *dying* of curiosity," she flicked, snake-tongue-like—

The thing is: she was laughing too—because of the low, burlesque notion that had sprung tacitly between *them* that between him and Miss Sly there could be—of all conceivable possibilities—a carnal connection!—the very idea!—causing their laughter, causing them as they stood there laughing and looking at each other to suddenly stop laughing and to step toward each other and with a Genesis velocity, to bodily collide and to kiss. To go on kissing. And then to separate, and to again stand apart, and in each other's eyes, to be astonished—

"I hadn't planned to fall in love," she said. "I'm thirty-eight years old," she said. "I liked my life as it was—"

—in his arms again, close, not kissing, close to tears.

"I promised you. I'll leave it to you to set the pace," he said, holding her. "All I ask is that you believe in me as I believe in you." And then, crazily practical: "We have to keep moving. The sun will be behind the mountain in a few minutes. We'll lose the light."

Now they walked down the steep slope hand in hand, arm in arm, thinking, frowning, shining, being still astonished, talking in spurts— the way the hawk had employed its wings after it broke the long suspense of its hover—talking in a vocabulary that flew. Afterwards, he could never remember the sequence of what they said, only its inspiration, and the rapidity of the exchange, and the overlapping. He would, however, never forget how she dazzled him as, in a voice that sounded increasingly of wonder, she talked about the three Greek sister-Fates who preside over everyone's life, over every single individual life—from birth to death: Clotho, distaff in hand, present at the moment one takes one's first breath outside the womb; Lachesis, at her spindle, spinning the designate thread of every event and action that will run through the tapestry of each (individual) life; and Atropos, the eldest of the three sister-Fates, standing by, holding the shears with which she will cut the thread of life. "The Fates don't consult the Fated; the Fates only *decide*," (she said). So have the Fates decided about us? (he asked). Yes, though we don't know their decision, and that we *don't* know it is what creates our unsolvable human riddle: What will our penalty be if we buck Fate's unknown-to-us decision? So in our ignorance, what do we do? (he asked). Oh, the only thing we *can* do: *believe* in each other, just as you said.

"You make me sublimely happy," he said.

"That could be a preparation for sublime sadness," she said.

"Isn't that—at its heart—what happiness is, sublime sadness?"

"Yes," she said: "Kiss me."

They were back in the clearing where they'd left the car, and just in time, for right there at the end they could barely see, darkness had so quickly descended. When he switched on the car's headlights she laughed and lampooned: "How far these little Mercedes candles throw their beams!" And then: "How long will it take to get to the inn?"

"Fifteen minutes or so."

"After we get there, and after I've combed my hair and changed into my proper shoes, is when you'll tell me about you and Zee," she stated.

"It's a saga. I'll do my best to compress it."

The inn diverted. It dated back to 1704. It had been built as the manor house of a New Netherlands Dutchman of the patroon aristocracy. Stone was what it was made of: fieldstone that had been back-breakingly gathered and put into primitive wheel-barrows and taken to the building site on a hill overlooking the Hudson, the stones then sized and chiseled and finally, one by one, mortared into place. The vertical beams and criss-crossed rafters that supported its roof were bark-stripped trunks and squared-off limbs of axed-down oak trees. A large, romantically rendered oil portrait of the (imagined) patroon hung on the wall just inside the inn's front door. Pictured was a big-chested, florid-faced, silver-buckled man wearing knee-breeches and a warm coat and a tri-corn hat—*The Patroon*—astride a horse, comfortable in the saddle—surrounded by a horde of tattered, driven, worsened men busy, back there in the dawn days of the eighteenth century, busy at building the house. Now, these 250-plus years later, the patroon's house was owned by a Swiss restaurateur who employed the *cordon bleu* chef who produced the fine food that gave the inn its starred reputation.

Morgan had requested a quiet table; the head-waiter had complied by reserving the retreat of a small, softly lighted room. They were the only people in it. They had studied the menu and ordered their food. The waiter had gone away to the kitchen. Sylvia said: "Now, Morgan: about you and Zee. Tell me first how long you've known her."

"Nearly twenty years."

"That long!"

"Maud and I met her over the matter of adopting a child. We had applied to Tilden-Herne for a boy. Thanks to Miss Sly's golden persuasion, we ended up with Julia and Caroline. We—"

Her eyes had widened. "They're *adopted*?" she exclaimed: "Julia and Caroline, *adopted*? I didn't know! It never occurred to me."

"There's no reason why it should have," he said. It's not something—"

She stopped him. "Please, Morgan, I must know: what's their birthdate?"

"April twenty-seventh, 1940."

She flung her hands across the table and gripped his and clung to them as if she were, life or death, *in* his hands: "Oh Morgan! If I am right, then it's all come full-circle home."

The look on her face, the mire of her sorrow, her hold on his hands, reversed their positions: he was the one now in *her* hands: "For God's sake, help me, Sylvia. How have I hurt you?"

She was immediate: "It's not *you*. Or me. It's what happened. And the ramifications. I might lose you."

"I'm not losable." But he was, to the point of vulgarity, desperate. "I don't give a fiddler's fuck about what the hell *happened*. I'm not losable. And stop crying. I can't bear to see you cry. Just tell me."

She blinked. She was fast and brilliantly intelligent about where she knifed in: "When I told you I have no brothers or sisters, it was a part lie. I never had a brother, but I did have a half-sister, Katherine, my father's daughter by his first wife. And if I am right in what I think—if everything I think is proved to fit—then Julia and Caroline are Katherine's blood children."

Now he saw it. Miss Sly's conduct at the Cleveland airport had prepared him for the appearance of *something*, something that had turned out to be *this*: the past *being*, as it was right now—being *seen*: having come (in Sylvia's words) "full-circle home."

"Morgan—"

He kissed her hands. He said for the third time: "I'm not losable." Then, quelling all he was thinking, all he was feeling, he said: "Listen, my love, we're going to have dinner and we're going to be peaceful and you're going to fill in all the blanks for me and we won't weep—either of us—and my promise will still pertain: I'll leave it to you to set the pace."

So what had begun as a history of his and Miss Sly's relationship became then a different history, Sylvia's to tell: the history of Julia and Caroline's conception.

"I'll tell you the hardest part first," Sylvia said. "Once I've done that, I'll be all right."

Katherine Phelps, dead at age twenty-four. Bled to death after giving birth to twin girls on April 27, 1940. That was the hardest part to say.

Now go further back—to 1915—the year Edgar Phelps's first wife died, leaving him at age twenty-six a widower: father of three-month-old Katherine. Next, go forward—to 1920—the year Edgar Phelps married Sylvia's mother; and forward further by eleven months, to Sylvia's birth on March 31, 1921. An age difference of five years between Katherine and Sylvia. For Katherine, doted on singly until Sylvia was born, Sylvia was no joy. Katherine's "resentment" of Sylvia had never "fully" been resolved. "Resentment," though, too malignant a word: erase it: try vexation or choler instead—or any other more forgiving, more childishly active word. Because the vexation or choler—call it what you will—abated when Katherine went off to college, and by the time, early in 1939, when Katherine was twenty-three and Sylvia eighteen—when Katherine met and became engaged to Richard Hamilton—she and Sylvia, older now, were: "Almost close: compatible enough to be able to laugh together." (It was at this point that the waiter returned, bearing on a tray their dinner's first course. They let go of each other's hands and picked up their soup spoons. "Odd, isn't it, to be presented with lobster bisque at the same time I'm telling you all this," Sylvia said. More odd, hunger itself, that they welcomed the food. "Go on," he said.) The date of Katherine and Richard's wedding was set for Saturday, August 5, 1939. The invitations had long been mailed. It was to be a large wedding, in its genteel way, elaborate. Sylvia was to be Katherine's maid of honor. There was a spate of festive pre-nuptial parties. Two nights before the wedding, driving home alone at a late hour, Richard was killed, his car—found—crushed at the bottom of a ravine. There were awful scourings of skid marks on the road. Surmise was that he'd swerved to avoid hitting an animal, a fox or a racoon, maybe a deer. . . . On the sea of her grief, for a terrible long while, Katherine floated, seemingly lifeless, on her back, staring up at the sky. No one could reach her. Everyone tried. Give her time, they said. In time, she will heal. How could they, knowing Katherine, have thought so? It was Sylvia's mother, Katherine's step-mother, who, four months later, in mid-December, "guessed" that Katherine was pregnant. And it was to Sylvia, then—at Christmastime—Katherine confided that she'd known for the past four months she was pregnant and had conspired with herself to keep it secret until it was—"too late for anything to be done." She would have Richard's baby. . . . Katherine's father, Sylvia's father—a conventional, Methodist man—viewed his daughter's pregnancy as a blemish on his image of himself. By Edgar Phelps's decree, Katherine would be sent away, be sent out of sight. He took the position that by the time the baby was due to be born, Katherine would see the sense of putting the baby up for adoption. His wife's oldest, dearest friend—his friend too— was Zenobia Sly. Zee (he said) could be counted on to save the situation. And so it was to Zee Katherine was sent: under Zee's loving care, in Zee's home, that Katherine spent the remainder of her pregnancy's term. . . . "What my father never knew," Sylvia said, "is that—against him—Zee and my mother plotted with Katherine that Katherine would keep the baby." . . . How had it been possible that the Cleveland obstetrician hadn't known—until that dire hour Katherine went into labor— that she was carrying two babies; twins? Katherine hemorrhaged. Within a few minutes of the second baby's birth, Katherine was dead. . . . Sylvia was nineteen, away at college in her freshman year at Radcliffe. From her mother, by telephone, she learned the two-fold tidings of Katherine's death and the twins' existence. "In a daze," she had gone home for Katherine's funeral. Of the long overnight train trip, she retained "only the mistiest memory." On the day after the funeral, her father—empowered to do so by the fact of his being Katherine's closest living relation—signed the legal document in accordance with which the infant twins, under the sponsorship of the Tilden-Herne Agency, were "placed" for adoption. The evening of the same day, Sylvia was present in the room—"when Zee swore to my father and my mother that she would undertake to find for the twins the best possible parents. 'I will risk playing God; *I* will choose who their parents will be,' Zee vowed." Sylvia remembered that one of the room's windows was open, letting in and making audible the first shrill springtime pipings of tree toads. "I remember thinking how usual the tree toads' pipings sounded to me—by some supreme law of continuance, how purely *usual*." And oh, the strangeness of it: how the pipings had nearly drowned out the voices of Sylvia's father and mother and Zee, who, from their human throats, strummed the fate of the five-day-old twins.

It became his turn, then, to speak: to tell Sylvia that head-to-toe, mind, heart, and gut, he and Maud had known they'd been chosen; been, by Miss Sly, *picked*. And to further say that the minute the twins were in Maud's and his hands, by the court's edict forever in Maud's and his keeping, all connection with Tilden-Herne, hence with Miss Sly, would—under ordinary circumstances—have been severed. Miss Sly had herself emphasized the efficacy of such disconnection—"For the reason of its psychological soundness." And certainly Maud had not only desired disconnection but had seemed, psychologically *and* emotionally, to absolutely require it. And so, under ordinary circumstances, and for all time, all sides would have honored such disconnection. *But for the war*. The war had played havoc with intention. "The altering war," Morgan said. Its dislocation, its loneliness, its terror. But for the war, he would never have written a first letter to Miss Sly. But for the war, Miss Sly would never have answered that first letter, nor permitted herself to write all those subsequent peculiarly inspiriting letters that had reached him in distant places now almost mythically remembered; letters he had read and re-read, in one of which was that Morphean incantation he had memorized and put himself to sleep by on enemy-infested seas whose exchanging waters lapped against the shores of the earth's seven continents—"One good hen, two ducks, three cackling geese, four plump partridges, five . . ." And when at last, at last the war ended and he came home and resumed a normal life—"to the degree there is such a thing"—he had called Miss Sly, called her with the trepidant expectation of being censored for the impulse, or of being told by her that, due to the war's end, further contact between them would not be possible. But no! She "welcomed" his call—by which word she acknowledged that the bond forged by those letters, was not to be cut. . . . Maud, though, protested the bond. He had tried to explain it. An impasse. He and Maud made a pact: between themselves, they would never speak of Miss Sly. . . . "Beginning then, Miss Sly became my secret life. . . . Even after that night at Carnegie Hall when we bumped as a family into Miss Sly, bumped into you—*Sylvia*—even after that, Maud and I never spoke of her." He stopped talking—suddenly impressed by the morality of the flashed thought that all of what, often stumbling, he had just told Sylvia, and all of what, often stumbling, Sylvia had told him—*belonged* to the past: was the past's rightful property: not theirs to rake over. . . . He said as much, then, to Sylvia.

She nodded, clear-browed, and affirmed: "That's my belief too, Morgan; and I want you to know I'll always be glad you said it first." She glanced down at their empty dessert plates, then back up at his face, into his eyes, and almost smiling, wondrously declared: "So here we're left! And look at us! At what a pair of gluttons we are! We've eaten everything that was set before us, everything, like well-brought-up children admonished by a nurse to think of the starving Armenians." And next, and quickly, with her near-smile vanished: "But before we go on from wherever it is we've been left, I must ask you: Is there such a recognized thing as a half-aunt? And if there is such a thing, isn't that what I am to your daughters?"

As a trust-and-estates lawyer, her questions were right up his alley. "Yes, there is such a recognized thing, and yes, perforce of agnate blood, that's what you are to Julia and Caroline: a half-aunt. And to quote my great mentor, Roger Chandler, 'Such are the scrambled eggs of family trees.'"

Her laugher came like the chimes of a striking clock. Its capacity updated her, updated him: placed them together in the present tense—

Consequence is what being alive is all about.

I love you—

The waiter appeared. Would they have coffee? Yes? No. Just the check, please.

Out of the inn, in the cold night (stars in the sky), they walked the short distance to the parking lot. In the car, away from anyone's sight, they kissed, this time erotically. Then he turned on the car's engine and they set off on the drive back to the city.

They agreed: "Not tonight."

"I'll call you on Thursday, the minute the plane lands."

"Be safe," she said.

They would meet on Friday evening, they said. He would decide where they would have dinner. And after dinner—

"*Then,*" she said.

He left her at her building's front door. From there, he drove to the garage, and from the garage walked home. Not out-loud singing. But singing, striding along in step with the pace she had, *now,* so wonderfully set.

⋄

Monday, November 9, 1959

Fasten seat belt. No smoking. Crab onto the runway. Wait. Rev the engines. Move forward. Accelerate. Faster, faster. LIFT. Ascend. Ascend.

Aloft, and the plane leveled off, he took a yellow pad out of his briefcase and, on behalf of his client, Patricia Forbes, began to draft the complaint that charged the Graham-Sorensen hospital with negligently permitting the suicide of her husband, the astrophysicist Dwight Forbes. In time, this lawsuit would become known as "the Forbes case," or, in court parlance, *Forbes* v. *the Graham-Sorensen Psychiatric Clinic.*

Work made the trip a fast one. Fasten seat belt. No smoking. Prepare to land. He put the pages of the drafted complaint back in his briefcase. Descend. Lake Erie below. Circle. Swing inland. Descend, descend. NOW. Touchdown. ("Be safe," Sylvia had said.)

A small crowd was clumped together at the terminal's entry-gate. His eyes lit on a wide-brimmed, flat-topped hat banded round by the feathers of a murdered game-bird. The hat's wearer stepped forward.

"Pa! What a surprise!"

"Me, or the hat?" Ansel Shurtliff laughed.

"Both. In equal measure."

"Letitia told me what time your plane was due in, and meeting you seemed a good way to have a bit of time alone with you. I worried you wouldn't see me—"

"With that hat, Pa, you're not to be missed. Where the hell did you get it?"

"A fright, isn't it? Fred Bingley brought it to me from Australia. I figured I'd wear it this one time. It did the trick: it caught your eye."

"It's truly—"

Ansel Shurtliff swept the hat from off his head. "Take it," he said. "I'd love you to have it. Among your vast acquaintance there must be someone you can give it to. Now that I think of it, I bet Caroline would appreciate it."

"Probably." Morgan laughed. "Probably Callie would."

"I'll get her a kangaroo to go with it." Banter. From banter to a quick scrutiny of his son's face, Ansel Shurtliff said: "You look in great form, son. *Happy.*"

"I *am* happy, Pa. Things are going well."

They walked briskly from the terminal to the parking lot. There, polished, shining in a last ray of late-afternoon sunlight was what Ansel Shurtliff called "my chariot" (i.e., his Jaguar). "Off we go." And fast. Through traffic, Ansel Shurtliff maneuvered his chariot in a masterful way. They sped along, talking about family and friends and current affairs—Cuba, gone Communist under Fidel Castro; Alaska and Hawaii becoming the forty-ninth and fiftieth states—

"Here we are."

Under the portico of the Grants' house, the chariot rolled to a stop.

৵

Tuesday, November 10, 1959

KISSEL, CHANDLER, SHURTLIFF & COLT

The brass name-plate never shone brighter to him than it did today.

He spent the morning with George Colt. Along with a crop of other firm matters, they discussed the legal complexities of the Forbes case.

"You have that hell-bent look you get on your face when you're on a high, Morgan."

"Oh?" (Thinking of Sylvia.)

"Well, it's pretty damn exciting, your Forbes case—"

Morgan laughed. "Yes," he said. "It's damn exciting."

❧

He opened the restaurant's door. "Miss Sly!"

This was the first time she had ever arrived at the restaurant in advance of him. It wasn't that he was late (it was only 12:15), but that she was even earlier—waiting for him, looking (he thought) burdened, standing there indoors in a coat too heavy for today's weather, that large black purse dangling floorward from its gripped strap. "Mr. Shurtliff." His hat removed, held in his right hand, encumbered, they embraced, rapidly and awkwardly. "Let me take your coat," he said. "I'll check it with mine."

He had reserved their usual alcove table. They decided to have a drink. Sherry on ice; two. "I'm not very hungry," she announced. "A plain omelet and salad will do for me." He echoed: "And for me." He said to the waiter: "Give us a few minutes to have our sherry, Vincent. I'll signal you when we're ready to eat."

In feel of relation to her, it was as if a field separated them.

She hung her purse over the back of her chair, checked with a hand-touch the eternal amber comb that secured the dome of her done-up hair, arranged around her shoulders the triangle of a paisley scarf. Fussing; not looking at him. Fussing, the way a committee-head fusses just prior to wielding the gavel and calling an assemblage to order. Her hands finally came to rest on the table. "There's a great deal we must talk about," she said at last.

(*Ah:* an agenda.) As a lawyer, trained not to assume but to listen, he settled into silence.

"I will be direct," she said. And immediately was. "The last thing I ever imagined would happen is that you and Sylvia would meet and become friends. Sylvia has told me you *have* become friends." She paused.

It wasn't quite a question, the way she said it, but he heard it as a probe for him to affirm, even perhaps to enlarge upon. He did not comply, thinking that do so would draw him prematurely in.

Her pause was twice lengthened, first by his retained silence, secondly by Vincent's placing before them their sherries. With Vincent's withdrawal, his silence, maintained, forced her on. "I find myself in the difficult position of needing to intrude myself into the progress of that friendship. You'll see why in a moment. But I must begin by asking you if the fact that your daughters are adopted is a fact known to Sylvia, because if she doesn't *yet* know—if and when she *might* find out, it's possible—because I'm the link—that she'll piece together *about* your daughters, that—"

Over her hesitation, he entered. "She does know they're adopted. As of day before yesterday, she knows."

"And when she found out, did she piece everything together?"

"To the degree I understand your question, yes."

"So now *you* know. How it all came about, I mean. Katherine. Everything. *Everything*—" she repeated.

She seemed preyed upon by—"everything." In some way the word's victim.

He took too long, wondering—

"And now that you know everything, will you go on seeing Sylvia, Mr. Shurtliff?"

He heard her question as an admonition. "Can you give me a reason why I shouldn't?"

"Why, because—it seems to me so obvious—because if you *do* go on seeing her, the possibility of your daughters finding everything out is greatly increased."

"How so?"

"Because as a impulse, the human sentiment to divulge can overcome one's better judgment, and—"

At a sudden boil, he stopped her: "Are you suggesting that I'd ever volunteer to disturb Caroline and Julia with any of this? My God, they've suffered the death of their *real* mother and the idea that I'd ever impose on them the initial death of their birth mother—surely you can't think I'd ever do that, or that it's in Sylvia to do such a thing—" He arrested himself. He'd heard the whip-tone of his voice, and regretted it. "Forgive my ferocity—"

She went white, but she did not slump. "I—I deserve your ferocity. I am grateful for it. It has set me straight. I wonder at myself that I could ever have gone so wrong." There were tears in her eyes. "I was taught never to weep in a public place," she finished.

He couldn't believe the speed of what had happened between them, the ignited way, within seconds of their being together, they had locked horns, and now, gazing at each other, the speed even faster, of reconcilement.

"Drink your sherry," he said. "We've passed our crisis. I'm not even sure what it was about—our crisis."

"Oh I know, *for myself,* what it was about: losing control. After all these years, losing control of everything I thought—*falsely,* I now understand—was up to me solely *to* control: all that I'd put in place after the twins were born: all that I felt responsible for: all those things I feared *not* to control." There were tears streaming down her cheeks, but in her great emotion, she was sturdy. "Thank you for assuring me our crisis has passed."

"Thank you for accepting that it has passed."

If it were a day in August, if they were outdoors lazing under a shade tree, if birds were singing, if—if they weren't here in a restaurant, if they had the longer time, they would have just sat, whole and at peace, maybe yawning, they were, in their deliverance, that exhausted.

She brought them back to where they actually were: In the restaurant, with its restaurant's sounds and busyness, and to Vincent, waiting to tell an aproned cook to begin to stir up their omelets. She it was who fully wakened him. "I've grown quite hungry," she declared.

He signaled Vincent—

With a tug at her paisley scarf, pulling him with her further along, she said: "Now about my sketches of Hannah, Mr. Shurtliff: I'll send a packet of them around to your office tomorrow. There's one my teacher deemed good enough to display for a few days on our classroom bulletin board, and that's the one, due to my inflamed amateur's ego, I've had framed for you."

"I can't wait to have it. To have all the sketches—"

"As you go through them, I do hope you'll see a sequence of improvement." She did, then, smile.

And he, then, smiling too, began to describe to her his father's extraordinary hat.

. . . Outside the restaurant, on the street, they embraced. Just before she walked away, her last words to him were: "Give my love to Sylvia."

❧

Wednesday, November 11, 1959

In the late afternoon, after the partners meeting, in a car borrowed from the Grants, he drove out to Hatherton to see Lillie Ruth and Tessa. He had called them earlier in the day: "I won't be able to stay more than a few minutes, but I'd very much like a glimpse of you."

They'd acquired a male puppy of a kind the AKC had no place for in its books. It was a terrier (of sorts), short-legged and curly-haired and mongrel-smart. It's name? "Charlie," Lillie Ruth laughed. There were sprays of bittersweet in a familiar vase. He had brought some chrysanthemums. Tessa arranged them in another familiar vase. Lillie Ruth gave him (to read) Julia and Caroline's most recently received letter. "Dearest Lillie Ruth and Tessa." Two paragraphs in Julia's legible handwriting; two in Callie's scrawl. At the letter's end, over their signatures: "Hugs." "Hugs." Tessa reported that Doctor Leigh "dropped by every week or so." Lillie Ruth had a new set of dentures. "They fit better than the old ones," she said. He told about the Leigh mantel, installed now in the New York apartment. And yes, he and Julia and Caroline would be coming to Cleveland between Christmas and the New Year, so they'd all be together then. . . . "But now I must go." He stood up; hugged Tessa. "Don't you get up, Lillie Ruth." He bent to her; kissed her. "Morgan," she said. Tessa saw him out.

In the car, he thought how memorable it was bound to be—that coming day when he would introduce Sylvia to Lillie Ruth and Tessa.

❧

Thursday, November 12, 1959

About an hour out from New York, they ran abruptly into fog, as it were through a door. Rain next. Turbulence. Fasten seat belts. Across the aisle there was a boy, age about five, traveling with his mother. The boy reveled in the bumps; he didn't know about danger. His mother was promptly, hugely sick. Morgan rang for the stewardess. She came at once. The seat next to Morgan was empty. "Put him here," he said to the stewardess. A deft transfer of the boy to the empty seat. The stewardess strapped herself in beside the boy's vomiting mother. "What's your name?" he asked the boy. "Cameron. Mom's got an upset stomach." The plane bucked starboard, recentered itself, bucked port. "It's like riding a horse," Morgan said. Cameron said: "It's fun." They leapt a fence. "Wow!" Morgan said. "*That* was the *biggest* bump," Cameron said. Morgan hoped there wouldn't be many more like it. "When will we get to New York?" Cameron asked. "In a little while." He signed to the stewardess to hand him Cameron's coloring-book and crayons. "By the time you finish coloring this picture, we'll probably be there." Three pictures later—lots of cows and sheep and birds and humans vividly crayoned over (far from neatly)—the plane's captain informed: "We're starting our descent." Cameron said he wished he could "see down." "There's nothing to see yet, Cameron." "Well, how much longer before we get there?" "How much of the alphabet do you know?" "All of it." "Tell it to me." "A-B-C-D-R-L-" "Let's start over. We'll say it together." "A-B-C-D-E-F-" Descend, descend. "Can you see New York yet? Mom said there'll be skyscrapers." Bump, bump. "When will we see New York?" "We won't see much of it, but we'll be there soon." Beneath them, suddenly, through the mist, ribbons of road and clustered houses. Descend. "I can see the runway," Morgan smiled at Cameron. Glide. TOUCH-DOWN. "We're here," Morgan said. "Hey, Mom, we're here!" From across the aisle, Cameron's mother waved to her son; waved too to Morgan. . . .

. . . Into the telephone's coin-slot, he inserted a dime and dialed her number. Two rings. "Hello—"

"Sylvia."

"You're safe. I've been worrying about you in this scummy weather. Are you tired? If you aren't, come by. I'll give you a drink."

"I'm on my way."

. . . If they had been younger, at an age when the power of mere sensation can't (won't) be curbed, they wouldn't have waited until tomorrow night. That they *would* wait was implicit in the transcended way they kissed (just inside her apartment door) with an older, informed passion enforced to endure. It was enough, right then, to be again together; to sit quietly for a bit, in each other's arms, on the couch: to anticipate: "Tomorrow night."

"It's nice to know you're not afflicted by triskaidekaphobia—"

"Dobson! What the hell is trisk—how do you spell it?"

"Tris-kai-deka-phobia. It's fear of the number thirteen. Tomorrow's the thirteenth, and a Friday too."

"Don't worry. We'll render both evils harmless."

"Tomorrow night—"

"We'll let Elsa give us an early dinner—"

"Then we'll come back here."

&

When it is combined with love, sex exceeds its own limitations. "Glorious," they said. There seemed no other word.

Between glorious instances, they talked. During one in-between interval, lying close, heads pillowed, faced toward each other, their eyes meeting clear in the light of a turned-on bedside lamp, he said: "We'll be married as soon as possible."

"It will be an eccentric marriage."

"Is there anything you can name, anything that counts as *life*—that isn't eccentric?"

. . . Friday the thirteenth had been superseded by Saturday the fourteenth. They parted at one-thirty A.M. When he was putting on his overcoat, he took up again the theme of marriage. Marriage would be to walk freely on firm ground. Marriage would provide greater space for, and make profounder the "eccentric." He said they should set six months as the limit of their "soon." Julia and Caroline would be home for the long Thanksgiving weekend, less than two weeks away. Sylvia would meet them then. "Six months will be long enough—" Kissing, they let the end of that sentence dangle.

He would be back: "At six this evening." They would go to some quiet place for dinner. Quo Vadis, maybe. Over dinner they would plan how this insanity of parting from each other at night would be made, soon, to cease. Garbed in the thick fabric of his overcoat he held her, silky in a dressing gown.

"I love you."

"I love you."

Outdoors, on the lighted avenue, a thin scattering of winter's first snowflakes were falling. They were large—the snowflakes—and they fell slowly, straight down. And there weren't many of them, so few in fact that you could almost count them as they fell. He reached out and captured one in his hand. It disappeared at once: melted away. Oddly, his lifted hand that had caught the snowflake, brought a taxi to the curb. He decided, quickly, to take the cab. He opened the door, got in, gave his address to the driver; sat back. He was marvelously tired. He was deeply happy. What he had supposed would never again happen to him had, in Sylvia, occurred.

❧

Thanksgiving Day, Thursday, November 26, 1959

He worked in the morning. Julia and Caroline slept late. (They had arrived from Bryn Mawr the evening before. Within half an hour they were unpacked and settled in, all in a way undoubted, as if they hadn't been gone for two and a half months.)

At two o'clock, by Julia's invitation, Bruce Wilson turned up, carrying over his arm in a dry-cleaner's bag the suit he would don later for the Puritan feast. Morgan and Julia and Bruce took a walk in Central Park. Caroline did not join them: she had to wash her hair, she said. At five, Lucy Blackett rang the front doorbell; then Geoff and Alan; then Whitney Aiken (called "Whit"), a lanky, self-confident Haverford senior with restless hands and an obstinate laugh: Caroline's "current."

At six, Elsa announced dinner. Seated in the dining room at the large, oval, candle-lit table: Lucy, at his right; Caroline on his left; between Caroline and Julia, Whit; Bruce at Julia's left; next to Bruce, Geoff; next to Geoff, Alan; next to Alan, Lucy—back to himself: the circle thus completed. Eight in all. (*Sylvia*. He hadn't seen her since Tuesday night. She was dining with friends whom he had not [yet] met. All through dinner he kept thinking of her, kept wondering what color dress she was wearing and how its color was influencing the irises of her eyes). The feast was a jolly, lengthy affair, in Alan's word—"Lucullan." After dinner, Caroline and Whit went off: they had a ten P.M. date with some college pals at a Village jazz place called "The Parrot." ("Be back no later than one, Callie," Morgan told her; told Whit. Callie said, "Yes, yes"—grimacing at being reminded.) Julia and Bruce sought the refuge of the library: they were far from talked out. The "grown-ups" went into the living room and lingered there together for another hour or so. It was when Lucy and Geoff and Alan were putting on their coats to leave that Morgan said to them: "If you're free on Saturday, come around for a late cup of tea or an early drink. Five-ish. Callie and Julia have asked some college friends to drop by. It would be nice for me if you could look in for a little while. . . . See how you feel. Play it by ear."

Geoff: "I'm game for a look in."

Alan: "I'll be here."

Lucy: "So will I."

He didn't mention the great point: that Sylvia would be there.

۶؟

The Saturday gathering was not a quiet affair. The front door was kept open. Through it came college friends in the company of other college friends in the company of "link-ups." About half of them weren't known to Caroline, but she greeted them all as if they were long-lost brothers and sisters. Julia and Bruce seemed a bit out of it. There were few surnames: most were Carols and Bens and Eds and Susies and Sheilas and Joes and Hals and Alices and Jims and Bettys. There was a Dorcas with a mass of curly, wiry red hair, and an Andrew in tails: he was going on to somebody's sister's coming-out dance. They were all ravenous, like racoons. They went at a huge baked ham and denuded it down to the bone in no time. They made sandwiches and cleaned up platters of cheeses and ate bowls and bowls of mixed nuts. "Ain't youth grand?" Geoff laughed. Lucy and Geoff were the party's at-large minglers. What pleased Morgan most was seeing Julia and Alan and Bruce and *Sylvia* sitting together in the library, talking, huddled close to hear one another's words over the background noise. (He had—earlier—told Julia he'd invited the author of *A Night at Dsiatzdavo* to the party. Julia had said: "I can't wait to meet him." *"Her,"* he'd corrected. "Her name's Sylvia Phelps. S. K. P. Dobson is her nom de plume." Julia's eyes had widened.)

Lucy and Geoff and Alan stayed until seven-thirty. In the hall, by the front door, Alan said: "Sylvia Phelps is a joy, Morgan. And it's a small world. She and I have several friends in common. Teachers, at Columbia. I'm looking forward to seeing her soon again." Geoff—no slouch—said: "I have a hunch you won't have to wait long, Alan." Lucy, buttoning her coat, was mute.

Caroline did, did, did abstract herself from the crowd and spend a few minutes with Sylvia. But it was a hasty meeting. New faces kept appearing. "Please excuse me, Miss Phelps—"

The young crowd was here to stay. Now they were playing records in the living room, pairing-off, dancing. Morgan's old records. Harry James, Shep Fields, Count Basie, Glenn Miller, Duke Ellington, Benny Goodman ("Benny the Good," Whit said), Jimmy and Tommy Dorsey. "The Man I Love," "In the Mood," "Autumn Leaves," "Troubled Waters," "Stompin' at the Savoy," "Cheek to Cheek," "I Can't Get Started," "The Thrill of You"—

It was when the tune and words of "A Slow Boat to China" came clear that he sang with the record to Sylvia: "I'd love to get you on a slow boat to China / All to myself alone / Out on the briny with a moon big and shiny'"—

—then, that he took her hand and said: "Come on, dearest. Let's get out of here." He caught Caroline's eye and waved. Julia and Bruce went with him and Sylvia to the front door. "I'm going to take Miss Phelps home," he told Julia. "I'll be back in about an hour. Don't let Callie turn the Vic up any louder." Sylvia shook Julia's hand, and Bruce's. Julia said: "I'm honored to have met you, Miss Phelps." (Ah, Julia.) Bruce said: "A privilege"—(shy and serious).

In the taxi, they kissed. "God, I've missed you so much, so much." At Sylvia's apartment they sat for a few minutes on the couch, Sylvia in his arms. As far as the world was concerned, today—in their view of it—marked their beginning. They had planned it so: that the busy world be given a six-month chance to notice them, however it chose to; however it would. . . . About Julia and Caroline, Sylvia, in a way searching, said: "It's strange, Morgan. Strange, that I can't see a trace of Katherine in them. Or of my father. No Phelps at all. I kept looking for something, anything—a mannerism or a voice inflection, but there was nothing to remind me. . . . They look a lot like you, and what's not *you* in them, must be Maud. . . . There's a hint, in Caroline, the merest hint, of Richard. Or I think there is—in the way she stands, sort of with her weight on one leg, the left one, as if she'd stopped herself in the middle of a step. Richard used to stand like that. Maybe Maud did?"

"No, she didn't."

"So maybe that's Richard in Caroline. But nothing of him in Julia. And—I can't get over it—not a hint of Katherine or my father in either Caroline or Julia. . . . It makes me wonder about myself. Is there anything in them that reminds you of me?"

"No, there isn't."

"It's strange. . . . Do you think we're blanking out on purpose?"

"No, my love, I don't think so." He kissed her. "Now about tomorrow. Julia and Caroline go back to Philadelphia after lunch—"

"Come here—around four?"

"Yes. At four."

4 ❧ Now

Getting to, arriving at, achieving the firm matrimonial ground on which they would freely walk was at some moments heart-stopping; poignant. At all moments, fascinating.

Regard the change! The *changes*: the plurals and combinations of astonishment and adjustment! Think of, and wonder at, all the intersecting lives, starting with his life as it intersected Sylvia's life, as his and Sylvia's lives intersected Julia's and Caroline's, and Miss Sly's, and Ansel Shurtliff's, and Letitia and Lewis Grant's, and Lillie Ruth's, and Tessa's, and Lucy Blackett's, and Geoffrey Barrows's, and Alan Litt's, and Sidney and Linda Aronov's, and Lawrence and Pamela Cuyler's, and Doctor Leigh's, and of the intersectings with Sylvia's friends who stood ready, beckoned by her, to meet him: to come to know him.

Hear those certain voices; see those certain faces—

—Caroline's and Julia's, when, in early March of 1960, he told them that he and Sylvia were going to marry. How they looked at him, as if they were seeing *him* for the first time. (Make that the second time: the first time had been when he returned from the war and was seen by them as real, and to their amazed eyes, in the flesh, had stood on his head. . . . That kind of really seeing *him*) . . . Caroline's voice and face: "She's not going to try to step-mother me and Julia, I hope." "No, Callie, Sylvia hasn't it in mind to do that." And Caroline's next question, earthed (it amused him) in Sex: "You and Sylvia—you're not thinking of having a kid, are you?" "No, Callie." And the way, then, Julia looked at Caroline and told her: "Come off it, Callie." And the way, next, Julia looked at him and said: "I think you and Sylvia are perfect for each other, Morgan."

—Ansel Shurtliff's voice and face: "It's thrilling."

—Lucy's voice and face: "Out of memory for Maudie, I wish I didn't like Sylvia, but I do, immensely. And how great for you, Morgan, that you won't have to hack through the rest of your life alone." The way, in that last sentence, Lucy anticipated the rest of her own life's loneliness. But that she would go on, hoping with her own eyes to spot in a night sky, a UFO. And the way, over Lucy's clean candor, he and she had embraced: intact.

—Geoff's voice and cognizant face: "It's *right*, Morgie."

—Alan's voice and face and straight words: "Maud was incredibly Maud. Sylvia is incredibly Sylvia."

—Lewis Grant's voice and face: "Bravo! Brava!" And Letitia's: "I have that framed set of gemstone intaglios—Greek gods and goddesses. I want to give them to Sylvia."

—The unsurprised look on Lillie Ruth's face.

—Tessa's face: the little white berry-spots on her cheeks as they converged over her smile.

—Sidney's voice and face as he murmured: *"Ashre ayin ver hot dos geshn."* "What does that mean, Sidney?" Sidney wrote out on a slip of paper what he'd said. "It's Yiddish. It means—'Fortunate the eye that has seen this.'"

—Lawrence's voice and face, in some way perpetually afrighted by change. Always hoping, though, for the best. "Blue skies, Morgan. Blue skies."

—Doctor Leigh, ever the stunner! "Well, well, Morgan! What a coincidence! I'm thinking of marrying too. Mrs. Kerr. You may have met her. She moved to Hatherton about six years ago. She's been a widow since 1951. She likes to travel. Now that I've begun to slow down a bit—professionally, I mean—I'll have the time to go places with her. There's Athens to be visited. And Mandalay, where the flying fishes play. Mrs. Kerr hasn't been to Mandalay."

—And Miss Sly. Zee. She was the one person unknown to any of the intersecting others. By her desire, she would remain to all the others unknown. "I shall be the loose thread," she said to him and Sylvia, then added: "And properly so. It is enough that I know you, Sylvia, and you, Morgan, and that you know me."

(And: as in memory they are alive, think of the ghosts: Katherine; Richard Hamilton; Sylvia's father; Sylvia's mother; Maud.)

ৰ্পু

About their impending marriage, Sylvia had but one proviso: "That I keep my apartment, Morgan. . . . Oh, no! *No.* I won't let you. S. K. P. Dobson will pay all the bills relating to my apartment. It's where I'll work, and when I've finished a day's work, I'll go home to you."

ৰ্পু

By the time April rolled around, Julia and Caroline were already deep in their separate excitements about the up-coming summer. Julia would be in England, at Oxford; she had sought and won a coveted place in an English literature college-exchange program. Caroline was going to "tour" Europe as a member of a group organized by a Bryn Mawr professor of European history. (And more about Caroline, in the form of her "announcement" to one and all: "I've made up my mind. I am going to be an anthropologist.")

ৰ্পু

Morgan and Sylvia beat their six months' imperative of "soon" by about two weeks.

They were married on Saturday, the twenty-third of April, 1960—four days before Julia's and Caroline's twentieth birthday.

It would be redundant to list the names of those who were present when they spoke their vows. Suffice to say that everyone vital to Morgan, everyone vital to Sylvia, was there.

Ah. Except Zenobia Sly. Yet that they did conjure her, looking at each other as they spoke their vows, did think of her—the binder who called herself—"the loose thread." Miss Sly; Zee: As in zed.

Today is the twenty-fifth of April, two days after their marriage, and they are in London. They flew across the Atlantic on a relatively new type of airplane—a so-called jet. They will return to New York in two weeks. The Forbes case is going to go to trial; Sylvia has started a new book, this one a novel. But right now, this morning, they are walking in St. James's Park. It is a fine, a beautiful day. The trees are in fresh green leaf, the grass shines in the sunlight. They hear a tinkling sound coming from behind them. They turn, then step quickly to the edge of the path to give greater passage-room to two red-turbaned Sikhs who are carrying—strung from a sturdy pole held horizontally at shoulder height—a huge crystal chandelier!

They stand in place, Morgan and Sylvia, gleeful and astonished. A moment. An intense moment. They know about the moment that it is in the process of becoming a beloved memory. A few seconds tick by.

Now they resume their walk.